RISE
OF THE
LYCAN QUEEN

RUBY K.

Dedication

To every woman who rebuilt herself from the ruins—your strength is your own revolution.

And for every man who has used his strength to uplift women—may your legacy be the fire that reshapes the world.

Contents

Playlist

The Woods— Lydia the Bard
Shameless—Camilla Cabello
Figure you Out—Voila
How it's Done—Huntrix
Queen of Kings—Alessandra
Chemtrails Over the Country Club—Lana Del Ray
Till Forever Falls Apart—Ashe, FINNEAS
Naach Meri Raani—Guru Randhwa
Eternity—Alex Warren
Step Into Your Power—Lenzspot

She is my crown, my oath, my fury. Harm her, and I will unmake him.

RotLQ
playlist——→

Chapter 1

Amara's POV

I drifted in and out of consciousness, the only reminder that I was alive being Asya's gentle hands on me as she kept me steady on the horse behind her. At times, cool water touched my lips. But my body was on fire. Even the clothes on my form seemed to burn my skin. My ears felt like they were bleeding, the smallest sounds grating against my eardrums.

This was awful, unending, heart-wrenching agony. And I was powerless to do anything as the skull-splitting pain in my head refused to let up.

"We are almost there, Amara." Her whispered words offered a glimmer of hope that seemed to penetrate the dark oblivion I was drowning under.

I hoped so. I hoped I was almost finished transitioning.

"Hold on, dear sister. I will get you the help you need," came her gentle voice, hands on my forehead checking for a fever.

I could not even open my mouth to tell her she was mistaken.

With every step the horse took, my grip on consciousness slipped further away. Images and memories flashed before my eyes like a fever dream, each one a blur of colors and emotions that tugged at my fragile state of being: Mother braiding my hair as she told me stories, Baba's kind smile, Asya's loving hugs, Zayed's gentle kisses. It was as if all the important parts of my life until now were being replayed. Was this because I was about to die?

Or perhaps because I was on the brink of a new life, one filled with unknown possibilities and challenges.

And then, just when I thought I could not bear it any longer, the heat that tormented me began to dissipate, replaced by a cool breeze that danced across my skin like gentle fingertips. I was on my back, the sand grains no longer painful as they brushed against my skin. Asya's hand cupped my cheek, comforting me as she called for the men to set up camp. We were taking a break. I could sense her worry for me.

"This is no normal fever," I heard Asya mutter as her hands smoothed the hair on my forehead.

I wanted to tell her I would be OK, to not worry, but my tongue felt heavy in my mouth. As I managed to croak out all would be well, I realized she had left me in a cocoon of soft blankets to go patrol the perimeter of the camp. I sighed, eyes still closed. My body was so tired, as if I had been running for hours and needed more sleep. But the agony, the searing pain, and the paralysis were slowly receding.

It was as if my body was adjusting to the changes taking place within.

The sudden low growl in the back of my head was the only warning I had before a pain so intense, so torturous, overtook my entire being as my arm twisted of its own accord.

The agony ripped through me without a moment's reprieve, the bones in my body shifting and contorting in ways that were unnatural. I could feel fur sprouting from every pore of my skin, sharp claws extending from my fingertips as if eager to slice through anything within reach. Tears streamed down my face, mixing with the sweat that dripped off me.

Screaming. I was screaming. But so was Asya.

Each muscle strained against its human confinement, yearning to break free in its beastly form. It was a battle between two worlds raging inside of me—a war I had not expected to be so ferocious but one I had no choice but to endure.

Asya's voice sounded muffled and distant amidst the chaos erupting within me. "Amara! Stay with me!" she cried out desperately.

The beast within me snarled, and I did my best to reign it back. Zayed had promised to be with me, to help me calm the beast within me. But he was not here. It was just me trying to stop myself from hurting my sister.

"STAY BACK!" I growled, my eyes flying open to rest on Asya.

I was in a crouched position, on all fours, as my back bent into an unnatural arch. Tears leaked from the corners of my eyes.

"No," Asya croaked out, shaking her head in disbelief as she took me in. "No...your eyes. They are red! Your body...no, Amara! Tell me you did not... You have become just like him!"

I wanted to reassure her that I was still here—that despite this excruciating metamorphosis taking place before her eyes, I was still her sister. But the words refused to leave my lips, coming out as a low, ferocious snarl instead.

Asya's face twisted from disbelief to horror.

She stumbled back, her hands trembling.

"Kill it!" came a voice from behind her.

I screamed as my body twisted further into unnatural angles, joints breaking and reforming. Captive in this transformation, words failed me.

My heart ached for her pain and disbelief, but there was no bridge I could cross to reach her in this raging storm of change.

My heart trembled as I watched Asya reach for her bow and arrow, and then she turned, pointing it straight to the source of the voice.

"Anyone who takes even a step toward my sister will find my arrow lodged in their neck. Touch my sister and die."

I let out another scream of pain, mixed with relief. Asya did not believe me to be a monster. My newly emerged claws dug into the sand, leaving furrows in the ground as I tried to maintain some semblance of control. I cried out internally for Zayed. My love, my husband. Would I be able to keep the beast inside at bay without him?

This pain was unbearable yet necessary.

"Stay back!" Asya called out in warning. "Stay back!"

I heard the plucking of her bow. She had just let fly an arrow at someone. "I SAID STAY BACK!" she boomed out, her voice tinged with panic.

My sharp ears picked up footsteps drawing closer, converging on Asya. They would not heed her warning for long.

"Move aside. We need to get rid of this beast! She will kill us all otherwise," a voice spoke sharply.

My chest heaved with each agonizing breath, every muscle straining as I tried to regain control over my newfound form. I felt my ears elongating, turning into those of a wolf. I opened my mouth to tell Asya I would not let anyone harm us, but it came out as an ear-piercing howl echoing through the air, culminating the completion of my shift as my half-formed snout began to elongate as well. The sharp gasps of everyone around me were picked up keenly by my Lycan ears. Slowly, I rose to my full height...taller now than everyone around me. It was akin to an adult looking at little children. I felt the beast growling inside of me, wanting to kill the men who were approaching Asya threateningly. She was my sister, and therefore the Lycan inside of me was protective of her.

Asya's voice quivered as she spoke. "Amara, I do not know who you are now, but I will protect you from harm." She stepped in front of me, her now-small body shielding mine from the approaching men. Oh, how I wished to thank her then and there. But how could I? My words were a low growl now, barely resembling the language we had shared for so many years. I watched Asya flinch in response to my growl.

It was dark, and yet I could see perfectly. I inhaled slowly, taking in the smells around me. Leaning down, I sniffed my sister, noting her signature citrus scent. I had to commit it to memory. She was not an enemy.

"A-Amara...it...it's me." Asya was trembling as she spoke. I could sense the fear in her.

"Looks like you are the main course for this beast tonight," one of the men jeered.

My eyes narrowed on him. I inhaled deeply, pinpointing his scent of smoky wood. He was an enemy. And I pounced without warning, pinning him to the ground, my claws digging deep into his sides.

He screamed in pain, his blood mixing with the sand as he squirmed beneath me. I held him down with all my strength, my newfound power coursing through my veins.

"No, Amara!" Asya yelled out. "STOP! THEY ARE ALLIES!"

Allies? They were ready to kill me! I wanted to spit the words out. Instead, I growled, letting my canines glint menacingly in the moonlight.

The other men froze, their eyes widening in horror as they saw their comrade pinned down by my monstrous form. The glow of the fire they had lit to set up camp flickered from the far right, casting a menacing glow on my form, wrapping around me in a shroud of sinister orange. I snarled in warning.

They all began to back away slowly, the fear in their eyes all too obvious. I released the man squirming under me and growled low, my canines bared. My Lycan would not spare anyone who harmed me or my family.

Asya slowly stepped forward, her eyes wide with a mix of fear and concern. She reached out a shaking hand toward me, and the sight of her calmed my beast.

"Amara," she whispered, almost in awe as she took in the sight of me. "You are...you are magnificent."

I lowered my head, allowing Asya to reach up and stroke the side of my face. Her touch sent a strange mix of emotions coursing through me — familiarity mixed with protectiveness. I had always been protective of my sister, but my Lycan was different. She wanted to kill, wanted to maim anyone who even looked at her the wrong way. This was what Zayed meant when he said I would forever have a beast living inside of me. But I did not view this beast as a stranger or interloper inside my mind. It was as if she had assimilated, adopting my feelings and viewing my people as her own. I whined softly at my sister's gentleness, keen to not show aggression.

Asya's eyes filled with tears as she looked at me, unsure of what to say or do. I knew she was terrified, but I could also see the love and admiration in her eyes.

"Can you...can you change back?" she queried softly.

The men behind her were whispering in fear and awe as well, my Lycan hearing easily picking up their whispers.

"Think of what we could do with a weapon like that on our side."

"This is an abomination. She is not to be trusted."

"We need to be careful. For all we know, she might be an informant for King Kadin's side and rat us out to him."

That last line made me look up sharply. I let out a low snarl at the mention of Kadin's name. Immediately, I needed more answers and, on pure instinct, lunged at the man who had mentioned him. He screamed as my Lycan form barrelled into him, the sand flying up around us as he hit the floor under me. I could not control the panic coursing through my beast. And the primal being within me did not have the power of rationality. It wanted to draw blood at the mention of Kadin being referred to as King!

"WHAT HAPPENED TO MY HUSBAND?" I screamed. But it came out as a growl instead. Even my Lycan was anxious at the mention of Kadin becoming king, ready to start tearing into the people around us unless we got some answers.

"Amara, no! Control yourself!" Asya screamed from behind me.

"Please...please do not eat me!" the man screamed. "I have little children! A son and a daughter! Who will feed them when I am no longer alive?"

I breathed in deep, realizing that I would not get answers in this form. I stared at the men before me, noting the vast dunes stretching endlessly beneath the cold silver glow of the moon. I needed answers. And to get them, I had to calm myself down first. I had to shift back into a human.

So I closed my eyes and concentrated on shifting back into my human form. I tried to reason with my beast, and she quietly relented, giving me back control.

The shift began, and I felt the popping of joints and breaking of bones. It was painful to say the least, though not like the first time, which had been unbearable.

The man under me managed to squirm away as I shifted into my human form. As my shift slowly completed itself, the fur receded, my snout shortened and formed into a human nose, and my claws retracted. I winced in pain as my teeth shifted and locked back into their original place. I now stood before them, naked in the dim glow of the firelight, our shadows dancing against the sand. My body ached from the shift, but I pushed through the pain for the sake of answers.

Asya threw a dull grey cotton cloak around my bare shoulders. My body still trembled from the exertion of shifting.

When I looked up, I saw trepidation, revulsion, and awe in the gazes of the men before me. I stood up shakily, my legs feeling numb.

"What do you mean, King Kadin?" I finally demanded. "Where is Zayed?!"

"All will be answered, Sister, I promise you," Asya vowed, an arm around my shoulders. "First, let us find you some clothes and I must patrol the perimeter. Then we will answer your questions."

An hour later, I found myself sitting in front of the fire, a cup of water and a strip of camel meat in hand. The rebels looked at me warily, their dark garb meant to help them meld into the shadows, but now, with my newfound Lycan sight, I could discern them clearly.

Everything was intensified now.

My sight, my hearing, my smell—even my sense of touch heightened dramatically. The world seemed sharper, more vivid, as if a veil had been lifted. I could feel the cool, textured clay of my water cup with remarkable clarity,

Each groove and ridge etched into my fingertips as though they were tiny canyons carved by time. The texture was palpable, as if every detail of the clay was whispering its story to my skin.

Is this what it was like for Zayed? Is this what it would be like for me from now on? I looked up, noting the way Asya came to sit next to me. She threw her torch toward a man I now knew was named Ronan. He was the son of one of the key leaders of the rebel faction. Ronan's sister had been the first to die. The first queen Zayed had killed. And Ronan looked at me with unconcealed distaste as he caught the torch in his hand expertly and left to go patrol the perimeter, no doubt to make sure Kadin's men were not closing in on us.

"Kadin has made himself king," Asya finally revealed. " Upon hearing the news of his queen's demise."

I jerked in surprise. How had Kadin fooled Zayed into thinking I had died? My hand went to where the green pendant was missing from around my neck. My lips curled into a grim scowl. Zayed trusted his cousin. And it must have been all too easy to fool him with the pendant in hand. Asya did not notice my reaction and was still speaking.

"It is said that Zayed lost his mind and transformed into a beast. Kadin told the people that his horrendous deeds of killing innocent women had caught up with him and the goddess has cursed him to walk the earth alone as a monster. His beast killed many of his own guards and ran off. There is a bounty on his head, and people have been warned to stay back should they see him."

"No, no, no," I hissed, shaking my head. "I am alive!" I screamed, realizing my husband thought I was dead. He must have transformed into his Lycan, unable to control the raging feral nature brought on due to the curse.

"Your death, along with the Grand Vizier's and Baghel's, have been laid at the feet of the rebellion and the chieftain of the mountains. Kadin has said it was planned to lure Zayed away so they could infiltrate the palace and kill the queen. He has proclaimed war on Chieftain Lamar."

My eyebrows furrowed in confusion. Why was Kadin so bent on attacking Chieftain Lamar? Especially when he himself was the one funding the rebel faction?

"This is not making any sense," I muttered to myself, shaking my head. "Kadin is greedy and would never want to waste money on a war!"

"Oh, he has found new ways to make money," Asya snorted disdainfully.

I looked at Asya with keen eyes.

"The Queen of Asser has refused to honor the alliance. She said her deal was with King Zayed. And due to the impending food shortage, Kadin has threatened to throw everyone out of the city of Ilm who was not born there. Only those able to pay exorbitant amounts of bribe money to the crown, traders and merchants, are able to stay within the city. He has also increased the taxes on the common man. Furthermore, each family must pay an additional harem tax," Asya spat out.

I gasped. "A...harem tax?" I echoed hollowly.

"It is an annual tax to maintain his harem. Those who cannot pay must offer a daughter to have the tax waived. A daughter to fill his harem," Asya explained venomously. "He has already carted a handful of peasant women off to be sold into sexual slavery. The money he earns from selling them will fill his coffers. Since they were given to him to fill his harem, he thinks he can do with them as he pleases!"

I gasped. This was...so much worse than what I could have ever imagined. And I wondered if it finally made everyone realize that under Zayed's rule, only one daughter had been in danger of being picked. Now, not even a single peasant daughter of Elamaria was safe.

And that was when another thought struck me.

"So much has happened...how long have I been unconscious?" I finally croaked out.

Asya gazed at me sympathetically.

"Two days with me," she replied evenly. "I did my best to make sure you consumed broth so you could get vital nutrients." Her hands shook. "I thought you had the plague, or something equally fatal—"

"Shhh!" I cut her off, my nose twitching as the scent of rotting flowers assaulted my senses.

My sharp eyes caught a movement beyond. The darkness itself seemed to twist and unravel and cold fury gripped my heart. Dark, ember-red eyes stared back at me from the black mist twisting and writhing, slowly making its way to our camp. My ears picked up on the whooshing sound of arrows just in time.

"Get down!" I screamed, shielding Asya as I threw her under me, taking the full brunt of the attack. The cold metal of arrows pierced my back, biting into my flesh. I gasped in pain, realizing that, with cruel precision, one arrow had sliced through my shoulder, its razor-sharp tip emerging from the front, glistening red with my blood in the dim firelight.

Chapter 2

Amara's POV

"You are hurt!" Asya gasped, trying to move from under me.

But I kept her pinned down with all my newfound Lycan strength. "I will be fine!" I hissed out, gritting my teeth against the agony.

I would heal. I had regenerative abilities. But it hurt, it burned, and it took all I had in me not to cry out in pain.

All around me, I heard the men falling to the ground with heavy thuds as the arrows found their homes in the hearts of the rebels. I had to do something. Or we were all dead.

With a steady hand, I reached behind me, feeling the sharp sting of pain as my fingers brushed against the arrow embedded in my back. In one fluid, practiced motion, I grasped the shaft of the arrow and deftly pulled it free, wincing as it slid out, leaving a hot trail of pure torture in its wake.

"Stay down," I ordered Asya sharply.

My muscles tensed with the effort I was exerting to move my body, every movement sending fresh waves of pain shooting through my opened wound where blood spilled out in torrents. But it would heal. I had to ignore the fiery agony for a few moments longer, because I could not afford to falter now!

In the shadows, I spotted Kadin's men taking aim. I was not as adept as Asya was with her bow, but I had one advantage they did not.

"Put out the fire!" I commanded, reaching for Asya's bow and arrows.

"Are you mad? We will not be able to spot the enemy!" Ronan argued.

"They will not be able to spot us either," I retorted, arching a brow in his direction.

Understanding lightened his eyes.

"Put out the fire!" he bellowed.

"If you think I am about to let you have all the fun," Asya muttered.

I heard her movements behind me and the unmistakable plucking of the string of a bow. She must have had an extra one nearby. My lips tugged up into a half-smile despite the grim situation. Trust Asya to always travel with extra weapons. Just like me.

"There," I whispered as the fire was snuffed out, plunging us into darkness. Shadows stretched long, swallowing the camp in silence. My eyes cut through the blackness, tracking our enemies with razor-sharp precision, as if daylight still bathed the earth.

"Fifteen men. Northeast of the camp, moving in a staggered formation. Closest one, twenty paces out—armed with a blade. The others follow, fanning wide, likely trying to box us in." I shifted my weight, pulling the string of my bow taught. "Take them out before they take us."

I let my arrow fly, relishing in the way it found its mark in the shoulder of one of our enemies.

"Tell your men to stay down, Ronan!" I hissed, hoping he was close enough to hear.

The night was our ally, a cloak of shadows that rendered us invisible. Asya and I moved in perfect synchrony, bows drawn, arrows notched. Asya could not see them, but she followed my lead without hesitation.

My next arrow sliced through the darkness, striking another man square in the throat. He crumpled without a sound. I whispered instructions to Asya, singling out her next target using my words. A heartbeat later, Asya's arrow found another target, burying deep into his chest. He collapsed, his fingers clawing uselessly at the shaft before going still.

We loosed our arrows again. More bodies fell, their comrades floundering in the dark, blind and disoriented. The night was thick with their confusion, their frantic whispers, their stumbling steps. They did not know where death was coming from, only that it was closing in.

I drew another arrow, but before I could fire, the air thickened, humming with an unnatural energy. A chill rippled down my spine. *Something was coming.*

"Asya—" I barely had time to warn her before the shadows themselves twisted, coiling into a shape too dark, too jagged to be human. The demon witch materialized between us, her eyes burning like embers in the night.

Then, with a flick of her wrist, she sent me hurtling backward.

The force of the demon witch's magic slammed into me like a tidal wave, sending me skidding across the sand.

Asya cried out from behind me, "I cannot...MOVE."

I cursed. Thankfully I still possessed the evil eye talisman, located in the folds of my clothes. As I initiated a shift into my Lycan form, I could not help but think over how this entire time, Elvira had been pretending to ward my rooms. Pretending to want what was best for me. PRETENDING TO BE MY FRIEND.

I threw my head back and howled at the moon, my frustration and shock echoing into the night. But beneath it all, there was pain—raw and undeniable. Because even if Sherazi had been a lie, she had been real to me. A confidante. An ally in a den full of enemies I had whispered my fears to. And now, that ally was no more. Had turned against me. Had always been against me! The pain of her betrayal cut deep.

Darkness curled around my fur, slithering like a serpent, and my narrowed gaze locked onto her. She stood with her back to Asya, who had crumpled to the ground, paralyzed by Elvira's powers. Asya's wide eyes shimmered with terror, her breath coming in short, panicked gasps.

Beyond them, Ronan and his warriors clashed with what remained of Kadin's army, steel flashing, bodies falling. The battlefield was chaos, but my focus was on the undead woman before me—the one who had orchestrated so much destruction.

Elvira's lips curled into a wicked smile, her voice a venomous whisper carried by the wind.

"So, you are now a Lycan Queen." She tilted her head, amusement flickering in her cold, soulless eyes. "That just makes your impending demise all the sweeter. And your husband? He is next."

Then she laughed—sharp and merciless, a sound that sliced through the air like a blade.

Rage shot through me, hot and unrelenting. I lowered my stance, claws digging into the earth. If she wanted a fight, I would give her one. And this time, I would not hesitate. I let loose a primal snarl and lunged, dodging the attack of her shadows, feeling the cold tendrils lick at my fur as I closed the distance between us.

My claws slashed through the swirling darkness surrounding her, tearing through the layers of magic she had cloaked herself in. She hissed, stumbling back, her skeletal fingers curling like talons. I could smell her rage, her desperation.

She flicked her wrist, and jagged shadows erupted from the ground, razor-sharp and aiming for my throat. I ducked low, my powerful limbs propelling me beneath her defenses. Scampering on all fours, I ducked her attacks and rose up again right in front of her. Her evil red eyes widened in surprise. She had not expected such quick reflexes. I was no longer a human. And Elvira, it seemed, had never fought a Lycan. For like the countless monsters before her, she thrived on the helplessness of her victims.

Taking advantage of her momentary shock, my jaws snapped around her arm, the taste of rotting flesh filled my mouth as I bit down. She screamed, her magic faltering, and I used the moment of weakness to pin her down.

She shrieked, louder this time.

"FALL BACK!" her voice boomed through the night.

But there was no one to heed her command. For Ronan and his men had disposed of what remained of Kadin's assassins.

I allowed the sense of utter defeat to envelop her, relishing the sight of her panicked gaze.

The demon witch looked at me, twisting, trying to disappear into her shadows, but I caught her by the throat, claws extended, before she could slip away.

I could end this. Right now. My fangs hovered over her throat, my instincts screaming at me to tear it open, to finish her like the monster she was.

But then I saw it. The demonic fire in her eyes dimmed and something more human took over. Pain. Grief. A hollow kind of loss that I recognized all too well. For I had seen it many times in Zayed's own gaze when he spoke of his mother and brother. In my own, too, when I was overcome by the memory of my own mother, whom I had lost too early.

I hesitated, my breath ragged as I stared down at her. She had hurt so many, destroyed so much. She had cursed Zayed and was responsible for the deaths of many innocent women! But beneath the hate, beneath the blood and the rage, was a creature who had once been something else. Someone else.

Her black lips trembled, but no words came. Her fingers twitched as though she wanted to fight, but even she knew it was over.

I growled low, my claws still pressing into her chest.

"Finish it," she gasped out, her shadows receding into her. She was admitting defeat. "You win, Lycan Queen."

I let out a low growl of frustration. I would not give her what she wanted, for death was too easy a punishment for this vile creature. I would not give her what she craved. Or maybe I would. If she told me what I needed to know first.

"What are you doing? Kill her!" Ronan boomed from next to Asya who he was now helping to stand up.

I shifted back into my human form and stood before Elvira, who lay on the ground as if my Lycan still had her pinned.

"You want to die, demon witch?" I snarled, towering over her, my bare skin bathed in moonlight, unashamed, unafraid. I wanted her to remember me like this—powerful, unbroken, the predator standing over its prey. "Then you shall die. But not before you lift the curse from my husband."

Elvira wheezed out a laugh, her mangled form trembling as she forced herself upright. I noticed her eye socket, where Asya's arrow had lodged itself into days ago, still held a jagged scar that ran straight through her eye. The red glow was dimmer there. It took me a moment, as I stared at her, to realize she could not fully heal from an injured eye. Elvira continued to cackle, her twisted mouth splitting into a manic grin. Her injured eye popped out of the socket. It pulsed an angry red, emanating dark magic, and I gasped in disgust, watching as she reached out a hand and lifted the red glowing eyeball, fitting it back into her hollowed and scarred socket with a squelching sound. Dark magic powered her limbs. She did not function like the living.

"Foolish girl," she rasped, her voice thick with cruel amusement. Clumps of her gray, stringy hair shook about her like snakes as she spoke. "You think I can undo what has already begun? No." She cackled maniacally. "I sacrificed my life to ensure the curse would be unbreakable. He will live out his days shackled to the hunger, forever battling the urge to destroy the one thing he loves most in this world..." She leaned forward, her grin widening. "You."

Her laughter tore through the night, jagged and raw, as if the very air conspired to carry her madness.

Filled with absolute disgust, I brought my claws out, extending them as I took on a partial shift. Then I drove one claw deep into the eye socket of her injured eye, watching as the blood trickled out. Her shriek of pain pierced the night. Without thinking twice, I twisted my claw, rendering her injured eye into nothing but a sticky, slimy mass of pulp. Elvira's screams rent the air. Claws still dripping with her blood and the putrid remains of her, I reached for her remaining good eye, clawing it out of her socket. With a sickening pop, her whole eyeball tumbled free and into my waiting, extended palm.

"I do not think it was a good idea letting her continue to live, sister," Asya said haltingly as she stared at Elvira, who was bound in chains.

I remembered the words Dornia had used to ward my room. I used those same words, imbuing the chains, now binding Elvira, with the same powerful magic. She was tied up, one eye socket bleeding dark puss while the other was a hollowed-out, cavernous, gaping hole.

Her remaining good eye rested safely in my pocket. And if I destroyed it, she would remain blind forever. It should be enough of a deterrent to keep her from trying anything further. For I had no qualms in letting her live blind for the remainder of her immortal life.

"I need her," I replied quietly, noticing the way Elvira's head shifted to tilt her ears toward us. "She is a vile creature. And I would sooner see her dead. But we need information from her. Not just on how to lift the curse, but on what exactly Kadin has planned."

"This is the witch who cursed the king? The one who is responsible for my sister's death?" Ronan exclaimed hotly from across the crackling fire. "She is an abomination!"

"I take first watch," I intoned, standing with sword in hand. "Rest while you can."

Everyone retired to their respective tents. I moved slowly to stand before Elvira. She could not sense me, but she could hear me...smell me...

"So, Lycan Queen...maybe you still believe me to be your friend," Elvira sneered in my direction.

"I would never think that," I scoffed. "You have more than proven you cannot feel anything for anyone. Your thirst for revenge has consumed you so fully that there is no room for you to feel anything else."

Elvira snarled, fighting against her binds.

"If you knew...you have not seen the cruelty of this world...what men are capable of. If you had, you would sooner join me on my quest than oppose me!"

"And yet you sided with Kadin." I tilted my head to stare at her. "The son of the very woman who helped orchestrate the death of your beloved Liliana."

Elvira suddenly stilled as if she had been doused with cold water.

"YOU LIE!"

I shook my head, feeling pity toward this hateful creature.

"He confessed everything to his father before killing him. Mera told the king Liliana had been unfaithful. Think, Elvira! Who else knew aside from Liliana? Mera had been helping her meet her lover in secret! The king rarely visited his wife and children. Someone had to have told him! Mera wanted her son to be king! It is why she sent word to you that Zayed's father murdered Liliana. She wanted you to end the line to pave the way for Kadin!"

"STOP LYING!" Elvira boomed, her gray, rotting form struggling harder against the binds. I watched the chains digging into her skin.

"Believe what you want. I tell the truth," I hissed out. "How does it feel...to know you helped the family who killed a woman who was like a daughter to you? And you have helped them orchestrate the downfall of her son? Is that what she would have wanted from you?" I pressed on, my voice filled with disgust. "If Liliana could see what you have done to her own blood..." I trailed off, shaking my head. "No amount of heartbreak can condone what you have done, you monster!"

Why was I even speaking to Elvira? She was an evil demon!

A wail like no other emitted from her lips as she keened, full of heartbreak.

"YOU HAVE NO IDEA WHAT MY LIFE WAS LIKE! You pretend you know pain. You know nothing, you pathetic queen," Elvira spat out, her hollowed eye sockets staring at me as they glowed a dim red.

"Have you been beaten to an inch of your life by your husband? While carrying his child?" she roared, red froth gathering at the sides of her mouth. "And when you finally managed to escape...did your father turn you away from his home, deeming you 'no longer his problem'? All because you ran off and married a man without his approval?!"

The ferocity of her words made me take a step back, eyes widening as her story unfolded. Elvira paid me no heed as she continued to speak, her voice taking on a faraway quality as if she was no longer here in the desert but somewhere very far away from me. I stared into the red, glowing, hollow sockets, feeling as if I too was being transported to another time as Elvira told her story...

"I clutched my belly, not yet swollen with child, willing my unborn child to stay safe inside me as pangs of hunger overwhelmed me. I walked the streets of my small village, miserable and bleeding. My father, who once held me on his knee and told me I was his pride, his little jewel, had turned me away. He said a woman who did not marry according to her father's wishes was a disgrace! When I stood before him, broken and begging for refuge, he shut the doors in my face, sealing my fate. My husband, the man who was supposed to protect me, abused me. I could not go back there, for I would not risk the life of my unborn child.

"So I walked. I walked under the cloak of night, tending to my wounds and broken arm as best I could. And when the blistering sun rose, and my sandals wore thin against the desert sands, I decided to make my way away from the village I had been born in to find a new home. Somewhere where no one knew that I was running from my husband. Or that I was a disgrace to my father. I walked in the desert alone, broken arm wrapped in torn fabric, my belly heaving from nausea due to the growing life inside me. Thirst burned my throat, hunger gnawed at my ribs, but I kept walking, because stopping meant dying!

"That was when I met her. The woman with eyes like storm clouds and a voice like the whispering wind. She sat by a dying palm tree amidst the vast golden sands and called me forward. 'You are lost,' she said, a smile on her face. 'But not yet beyond saving.'

"She taught me magic. Not the kind that moves mountains or bends men to your will, but the kind that makes the rains come, the kind that heals wounds others would leave to fester. With each passing day, I grew stronger—not in body, but in spirit. My arm healed slowly as did my heart. I thought luck had finally smiled upon me. Slowly, she taught me the darker side of magic. One that demanded blood sacrifices. Unable to continue down such a path, I decided it was time for me to leave. I thanked her as I bid her farewell, knowing I could not stay with this woman. She only smiled. 'All things in this world take something in return,' she said. I did not understand her words, not then.

"I traveled far and wide, my belly ever-growing as the months passed. In each village I stopped, I used my magic to earn a day's meal, a night's stay. And then, when I could walk no longer, due to the impending arrival of my baby, with only three months left, I arrived in a strange town. It was the great Emir's city, where I heard the man was a just and kind ruler. He had set up shelters in his small city for the homeless, and there I was able to find lodging. Unfortunately, as a pregnant woman travelling without a male chaperone, I was turned away in the middle of the night.

"However, even then, I did what I could to survive. I used my magic to heal small wounds, to ease pain, to help where I was allowed. I sold my magical labor for scraps of bread. Slowly, I was able to hire men to make a small hut for me where I could reside. I became known as the witch who could heal all wounds. Thankful for the magic I had learned, I prepared for the birth of my baby. And then, one night, under a pale, silver moon, my body betrayed me. The child was coming an entire month sooner than expected. And when I tried to ask for help, no one came to my aid. The doctors refused my money. They all believed my child was the product of *an illicit liaison. A child without a father in the land of Elamaria is a child without the refuge of shelter during a sandstorm.*

"I had no one! No mother, no sister, no midwife to hold my hand and tell me to breathe. I bit down on my screams and labored alone in the dark. Hours passed, then days. The pain became unbearable. My body shook, my mind blurred, and still, I fought.

"Until at last, my child was born.

Silent.

I waited for the cry, for the first gasp of breath, but there was nothing. Only the hush of the wind and the breaking of my heart. My son. My perfect, beautiful son.

I held him against my chest, rocked him, wept over him, begged whatever gods there were to take me instead. But there was no answer, no mercy.

In the end, I wrapped him in the only cloth I had and buried him with my own hands beneath the shade of a palm tree. I whispered his name, the name I had chosen long ago, the name no one else would ever know. And when the sun rose, I was still there, kneeling in the dirt, alone.

All things in this world take something in return.

The magic had given me the strength to survive, but it had not been enough to save my son.

I stood, empty and broken, and walked forward into a world that had already taken everything from me. But I would not let it take my soul.

I would survive. And one day, I would make them remember me. Nobody mourned the loss of my son. Everyone said a child without a father was better off dead. It was the penance I must pay for my crimes.

Two days later, when the great Emir discovered I had lost my child, he brought me into his home and offered me a position as the wet nurse of his newly born daughter. Liliana. She was a tiny baby, her mother having passed on during childbirth. Liliana was my life. My everything. She was a balm to this cold heart that had forgotten how to feel. She brought color back into a world that had been gray. My breasts, hard as stone and filled with milk for a baby that was dead, fed and sustained Liliana.

I found purpose in my life once again. She was to be the queen of Elamaria. And I would protect her, nourish her, raise her to be queen. My daughter...my little flower....she could not completely replace what I had lost. But her soft smiles and the way she clutched my fingers whilst drinking my milk made the ache in my heart diminish until it was no longer a gaping wound but a quiet, constant ache—one I could live with.

The world had stripped me of everything, cast me aside like a broken thing, yet here, in the quiet moments with Liliana, I found fragments of myself again. She was not my blood, but she was my salvation. The warmth of her tiny body against mine as we slept, the way her fingers curled around mine with innocent trust—these were the only truths that mattered now.

I was a woman forgotten, a mother robbed, a soul condemned for sins I did not believe to be sins at all. But in Liliana's laughter, in the way she looked up at me with those wide, trusting eyes, I found something that no man, no fate, no cruel god could take from me.

Love.

And I swore upon the grave of my son—I would protect this girl with all that I had. I would raise her into the queen she was meant to be. The world had stolen my child. But it would never take Liliana from me!"

Elvira paused, and just like that, I was pulled from the trance of images moving before my eyes.

"Until...he killed her!" Elvira roared, and it was then that I realized she really had put me under a trance with her voice as she told me her story.

She was free of her binds, my own hands being the ones to undo them.

"What?" I murmured in confusion as I tried to shake myself of the stupor I had been under.

Elvira moved with quickness and agility, and I jolted back, realizing I had been brought under a spell by her magic. A rush of air brushed against my body, her passing seeming to ripple the space around me. And when she disappeared into the shadows, my skin tingled, as if her touch lingered for a moment.

It was like being jolted back from a dream, the images and emotions fading away as reality came back into focus. But even as I felt the world returning, the story that Elvira had woven with her words remained vivid, hauntingly etched into my mind.

But one thing remained startlingly clear to me. She had not tried to kill me, even though she had her chance whilst I was under her hypnosis, and I could only hope it meant she had believed me when I told her Mera was responsible for Liliana's death.

Chapter 3

Amara's POV

"How did she manage to get you to untie her and take her eye from you?" Ronan queried testily, staring me down.

I expelled a frustrated breath. It was the next day and we were travelling again, trying to reach the rebel hideout.

"I told you," I bit out. "She used her magic on me. I was in a trance!"

Ronan scoffed. He had asked me the same question multiple times before as we trekked across the desert, and I gave him the same answer each time.

"I am positive she is blind now from the one eye I crushed," I added feebly, wondering if that would make a difference to Ronan.

I knew he did not trust me. But what would I gain from helping Elvira? The same demon witch who wanted to kill my husband?

Ronan muttered under his breath that unnatural beings like her had the ability to heal themselves by killing living creatures. Death powered their magic. Perhaps he was right. But I was not going to sit here and listen to him grumble the entire way.

"How much farther?" I asked, searching the vast expanse of the desert as I travelled behind Asya on a camel.

Asya glanced over her shoulder at me, her face etched with concern as she scanned the desolate landscape. "The rebel hideout, or at least one of the many hideouts they have, is an entire day's journey. We should reach it by nightfall. "

I released an exasperated breath, incensed at this news.

"Another day that I am unable to find my husband," I huffed out.

Asya looked at me apologetically.

"Amara, I know this is not what you want to do, but we need their help to find him. We cannot blindly traverse the desert without any information. The rebels have men installed all across the city of Elamaria, spies who are able to relay information faster than a messenger on foot," Asya explained.

My eyebrows bunched together.

"How can they relay information so quickly?" I queried.

Asya stared at me before pointing up into the sky. Of course. My mind went back to the raven I had seen on my balcony in the palace. Had Elvira been passing information on to the rebels even back then? Of course, she might have pretended to be on their side, relaying information about the queen who had managed to stay alive. Elvira had played everyone.

"How are you so sure they will help us?" I finally asked.

"I believe everyone is realizing who the better ruler is between Kadin and Zayed. And this might come as a surprise, Amara, but if you can make the killings stop, there is no one else the common man would rather have as a queen than one of them...one of us," Asya corrected. "You understand the struggles of the people, and the reforms you brought about during your time clearly reflect that with you as queen, the dark times might be behind us."

Asya's words hung in the air, heavy with their implications. I glanced up at the vast, empty sky, my thoughts swirling with the possibilities. Could I really be the queen that the common people would rally behind? Did I deserve it? What if I let everyone down?

I took a deep breath, feeling the weight of the world on my shoulders. But I knew that if I could stop the killings and bring peace to Elamaria, it would be worth it. Not just for me, but for everyone who had suffered and might continue to suffer.

As I pondered these heavy thoughts, the heat of the desert seemed to bear down on me even more intensely. The endless expanse of sand and sky stretched out before me, offering little respite from my internal turmoil.

The desert was unforgiving, the heat endlessly suffocating as we trudged along on our camels.

However, I refused to be stopped by the heat of the desert, fear of failure, or the doubts that threatened to consume me.

"You have a strength within you, Amara," Asya said softly, her eyes meeting mine in the sweltering sunlight. "A strength that has brought you this far."

But it was only worth it if I could find my husband. I looked back at the horizon and clenched my fist, feeling the weight of my destiny pressing down on me. Whether it was fate or simply the choices I had made that led me to this moment, there was no denying what must be done.

"I promise you, sister, we will find him," Asya vowed.

Tears began to sting my eyes.

"How can someone I have only known for two months become so important to me?" I whispered, blinking my eyes and allowing my forehead to sink down into my older sister's shoulder.

The camel stilled and Asya turned to hug me. She held me as she had held me many times before when I was a little girl, sobbing.

"Because he is your husband, and the man you love," Asya whispered, patting my back soothingly.

"He is my everything, Asya. I have to find him," I whimpered.

She held me, offering me the warmth of her comfort as late afternoon settled into evening.

"We have to keep moving, Amara," Asya whispered apologetically. "The rebel hideout is not far from here."

I nodded, wiping my eyes.

I was determined to find my husband, no matter the cost. But Asya was right, we needed information. The two of us travelling blind in the desert was of no use to anyone.

It was nearing nightfall when we stilled, Ronan holding up a hand to halt our descent.

The faint electric hum of activity buzzed in the air as we peered across the desert and spotted a sandstorm building. Asya cursed. But when you are caught up in nature's fury, there is only one thing to do: survive. There was nothing but emptiness stretching out on either side of us. We had to work fast, setting up tents to take cover under until the sandstorm passed us.

As the wind began to pick up, sand stinging our faces, we struggled to keep our footing and hastily pitched our tents.

Asya's mouth was an unguarded slash of frustration. "This is not good," she muttered, dust coating her face and hair.

I gritted my teeth and fought against the stinging in my eyes.

I grabbed the fabric of a tent and thrust it into the sand, feeling the grains cling to my hands as I tried to secure shelter.

One of the men behind us screamed, falling as his feet slipped. I caught my sister's eye and jerked my chin in the man's direction. She understood and left to help him. I had done this before. Many times Ashad and I would get caught in a sandstorm outside the city of Ilm while we practiced sparring. Often we would race to see who could pitch a tent the fastest. A tent that would provide us refuge from the sandstorm.

Lightning streaked across the sky, and I let out a yelp of surprise. Asya was right, this was not good at all! The world around us was enveloped in a swirling vortex of sand and chaos.

"Get inside, Amara!" Asya yelled from where she was, moving to get inside the tent she had helped pitch.

It was too risky for her to make her way to me now. I nodded, knowing that right now this was the only option we had. As I sat huddled, I wondered how long it would last. Maybe all night? I sincerely hoped not.

As the wind and sand battered against the tents, my heart pounded in my chest. The storm seemed to go on for hours, its relentless force pushing us to our limits. I hugged myself, trying to gain some warmth as the chilly night air crept in through the flapping fabric.

I do not know when I dozed off, cocooned in the safety of my tent. But at some point, with the sandstorm raging around outside, I fell asleep. And when I awoke, it was to a primal howl of something that made the beast, dormant inside of me since my first shift, awaken. The hair on my arms stood up, and I could not help but inhale deeply. I smelled...I smelled something familiar yet so different from what I was used to.

My beast snarled inside my head, fighting against me to be let out.

I remembered Zayed's words when he had been preparing me for my shift.

There will be moments when the beast takes control, when the primal instincts surge unchecked, drowning the whispers of humanity. And in those moments, the battle is not against the world, but against oneself.

Those words rang true as I struggled to maintain my human form. I fought the ache in my gums as my canines begged to be let out. Snarls erupted in my brain, and an instinct so overpowering it made me scream in pain seemed to take hold of me.

Outside this tent, I heard screams and shouts. Something was wrong. The tent I was inside flapped violently as the wind picked up, sand battering mercilessly against the fabric of the tent.

I held onto my human form with everything I had, gripping my soft white chemise so tightly that my knuckles turned white.

My body felt foreign, as if the Lycan within me was straining to break free, to embrace the chaos outside. "Not now," I whispered, clenching my fists, trying to ground myself in my humanity. But the howling grew louder, entwining with the furious winds, calling to the beast lurking in my veins.

Suddenly, a bone-chilling roar cut through the storm, and I knew immediately that it was him.

I could not help myself, my beast urging me to emerge from the tent. I was still newly turned, still learning how to control these instincts, and I could not stop my feet from carrying me out of the tent and straight into the merciless sands.

Shadows moved through the swirling sand, Ronan and what remained of his men running closer to my tent. Behind them... I saw him—a massive figure, muscles rippling under a thick coat of fur, his eyes glowing like embers in the storm. He was a force of nature, tearing through the tents with a ferocity that sent panic rippling through those around him. He was attacking the camp.

I whipped my head around, instinctively realizing he was making his way here—to me. And behind me was Asya's tent.

I turned toward Zayed's Lycan, yelling for him to stop. But he either could not hear me or was too far gone in his feral madness.

I tried yelling his name again but my shift washed over me like a tidal wave, sweeping me away in its ferocity.

My bones cracked and reshaped, fur sprouting from my skin as I transformed. I was a creature of the night, powerful and fierce, and I charged at him, the wind no longer a barrier but a guide as I followed his scent, sprinting toward the Lycan King.

The howling of the wind seemed to dissipate around me, leaving only his primal roars ringing in my ears.

He was inches away from me now, his glowing eyes fixated on his prey, a lone man pleading for mercy as he stumbled in the sand. In one swift motion, I lunged at him, tackling him with a howl. We rolled around on the sand, our bodies twisting and clawing at one another. I was not in control. I did not want to hurt him! But my Lycan had something else on her mind. I felt a fierceness in me, a stubborn will to not lose to him. I could sense the last bits of humanity fluttering within me as we fought. Was I losing myself to the same rage that consumed Zayed? Is this how he had been driven to his darkest depths?

I ended up pinned under his Lycan, his canines snapping at my throat menacingly. Immediately, my powerful form bucked under him. I had to drive him away from the camp, from the people I loved. Because if we truly were about to lose ourselves to our Lycans, I did not want my sister harmed.

He landed with a heavy thud next to me, the wind knocked out of his Lycan. I took this opportunity to run. Taking off with my newly acquired speed, I shot off into the dark, the Lycan King hot on my heels.

The storm raged on, the sand sweeping across the desert like a thousand tiny daggers. Lightning struck behind me as my paws pounded into the sand, my beast desperate to outrun the Lycan King behind me who was quickly eating up the space between us. Our howls had ceased; in their place were only two strong-willed Lycans running against the tide of chaos that surrounded them.

A snarl ripped from my throat as another gust of sand battered my face, stinging tears filling up my eyes in desperation-driven haste before sliding down into nothingness. A sheer primal instinct propelled me forward without pause for breath—or fear—of what lay ahead for either one of us out here under these cruel skies, which crackled with lightning bolts that struck viciously across the midnight darkness.

Something in me knew it was only a matter of time before the Lycan King caught me. But the beast in me wanted to keep running. I did not know why this instinct was at the forefront. Maybe she sensed something I did not. So I continued to flee, winding my way deeper into the vast expanses of the desert.

It did not take long before the terrain began to change under me; tall dunes loomed over us like ancient, ominous sentinels. I could feel the sand shifting beneath my paws, becoming coarser with more patches of vegetation visible. I let out a roar of frustration when he tackled me to the ground from behind.

I turned; snapping my canines furiously. He let out a growl of warning.

The beast within me raged, trying to squirm out of his grasp.

The lightning seemed to flash in synchronization with the gusts of wind that whipped around us.

He could have ripped into me, his canines snapping dangerously close to my neck. But he did not. He was warning me to stand down...*to submit.*

The beast in me snarled, an ancient instinct telling me he had to earn the right to dominate me.

I growled back at him, refusing to let him win so easily. My eyes blazed with the fire of defiance, the same primal urge that had driven me away from the camp, the same wild spirit that now made me refuse to submit to him. His paw over my neck applied pressure, his eyes glowing feral red...the pulsing hardness against my inner thigh more pronounced now.

And I suddenly realised, this was not about winning a fight. This was...something else entirely.

The mating run...

Zayed had told me about it.

The male Lycan gives chase, proving his strength, his cunning, his worthiness to claim his mate. Only when he has earned her respect, when she has seen the raw power in his movements, the unyielding devotion in his pursuit, does she surrender. Not in weakness, but in trust. She submits to the one worthy of her—the one strong enough not just to take her, but to cherish her, to protect her, to breed her. For Lycans do not mate lightly. They mate for life, bound by a passion as fierce and unrelenting as the wild heat of the desert itself.

This was not just a fight; it was a ritual, a test of his worth and mine.

The naked plains of the desert and the night-shrouded sky bore witness to our ancient dance, the wind whispering secrets known only to those long gone. I bared my canines, growling in anger, refusing to back down. My beast moved under him, attempting to free herself of his hold. I succeeded, but was only momentarily able to wriggle out of his grasp. Right as I turned to run, he pounced on me again, growling low against my ear from behind.

I gasped as he exerted more of his weight on my body, pinning me so efficiently that I could barely move now. His canines grazed my jugular and one paw came firmly over my neck, a silent message.

Submit. If I had wanted you dead, you already would be.

This was how our kind chose their mates; how we formed unbreakable bonds that would last lifetimes.

He is worthy.

The feeling washed over me. My growls turned to soft whines, and I relaxed under his hard body.

As I softened against him, surrendering to the inevitable, he released his paw on my neck and drew back slightly. I gasped, able to breathe freely. His snout burrowed into the crook of my Lycan's neck from behind me. He inhaled deeply, and my Lycan mimicked the action, turning my head and burrowing my snout into his forearm, taking in his scent. Cardamom and spiced sandalwood. We stayed like that for a few moments, his body caging mine, snout slowly trailing down the expanse of my neck. The storm had passed, but the lightning continued to illuminate the sky above us.

There was something profoundly intimate about this exchange as we committed each other's scents to memory, ingraining it into our brains for all time.

His body, previously tense and poised to stop me should I try to escape, was now relaxed against mine. I felt his steady heartbeat as his chest rested against my back. He let out a low hum of satisfaction. He had his prey. Relief poured through me in waves. I was with my husband, my mate. We had found each other. Now, I felt as if I could face anything with him by my side. And here, right now, amidst the wild elements of the desert, our union was entering an entirely new phase of intimacy that went far beyond physical copulation. It seemed almost symbolic—two wild beasts entwined together under the stark moonlight of this unforgiving desert landscape; powerful forces clashing yet blending harmoniously within one another to create something extraordinary and magical.

And then...the sweetest sensation overtook me as he let out a wild howl and entered my Lycan from behind, claiming me at last, marking our bond for eternity.

My entire world came crashing down into sensations: the sand as it grated against my furry body, the steady rhythmic movement of my mate above me, the indescribable bliss that enveloped me in waves as we mated under the fearsome sky lit up by shafts of lightning bolts striking from above.

Our movements slowed as the need to mate was finally assuaged.

I nearly sobbed from relief, feeling my beast slowly recede and give dominance back to my human side. I was home. I was with my husband, with Zayed. We were together again.

I attempted to turn, to burrow further into the safety and security of his body. But my mate suddenly stilled above me and the scent of blood hit my nostrils. He let out a howl of pain right as I turned to see a silver arrow protruding from his neck. Blood spilled from his lips, and suddenly, he was shoving me down under his body, protecting me from the volley of lethal arrows that pierced his back.

"NO!" I screamed, and it came out as a howl.

"KILL IT!" I heard the screams of men. The voice...was Ronan's. "KILL IT BEFORE IT KILLS US!"

I let out a horrified, blood-curdling howl as one of the arrows pierced his torso and went straight through, grazing my own furry body.

They were killing him! I tried to push him off me, but he was too strong. Rivulets of his blood ran through the sand, staining it crimson red as I snarled and bucked under him in protest. Yet he would not budge! Zayed, ever the protector even in his Lycan form, used the last of the strength in him to keep me completely covered. I did not know Lycans could cry, until my tears mixed with his blood drenching my body. He was sacrificing himself for me.

If ever there is one thing in which I am selfish...let it be this...let it be you.

Chapter 4

Zayed's POV

When Kadin told me Amara was dead, I believed him. I shifted in a rage, my Lycan coming to the surface, uncontrollable anguish and anger consuming us. He, too, had grown to care for her, to love her. And as we killed mercilessly, giving in to the feral blood lust, my human consciousness retreated with the will to live completely gone. And then... we picked up a scent. The scent of my wife. My queen. And we followed it. As we tracked her down, it gave me time to put things into perspective. Kadin had been the one adamant about letting Amara live after she volunteered. He was the one who told me she volunteered as a member of the rebel faction and we could use her to glean information on who was backing it.

He was the one who suspected Amara as part of the rebellion from day one. He was the one who constantly reiterated that Amara might be betraying us. And how had the cheap trinket around my wife's neck managed to escape the fire completely unscathed when her body had been burned down to the bones? Things did not add up.

Which meant Kadin had been lying. Which also meant he had betrayed us. We had played into his hands, following his tune. The anger of betrayal coupled with the scent of Amara's blood in the sand drove me further into a rage. I wanted to kill whoever had harmed her.

We sensed her shift, the change in her scent, and it sent my Lycan into a frenzy. He wanted to claim her as his mate, and I could no more stop him than I could stop myself from loving the woman who had completely and irrevocably captured my heart. For the first time since I had acquired my Lycan, he and I were on the same page regarding Amara. She was our everything. And I would raze the world to keep her safe.

Up until now, I had made the right decisions. Protected my kingdom, gladly taken on the mantle of villain to keep the drought at bay, forged alliances based on the betterment of the people. I could just as easily become the monster they all believed me to be, if it meant my wife lived.

Kadin had, up till now, seen the part of me that loved him as a brother. He had not seen my dark side. The Lycan that revelled in spilling the blood of enemies. But he would know sooner rather than later that he had trifled with the wrong man. I cared not for the crown. I cared for my wife.

And when I finally found her, our coupling was more beautiful than I could have imagined. My feral bellow of completion died on my lips, however, when I sensed danger nearby. And then my world went black with rage. Arrows seared into my flesh from behind as I fought to protect my mate.

I was losing blood and fast. The silver arrows were not letting me heal. I grimaced. Fools. Did they not realize? A man willing to risk it all—his life, his very soul—to protect the one he loves is the most lethal weapon ever forged, more dangerous than any blade, more unstoppable than the breaking of dawn itself.

I let out a mighty roar as the next arrow buried itself in my arm. I caught the slightest glimpse of Amara's transformation as she changed into her human form.

Another arrow struck home, sinking into my thigh. Pain exploded, a tidal wave crashing through me, but I was not going to let that stop me from protecting my woman.

"STOP!" Amara cried out, moving swiftly from under me.

I reacted without thinking, moving faster than a blur. They would kill her if I did not act fast. I crashed into our assailants, hitting them like thunder, claws ripping through flesh as my entire body burned from the pain of my wounds.

They had not expected this; they thought me finished before I had even begun.

But they underestimated me. My blood mixed with those of my enemies, leaving crimson trails across the sand. Only three men were left of the original ten. I could not help the sadistic grin stretching across my lips.

One of them notched an arrow; trained on me. "He's insane!" the pathetic fool yelled. He was not wrong.

I rushed at him as his weapon released, catching the arrow in my shoulder before slicing through his throat.

Another man fell to my claws, hot liquid pouring onto my hands.

I turned to Amara. She was running toward me, her eyes wide with panic and concern, all mingled into one perfect storm of a woman.

Not for her life—for mine.

"Behind you!" Amara screamed, her voice shrill with desperation.

I whirled around in time to see two arrows flying toward me. I caught them with my lightning reflexes, one arrow in each clawed hand. Then I sent them hurtling back toward the poor fools who had thought to best me. My vision blurred, the blood loss finally getting the best of me. I staggered momentarily, realizing that I had to move quickly. My wounds were not healing due to the silver. I might not survive, but with my final breath, I could annihilate this threat. However, instead of charging into the men like I had hoped to, my Lycan stumbled and I fell to the sand, the sand dunes spinning around me.

A figure approached, blade drawn and aimed straight at my neck. For a moment I thought it was Amara. It took a moment to realize that it was her sister. And her eyes gleamed with the intent to kill as she took aim at me. I could not muster the strength to move out of her way. I blinked, realizing this was the end. I would die by the hand of my wife's sister. Because surely, if I attempted to defend myself, Amara would never forgive me for killing Asya. And the heartbreak she would endure over the loss of her sister would break her. I hung my head, ready to face the final blow that would end my life. I could kill mercilessly without batting an eye. But I could not kill the one person whose death would result in the spilling of my wife's tears. I would not be responsible for the loss of her kin.

I love you forever Amara-jaan, I thought to myself as I heard Asya's sword swipe through the air.

"NO!" There was a whoosh of air, I heard her shrill scream, and looked up abruptly to see Amara towering over me. Like a goddess of the desert, she stood, a blade in hand, scraps of clothing barely covering her naked body. She had stopped Asya, using her weapon against her sister.

My vision dimmed, pain reverberating through me like a relentless drum. But the sight of her shielding me with her body, blades crossed against her sister, would forever be ingrained in my mind's eye.

"Do not touch my husband," Amara hissed, throwing her might into her sword and making Asya fall back.

"He...he attacked the camp! He was attacking you!" Asya countered, moving to draw and point her silver tipped arrow at me.

"If you try to attack him, then we fight," Amara gritted out, back to me as she took a menacing step forward.

"Amara! Have you lost your mind?" Asya replied, breathing hard, her eyes wide with disbelief. "He has gone feral! He was attacking you!"

"Enough!" Amara's voice cut through the night, fierce and unyielding. "It was not what you think!"

I staggered to my feet, the world a haze of pain and war cries, Amara's silhouette blazing bright in my vision.

"He will destroy us all! He—"

Two arrows pierced into my chest, knocking me off my feet.

"NO!" Amara shrieked, falling down beside me. Her hands were on me with not nearly enough pressure to stop the bleeding.

"He needs to heal!" she screamed as she ripped the arrows from my flesh.

However, there was too much blood. Blood that poured free and fast from within me.

"Stay with me!" Her voice wavered.

I groaned, forcing a shift when the last arrow was pulled free of my body. Her gentle hands cradled my head in her lap.

"Zayed!" she cried out. "You cannot leave me now!"

Her lips pressed against my forehead, her hot tears falling on my skin. I wanted to tell her there was no better way to die than with her arms around me, but before I could, blackness finally overtook me.

When I came to, my entire body burned as if it were on fire. There was a tangy, bitter taste in my mouth, as if I had been force-fed medicine. By all logic, I should have been dead. Maybe I was.

Amara's soft hands were on my body, her touch more soothing than the cool salve being applied to my wounds.

"Get out! You were the one who told them silver was lethal! I trusted you, sister!"

Amara's voice was full of venom as she spoke. Where were we? Hopefully somewhere safe. I tried to use my sense of smell, but all I smelled was the pungent scent of medicinal herbs.

"I thought he was attacking you! Amara, he attacked the camp! I was afraid he was going to kill you. And from our vantage point, it looked as if he was about to rip into you."

"Like I explained before, we were mating!" Her voice was shrill.

"I did not know," Asya replied tearfully. "Amara. Please...let me help. I can grind the powder for the medicine—"

"You have done enough, Asya. We are lucky he is still breathing. I am thankful for your help in setting up camp here so I can heal him. But please get out. I am very angry at you right now. We will speak further once I am sure my husband is well. He needs me right now."

"But—" Asya began, and Amara's growl was enough to silence her. "Amara, I love you. I was only trying to protect you!"

"And I was only trying to protect my husband," Amara replied with finality.

Blinking away the darkness, I was able to open my eyes and view the tent I was inside of. Amara was wringing a wet cloth, the water trickling into a bowl. Asya left quietly, the flap of the tent shutting behind her. I blinked, my eyes settling on my wife, who was now pressing the warm, wet cloth to the wound on my shoulder. Her eyes were firmly trained on my body, on my wounds.

"Amara," I rasped out, finally finding my voice. "You are alive!"

She stilled, her eyes meeting mine. Tears sprang to her eyes as she threw her arms around me.

"And you are a fool!" she sobbed.

I winced as she jostled my wounds. But it was worth it to hold her in my arms like this. I grabbed her, pulling her against me more firmly.

"Shielding me the way you did—" she choked out onto my shoulder, sobs overcoming her. "Zayed, you are the king! You cannot do that."

I pushed her away gruffly, my hands clutching her shoulders.

"I am not a king. I am your husband first, and I will always, always protect you first. Damn everything else to hell," I gritted through my teeth, trying to ignore the fiery pain of silver-inflicted holes filling my back and front. "Listen to me, and listen well—if you ever dare believe your life is worth less than mine, you are gravely mistaken. You are the most precious thing in this world, my tigress. Do you not understand? No king, no kingdom, no alliance, no power in existence holds more value than you. I thought you were dead." The words came out raw, each syllable tearing through the pain. "And I wanted to kill everything in sight."

Her delicate hand came up to rest against the side of my face. Her gentle touch grounded me, and I breathed in, grateful for her.

"You should have known better. You should have known I would not give up that easily." Her words held all the fire and conviction that I had come to love so much in my wife.

The relief I felt at seeing her consumed me, overriding the sting of the arrow wounds.

"You shifted," I said, wonder and pride creeping into my voice despite the agony. "Your Lycan is beautiful," I breathed, moving to cup her face in mine. "My love, you are here."

"And our Lycans mated," Amara whispered, her body draped over mine.

Her soft lips were inviting, and I could not stop myself from claiming them in a possessive kiss. It had been so long since I held her in my arms. Our bodies intertwined, relieved to have found each other after such despair and distance.

"My queen," I murmured as the world threatened blackness once more.

"Your wife," she corrected fiercely. Her hands came to cradle my face in her palms. "Sleep, husband. The medicines are working to help heal you."

I slipped in and out of consciousness under her care, Amara's touch never leaving me as she fought to keep me grounded in both body and spirit.

Amara's POV

Watching Zayed teeter between life and death nearly broke me all over again. His blood soaked the makeshift bed in the tent where I had laid him.

The traitorous remnants of metal still clinging to his body smelt acrid to my heightened senses, mocking my every effort to heal him.

Every time he slipped into unconsciousness, it felt like losing him anew.

For hours I battled death itself to keep him tethered to this world. Asya hovered outside like a remorseful ghost, kept at bay by the ferocity of my grief and anger.

His breathing slowed at one point; panic crushed my chest until I could not breathe either. But luckily, as time progressed, I watched Zayed slowly begin to heal. We were so fortunate that when he was injured by the silver arrows, the hideout that we were supposed to reach was close by. It was only a few hours' journey, and Ronan, despite his anger over the dead men, was able to travel there and get us the medicines we needed to heal Zayed. However, the hideout's proximity was another reason the rebels had readily let their arrows fly on Zayed. They had been afraid of him attacking the hideout where some men housed their families.

As I sat next to my husband, exhausted and wanting nothing more than to fall asleep myself, a man I had not expected in a million years to see here entered the tent.

"What are you doing here?" I screeched, standing up to stare at the intruder. My eyes narrowed on the man before me.

"Amara...we are all worried for you. You have been here for twenty-four hours. Your father is waiting for you at the rebel hideout. He sent me here to check on you. Would you delay meeting your own sire...all for him?" Ashad jerked his head in my husband's direction.

Exhausted and completely fed up, I threw the bloodstained rag I had used to clean Zayed's wounds in Ashad's direction. It hit his chest before falling to his feet.

"Yes, for him," I sneered. "I love him. He is my husband."

"Amara, you do not have to honor your vows any longer. Please see reason. He is no longer king. The title is now Kadin's. We can annul your marriage to him and—"

"Why are you here, Ashad?" I asked wearily, passing a hand over my face. I was surprised when Asya told me of Ashad's involvement in helping the rebels. Apparently, he had been one of the people who helped the rebels infiltrate the palace. Ever since the altercation in the gardens, he had made himself scarce. I thought it meant he was no longer trying to win me over. How utterly wrong. Instead, he made his way here and drew out a map for the rebels so they could easily get into the palace and get me out of there.

It was the same map Asya and the rebels used to stay hidden, waiting for a chance to get to me. When I told Asya to take Baba and go into hiding, I had not meant for them to go join the rebels working to take out the crown. But that is exactly what they did. And so did Ashad. He had done it in hopes of winning my love once Zayed was out of my life. However, he had not counted on my husband arriving with me.

"Why do you not understand?" I huffed, crossing my arms. "I love Zayed."

"No, you do not. You are just a naive girl who believes she has to honor her wedding vows. Amara, stop thinking you have to stay married to this man. We can be together," Ashad pleaded.

I blinked, realizing Ashad was something more than merely delusional.

"You are insane," I finally said, shaking my head.

"Amara," he implored, voice full of frustrated longing. "You have been lied to by him. Surely, you must know of the curse by now. He tricked you and trapped you into this marriage."

Anger made my hands clench.

"He never lied to me," I whispered. "Not like you!"

"So that is what this is all about? You are angry I did not tell you I was a noble."
He crossed his arms and looked at me with remorse. "I am sorry, my love. Please,
let us put this all behind us and move forward to begin a new life together."

My Lycan stirred, ready to unleash her rage on him.

"Get out."

I bared my teeth at him, lost in the animalistic rage that pulsed through me. I
did not recognize the angry growl that ripped from my throat, but it sent Ashad
retreating a step. He stared at me with wide, fearful eyes .

"What has he done to you?" Ashad breathed. "He has turned you...into a monster..."

There was a rustling sound as the flap of the tent opened and my sister walked in.
Asya's eyes narrowed on Ashad.

"I told you to stay away," she hissed.

I let out another warning growl, not bothering to hide the feral red glow of my
eyes.

He held up his hands placatingly, as if I were a wild creature who might leap and
attack him. "Very well," he said quietly. "I will leave for now."

When he was gone, a tremor ran through me, the energy of my fury cooling back
into exhaustion.

"I am sorry. I went to get some rest and he must have slipped through," Asya
muttered.

I did not reply, merely letting my head sink into my hands. I could not trust
anyone. It was Zayed and me against everyone else right now. At least that is what
it seemed like. No one wanted me with him. Even my sister had tried to kill my
husband.

"I should have killed him when I had the chance." Zayed finally spoke up darkly
as he suddenly moved into a sitting position.

I could not help the sob of relief that wracked through me. Unlike the last time he had woken up, his wounds were nearly fully healed now.

"Better yet, let me kill him now." He was suddenly standing before me, naked save for a cloth around his waist; virile strength radiating from him in waves. His beard had grown out, and his hair was slightly longer. But he was still the man I loved.

I threw my arms around him, clinging to his warmth. He nearly toppled from the force, laughter rumbling in his chest.

"I thought you were asleep," I said against his shoulder, inhaling his familiar scent.

"And miss watching you scare that wretch into cowering?" He tousled my hair with a grin. "Never."

I pulled back enough to look at him, my fingers tracing where his wounds should have been. "I almost lost you." The words were softer now, laced with the terror I had felt. "I thought you were going to leave me alone. I cannot fight Kadin without you by my side."

He lifted my chin with a gentle hand. "You will not need to. We fight them all, together."

"Together," I acknowledged with a smile.

"But first, let me see to this man who is coveting my wife," Zayed said with a grim set to his mouth.

"He is integral to the rebel faction. His family helped weed out Kadin's men. We cannot harm him," Asya hedged, finally stepping forward. "He is also the one who made sure the medicines Amara required were sent straight away. Without him advocating for the two of you, they might have executed Zayed for the men he killed while he was in his Lycan form. For all Ashad's faults, he is doing everything for your benefit, Amara."

I scoffed and gave a shake of my head. Ashad was only doing this because he still hoped to win my love.

"Zayed, I am so sorry for the attack. I thought your Lycan was attacking Amara. If I had known...I would not have let Ronan and his men take aim."

Zayed looked at Asya, his arms still around my waist.

"Your every decision revolves around protecting your sister. I cannot fault you for that. But please know, the last thing I or my Lycan would ever do is harm Amara."

"Even though the curse demands it?" Asya pressed.

Zayed inclined his head.

"We have mated. And that is stronger than any curse's demands. My Lycan does not want to harm her."

"Does that mean the curse is broken?" I breathed out excitedly.

Zayed's apologetic gaze was all I needed to see.

"No, my love. The curse still exists. For famine and drought will not let up until the curse is assuaged. I feel its darkness residing within my soul, tearing at the edges of my consciousness. And its malevolence grows stronger with each passing day. One way or another, the curse will bring death and destruction. However, I would rather see them all wither away into husks than ever give in to the demands of it."

He kissed my forehead, sealing his promise with warmth. I wanted to believe that our love could defy anything, even breaking this curse in the end. I could not help the desolate sigh that escaped my lips. Despite everything, the curse still persisted.

"Amara, I know you feel like everyone is against you." Asya's voice was gentle now. "But we are not your enemy. Even Ashad is acting out of care, no matter how misguided."

I let out a shuddering breath. The anger inside me flared again at the thought of him, but it was more controlled this time, tempered by Zayed's presence.

"No," I said, my voice steadier now. "Ashad wants me for himself. He will stop at nothing to tear us apart."

"He believes you are being forced. We will make him see reason," she assured me.

"He will never listen, Asya. He wants to be the grand hero who saves me from this so-called monster," I replied bitterly.

Zayed let out a low growl, his grip tightening protectively around me. "I will deal with him. Whether it is with words or claws is up to him."

"We need Ashad and his men on our side. We need them if we are to fight Kadin's men," Asya replied evenly. She passed a hand over her face. "Rest for now. And tomorrow we will make our way to the rebel hideout. Can I get you anything to eat?"

Zayed's response made me blush bright red to the tips of my ears.

"The only thing I want to eat right now is my wife." And then he crashed his lips into mine with such fervor and passion that if I had still doubted his recovery, there was no way I could doubt it any longer.

Chapter 5

Amara's POV

I could not breathe as his mouth slanted over mine, so intense were the feelings surging through me. I sensed Asya retreating, a small giggle escaping her lips. Zayed lifted me up into his arms, and I adjusted myself so my legs were now wrapped around his waist. But suddenly I pulled back from the kiss, staring up at him warily.

"You still need to heal—" I began

"I need to claim you in every way a man claims his wife," he grunted, lips going to my neck, where he began to kiss and suck his way slowly up to my ear. "And I need to make you scream loud enough for that fool to hear you and know exactly who you belong to."

I gasped as he nipped my earlobe in response before I found myself laid out in the very spot he had been laying moments before as I tended to him.

I was wearing the black and silver garb of the rebel faction, a loose shirt and pants. Conducive for fighting in the desert and camouflaging oneself at night. He ripped it down the middle without batting an eye.

"I can smell the scent of the man who this belongs to," he growled.

I was unable to get a word out, in feeble protest, that it was a man who Zayed had already killed when we had been attacked. His mouth descended on my breast, and I was lost in a sea of bliss. His scruff scraped against the sensitive skin of my chest, heightening the sensation of his tongue flicking my nipple.

"Zayed," I breathed out, fingers burying in his locks.

"Oh, my love," he groaned into my skin, each vibration sending a jolt of ecstasy through me.

He held nothing back, raw and unrestrained as his mouth moved lower, lavishing attention down my body. I arched into him, a breathless gasp escaping my lips each time he found some new place to claim as his own. Just like he had sworn, he brought me so close to the edge that every pulse of pleasure seemed to echo around me.

His fingers came away from between my legs doused in my arousal.

"See how ready you are for me," he whispered, showing me his glistening digits before drawing back momentarily. There was urgency and heat in his gaze as he undid the cloth around his waist.

There was a wildness about him that sent a thrill through me, but beneath it all was an unyielding tenderness that made my heart swell. He brought his hardened cock to tease my entrance, swirling around it at a torturous pace.

"Say it," he commanded, voice low. "Say you are mine."

"I am yours," I whimpered out as he drove into me, filling me completely.

My back arched, and I clung to him, fingers digging into his shoulders. He held still for a moment, an unmistakable grin on his lips at my response.

Then he began to move.

Each thrust was deliberate and deep, and every sensation blurred into the next until I could not tell where one ended and another began.

I clapped a hand over my mouth to muffle the sounds he elicited from my lips.

"No." He jerked my hand away, pinning it above my head in one deft move. "No. Let me hear what I can do to you." He gave a particularly harsh thrust as he hovered over me, and I bit my lip.

"They will he-hear us," I panted.

We had set up camp close together, the tents next to each other to maintain strength in numbers and unity lest we were attacked in the dead of night. Asya was on the first watch. But Ashad...he was...close by. Asleep most likely. But if we kept this up, he would wake.

"Let him hear how well you take my cock inside you," he growled, pulling out and pushing back into me with renewed fervor. "I want him to hear you scream my name as I thrust into you and empty my seed inside you."

He kissed me, swallowed my moans as we moved against one another.

My pulse beat wildly in my ears, drowning out everything but Zayed—his breath mingling with mine, his body against mine, the words he spoke between ragged breaths.

"I will never let him have you," he vowed. "I will kill any man who tries."

My body responded long before my voice could; I gripped him tighter, urging him deeper.

But he stilled above me, my one arm still pinned above my head as he glared down at me.

And then, before I could even react or process what he was doing, he pulled out of me and flipped me onto my stomach in one quick move.

He lifted me by my hips, pulling me even closer so that there was not a single space between us as he drove into me with renewed fervor. I felt his resolve behind every movement—a need to prove something, not only to Ashad, but to himself. To me.

"This is all mine," he grunted as my hands curled into the blanket under me.

"Yes," I gasped between thrusts. "Yes. Yes!"

I no longer cared about anything but the way he was making me feel as he thrust into me from behind. He squeezed my hips tighter, his pace slower than I needed to find my release.

"Faster...please," I begged, like a needy bitch in heat. And maybe I was. He had me on all fours, a position I had never experienced in human form. One I would have thought degrading. But with him...it was not. It felt good.

"Beg me." His hand wrapped around my long flowing hair from behind, his hard, pulsing manhood rested teasingly against my entrance.

"Zayed, please!" I cried out.

Suddenly, I was pulled upright so my back pressed against his chest. One hand was firmly tangled in my hair, the other around my waist. This was different. He had been so controlled before. Had he been holding himself back? Or was this a new side of him after everything we had been through? I screamed his name again when he entered me, holding me upright so I was impaled over his cock as he sat back in a sitting position. One of his hands went to fondle me between my legs while the other released my hair to pinch my nipple.

"Move, take what you want from me. Find your release like a good girl."

I was lost in the haze of frenzied desire he had created. I moved against him, enjoying his hands on me as I gyrated over him.

"You move so beautifully with my cock deep inside you, Amara," he whispered into my ear, rolling my nipple between his thumb and forefinger.

My eyes rolled back into my head as my world shattered, and I screamed his name so loud, the heavens themselves probably heard it.

But my husband did not give me a moment's reprieve. I was on my back again, with him thrusting inside me mercilessly, sending me spiraling into a new wave of pure bliss.

"I love you," I told him breathlessly, my hands trailing up his chest as my orgasm waned. Another one was building quicker than I could comprehend. My body was flushed and I felt hot, like a fever had taken hold of me. But this was no fever. This was the result of the lovemaking between me and my husband after he had thought I was dead.

"I love you too, Amara. More than life itself," he groaned as he moved above me, sweat beading on his forehead.

We moved together frantically, lost in the storm of our emotions. Each ragged breath and low moan was louder than before. He pulled me into a sitting position so I was on top, straddling his hips. I gyrated on top of him, and his tongue came out to lave one of my nipples. He sucked on it, sending white hot pleasure to coil in my belly. A pleasure that mounted with each thrust and undulation of our hips as his cock hit a spot inside me that made stars dance before my eyes. We kept going, the sound of our panting and skin meeting skin filling the tent until finally I had no choice but to scream his name again. He shuddered under me, and then we were falling, shattering from the intensity of our respective releases.

His arms wrapped tightly around me as if to fuse us into one being, riding out the waves of desire as they crested and waned.

Finally, spent and sated, we burrowed into each other, tangled in the tent beneath the stars.

Zayed's POV

Holding her like this—feeling her body pressed against mine—was more potent than any balm or healer's touch could ever be. Amara's breathing evened out slowly until she was sleeping soundly in my arms. I pressed a kiss to her temple. My wife. We were together again, finally.

I buried my nose in her hair, deeply inhaling the scent of jasmine mingled with the faint coppery betrayal of blood that seemed to linger on us now—both hers and mine, but mostly from our enemies.

The sun was ruthless when morning came—a blazing reminder that we were still very much in a desert filled with many people who wished us harm.

Amara stirred beside me as light filtered through the thin fabric of our tent, but she did not say anything at first, just nuzzled closer like she never wanted to leave the safety of our little haven here.

"Good morning," I murmured against her temple.

Her lips curved into a smile though her eyes remained closed—a lazy expression that made it clear exactly how content and smug she felt this morning, given what had taken place last night.

"Are you hungry?" she asked after a few moments had passed in sweet silence.

I grinned mischievously.

"You should not say that when you are pressed up against me completely bare," I whispered huskily into her ear before slowly trailing a path down her beautiful body with my lips.

"Zayed, wait," she rasped. "I-I...I am no longer doused in expensive perfumes and oils, you might not enjoy—"

I silenced her when my tongue flattened over her clit. Her back arched, her head fell back and she began to melt like butter under my ministrations, all protests dying on her lips as they were replaced by her needy pants.

I pulled back momentarily, spreading her womanhood to stare at the evidence of how much she was enjoying my tongue inside her.

"All mine," I growled and gave one long lick up her seam. "Perfect. Wrap your legs around my neck, tigress. Let me enjoy my breakfast."

Every inch of me was burning, but it was a sweet fire, one I never wanted to end. Her nails raked across my shoulders as she held me, unconsciously, at the angle she wanted. At the angle that gave her the most pleasure. I groaned, deep and ragged, plunging my tongue inside of her.

My cock was hard and throbbing, but I focused only on her, on the way her breath hitched each time I moved my tongue against that perfect spot. Her hips moved against me desperately, and she chanted my name—Zayed, Zayed, Zayed—as she came apart around my tongue.

I brought her down from her high slowly, gently. I peppered her body with kisses, working my way up her thighs, her navel, her breasts and her neck. Until finally, she lay limp and boneless beneath me.

She reached for me, pulling my face away from her neck and toward her lips to kiss me—hard—so hard she must have tasted herself on my lips.

"I hope you are not too attached to this tent," I whispered darkly into her ear as I pinned her beneath me once more.

Her pupils dilated when my arousal pressed insistently against her thigh. She then wrapped her legs tightly around me like she might never let go again—as if neither Ashad nor any other foe could pry us apart when we were woven so completely together.

"Oh, I am not," she gasped between kisses, her breath ragged against my cheek as I slipped inside her. "Not even remotely. We can leave as soon as possible."

"Good," I teased as my hips pistoned against hers, my words daring her to tell me to stop so we could leave.

Her cry vibrated through me and out into the world.

But she did not say it was time to leave.

So I pressed into her once more, hard and deep. She cried out my name in ecstasy, eyes rolling heavenward. We were not going anywhere anytime soon.

I grinned, not caring how uncouth it might be of me to claim my woman in every way imaginable. I might not be able to battle that fool, but by the time we emerged from our tent, everyone would know she was mine, and no power on earth could take her away from me.

They would have to kill me first if they wanted me gone from Amara's life.

Amara's POV

The sun was high by the time we finally emerged—long past the hour when even the laziest among us would have risen.

"Amara," Asya called, waving us over to where she sat.

I noted Ashad sitting next to her, a surly expression on his face.

Asya tossed me a skin filled with water before passing dried camel meat to Zayed. "Eat up. We have to make our way to the hideout. It is not far from here."

We both sat down. Zayed offered me a piece of his meat and I gave him a sip of water.

"I have never seen you this...thoroughly conquered," Asya settled on saying, a small smile playing across her lips.

I could not help my reddened cheeks at her play on words. A hand went to my hair. I had done my best to make myself look more presentable. To make it look less like I had spent the entire night tangled up in a passionate embrace with my husband. But without the bevy of maids who usually helped me to accomplish that feat, it was nigh impossible. Especially out here in the middle of the desert. I glanced at Zayed. The wildness suited him. His unkempt hair, his roguish beard...

But me...I looked at my hands absentmindedly, noticeably lacking henna. He had never seen me dressed in anything but my best. I peeked at him sideways. Would he still want me, bare-faced and in rags? But this was who I truly was. I was a peasant. A simple girl who could not afford the luxurious life his palace had provided. And I was a warrior. A woman who had been taught that in vanity lay weakness. Why then, was I becoming so superficial?

Zayed's arm slipped possessively around my waist, pulling me close on the ground where we sat.

"She puts up more of a battle than you would think," he said, warmth in his voice.

Heat rose to my cheeks, spilling down my neck. But there was a strange thrill, too—seeing Ashad's frustration at such an overt display of Zayed's claim on me. The vindictive side of me that wanted Ashad to stop being so delusional was appeased.

Once we finished eating, I stood and dusted off my clothes as best I could. Clinging to vanity even as I rejected it.

Asya shook her head, but the corners of her lips turned up in an almost-smile. "Come on," she said.

We packed up and followed Ashad, who led the way across the sandy dunes toward the hideout. My heart hammered in my chest. Baba was waiting for me there.

No one spoke, and I was thankful for that. We travelled on foot, choosing to allow the one camel we had to bear the weight of our camp supplies that we had packed up.

The silence was broken when Zayed looped an arm around my waist in the blistering heat.

I found it impossible not to lean into him. To crave even more of his touch.

He kissed me, and the world blurred until all that existed were his lips on mine.

Asya sighed dramatically. "You two can do that later."

"Much later," Ashad added dryly, glancing back at us with irritated eyes.

"Not if Amara has any say in the matter," Zayed whispered against my ear, sending a wave of heat through my stomach.

I swatted him playfully but let my hand linger in his.

It was long past midday when we reached the hideout. A cave on the edge of the desert close to the mountains.

It was nestled in the cliffs, almost invisible to any passing eyes. My heart skipped a beat as my eyes fell on a line of men standing before the entrance. And in front of them all stood...

"Baba!" I called, my heart soaring.

He looked older than when I had seen him last. Had a few months affected him so much? But still, his familiar smile with his blazing white hair and fierce expression was enough to bring an answering smile to my own lips.

I ran to him, my feet kicking up sand as I went.

"Amara," he shouted, his voice booming across the distance between us.

We met halfway. The old man caught me in a tight embrace, and I breathed him in. A father is meant to be a girl's first shield against the world. His home, the fortress that keeps the darkness at bay. His arms, the refuge where she learns the meaning of safety. He is her first hero, the unwavering guardian of her well-being.

My Baba was everything and more for me.

He pulled back, his eyes searching mine, his face a mixture of relief and something graver.

"Amara," he breathed. "My child, my fierce lion. You are safe. You are here. You are alive!"

He brought me into his arms again, though old and frail now. There had been a time where they held the strength of a thousand men. Or so it seemed to a little girl of five.

The others caught up, and Zayed came beside me, almost bristling with protectiveness. I raised an eyebrow.

"Idris," he greeted my father respectfully but with a tone of familiarity that sent me reeling.

"Zayed," my father replied wearily, raising a hand to his brow absentmindedly. As if from a long-ago habit. Awareness prickled my brain. This exchange was not of two strangers meeting for the first time. "When I retired from the palace long ago, never had I imagined we would meet again, with you as my daughter's husband."

His comment left me reeling. They knew each other?

Chapter 6

Flashback

"Master Idris," the young boy of fourteen looked up at his tutor from the scroll before him. *"Why does the king wish to disband the Blade-Callers?"*

Idris cupped his chin, looking down at the child pensively. The crown prince was astute. And though the king had attempted to brainwash his son and fill him with hate, Idris did his best to instill empathy in the young boy. If he could even make a small difference to ensure that the next king would be a just ruler, it would be worth it all.

"Because, Prince Zayed, we both know he does not think women should be allowed to fight. He believes their place is in the home, submitting to a man."

"Is he right?"

"Do you think he is?" Idris asked calmly. He motioned to the women in their white garb surrounding the courtyard where they sat. "Do you think these women do not deserve to be here after relentless hours of training? After devoting their entire lives to achieving their dream?"

Prince Zayed set his quill down next to the scroll of parchment and thought pensively.

"I think..." His eyes suddenly became sad as the memory of his mother entered his brain. "I think...women should be allowed to choose whatever makes them happy."

"And disbanding the Blade-Callers would take away the choice of becoming warriors," Idris chimed in on a gentle whisper.

"It would...?" Prince Zayed murmured.

"Remember, women were not made to live beneath us, young prince. They are to be cherished and protected, yes. But they are never to be subjugated."

"Father says men are stronger," Zayed replied evenly, though his voice held disdain for his sire as he spoke. *"He says that, as the weaker sex, women are beneath us."*

"Weakness is subjective, young prince," Idris pointed out with a chuckle as he patted his white beard. *"If strength is all it takes for one person to be deemed more worthy, then I should be serving all these wonderful women stationed around the courtyard for your protection. For surely this old man is not stronger than these young women with the reflexes and strength of mighty lions. In fact,"* he chortled, eyes twinkling, *"my own wife could probably trounce me in hand to hand combat. She used to be a Blade-Caller too,"* he whispered with pride in his eyes and not even an ounce of embarrassment over a woman's ability to best him. *"She was so skilled in her time that your grandfather awarded her with the sword of honor for her service to the crown."*

"The sword of honor was awarded to a woman?" Zayed had all but forgotten his assignment, now looking eagerly at his tutor. *"I have never heard of that ever happening!"*

Every ten years, the Crown bestowed a sacred award upon the bravest of its warriors—The Sword of Honor. Made in the heart of the royal forge and inlaid with gleaming gold, its hilt adorned with the fierce image of a lion, The Sword of Honor is a symbol of strength, courage, and unwavering loyalty.

But this is no mere weapon. It is a testament. A declaration that the bearer has faced the gravest of trials and emerged not only victorious but unbroken. It is given to the best among the best—those whose valor has written itself into the annals of history.

To receive the Sword of Honor is to be more than a soldier. It is to be a protector of the realm, a defender of its people. It is earned through acts of extraordinary bravery. Acts done not for glory, but for the good of the Crown and the kingdom. Battles fought in the name of justice, sacrifices made without hesitation, and choices that placed duty above all else.

When the ten years pass and the time of selection draws near, the air always grows thick with anticipation. From every corner of the realm, stories of heroism are brought forth. Yet only one name shall be etched into legend.

Before the gathered court, the sovereign themself presents the sword, the lion's golden eyes gleaming as though alive. As the blade rests in the hands of its rightful owner, the realm echoes with the resounding truth—that true honor is not merely won on the battlefield, but carried in the soul of those who serve.

The Sword of Honor is more than a prize. It is a legacy. A reminder that courage may shine brightest when all else has fallen dark. And Idris was mighty proud that his wife had been the recipient of it. Unfortunately, after her, no woman had ever been awarded it again.

"Because your father does not wish to acknowledge it. Ever since his reign started, the sword of honor has only ever been awarded to males," Idris explained gently. "No matter how well the female counterpart might perform."

"But that is not fair!" Zayed exclaimed, his face red with anger. "When I am king, I will make sure that does not happen. Every ten years, the sword must be awarded to whoever performs the most heroic deeds! Gender should not be a deciding factor."

"Keep your voice down, young prince," Idris implored, realizing Zayed's voice was echoing in the courtyard.

"In fact," the crown prince plowed on, his voice excited as thoughts overwhelmed him. "Maybe I can talk to my uncle. Maybe I can convince him to make Father agree that there should be two swords of honor awarded every ten years. One for women, and one for men. After all, how can we expect women to contest equally when we do not treat them as equals? It would—"

"Enough of this nonsense!" The king's angry voice echoed through the courtyard. He strode forward from the shadows, face red. "I had a feeling you were feeding my son these ridiculous ideas," he fumed at Idris, his words sharp as daggers.

"Father," Zayed stammered, uncertain but defiant. "I was merely saying—"

"I know what you were saying!" the King interrupted fiercely. His pale, haggard face held the effects of the curse placed upon him. Soon, he would be dead, and he would not leave behind an heir with such preposterous notions. "And I will not have it! Not in my kingdom, and certainly not from my heir."

"If that is what you call me," Zayed shot back, "then maybe you should take my opinions seriously!"

The king's laughter echoed bitterly. "You think your opinion matters when you will be king only because I have no other choice?" He looked at Zayed with disdain. Then his eyes fixed on Idris. "Your services are no longer required, Idris. You may opt for early retirement or else find your head on the executioner's block at dawn. I do not wish to see you in my palace any longer. If the crown did not owe your wife a life debt, you might already be dead. For I surely would like nothing more than to drive a sword straight through your heart for teaching my son to be weak!"

"But Father—!"

"Silence, boy! If only I was not impotent! I could have sired another heir. But you will have to do, and l will be damned if I let this fool scribe fill your brain with useless rot!"

The king stomped over to the desk Zayed had been sitting at and glared at the scroll. His assignment had been to write an essay on how the current laws impacted the rights of women. The king grabbed it, shredding it to pieces.

"No more of this foolish brain rot!" The king was frothing at the mouth, his breathing heavy from the exertion required. "Get out, Idris. Out, now! I will find a tutor more suitable to my needs. Someone who will align with our values!"

Idris hesitated, fearful for the young boy. But then he slowly retreated. His family needed him. He had two little girls and a wife who were dependent on him for their livelihood.

"We will meet again one day, young prince," Idris murmured with a bow, before moving away.

The crown prince looked on, shattered, angry defiance rolling off him in waves. One day, he would not be little anymore. One day, he would be able to right the wrongs his father had done.

And when that day came, the sword would no longer be a prize only for the ones his father deemed worthy.

No words were spoken between father and son as the king watched Idris leave. The silence stretched, heavy with their unyielding differences, until finally the king stormed off to brood in solitude. His days were numbered, and ever since Elvira had placed the curse on him, despite all his attempts, he could no longer sire heirs. Prince

Zayed remained in the courtyard as if rooted by defiance, gathering the torn paper scraps like fallen petals.

End of flashback.

Zayed's POV

I had not put two and two together until I saw Idris. He looked older. Much older, as he held his arms out for my wife and embraced her. Where there had been flecks of black still peppering his hair, now his head had turned entirely gray. The crinkles at the corners of his eyes had become more pronounced. And there was a weariness about him that I had not seen before. Or maybe, as a child of fourteen, I had never noticed.

"You two...know each other?" Amara queried, aghast as she leaned against her father.

My heart went out for the man before me. Because, in the time since I had seen him, he had lost his wife. The woman he had spoken of with such pride.

"Part of my scribe duties during my final years was to tutor the crown prince," Idris said smoothly, eyes going to me.

"And I am the reason you had to opt for retirement before your time," I grunted, sadness filling my being. Maybe the financial troubles Amara had spoken of would not have befallen her family if not for me.

"It was not you, but your father who demanded it. We are not to be held responsible for the mistakes of our sires," Idris said gently, placing a kiss on Amara's temple.

"You...had to take early retirement?" Amara asked in surprise. This must have been the first she had heard of it. Of course, back then, she was an eight-year-old and too young to understand. "But why?"

"The king did not agree with the syllabus I was teaching his heir," Idris informed Amara. "He found new tutors, those who had values that aligned with his. And I must admit...I thought the king had succeeded in his aim."

I grimaced, realizing that the killing of innocent women must have been something Idris assumed I did as a result of my father's upbringing.

I had wanted Amara's father to like me. Yes, that much was true. But now, seeing him for who he truly was—the man who had shaped the very foundation of how I saw the world—the need for his approval burned within me, fierce and unrelenting, more powerful than ever before.

"Come, let us go inside and talk further," Idris murmured, motioning toward the caves .

But at once, a line of soldiers moved to block the entrance.

"Your daughter is free to enter, but the man who murdered our people is not," A new voice spoke up, loud and firm and full of anger. Anger and hate.

I took a step back in surprise at the familiar face. An elderly man stood before me, older than Idris, but more muscular and powerful. I knew him, with his broad shoulders and fierce angry brown eyes. They still seethed with the same hatred they had ten years ago at his daughter's funeral. He was the father of my first wife. I closed my eyes, regret seeping through me. For guilt had always plagued me over the deaths of my previous brides.

"Murderer of innocents!" he raged. "I will be damned if the man who killed my daughter is allowed into the rebel hideout! Be gone from here, you evil scum. I am the leader of this rebellion. And we will save our kingdom from your entire family! I will be damned if I allow you to join us!"

"Sorrin, we already agreed to give them asylum," Idris said placatingly. "We must remain calm and think rationally. We have no chance of defeating Kadin without a ruler to take his place. Zayed is someone the nobles will rally behind as the rightful king. Kadin had been secretly funding the rebellion, if you recall. We thought it was a benevolent noble who wished to see the king's downfall, not Kadin looking to usurp the crown. We need the wealth and resources of influential people. Without their backing, we are fighting a losing battle. Only the true king can help us win."

Sorrin sneered, eyes on Amara before going to Idris.

"Easy for you to remain calm, Idris! Your daughter lived! Putting her husband back on the throne will make her a queen! My daughter was queen, too! But mine paid with her life for being wed to that—filth!" Sorrin's voice cracked, his trembling finger stabbing the air toward me. "I can never hear my little Sheila sing again. All because of him! I do not care if there was a curse! My daughter did not deserve to die!"

"She sang on her last night in the palace," I murmured, though the words barely felt like my own. "When I told her what had to be done, she sang, and she did not weep." I swallowed hard, the memory burning. "Sheila knew the cost. She knew her death would save the kingdom. And she bore it without hesitation. She gave her life so thousands more could live. She did it gladly, Sorrin."

"Gladly?" Sorrin spat, his face twisting in pain. "Why did she have to be the one? Why not Idris' daughter? What made her so special?" His voice broke as he lurched forward. "Is it because the king loved her? Because she was a woman you wanted as a companion? While mine was merely a pawn to be sacrificed? Who gets to decide whether one life is more precious than the other!? It is not fair!"

The air was heavy with the weight of his words. Amara's guilt-wracked visage made me look away, a tick in my jaw. I hated to admit it, but Sorrin was right. The only thing that separated Amara's fate from Sheila's was because I had fallen in love with Amara. The echo of Sheila's song lingered in my mind, her voice trembling but unyielding. Even as fear must have clawed at her heart, she chose to stand. She chose to sing—her voice a final gift to her people, to the kingdom she cherished. Even the servants had paused in their duties to listen to her lilting voice.

"Sheila will not be forgotten," I rasped softly, the promise tasting bitter. Empty. For I could not promise him his daughter back. "Her name will be sung in every corner of the kingdom, in every corner of the palace for generations. Her sacrifice, just as those who came after her, will echo in every stone, in every heart that still beats because of her."

But Sorrin shook his head, tears gleaming in his eyes. "And yet I will never hear her voice again."

The silence that followed was unbearable. No amount of honor or remembrance could mend the hollow emptiness of a father's grief. I understood it. Sorrin would burn the world to cinders if it meant bringing Sheila back. He would see a thousand souls perish just to hear her laughter one last time. And as much as I wanted to fault him for it, I could not. For I would do the same.

I would sacrifice kingdoms, armies, and every innocent life for the sake of my wife. Love, whether that of a parent or a lover, was unyielding—a force that defied reason and morality. It was selfish and pure, terrible and beautiful. And in that terrible beauty, we both stood ruined. My eyes went to Idris.

Idris' voice trembled, the weight of sorrow dragging each word from his lips. "If you must place blame, Sorrin... blame me. It was I who taught Zayed that sacrifice for the greater good is the price of a kingdom's survival," he whispered, tears tracing mournful paths down his face. "Believe me, had I known of the curse, I would have given my daughters willingly for the greater good. And they would have died proudly."

"Baba is right," Amara breathed, placing a hand on my shoulder. "When I discovered the nature of the curse, I told Zayed that for the survival of our kingdom, I was willing to sacrifice myself. I did not shy away from the task."

"In the end, the world is a fleeting shadow. What remains is the memory of those who gave their all for others." Idris quoted one of the ancient philosophers he taught me about during his time as my tutor.

Amara was nodding along dutifully, and I knew she must have been imparted with the same knowledge from her father. Is that the reason I had gravitated toward her? Because she embodied the same values I had strove so diligently to achieve? She had been familiar, no doubt, like coming home. Some of my fondest memories were of Idris and me sitting in the courtyard. However, I had failed terribly as his pupil.

Idris' words burned brightly amongst the clearing, but my resolve burned hotter. My voice was low, yet fierce, like the growl of a storm. "Then I have failed you, my dearest mentor," I said, the truth tasting bitter. "Because I would sooner see this kingdom reduced to ash than let you offer your daughter. I would tear the sky apart, drown the world in fire, and rip the very heart from my chest before I let anyone sacrifice my wife."

A tinkling laugh from the shadows at the mouth of the cave made the hairs on the back of my neck stand on end. It was distinctly feminine. Distinctly familiar. A figure emerged, walking forward with the same graceful sway of her hips that I remembered as a teenager.

"My, my Zayed. It is just like I always said," she spoke with arrogance, her perfect crimson lips curling upwards into a delicate and beautiful smile. She arched a perfectly shaped brow in the direction of my wife, who seemed to be staring at the woman before us curiously. "When you fall in love, you fall in love with your entire heart."

She laughed again, a perfectly practiced laugh honed from years of training. She gave a toss of her head as chuckles escaped her lips, and her hair, with streaks of gold, created the illusion of sunlight dancing on the surface of a deep river, cascaded over her shoulder like a waterfall of dark honey.

"Katarina," I replied evenly with an incline of my head. Shock was bursting through my very being at her presence here. And yet...I should have known.

"How are you...my lion of the desert?" Katarina purred, walking forward with purposeful strides. She wore a short top, baring her midriff, and loose trousers.

An outfit not meant for battling at all. And yet, here she was, hiding amongst a camp of rebels who had, until now, been working to overthrow my reign.

Amara bristled next to me.

"Lion of the desert?" my wife hissed, eyes glittering with rage now rested on me. "Who is she?"

Katarina laughed again, stopping short a few feet away from me. Her pearly white teeth glinted in the sunlight. Teeth she bleached and polished every morning to maintain the pearly sheen. I knew because she had done it many times in front of me.

"Ah...I see she does not know...interesting." Katarina's eyes slanted toward Amara and then back to me. She sighed and extended her hand, nails dyed deep blood-red from henna. That, too, I knew because she had often created the paste late at night in front of me. "Well, since he is struck mute, as men often are, let me introduce myself. I am Katarina, my dear. The woman your husband disbanded the harem for. So I could be free."

"I did not do it just for you," I scoffed, shaking my head. "I did it to free everyone there!"

"Oh, but we both know what you wanted, Zayed. You hoped, with my freedom, I would stay back and choose to remain your mistress," Katarina responded evenly, her tone taking on a hard, brittle edge. "Because you loved me."

Out of all the things I had expected Katarina to say, outright telling my wife of our past was something that completely caught me by surprise. And judging from Amara's sharp gasp, it had blindsided her as well. My eyes went straight to the mouth of the cave, wondering who else was going to emerge from my past. I would not be surprised if Father himself materialised out of nowhere given the circumstances.

Chapter 7

Amara's POV

Everyone had a past. And it would have been extremely hypocritical of me to be angry at Zayed over his past with Katarina. Especially when my own former betrothed was constantly a thorn in our side.

However, the relationship I used to have with Ashad was vastly different from what Katarina claimed to have had with my husband.

They had been lovers.

He had loved her.

This was not a few stolen kisses in the desert amidst sparring matches.

This was her knowing exactly how Zayed made love. How he looked right before he fell apart. How he moved when he was over me...

This was them spending countless nights in each other's arms...

This was Zayed setting an entire harem free because he wanted Katarina to choose to stay with him rather than stay with him because she was his slave. How long had they been together? Certainly longer than the few months I spent with him.

When you fall in love, you fall in love with your entire heart.

She knew what it was like to be loved by Zayed.

That was what hurt the most in Katarina's quick revelation. The way he appeared to love her so openly. So freely. Without the looming spectre of a curse and a kingdom to run on his shoulders.

Katarina stepped closer, her presence electric, intentional. She was beautiful, and the floral fragrance that clung to her body reached my nose. This was a woman who spent a great deal of time on her appearance. And yet, she did not carry herself as a slave in a harem. She carried herself with all the grace of a noble woman.

"And now he loves you," Katarina said, voice dripping with a mix of condescension and intrigue. Her eyes stayed steady on me, assessing. Perhaps she was wondering what kind of woman had taken the place she once occupied? For a moment, I thought a hint of jealousy flared to life in her eyes.

"It seems so," I replied with more confidence than I felt. The words tasted heavy on my tongue. I squared my shoulders, refusing to let her see the wound she had so neatly cut open.

Katarina was beautiful. Stunning. Soft. Unlike my calloused hands from sword fighting, hers were soft and smooth.

For a moment I wondered if now, with the option open, Zayed would want her again.

"How quaint," she mused, turning her gaze back to Zayed as if gesturing to a trinket from an old life. "Have you told her how we met? How enchanted you were? How you took one look at me and—"

"It hardly matters," Zayed interrupted sharply, his eyes never leaving mine. An unspoken apology lingered there, raw and sincere.

"What are you doing here?" he asked abruptly, voice slicing through the tension.

Katarina tilted her head coyly, her beautiful hair falling to one side, shrugging her bare shoulders. "Why do you think I am here, my darling?"

Zayed blanched, taking a step back as she took one forward.

Darling. Is that what she would call him as they lay entangled in each other's arms after a night of love making? I shook my head, trying to rid it of these thoughts.

She leaned forward slightly, as if sharing a secret. "I heard your lovely wife is a Lycan now. You turned her. And yet, you refused to turn me."

The bluntness in her words sent my stomach lurching. She knew more than I thought. Further cementing my belief that their relationship had not been a mere dalliance.

"Allow them in!" Katarina's voice was commanding as she stood to her full height and glared at the rebels lined up outside the cave. "If you want my continued cooperation, you will give them shelter."

The blades were lowered, and everyone parted to give us passage. Even Sorrin did not argue.

"Why are you helping us when you so clearly were part of a faction working to overthrow me?" Zayed queried as he watched Katarina walk away.

"Because despite everything," she called over her shoulder, "we are on the same side now." She paused briefly. Her back still to us, fists clenched at her side. "If you had only told me you were cursed, things could have been different. I thought you did not want me to be your queen because I, the daughter of a defeated chieftain, was not good enough to be your wife."

With those parting words, she left us.

And I was left with more questions than ever before.

This was most assuredly a deeper connection and relationship than I had ever shared with Ashad.

Asya led us through the intricate network of caves, explaining to Zayed how the rebels moved through the existing passageways and never stayed in one location too long.

This is why they had gone undetected for so long. And why it was so hard to find them. They switched locations often, cycling through them. Divided up into multiple groups, they rotated between their hideouts to keep confusing those on their trail. At any single time, three out of seven of their hideouts were in use.

They had carved out or expanded existing chambers within the caves to create functional spaces like living quarters with doors made of plywood, storage rooms, kitchens, and meeting rooms.

We stopped inside a living quarter Asya explained would belong to us during our stay here. She could tell I needed some privacy after Katarina's revelation.

"Please talk to me," Zayed pleaded, eyes on me now that we were alone.

"So...you had a mistress," I shrugged with nonchalance even if Zayed could easily see through my façade, "I do not know whether to thank you for freeing her before we married or be angry with you for never thinking to tell me about a woman you discussed marriage with."

Zayed winced at my words.

"I did not expect to see her here," he revealed, moving forward to grab my hand.

"She is the reason you freed your harem," I whispered, stating the words outright.

"No...she is not the only reason," Zayed responded evenly, passing a hand over his face before expelling a resigned breath. "Come, sit." He pulled me over to the makeshift bed.

The living quarter was sparse, with nothing but a bed and some blankets. A pewter wash basin containing water was situated in a corner of the tiny room. Three torches lined the walls of the cave, flickering dimly.

Here in the dim lighting, it was easier to hide how I felt right now. Like I was not enough.

Katarina was the daughter of a chieftain. She was a princess! She was everything a king like Zayed would need. I shook my head, wondering why I was letting my insecurities rise to the surface like this.

Back in the palace, I had never felt this inadequate. But it was easier to feel like you belonged when a bevy of servants worked tirelessly to make you look every bit the queen you were supposed to be. And when people like Kadin and Sherazi had your back. The Amara that entered the palace had never been stabbed in the back by those she trusted implicitly. My heart now burned with the pain of betrayal. A woman I thought was my closest friend was a demon witch in disguise. A man who I thought was my staunchest supporter quite literally tried to kill me.

"She wanted you to turn her," I finally said.

Zayed squeezed my hands affectionately. "Amara, look at me."

I raised my eyes to meet his, my own turmoil reflected in them. I did not like the fact that my husband used to have such an intimate relationship with another woman.

"It would not have lasted," he said gently. "Even if she had turned, even if I had made her my queen, it would never have worked out." He fixed me with a long gaze, willing me to understand his sincerity before he uttered his next words softly. "She was not you." He watched me intently as I took in that simple statement.

He pulled me into him then, closing the space between us on that makeshift bed. My heart started to settle once he wrapped me in his arms and I breathed in his distinct scent.

"Nevertheless," I said into his chest, anchoring myself to his words that had stalled my insecurities. Even if Kadin betrayed me. Even if Sherazi had been making a fool of me, it did not mean that Zayed would do the same. No. He loved me. "I would like to know what happened between you two so her words do not take me by surprise any longer. What did she mean—" I stopped mid-sentence and pulled away to look at him, my hands still fisting the material of his shirt as they rested over his chest. "She said you were enchanted by her the first time you met?"

Zayed scoffed, shaking his head.

"You are the only woman I was enchanted by, Amara, upon first sight. With Katarina I was..." he trailed off hesitantly.

"Tell me," I implored.

"It was lust, nothing more," he revealed flatly, hands gripping my waist tighter as if I might pull back. But I did not. "You need to understand. My father had an archaic custom. When women are brought into the harem...they must dance. If they are able to please the king, they stay on as his concubines. If they cannot..." Zayed paused before plowing forward. "My father either had them sent to work as maids or merely had them beheaded."

I gasped in horror. They had to quite literally dance for their lives. It was archaic. Barbaric.

"But Katarina is the daughter of a chieftain." I blinked in confusion, trying to make sense of his words. Why would a daughter of a chieftain be a slave in a harem?

"The daughter of a chieftain who was defeated by my father. A chieftain of a small village on the outskirts of the kingdom of Elamaria. He refused to pay homage to my father and his entire village was attacked. All were taken as slaves to work in the palace. But the daughter of the chieftain was admitted into the harem and gifted to me."

My eyes widened in surprise. Her father had been murdered by Zayed's father.

"By taking her as my concubine, Father hoped to quell any remaining rebellions. For even a mistress of the crown prince has quite the social status." Zayed's lips turned into a cruel smirk. "Katarina knew what she had to do if she wanted to survive. Bed the crown prince who would eventually become king." He shook his head. "She hated me at first, thinking I was exactly like my father. And I abhorred the attraction I felt for her. But I did not want her to meet the same fate as her father. So...we pretended," he said bluntly. "We put on a show for my father so he thought we were sleeping together. Bastard died within a year, when I was seventeen. And by then, Katarina and I were no longer pretending," he explained.

Zayed sighed with resignation, eyes a stormy green as he cursed his father. "She wanted me to marry her. I knew the curse that loomed over me. I could not, would not, put her life at risk. And I also wanted her to stay with me, not because she was a slave, but out of the love she claimed to feel for me. So when I turned eighteen and felt the onset of the curse, I set the entire harem free. The elderly women who had been my father's concubines had nowhere to go. I arranged for them to be well-looked after within the city of Ilm. Those who wished to leave were given a sizable amount of gold coin so that they would not need to sell their bodies to make ends meet. I could have freed just her, but I freed the entire harem because it was the right thing to do."

Zayed gave me a sad smile. "Katarina stayed on. But as famine ravaged my kingdom, I knew I could not merely live in my own little world with the woman I thought I loved. The four walls of her room might block out the hungry cries of my people for brief moments in time, but that did not mean people were not suffering. I knew I had to marry. And I hoped marrying would be enough to staunch the flow of the curse and blood lust of my Lycan. On the eve of my marriage to my first bride, Katarina left. She took the gold coin promised to all women who had left the harem and left behind a note, making it clear that she took my wedding announcement as an insult. She would either have all of me, or none of me. She deserved to be queen, not a mistress."

Zayed ended his story, staring down at me intently. He had never revealed the curse to Katarina. That much was clear.

"You never went after her?" I wondered. "Even after your first bride was...when the curse claimed her?"

"I had no time to implore Katarina to come back, because I needed..." Zayed's words wavered, but he did not break eye contact with me as he admitted the truth. "I did not need her, Amara. I needed a wife who could stop the madness of my Lycan. A queen who could save my kingdom. I needed you," he murmured, brushing a thumb tenderly across my lips.

"I think she wants you back," I whispered, voicing my fear finally.

He pressed his forehead to mine.

"It does not matter what she wants, Amara," Zayed insisted fiercely. "No other woman matters aside from you."

He growled low in his throat, voice guttural with conviction and something feral that made goosebumps rise along my arms before his tone softened once more. "She might be on our side because she realizes that with Kadin in charge, her own kinsmen are in danger. I told you, her people were enslaved by the crown. I set them free, and most stayed on as paid servants in the palace. Servants who have most likely been put back under the status of slaves. That is why she is helping me now."

I shut my eyes against a hot rush of emotion. Anger and jealousy mixed together. But I did not dare speak, because all these feelings might spill out in graceless heaps if I opened my mouth at all.

"She is a beautiful woman," I acknowledged after a moment's pause to gather my bearings.

"Yes," he agreed, thumb tracing slow circles over my hips, "but nothing compared to you."

I flushed at his words, feeling heat spread through my cheeks. His gaze was sincere, and I wanted to believe it—to believe him.

"Amara." My name on his lips was a plea and a promise all at once. "The only woman I want is you." He smirked, placing a finger under my chin to tip my head up slightly. "Do you remember what I told you? In the antechamber to my throne room? Where I fucked you while my nobles waited in the throne room for us to hold court?"

My blush deepened. He had never used such language with me before. But I found I rather liked it.

"You told me..." I faltered for a moment, recalling exactly what he had done. When he had made me fall apart with his tongue inside me while on his knees.

Arousal flooded my veins. "You told me I was the only woman you would ever kneel for," I murmured.

"And it is the truth. You are the *only* woman I will ever kneel for, I *have ever* knelt for."

He kissed me then, before any more doubts could creep in or rear their ugly heads. Warmth unfurled in me as I found my back hitting the bed, his hands insistent as they trailed up and down my body.

I was breathless by the time his mouth broke free of mine, heart racing and blood singing under the heat of his touch. "I cannot lose you like I have lost my other brides. I will not," he muttered roughly, turning his head to press kisses down the slope of my neck and across my shoulders.

I bit back a moan as his tongue laved over the sensitive pulse point at the base of my throat. His mouth was hot and urgent, and my body arched toward him instinctively.

With Zayed above me, his dark eyes fierce with intensity and hunger, his thumb tracing gentle circles over my hips and down along the curve of my waist, it was easy to forget everything and just concentrate on the feel of his body over mine.

My hands tangled themselves into his hair, and this time it was me who closed the distance between us—me who kissed him soundly until he groaned low in his chest and rolled us over so I straddled him atop the bed covers.

His hands wrapped possessively around my hips, causing a shiver to run through me. I knew I should pull away and rest, but I could not stop or silence the sounds of pleasure slipping through my lips as his hands slipped under the folds of my tunic and hit bare skin. His fingers skimmed gently over my stomach.

"You are so perfect," he breathed, staring up at me. "Like a painting come to life. My warrior queen of the desert."

I bit back a moan when his hands reached higher to cup my breasts.

His thumbs toyed idly with my nipples, and a thrill of pleasure shot straight down my spine making my toes curl.

"I love you, Amara. Now and forever. Since the first moment our blades crossed, I was enthralled. Not only by your body, but by your heart, by your determination.

I could not help but wonder how a creature as lovely as you could be so fierce and so breathtakingly beautiful all at once."

He pulled me down for another kiss, lips crashing into mine hungrily, and I knew then just how much weight his words carried. How deep the trust was that he offered me now. But more importantly—I trusted him too. My hands skirted over his chest and down to his waistband, fingers dipping dangerously low, teasing at bare skin beneath. With a quick yank I pulled loose the tie there, heat pooling inside me as he gasped under my touch. Only for me.

"Zayed," I murmured against the corner of his mouth as his hands moved insistently over every inch of skin they could reach. It made my head swim and my breath come short. But right now, I wanted to make him feel everything he had made me feel.

I moved slowly, like a tigress hunting her prey.

"I have wanted to do this," I whispered firmly, freeing his hardened member from his loose trousers and taking it into the palm of my hands.

"Wha—" he began breathlessly but gasped when my lips closed over his cock.

Everything was him: the heady, masculine scent; the hard muscles tensing beneath me; his fingers tangling in my hair as he let out a long, shaky breath. "Amara..." It was a soft sound, almost reverent, that sent a thrill of satisfaction and desire spiraling through me. I took him deeper, savoring every husky groan and shudder. His chest rose and fell rapidly, stretching tight the thin fabric of his tunic as his control slipped deliciously away. I swirled my tongue around the head of his cock and he bucked under me.

He was trying not to move, I could tell—trying to let me go at my own pace—but I did not want careful right now, I wanted reckless. Wild. I took him deeper still, and his hands clenched into fists and released again in my hair as he gave a ragged sigh.

"Goddess above..."

The tight, breathy words were almost a growl. He was close, so close; I could feel it in the way his muscles tensed beneath me.

"Amara, I am going to—" he warned, but his voice broke when he came in a rough torrent that left me dazed and breathless. I swallowed greedily, tasting salt and spice, while savoring the way he shuddered and gasped under me as though my name were some sort of prayer.

At last I released him, feeling sinfully pleased with myself, and moved up his body to lay against his chest. His breathing was ragged as his arms wound around me, holding me close with a possessiveness that made my heart stutter.

"How," he began after a moment, voice still heavy with disbelief and satisfaction. "How did I ever become so fortunate?" He kissed the top of my head, a gentle contrast to the wildness we had just shared.

"I am the lucky one, remember?" I murmured into his shoulder, letting the warmth of our tangled limbs seep deep into my skin. "You saved me."

"You saved me first." He chuckled darkly, running his fingers lightly along my spine until I shivered and pressed closer to him.

"No more doubts, my little tigress," he murmured into the crown of my head

I nodded and captured his lips with mine once more in affirmation before pulling back only slightly to watch his face as fatigue took over and heavy lids threatened to drag my eyes closed. I had not gotten much sleep the night before, and now the lack of sleep was catching up to me.

"Right now," I breathed lazily into the crook of his neck, "all I want to do is sleep."

I felt rather than saw the smile stretch across his lips as both of us melted into each other's warmth. "Then sleep," he whispered against my hairline with infinite tenderness.

The last thing I remembered before dreams swept over me like a merciful tide was how steady his heartbeat was under my cheek and how calming the rhythm made everything feel.

Something was wrong. The instinct sent adrenaline coursing through me long before any sound breached consciousness. It was second-nature—a warrior's instinct—a fear so deep that it thundered in every pulse point even in sleep. My eyes flew open.

Zayed was not beside me.

A muffled crash shattered what remained of the silence. I was throwing off the covers before noise registered fully within my waking mind: danger loomed near.

Beneath that knowledge, another thought lurked—the sensation from earlier that night of Zayed's arms wound tightly around me... now gone.

I stumbled across our dimly lit chamber, each step quickening the frantic beat beneath my ribcage.

I yanked open the flimsy door and stopped short. Nothing could have prepared me for what I saw. Zayed was there, but he was not alone.

Two men stood on either side of him, caught in a freeze-frame of violence. One grasped his shoulder, and the other had a silver dagger poised at Zayed's throat. Torch light glinted off steel like moonshine on water.

Horror clenched around my ribs, and I opened my mouth to scream—to warn everyone—but Zayed's eyes flicked to mine, fierce and commanding. *Wait.*

One heartbeat passed. Two.

On the third, he exploded into motion.

He slammed an elbow into the ribs of the man with the dagger, their bodies jolting apart so quickly that everything blurred. The other man lunged, but Zayed was faster; he twisted away from their grasp right as the dagger flew at him, missing him by a hair's breadth and came straight for me. I dodged it just in time as it clattered against the wall beside me in the narrow passageway.

"Amara!" Zayed's voice was a whip crack of urgency as he grappled with his attackers. He successfully slammed one back into the wall, his assailant's head hitting hard stone and leaving a trail of blood flowing from his temple.

"You will pay for killing my sister!" he rasped as he threw himself at Zayed despite his obviously cracked skull.

The world snapped back into focus as I registered that this was clearly an assasination attempt on my husband. I reached for my own dagger, still secured against my tunic.

I threw it without hesitation straight toward Zayed's struggle, where the man behind him was trying to secure him into a headlock.

He ducked aside at precisely the right moment, bringing the still bleeding man to the ground with him, letting my dagger fly past him and bury itself deep into the assailant's gut with sickening precision.

"Are you hurt?" we asked in unison—out of breath, yet unbroken—and met halfway between death stains spreading red across the floors of the cave. Both men were either dead or unconscious.

I buried myself against him, inhaling the steady scent of cardamom and mint, feeling the hard reassurance of his hands on my back.

"Not a scratch," I said. "You?"

"Same," he breathed back, even as he was glancing over my shoulder for any sign of movement beyond.

Fear still clutched my gut in a tight fist, though adrenaline was beginning to ebb from my blood with heart-thundering slowness.

"They came to kill me while everyone slept," Zayed admitted wearily. "Said they wanted retribution for the women I had killed. I did not want to kill them, which is why I stopped you from interfering. But nothing is worth endangering your life. When that dagger nearly hit you, I knew I could not hold back anymore. *We* could not hold back," he corrected.

I nodded into his chest. Was this how it was always going to be? Us looking over our shoulders for people trying to kill Zayed?

I squared my shoulders and moved away from him, my tunic now stained with the blood of the men we had killed.

"Where are you going?" Zayed asked, following me as I made my way down the cave passageway.

I had not been paying much attention when Asya had brought us here. But I distinctly remember her pointing out the living quarters that my father occupied. My father, who held considerable weight within this rebel faction, or so I hoped.

"It is time to call a meeting. I am done letting everyone blame you for something completely out of your control," I hissed, determination laced through every word I spoke. It was time to expose the real culprit behind all of this. The one truly responsible for the queen's death and the curse that had been placed afterwards. She might be dead, but at least people would know her true face.

Chapter 8

Zayed's POV

"What did you expect?" Katarina asked impatiently, staring at Amara as she pulled her robe tighter around her body.

I glanced at Idris, then at Sorrin, then the other people gathered in the meeting room.

Amara had recounted everything to us that had happened. How Kadin had killed my uncle. How her maid had been Elvira. How Kadin had tried to kill her. I wish my Lycan had killed Kadin back in the palace when I had gone feral. He had tried to kill my wife and then pretended to be sad over her supposed death.

When Amara relayed Mera's part in everything, however, she did not get the desired result. Amara's revelation about Mera did not shock me. For I knew my uncle was not the one who must have fostered Kadin's thirst for power, which left Mera as the culprit. And if she was the culprit, it most likely meant she had played a larger role in everything that occurred. However, even I was surprised to learn she was the one who betrayed my mother.

Another stab of the pain of betrayal sliced through me. Had my entire family been nothing but backstabbers?

"But he is not at fault!" Amara gestured toward me wildly.

My lips twisted into a scowl. Amara had hoped revealing Mera's involvement would absolve me.

I understood my wife's reasoning. But it did not take away the pain the majority of the rebels felt over losing loved ones. And when people were in pain, they wanted to punish those who had caused it. I was an easy target. It did not matter to them that I was cursed. Or that my aunt was behind the curse because she wanted her son to be king. All that mattered was that their daughters, sisters, cousins had all died by my claw.

"No one held him at knife point and forced him to succumb to the curse. Better to let the kingdom fall to ruin!" an elderly rebel exclaimed. I remembered him. He was the father of one of my brides. "I was powerless to save my daughter. And that feeling of helplessness, of being at the mercy of those more powerful than you, of being forced to sacrifice your own blood..." He swallowed and wiped his eyes.

The truth was that each and every one of them would have rather seen the kingdom burn than see their daughters die. I closed my eyes, letting all the emotions I had bottled up inside of me for so long flow over.

"I remember Zana," I finally said, nodding to the man who had spoken. There was gray at his temples and sorrow etched in his brow. "Your daughter wore the color blue at our wedding. Not the traditional red. She said red made her look like she was trying too hard to be brave. But in blue, she said, she could be herself. I told her she was radiant either way—and she laughed at me."

I ran a hand through my hair, feeling the burgeoning guilt seep into my bones. The guilt and self-loathing I had always kept at bay. I let it spill over; ooze from my every pore.

I turned to another man, his fist clenched around a worn ribbon. "And your sister, Rhea...she wrote me a letter before the sacrifice. Said she was not afraid. That if death meant a future for her little brothers, she would greet it with open arms. For I left her a letter, telling her the truth of the curse."

The man before me blinked, tears streaming down his cheeks.

"Rhea!" he choked out.

"I left them all letters. They knew their deaths were not merely to assuage a mad king's blood lust," I announced to the entire room.

They had never mourned. Not properly. They had been too filled with hate for me. And I could not blame them. I hated myself, too, for what I had done.

"Liora," I whispered, moving to another, younger man. "She had a laugh that could bring light into the darkest day. She was my third bride. And she told me about you. You two were in love," I whispered. "But she knew her father would not let her marry you."

"If he had, she would not be dead!" he choked out.

"She used to say if you could not find a reason to laugh at least once, the day did not count," I said somberly.

He nodded, closing his eyes in heartbreak.

And so down the line I went, heart aching as I acknowledged the sacrifice of each and every woman that had come before Amara. Before, I had shoved their names and personalities into a corner of my mind. But now, I let it all flow out. They were no longer nameless, faceless brides, but people. Beautiful souls whose lives had been snuffed out far too early. Lights extinguished before they ever had a chance to truly burn bright.

"They are not just names on a headstone! They were storms. Suns. Flames that burned for this kingdom. Died for our kingdom And though they are gone, their light remains." I lowered my head. "I will carry them with me. Always."

Sorrin snarled, his fingers curling into fists as anger lashed out in gusts around him. "You expect absolution for this? To parade their memories and claim what—a clear conscience?" The words ripped from his throat, raw with grief and rage.

"No." My reply was steady, the ghost of each woman shimmering in my eyes, the guilt of taking their lives consuming me."I expect nothing but your hatred—I deserve nothing less." I met every furious gaze head-on. "But know that they did not give their lives for our kingdom to crumble, as it surely will under Kadin's rule. Do not let their deaths be in vain."

"They were brave," Amara's voice rang out, sorrow riding her breath. "But they are not dead because he had them killed out of wanton cruelty! He had no choice."

"There is always a choice, girl!" Sorrin replied gruffly. "I would rather he have killed himself than my daughter! His death would surely end the curse!"

And there it was. The theory that had often gone through my own head. The theory I had more than once been tempted to try.

"So what do you propose?" Katarina cut in angrily. "That he should die so Kadin can remain king?" Katarina shook her head. "With Kadin in charge, none of the daughters of Elamaria are safe. My sources tell me he is now forcing any servant girl he develops a fancy for to become part of his harem." Katarina's eyes misted over briefly. "We need the backing of the other nobles if we plan to take him down. And that backing can only be garnered through the rightful king." She gestured to me. And that was when realization struck me, more intensely than a lightning bolt.

"Your...sources..." I echoed, analyzing Katarina's features.

She watched me stoically and I let out an incredulous laugh. "It is why you are part of the rebel faction. Because your fellow tribesmen probably helped spy on me for you." I shook my head in disgust. "I should have known you would go off to join a faction intent on overthrowing my reign, then use any vital information gleaned as leverage to convince me to make you my queen, or else you would use the information against me."

I crossed my arms, staring her down. Katarina had always gone after what she wanted with deadly precision. And this was one such instance. She had been trying to become queen through her network of spies.

"It does not matter what I planned before," Katarina responded swiftly. "What matters is that my tribesmen who still work in the palace are in danger. Everything I have done has been done to protect my people. You and I are no different in that regard." Katarina's eyes went to Amara.

I let out a snarl. The two could not be more different. Amara was my sun.

"If you are truly on our side," Ashad said, his expression tight and conflicted as he looked directly at me for the first time since we convened, "then prove it."

"How?" I asked sharply.

Ashad's gaze was full of challenge. "We need to get the tribal chieftains of the mountains on our side. They are unhappy with Kadin's reign, and we all know they do not want you on the throne either." His words were deliberate, each one resounding like an unspoken dare. "Think you are capable of appeasing Chieftain Lamar and obtaining his backing? So they can help us in the fight?"

I could feel Amara tense beside me. I glanced her way, and then back to Ashad. My relationship with Chieftain Lamar was complicated. I was sure to get Queen

Serafina's support. But Chieftain Lamar was an entirely different story. My father had killed his nephew.

Before I could answer, Amara squeezed my hand tightly, possessively, and spoke fiercely, "Both of us can."

The shock that traveled through the cave was palpable. Ashad blinked in surprise, Sorrin's eyebrows shot up, even Katarina looked taken aback. Women were usually not involved in such diplomatic missions. It was thought they were safer back home. But Amara had a point. Chieftain Lamar did not like me. Maybe Amara could convince him.

"Just like her father," someone muttered among the assembled rebels.

"Yes," I said, my quiet conviction echoing through the stone walls. "Just like her father."

I exchanged a glance with Idris, who stood closer to the head of the table. He looked at his daughter before switching his gaze to me. I could see the wariness in his eyes. He did not trust me fully. But he was willing to trust me for the sake of his daughter.

Once the meeting was over, we left the meeting room with my hand still tightly gripping Amara's.

I had held Amara's hand during the remainder of the meeting, making a point to everyone before us. We were both equals and in this together.

"Amara," Idris spoke from behind us. We stopped in the narrow passageway and turned to look at him.

His eyes went to our joined hands, his face solemn. "Daughter, I wish to speak to you alone."

I could not help but let out a feral snarl, fighting the canines wanting to erupt from my gums and tear into the man who tried to take her away from me. It did not matter that he was her father. I was loath to let Amara out of my sight.

Her hands came to rest gently on my shoulders.

"Zayed, he is my father. I have not seen him in a very long time," Amara whispered gently, her voice calm and soothing. "Go back to our room. I will join you there soon."

"Whatever he has to say to you, he can say in front of me!" I pushed aggressively.

"Young man, would you deny a father a few moments of privacy with his own daughter?" Idris asked incredulously, raising an eyebrow in reprimand. He had that tone. Like I was still his student and he was my teacher, and I had failed some sort of test.

"SHE IS MY WIFE!" I roared, pulling her into my chest. "I do not trust the rebels to not harm her in a bid for revenge against me!"

Idris shook his head, his tone full of frustration.

"She will come to no harm when she is with her father."

"You are too old and frail to fight off anyone who comes for her," I retorted.

Amara gasped.

"But I am not!" she responded in ire, unsheathing her dagger. "I can protect myself, you know this. Zayed, calm down," she urged, eyes full of reprimand.

I breathed deeply, willing myself to stop overreacting.

"I let you out of my sight once," I whispered. "And almost lost you."

Her eyes lightened in understanding. I had left her, and Kadin had tried to kill her.

"If I had not been paralyzed due to my shift, I would have been able to defend myself against even Kadin," Amara replied gently. "I am stronger now. With the fast reflexes of a Lycan. Do not worry, Zayed. You know," she said, her voice taking on a teasing lilt. "I am starting to think you have a habit of letting women think they are free while they really are not."

It was meant lightly, teasingly, to make me realize she was free to go with her father. But there was a trace of seriousness beneath her words that made me stop and pull her close.

"Amara, we are two souls bound together against everything in this world that might tear us apart," I whispered in an undertone, lips close to her ear. Because I knew Idris. Marriage vows did not matter to him if his daughter was unhappy. Even if it was marriage to a king.

Her hand came to touch the side of my face.

"I will never leave you, Zayed. I love you. Please know that."

Those words, reassuring and strong in conviction, eased the tremors in my heart.

I smiled down at her. She was my everything.

"You are free to leave whenever you choose...but if you do—"

I dipped my head until our foreheads touched, emotion catching fire along every nerve—a wild combustion of the fear over losing her and elation at knowing she would not go.

"—you will have one extremely feral Lycan hunting you down forever."

The smile she gave then was radiant enough to make all doubts evaporate completely into thin air.

My wife laughed—a sound so rich and deep it could have sustained the soul of a parched man lost in the desert, the kind of laugh that quenched thirsts no water ever could and made you believe, just for a moment, that the world was whole again.

Amara's POV

Torchlight cast a warm glow over the stone walls of my father's chamber. I sat cross-legged on the floor by his feet, a light throw draped over my shoulders, my head tilted back against his chair as he absently braided a strand of my hair—something he had done for me since I was a little girl. The movement was comforting as we talked. As I told him of my time in the palace. Here, I was not a queen in exile. I was not a warrior. I was his little girl. And the poignancy of the moment was something I had needed after everything we had gone through.

"I told him Mother's stories," I admitted to Baba. "I would try to end it on a twist, hoping he would let me live another night to complete the tale. And it worked."

Baba's eyes flared at my ingenuity.

"You always did prefer your mother's stories over mine." Baba's voice rough with age, threaded with solemnity. Was it me or had he aged drastically in the last four months we had been apart? The lines on his face seemed more defined now, the weariness in his eyes exponentially more than when I had left our mud home that fateful morning. I had expected to return by sunset.

I twisted to look up at him, determined to keep the moment between us light and cheerful.

"That is because hers were *good*," I grinned. "They had magic carpets and shapeshifters and women who ran faster than the wind. Yours were about philosophy."

He chuckled, the sound deep and comforting. "Fair. Though I suspect her stories had more truth than we ever gave her credit for."

I blinked. "What do you mean?"

He leaned forward, placing a steady hand on my shoulder. "Your mother was not just a dreamer, Amara. She served Zayed's grandfather. Went on missions I still do not know the details of. She traveled far beyond the sands, into the mountains. She served kings who were more beast than men. She must have known that Lycans walked among us. She knew Lycans. She knew shifters."

The scent of sandalwood filled my memory, and just like that—I was no longer sitting by my father's feet. I was six again, curled up in my mother's lap under a woven blanket, her long hair cascading around us like a curtain of silk. Her voice, soft and thick with magic, echoed in my mind.

"Do you know how the first Lycan came to be, my tiger?" she whispered, her fingers tracing idle circles on my arm.

I shook my head, eyes wide.

"There was once a king who loved his kingdom more than life itself. But his kingdom was under siege. He was a king on the brink of ruin. His enemies surrounded him. His people were starving. On the eve of what would have been his last battle, he cried out to the goddess for help. He begged, not for victory, but for the strength to protect what little remained.

"The Goddess heard him. Moved by his plea, she offered him a gift but warned him it came with a cost. She gave him a beast that would live inside his skin: rage and instinct fused into muscle and bone. Thus, the first Lycan was born. No mere shifter, but something far more primal. A king with the power to destroy legions, but always teetering on the edge of losing himself."

I gripped her sleeve, awed by her tale.

"After a time, the king grew tired of being alone. He longed for warmth. For a companion, a woman who could complete him. Someone who could bear his power without breaking. So the moon goddess, among mortals, hid one woman whose soul could survive the Lycan bond. The queen he sought. But not every Lycan would find her. Not every woman would survive him."

"Did he ever find his queen?"

My mother smiled, brushing hair from my brow. "That is the question the story never answers. But I think...he must have. For you are here, are you not?

I wrinkled my nose in confusion, but was eager to hear more.

"What about the wolf shifters you talk about?" I asked.

She had smiled, a wistful look in her eyes. "They were born from love, not war. The goddess wept for the burden she gave the king. So, from her tears, she created the first wolf shifters—beings who ran wild through the forests, whose hearts beat with compassion, not wild ferocity. They were not born into royalty, but chosen by the stars to protect it. To help the Lycan rule over his subjects. They are loyal, fierce, and kind."

I blinked, the present pulling me back to the warm chamber.

"She always made it sound like a fairytale," I said aloud, almost to myself as I realized there was so much more to her stories than I had originally thought.

"She wanted you to remember it that way," Baba murmured patiently

My breath hitched slightly. "And she never told you the truth?"

"She told me in the only way she could—through stories. Warnings wrapped in wonder. Truth veiled as fantasy. She was trying to prepare you, I think. For we both saw the fire in you, Amara. I always thought your mother meant you would be an accomplished warrior like her. But maybe...she saw something in you I did not...knew you would need these tales to guide you when you were older..." Baba trailed off, letting his words and the memory of my mother linger in the silence between us. "Maybe she knew you, a mere peasant girl born in a tiny mudhouse, had the heart of a queen."

The words hung between us. Mother could never have predicted what would happen. Right?

I closed my eyes, feeling the pulse of ancient truths in my blood. These were not merely fanciful stories.

Suddenly, Baba's tone shifted—gentle, but serious.

"Are you happy, Amara?"

My eyes opened slowly. "With Zayed?"

He nodded, his hand still resting lightly on my shoulder. "If you are not, you may leave him. I will shelter you. No one will question your choice."

I turned to face him fully, emotion tightening in my chest. "You would do that? Even if it meant angering Zayed? We might lose the one person who could help this rebellion and overthrow Kadin."

"I would," he said, his eyes glistening. "Because you are not a bargaining chip. You are my daughter. And I will not see you live in a gilded cage."

Tears threatened at the edges of my eyes. "I love him, Baba. I *chose* him. I chose to become a Lycan for him."

Baba searched my face for any sign of uncertainty. Finding none, he smiled.

"Then I will stand by you. And may the gods protect the man who ever tries to take your freedom. I might be a frail old man, but I will fight for you with all I have, my dear daughter."

I let out a watery chuckle, realizing he had heard some of the conversation between Zayed and I in the cave passageway. Slowly, I leaned into him, pressing my forehead to his chest as his arms folded around me.

In the warmth of his embrace, I felt the power of two legacies within me—my mother's strength of a warrior and my father's steadfast love.

Chapter 9

Amara's POV

I watched my father as he spoke to the children gathered in the cavern; his voice was steady and warm amidst the flickering torchlight. There was something so comforting about the way he spoke, about the way he taught, and I could see the eagerness in the children's eyes as they absorbed every word. So much like me as a girl when Baba tried to teach me. Had Zayed also looked at him the same way? I turned to look at my husband and saw the way his eyes danced with familiarity as he gazed upon the children. Something in my heart clenched. Seeing him here made me think of what kind of king he truly was. Everything he had done was for the little lives sitting on the stone floor of this cave. He wanted to give them a future to live in. Not a famine to starve in.

As the lesson came to a close, and Baba gave the children their assignment for the day, I noticed the assistant teacher who was nodding dutifully.

"You must take over from here," Baba instructed, moving toward the door frame I was leaning against.

"Let us go; it is time to meet with Sorrin," Zayed muttered from behind me. "They plan to rotate hideouts tomorrow and we must strategize our own move. Word is that Kadin has declared war against the mountain tribes. War, when people are starving as it is."

The weight of his words settled upon me; we were all too aware of the turmoil that lay beyond our hidden sanctuary. I knew we could not remain here for much longer. Eventually Zayed and I would have to play our part in defeating Kadin.

Zayed, Baba, and I walked along the narrow passageway.

"We predicted Kadin would turn his eyes on Chieftain Lamar. But so soon? Is he so desperate to deplete the royal coffers?"

"Desperate," Zayed agreed. "He stirs war and terror, not to defend the people, but to distract them. It is a tyrant's game to fuel fear of an invented enemy so no one dares to look too closely and see the empire of lies he builds atop their suffering. All eyes will now turn outward, not inward."

"But if he cannot feed his soldiers, they will turn on him," I pointed out hopefully.

Baba paused, thoughtful, as he mulled over my words. "He will force their hand upon villages for food and claim it is their own hunger for victory that drives them."

His voice echoed on the stone walls, "Soldiers, too, are ensnared—fed tales of honor, enemies to hate, and the sweet taste of victory. As long as they fight an outside enemy, they will never realize their true chains."

I paled and exchanged a look with Zayed.

"More than swords and soldiers," Baba said slowly, his pace unhurried. "The people must see the truth with their own eyes. Otherwise, we are naught but another threat in a world already too full of them. Trust in your people, trust that they will know who to side with. Do not give them another king to hate, but the truth of the curse that has plagued our kingdom," Baba ended.

"And what if the truth is not enough?" Zayed's expression was unreadable.

But I knew what lurked behind that mask. He was afraid. Afraid that, despite everything, the people would still hate him. Still blame him.

Baba stopped walking and gave Zayed a hard look.

"Young man, the strength of a nation lies not in the hand of its ruler, but in the hearts of its people. Trust them—and they will rise higher than fear, louder than lies. They will rise, not in chaos, but in courage. Give them the truth, and they will forge a path brighter than any ruler could alone."

He began walking faster this time, leaving Zayed and I to stare after him momentarily.

"He is right," I whispered.

Zayed turned to me, his eyes alive with the spark of a new idea. "Then we must show our people where their strength truly lies."

We rounded the final bend and came to a stop at the meeting room. Baba had told us that the next hideout we were supposed to travel to would not be revealed until tomorrow. Once revealed, everyone would be given an hour to finish packing up, and then we would start to move. This was to prevent word getting to the enemy of us changing locations.

"Why do you put the families at risk by hiding them with the rebels?" Zayed queried once we filed into the meeting room. His eyes met Sorrin's as he spoke. "The children would be better off living in a remote village, far away from this chaos. They do not deserve a life living in caves and studying in candlelight. They deserve to live in the light, play under the sun, and learn by the rays of the sun."

Sorrin's lips twisted into a scowl. "We have no other place for them. We do not have unlimited funds to place families in homes. So where we go, the women and children must also go."

Zayed shook his head.

"What if I could give you a better alternative? I am sure Queen Seraphina would not mind granting asy—"

"You are not king here!" Sorrin yelled, interrupting Zayed, face red. A vein throbbed in his temple and I feared his heart might give out, such was the palpable rage radiating from him. He did not like Zayed. And he was letting his personal dislike get in the way of making rational decisions. Even I could see that much.

"Do not question the decisions of our council! You think others have not offered the same? For now, this is the best option. I am the leader here, not you! Murderer!" Sorrin spat out the last accusation, eyes clouded with anger.

Zayed's lips formed a scowl, his eyebrows bunched together.

"The true measure of a leader is their ability to be fair and not let personal grudges cloud their judgment. You know I speak the truth, Sorrin."

Sorrin took a step forward menacingly in Zayed's direction. I tensed, ready to fight.

"Here, my word is law. And I will not entertain the notion of sending off the families of our fighters to a far off land where they might not see their parents ever again."

"So you would rather put them in danger?" Zayed retorted incredulously.

"They are not in danger! Our system is specifically organised in a way to prevent danger!" Sorrin was screaming again, so loud that his words bounced off the walls and echoed around us.

"Even you must admit that in war, nothing is predictable. Kadin's men are tracking us even as we speak–"

"Which is why I was against allowing you to enter the hideout in the first place!" Sorrin screamed. He pointed a finger at Zayed and then at me. "If anything, it is you two who have put us in danger with your arrival!"

"Regardless," Zayed replied calmly and I marvelled at his ability to keep his cool in the face of a screaming, irrational man. "That is not what we are discussing. We are discussing a better possibility for the families of the rebels fighting for a good cause."

"Actually," Sorrin spat out, lips curled into a sneer, "we are here to discuss patrol schedules. You live here, with us, you follow our rules. And every person must be put on the duty roster. Even the noble king and queen." He stared at us, daring us to disagree.

But we did not. And we did not protest when Sorrin declared that Zayed and I would be patrolling the perimeter for six hours rather than the customary four assigned to everyone else.

Sorrin said it was to make up for the shortage of people due to the men Zayed had killed. But I had a feeling it went deeper. He was purposefully being difficult. Especially when he assigned Zayed cleaning duty in the kitchens.

I glanced at Zayed, a man who had once held the title of King of Kings. He took the assignment with nary an argument, agreeing to manual labor when he had never done it in his entire life. But I could tell the potential danger that innocent children were in still plagued him. He shared his concerns with me later that day as we patrolled the perimeter of the caves.

"We cannot force them to trust you," I replied mournfully, sheathing my dagger after sharpening it carefully. It was silver, and even the sight of it seemed to sting my eyes. But I was loath to part with it. As long as I was careful, the silver blade would not harm me. I could not touch it like I used to, due to being a lycan now. However, the hilt was gold, so I could still wield it.

"I understand that their resources are limited," Zayed replied, looking out into the blistering heat of the desert. He turned to look toward the far-off mountains, closer from here than they had ever been in the city of Ilm. "But I have connections and influence. Whether they like it or not, I am the rightful king. Nobles will listen to me. Monarchs of other kingdoms still respect me, despite the tumultuous relationship I have with Chieftain Lamar."

"Sometimes, I think they do not want a king in Elamaria," I mused, looking at him sideways.

Zayed made a noncommittal sound in the back of his throat as we resumed walking.

"If that is the will of the people..." he trailed off, lost in thought.

I wondered, however, if our kingdom could ever thrive in such an environment. For before the monarchy, the country had been littered with small pockets of tribes that constantly warred against each other. They had only been subdued by Zayed's forefathers. The mighty Lycan King who had made the tribes bow to him. But too much power often corrupts. One needed only to look at Zayed's father for proof of that.

My eyes went to Zayed again. Would he have been the same? A corrupt ruler, had it not been for the curse that plagued him? No. I refused to believe Zayed could ever be capable of the same atrocities as his father.

"Yasmin and Farid went to face the evil mage in his lair—a fortress carved into obsidian rock, where screams echoed and magic turned to poison."

Zayed's eyes narrowed with intrigue. We sat outside, under the stars, our hands clasped together. We were both thoroughly exhausted after an entire day and half a night of duties assigned by Sorrin. Tensions still ran high and we both could not sleep, so we ended up out here. I hid a smile as I saw one of the patrolling men angled toward us so he could catch my words. It seems I had more than one person's ear tonight.

"*They fought together,*" I continued, leaning into Zayed as he wrapped an arm around my shoulder. I burrowed deeper into him, inhaling his familiar scent. This was a much better way to tell stories. With my head on his shoulder and his arm securely around mine. I continued after a brief, contented sigh, "*Yasmin with her blade, swift and sure, her movements like lightning through the night. Farid with his sword and shield, his heart aflame with fury. But the mage was stronger than they had imagined. He bent the air to his will, turned shadows into monsters. The sky above the fortress split with thunder as he summoned a storm of raw sorcery. Bolts of dark energy slammed into the ground, scorching the earth, shattering Farid's shield.*"

My voice tightened as I neared my favorite part.

"*Yasmin was struck. Thrown across the battlefield. Her blade flew from her grasp, and she crumpled to the ground. Farid cried out and ran to her, but the mage descended like a phantom, ready to finish them both.*"

My eyes gleamed. "*And then it happened.*"

If we had been in the palace, this was when I would have stopped, hoping to end on a plot twist and be allowed to see the dawn. But things were different now.

"*He roared. Not in pain, but in fury. The sound shook the very walls of the mage's fortress. His bones cracked, his form shifted, muscle ripping through skin as his body reshaped itself. Before Yasmin's stunned eyes, her lover transformed. Not into any beast—but a wolf. His eyes were silver like the moon and his fur was as dark as night. He lunged at the mage. Magic collided with claws and fangs. The mage screamed incantations that turned the sky red, casting chains of fire and smoke, but Farid was unstoppable. His jaws crushed the necks of the mage's minions. His claws carved through summoned beasts. He was vengeance made flesh.*"

I paused for a moment and noticed that more of the men patrolling seemed to be circling the area where Zayed and I sat. I knew he noticed it too, but he merely brought his cloak up around my form protectively. I could not help but hide a smile. He truly was constantly wanting to shield me from any possible threat. What threat could a few men listening to my story ever pose?

"*And then, Yasmin rose,*" I said impactfully, lowering my voice for effect.

"*Bleeding, breathless, she retrieved her blade and fought beside Farid. Her movements wove together with his, two halves of a whole. Her sword struck where his teeth could not reach, and together, they drove the mage back.*"

Zayed leaned forward, enthralled as I paused my story.

A voice from behind us spoke up, one of the patrolling men eager to hear more. "Did they kill him?"

I shook my head, glancing in his direction. Slowly I continued the story.

"*As the mage Harun lay defeated and at Farid's mercy, Yasmin placed her hand on Farid's furred shoulder and begged him to stop. 'There must be another way,' she said. 'Killing him will not solve anything.' And Farid obeyed. With a growl that shook the stone beneath them, he stepped back.*"

"Yasmin should have let Farid kill the mage," Zayed said disapprovingly.

The men around us murmured in agreement. I ignored them pointedly, relaying the rest of the story.

"*But Harun, even broken, did not weep. He laughed. A terrible, bitter laugh that echoed off the walls of the fortress. 'Your mercy is weakness,' he spat. 'My descendants will never forget. Your kingdom will never know peace. One day, the carpet will be returned to us.'*

Yasmin and Farid left him there and returned to their land. They sealed the carpet deep beneath their palace, hidden behind stone and spell, guarded by generations sworn to secrecy. Only to be used at the right time by one who is worthy."

Zayed was quiet for a long moment, the moonlight playing against the sharp lines of his face. The patrolling men dispersed, going back to their posted stations now that the story was over.

"You speak of it as if it is more than a tale," he said finally.

"Maybe it is," I replied. "Maybe some legends are really truths the world is not ready to accept."

That was what Mother always said.

He turned to me, his expression unreadable. "And if it is true—then that means there is a carpet out there capable of crossing vast distances faster than any living being."

I shrugged, imagining how beneficial a magic carpet would be right at this time. Especially for people like us in a rebel faction.

"Why are there so few Lycan females born?" I asked, looking at Zayed. "You had to turn me. And something I remember in my mother's stories tells me that a Lycan female is rarely born."

"Some daughters are born with the Lycan gift. But not all. For not all can bear it. The beast overtakes them, overpowering the human side. My mother once told me that female Lycans are rare, not because they are weak—but because they are wild. Harder to tame. Fiercer in love and war. Only a mate worthy of them can tame the beast inside them," Zayed explained, running a hand through his hair.

He glanced at me, giving a rueful chuckle.

"Sounds like someone I know."

I nudged him playfully and then leaned my head against his shoulder. After a long moment of silence, Zayed finally spoke.

"Are you happy, Amara?"

I looked up at him. "With you?"

He inclined his head in the affirmative, expression solemn. "I am no longer king. And I do not know if I will choose to be king again if...when we defeat Kadin. You might never be queen again."

I reached for his hand and laced my fingers through his. "I love you. I choose you. And no curse, no crown, no decadent riches, will change that."

Zayed kissed my temple, the moonlight catching in his eyes.

And far off in the distance, the stars shined brightly, sealing our promise forged in love.

Chapter 10

Amara's POV

The sun bled fire across the jagged horizon as I finished my patrol, sweat clinging to my back like a second skin. There was no wind, only the relentless heat of the sun. It was thick, cloying, and still. I paused at the mouth of the cave in order to rest in the meager shade, letting my eyes adjust to the dim interior. The patrol had been uneventful, just heat, silence, and the far-off whisper of the desert breathing. Since we would be changing locations in another day's time, everyone was busy packing what little essentials they could travel with.

I sheathed my blade and rolled my neck, ready to report in and switch duties. As I stepped deeper into the cave entrance, a familiar voice drifted on the dry air.

"Finished already, Amara?"

I turned. There she was—Katarina—perched on a smooth rock like a desert goddess, legs crossed, her long hair catching fire in the sunlight. She was brushing it deliberately, each stroke slow and sensual, as though she expected someone to be watching. Did she? It was no secret that Zayed patrolled with me. But today he had been pulled for cleaning duty. Another way Sorrin lorded over my husband that he held no position here. However, it was not lost on me that Katarina was never assigned duties.

Katarina's eyes studied me with amusement.

"What are you doing out there?"

"I sit here every afternoon," she said, tilting her chin. "The sun gives me these natural blonde streaks Zayed always loved. You know, before he got...*distracted*."

I arched a brow but said nothing. Not yet.

She smiled, the kind of smile that was meant to be condescending. "You know, I was his first love, Amara. His first everything. Before he even knew that *you* existed. He used to say I smelled like wildflowers after the rain."

The condescension in her tone dripped thicker than the sweat on my skin. I did not flinch, did not even blink. I simply stepped forward, my voice like cooled steel.

"But he did not marry you."

Katarina's brush froze mid-stroke. Her smile faltered.

"He did not turn you into a Lycan," I continued, my voice lowering, the lycan rumble threading beneath my human tone. "His Lycan did not mate with yours," I added, a satisfied smile crossing my features. "You might know what it felt like to be his first, but you will never know what it feels like to be his last. To feel the power of his Lycan over and under your body."

I could not help the curl of my lips as I watched the brush go slack in her hand.

Something in my body shifted subtly, the air pulsing with the pressure of my Lycan stirring. My eyes flared red briefly, long enough for her to *feel* it, to *remember* her place. To remind her that I was the one Zayed loved now.

She looked away first, lips tight, brushing again, this time a little faster.

I left her in silence, feeling utterly content. Bullies like her needed to be put in their place. Zayed had told me Katarina thrived on feeling like she always had the upper hand. I hoped my words were enough to quell her arrogance, at least for a while.

I stepped deeper into the coolness of the cave, a welcomed reprieve from the oppressive heat.

Reaching the chamber where we checked in after patrols, I found Ashad, his dark eyes going to me from where he sat with Sorrin. He stood up, the flickering light casting strong lines across his jaw.

"Nothing to report," I informed Sorrin. My gaze flicked to the duty roster, which was kept on Sorrin's person at all times. It lay on the table between Sorrin and Ashad. "Where is Zayed? He told me he was reassigned to a different duty."

Ashad cleared his throat and exchanged a glance with Sorrin that had me realizing I would not like the answer.

"He was assigned to gather the waste water and refuse in the bathing rooms," Sorrin grunted, looking at me challengingly. "Everyone must play their part. Do not expect me to take it easy on him."

My fists clenched in anger. Sorrin was purposefully assigning Zayed these types of duties. It was not lost on me that warriors were exempt from them.

"So the resident enchantress gets a free pass and is allowed to while the entire day away brushing her golden locks in the sun, while we are overworked and treated like slaves?" I hissed.

"Exactly," Sorrin replied, an infuriating smirk creeping across his lips. "Katarina contributes to our strength in more ways than mere labor. Your husband is not special."

Ashad shifted uncomfortably, avoiding my gaze. I could see the internal struggle within him, caught between the loyalty he owed to Sorrin and our friendship.

"This is not fair!" I burst out.

"You know what is not fair?" Sorrin asked, standing to glare at me. "That my daughter ended up nine feet under because the king never fell in love with her. And you stand before me, proof that he could have fought the curse had he so wished."

"Sorrin!" Ashad cried out. "We agreed to no longer discuss this!"

"No. You agreed to it. This is not a democracy. And I decide who gets assigned where. You would do well to remember that," Sorrin ended, eyes on me.

I took a step forward, the heat of my anger rising alongside the Lycan itching under my skin. "You do not deserve to lead when your anger is hindering your ability to be fair and just," I spat at him.

"Amara!" Ashad gasped, eyes on me in disbelief. "This is not going to end well if you keep pushing." His voice was cautious yet firm, trying to be the mediator. "Come, let us go grab a bite to eat in the kitchens."

His hand came cajolingly over my forearm in an attempt to steer me away, but I wrenched it free from his grasp.

"I am not afraid of him," I replied sharply to Ashad. "And I am going to go find my husband!" I snapped, turning to leave.

I found Zayed near the back of the cave system, in the bathing rooms—the warm, musty air thick with moisture and soapstone. He was crouched by the basin drain, lifting a heavy wooden basket filled with waste water.

As he hauled it up, the wood groaned, then snapped.

Water exploded over his chest, drenching his shirt, the linen clinging to the hard muscle beneath. He froze, blinking through the splash, dirty hair plastered to his brow.

My heart kicked. This man, this king...

"What are you doing?" I snapped, storming toward him. "Why are *you* the one cleaning this filth? You are not a servant—"

He looked up and smiled, cutting me off without a word. He stood, slow and deliberate, water sluicing down his arms, his shirt now transparent against his skin.

"It is all right, Amara," he said with a shrug, wiping his face with the back of his wrist. "It is just dirty water."

"It is *not* just water, Zayed. They are trying to demean you. You are the strongest person we have, a Lycan, and they—" I stopped, breathing heavily in anger. My eyes went to the basket, noting that the splintered wood was rotten. I shook my head. "Why do you let them do this to you?" I asked, looking up at him angrily.

Zayed shrugged again.

"Because perhaps it makes them feel better, Amara. They are hurting. They are hurting for their daughters. I will not fault them. If covering me in dirty bathing water helps lessen that pain, let it."

This man—this king—had been given a rotting wooden basket, knowing it would snap, knowing it would soak him in wastewater, like some twisted show of dominance. It was not a mistake. It was orchestrated humiliation, calculated down to the last splinter. But Zayed...he did not flinch. He stood there, drenched in filth, muscles tense, eyes calm—unbent, unbroken. They wanted to strip him of dignity, to drag a king into the dirt and call it obedience. But all they did was reveal the steel beneath his skin. They thought they could shame him. All they did was remind me why he was meant to lead, not because they let him...but because no one, *no one*, can crush what he *chooses* to carry.

"You are covered in wastewater now," I said sadly. "You do not deserve this, Zayed."

He gave me a smirk.

"Then help me wash it off," he said, voice husky, eyes glinting with mischief and something darker. "You look like you could use a shower yourself, smell like it too."

My anger simmered, then cracked—a small, involuntary laugh slipping out as he moved toward the wooden tubs filled with fresh water.

Zayed's teasing grin tugged at my heart, and for a fleeting moment, the raging storm of indignation faded, replaced by a warm flicker of intimacy.

I watched as he removed his dirty clothes and moved toward an alcove carved into the back of the bathing rooms. He was able to move one of the wooden tubs of freshwater toward the alcove. My eyes strayed to the muscles rippling across his chest as he exerted his strength.

"I have heard the next location might have a spring inside the caves. We might finally get running water," he mentioned offhandedly, reaching for a small wooden cup used to scoop up water. He filled the cup, and for a moment, he just held it there, glancing back at me briefly before throwing the contents over his body. "Come join me," he called back to me as he began to wash himself.

I could not help the way my eyes went to his perfectly rounded backside before roving over his muscular thighs.

"I think I would prefer to enjoy the view from here," I retorted lightheartedly, but I stepped closer nonetheless.

He looked back at me with a smirk and then dipped the cup into the water once more before stepping into the alcove where shadows swallowed him up like secrets.

I followed, my heart racing with anticipation as he poured water over himself, droplets glistening on his skin like jewels.

"Come here," Zayed beckoned softly, using his free hand to gesture toward me.

With every step closer, I found myself slipping into that space where only we existed—a cocoon woven from familiarity and yearning. "What now?" I asked playfully as I reached him.

He grinned mischievously, turning to face me. My eyes roved over his form appreciatively as water dripped down his body. "Now," he whispered, leaning forward conspiratorially, "you let go of all that anger and your clothes."

He stepped closer, a predator closing in on its prey, and the cool water trickled down his body, creating rippling patterns over honed muscles that seemed to beckon me forward.

With a playful flick of my wrist, I pulled at the laces tying my tunic together. The fabric slipped away and fell softly around my ankles.

The coolness of the cave air embraced my bare skin as I stepped out of my clothes and into the alcove with him.

Zayed's breath caught as he took in the sight of me standing naked before him. The flickering shadows danced across our bodies as we inched closer together. "You are so beautiful," he breathed out, and in those hushed words lay something deeper—admiration and desire interwoven like threads in a tapestry. Water flowed down his taut muscles like liquid silver, and my hands itched to touch him.

"Now," he said, voice thick with temptation, "let me wash away the remnants of today from your skin."

The way his gaze burned into my own spoke volumes, more than words could.

A wicked smile curled his lips. Then he dipped the cup in water and approached me, water glistening on his fingers as he cocked an eyebrow in my direction.

Gently, he poured water over my head and shoulders. The coolness contrasted against my skin but soon warmed beneath his touch as rivulets cascaded down my arms and back. A soft gasp escaped my lips at the sudden rush.

His eyes flickered with delight, watching every reaction on my face as his hands glided over me with practiced ease. "See?" he murmured, leaning in closer so that his breath brushed against my ear. "Merely let the water wash it all away."

The heat of arousal rose from within me as goosebumps danced across my skin under his gentle ministrations.

Zayed's gaze roamed over me with a reverence that stole the breath from my lungs. Water still clung to my skin, glistening in the low torchlight, my hair heavy and wet against my back—and yet the way he looked at me made my breath catch. I had never been pretty or dainty or petite. I was a warrior with toned muscles and a build that many men might have found off-putting. But my husband looked at me as if I was the most beautiful woman he had ever set eyes on. His voice was a murmur, raw and reverent.

"You are beautiful, Amara...like a goddess stepped out of the old world. So fierce and untouchable. Your skin gleams like gold kissed by the sun, and your hair..." He reached out, fingers brushing a soaked strand from my cheek. "Whether it is drenched from the sweat of battle or water, you leave me undone. No crown I could ever wear compares to the way you look at me. Compares to the feel of you in my arms."

"But Zayed," I breathed, momentarily lost in the depth of his gaze, "you should not have to endure what Sorrin puts you through."

His hands stilled for a heartbeat before he resumed with a steady rhythm, massaging soap into my arms, my stomach, and finally my thighs. "You know as well as I do that some battles are fought in silence."

"But," I whispered, daring to break the spell of intimacy with my concern, "your dignity—"

"Is intact," he interrupted softly, brushing his lips against my forehead briefly before dousing me with water again. "My kind of dignity comes from strength and choice, not from their twisted perception of worth."

I reached up with nimble fingers, seeking to return his caresses. My fingers grazed over the slickness of his wet skin. Slowly, I traveled the contours of his chest where water pooled like diamonds against bronze skin.

Zayed closed his eyes, surrendering to my touch.

"Now, what do you need from me?" I asked coyly, my own voice a husky whisper.

He chuckled softly, eyes glinting with mischief as he held the cup toward me. " Take this and pour it where it belongs." His thumb brushed over my wrist, and electricity sparked between us as he guided my hand to the scoop.

I took the cup and hesitantly stepped closer still, our bodies brushing together, flesh against flesh, sending a delicious jolt through me.

I tilted the cup to pour water over his shoulders.

My eyes appreciatively followed the curve of his muscles, with the cool water cascading down his body.

Leaning in closer, I let my lips brush against his shoulder. The scent of soap mixed with something uniquely Zayed enveloped me. It was earthy and heady, with a hint of cardamom.

"Would you be surprised if I told you that I have dreamed of moments like this?" His voice dropped an octave lower, wrapping around me like a spell as his arms wrapped around my bare waist and brought me closer to his body. His lips found my throat, and he began to place tiny kisses down the column of it.

"Of me bathing you?" I asked blankly.

He chuckled against a pulsepoint at the base of my throat, his beard tickling the sensitive skin there.

"Of fucking you while we showered together," he corrected. "It was not possible at the palace. Not with our busy schedules and separate bathing rooms. Not to mention the bevy of servants and guards posted around my bathing room," he added in an undertone.

Heat bloomed deep in my core at his words. I melted completely into him, sighing as he continued to kiss his way down my body. His lips trailed down my collarbone, over my breasts, my navel, until he was on his knees before me.

"Put one leg over my shoulder," he ordered, lifting my right leg to do just that. I gasped when his lips went over my womanhood. He gave one slow torturous lick as he tasted me.

My fingers tangled in his wet hair as the heat built, each flick of his tongue sending electric pulses through my body.

"Zayed," I breathed, barely able to form coherent words, "you have no idea what you are doing to me."

He looked up at me, mischief dancing in those dark eyes, the glint of challenge evident. "Oh, I think I do." His voice rumbled through me, vibrating with a dark hunger. The warmth of his breath sent shivers down my spine as he plunged back into his ministrations, licking and teasing with expert precision.

With each flick of his tongue, heat pooled deeper within me, igniting a fire that had long been dormant. It was intoxicating and consuming, drawing me closer to the edge with every moment. I could no longer think, all reason slipping away.

"Please," I whimpered as his tongue swirled inside me.

Everything else faded—the weight of Sorrin's taunts and Katarina's spite dissolved beneath the heat of desire pooling in my belly. Here, in this moment, illuminated by flickering shadows and water glistening off our bodies, nothing mattered but him and the exquisite pleasure he offered.

He pressed deeper, a low growl emitting from his throat that resonated through my core. I tightened my grip on his shoulders as waves of ecstasy washed over me. "Zayed!" My voice broke as another surge swept through me like a wild current, pulling me further under as my pleasure crested.

But he did not stop. He kept swirling his tongue with tantalizing slowness until my thighs began to shake. The one leg still holding me up threatened to give way under me as the leg hooked over his shoulder inadvertently pulled him closer, my body wanting so much more of him.

He pulled back slowly and stood, pinning me against the cool stone wall of the alcove. My heart raced as Zayed gazed down at me like I was a treasure waiting to be claimed.

"I want you," he murmured, pressing himself against me with a heat that made all thoughts scatter from my mind. His hands went to my wrists, grabbing them and pinning them over my head. "I want you now."

I blinked, momentarily recalling the last time I had been in this position with my hands pinned over my head by him. It had been when I had thought he was going to force himself on me. The one hand holding my wrists against the wall slackened slightly, and I saw the darkness in his gaze warily retreat.

I pushed my body against his, showing him how much I wanted him. Showing him it was fine to do this to me.

"I am yours," I answered breathlessly, assuringly. That was all he needed to hear. His grip tightened on my wrists while his free hand squeezed my hip before falling away. Leveraging his free arm, he hoisted me up so that my legs could easily wrap around his waist. Then he plunged inside me with a force that made stars explode before my vision. The world outside seemed to vanish entirely as we became nothing but flesh and fire and began to move together in a dance written in rhythm and longing.

Each thrust was both fierce and tender, a symphony of passion echoing against the stone walls. My back arched instinctively against him; our movements became a melody composed of shared breaths and whispered praises.

"You take me so well," Zayed growled low in my ear between ragged breaths. "Can you feel how much I need you? How hard you make me?"

"Yes!" I cried out, the intensity surging beyond anything we had ever shared before. Desire clawed at us both as we reached higher and higher toward an inevitable climax.

"Do you like it when I hold you like this?" he grunted, grip on my wrists tightening. "When I restrain you?"

"Yes...yes...yes! More!" I gasped, rolling my hips against him as white light seared across my vision.

"My little tigress likes it hard and rough," he grunted, hips snapping into mine forcefully.

"Yes... Please..." I whimpered, sobbing from want. "More!"

I wanted him to fill me so completely that I would feel it long after he was gone from inside me.

The cave filled with my cries and his dirty words as he spoke utterly filthy things in my ear. Words that sent heat spiralling through me.

His smile was wicked as he coaxed begging moans from me, each one deeper than the last. The pressure inside me coiled tighter, ready to burst like a dam crumbling under the weight of too much water. I cried out his name, pleasure building toward an inevitable peak.

The sounds of my pleas and his curses bounced off the walls, and together we spiraled into a blissful abyss where power and love met in an explosion that reverberated between us. He came inside me with an animalistic growl.

His name echoed in the alcove like a prayer leaving my lips. My legs fell away from around his hips and yet he continued to hold onto me, keeping me from collapsing onto the ground.

Slowly, we descended into tranquil silence, and Zayed held me close against him, our bodies slick with water and sweat.

He rubbed his chin against the top of my head before speaking.

"I want you to know that though they might try to demean me out there, in moments like this...none of it matters."

I melted into his embrace beneath the gentle cascade of his warmth. There was no pain and no unfairness; just us—two souls intertwined in defiance of every obstacle thrown our way.

I cupped his face in my hands and stared deep into those hazel green dark pools filled with determination and love. "You are not alone in this," I vowed softly. "We will weather whatever storm they try to conjure."

His lips curved into a genuine smile now—one that chased away any shadows lingering in his eyes. With a spark of renewed energy igniting between us, Zayed leaned down until our foreheads touched.

"I know," he whispered, closing the gap just enough for our breaths to mingle. "It is why I am lucky to have you by my side," he said, voice low and certain, as if the truth of it was carved into his very bones. "You are my anchor, Amara—steadfast when the world tries to shake me, loyal when others falter. There is no one else I would trust at my back...and none I would ever want at my side. I would choose you, again and again, in every life, in every war, in every storm. A thousand times over—and still, it would never be enough."

Then his lips met mine in an ethereal kiss that was gentle yet electrifying.

I did not have an extra set of clothes in the bathing rooms, but Zayed did. He pulled his clean shirt over my form while he opted for simply wearing his loose trousers through the cave passageways as we made our way toward our room.

We stopped short when we ran into Katarina, a trail of helpers following her with baskets of what looked like essential oils and aromatic soap.

She froze mid-sentence, her cheerful chatter to her helpers faltering as she caught sight of us.

The princess' assessing gaze flickered between Zayed and me, her expression morphing from surprise to something sharper—obvious jealousy layered with disdain. I did not miss how she took in the way I was dressed in Zayed's shirt, or how she noted our damp hair.

"You do know that couples are not allowed to bathe together," Katarina sniffed.

Zayed's posture stiffened, but he was quick to mask any response with an easy smile that did not reach his eyes. "Katarina," he replied evenly, noting the tension thrumming in the air. "All things considered, it is no concern of yours."

Her brows arched in feigned innocence, but there was a gleam dancing at the corners of her mouth that suggested otherwise. "I just do not want you to get in trouble. We do not want Sorrin placing more undesirable tasks on your shoulders, do we?"

She stepped closer to me, practically oozing sweetness. "You are welcome to try some of my bath salts, Amara. Surely, they will help make you more desirable to your husband."

"Any more desirable and I might not have been able to tear myself away from her," Zayed grunted, pulling me closer into him. "Amara has no interest in frivolous, vain pursuits when war is looming. And neither does she need them when it comes to me," he ended pointedly.

I took in the carefully concealed barb. The dig that maybe Katarina needed them, but I did not.

Katarina's eyes darkened momentarily before she composed herself, plastering a facade of sweetness back on her face. "Ah, well, it seems we are all entitled to our choices." She turned to walk away but then threw over her shoulder with faux casualness, "Just remember that sometimes people do not stay...even when we wish they would."

Her words hung in the air like a warning. But beneath it all was the echo of her jealousy that came alive when faced with the bond Zayed and I shared.

Once she rounded the corner, Zayed exhaled beside me, tension easing from his frame as soon as she was out of sight. "Ignore her," he muttered after a beat.

"I am trying," I replied honestly.

Would Katarina ever relent? Would she cling stubbornly to every opportunity to undermine what we had? The thoughts gnawed at me persistently.

We were back in a part of the caves which was supposed to be the meeting room.

We were supposed to be planning our departure. The location of the new hideout had been disclosed and we had to leave within the next hour, once the children had finished their lesson for the day. However, Sorrin and Zayed were arguing again, Sorrin refused to relent.

"I will not allow the families to leave!" Sorrin exclaimed angrily, fists clenched at his sides as he bore into Zayed with a steely gaze.

"There is nothing wrong in giving them a choice," Zayed retorted calmly, standing tall with his shoulders squared.

Zayed was a force to be reckoned with—not because of his lineage, but because of his heart. And I knew some of the warriors listened on with interest. Some were obviously rehashing the merits of letting their families move to safer lands.

Sorrin opened his mouth to argue.

A deafening crash interrupted him, cutting him off.

Then another struck, more intense this time, shaking the walls around us. Dust and debris fell like a rainstorm, and panic erupted in the room. "We are under attack!" someone shouted.

My heart lodged in my throat.

"Our location has been compromised!" Baba exclaimed, face pale and worry marring his features.

Asya cursed, grabbing her bow and arrow.

Sorrin quickly regained his composure, his voice cutting through the chaos. "Everyone! We must evacuate now! Move to the secondary exit! We have practiced the evacuation procedure before. Those meant to hold off the enemy, move to your posts!" His urgency was clear, and my own instincts kicked in. I had not practiced evacuation with them, but Zayed and I could easily follow Asya's lead and go hold the enemy off. As my husband and I moved as one to follow Asya, a breathless messenger rushed in, eyes wide with terror. "The room where the children were studying...it has caved in! We cannot reach them!"

Those words sucked the air from my lungs. A heavy silence fell over the room, and my heart dropped into my stomach. The thought of the children trapped beneath the rubble was unbearable. I saw Zayed's face pale with horror.

"We must attempt to free them!" Zayed stated emphatically.

Sorrin's expression hardened. "We will save who we can. We cannot risk the lives of everyone for a few. We have to get out now!" His voice was firm, but a mix of despair and anger bubbled inside me.

"No!" Zayed's voice cut through the tension, fierce and defiant. "I will not leave them! They are just children!"

"They are only ten children out of the forty living in these caves! We must get everyone out lest the walls fall on us all."

"No," Zayed retorted, taking steps to exit the conference room. "You are not my leader, Sorrin. I have not pledged loyalty to your faction. And I will do as I see fit."

Pride bloomed in my chest. For Zayed was not meant to follow. He was meant to lead.

I watched him turn away, ignoring Sorrin's desperate calls to stay back.

"Your skills could be used to evacuate the others!" he boomed out. "We need a Lycan's skill to keep the enemy at bay!"

Typical. After demeaning my husband at every turn, he now admitted that Zayed was crucial to the cause. But Zayed paid him no heed. And I followed him, realizing that I, too, had not pledged loyalty to Sorrin's cause.

Chapter 11

Zayed's POV

The ground still trembled beneath our feet from the last explosion, the cave groaning like a wounded beast. Dust swirled in the narrow tunnel ahead, and I could already sense the collapsed chamber where the children had been hiding. Buried but hopefully still alive.

Amara was right beside me, her curved blade drawn, her eyes scanning every shadow. Her breathing was steady, and outwardly she was calm, but I could sense the strength thrumming inside her, waiting to be unleashed should the need arise.

Deafening crashes rang out and echoed around us, each more menacing than the last as we pushed further into this nightmare. My heart pounded with fear but also with resolve. We would reach the children. We had to. Everything I had ever done was for our future. These children were the future of Elamaria. I would not let even a single precious life be lost if I could help it.

Footsteps echoed behind us. Asya and a handful of warriors were sprinting to catch up. She halted just behind me.

"Front lines are holding," she said quickly. "Barely. The east path is collapsing, too."

"Go," I grunted. "You need to keep it that way. Defend the entrance. Use your arrows to shoot them from afar and keep as many of the enemy as you can from getting in!"

Asya nodded, turning to follow my bidding.

I turned to the warriors who had trailed behind her, undoubtedly throwing in their lot with me rather than Sorrin. "Three of you, go left down the lower corridor. Look for any trapped children or elders. Evacuate anyone you find. Avoid contact with the enemy, if you can. Fight only if cornered."

They nodded and peeled off down a crumbling side path, weapons ready.

A group of civilians stumbled around the next bend—faces bloodied, eyes wild. One man was limping, carrying a child in his arms.

"Do not go east," I barked. "Take the west path—it has not collapsed yet. "

They fled, and we pushed forward.

Then we heard it.

Boots on stone running toward us rather than away from us and toward an exit.

A moment later, they emerged from the shadows. There were dozens of them, armored in leather and iron, silver blades drawn, some already bloodied from earlier skirmishes. One of them grinned when he saw us.

And then the cave was rocked with another explosion.

The walls shook violently. Rubble rained, and I heard the screams of children farther down this path. The goddess only knew what these explosions were doing to the children already caught under the collapsed portion of the hideout.

Amara dove to the side behind a chunk of fallen rock, dodging falling debris. I barely flinched—already lunging into the fray.

The first attacker came fast. I met his blade with my own hand and twisted hard, crumpling the metal in my grip. Blood trickled down my arm from the cut on my hand, and my skin hissed at the contact of silver against my flesh. Maybe it was the rush of the fight, or the resolve in me to save the children, but the silver did not burn as much as it should have.The clang of metal rang out as Amara fought next to me with her sword. I shoved my opponent backward with my shoulder. He stumbled. I slashed across his throat with my claws before he could recover.

Two more charged.

I ducked and rolled beneath one's strike, came up behind him and raked my claws down his spine. He shrieked, collapsing in a spray of red. The second tried to grab me from behind—I let my Lycan rise.

My bones shifted. My muscles tore and reknit in the blink of an eye. My jaw lengthened. My senses sharpened into clarity.

I spun and smashed the man into the wall mid-shift. His ribs caved under the force. I did not wait to see him drop.

Amara was a whirlwind beside me—fluid and deadly. Her blade gleamed with deadly precision as she carved down one, then another. She fought like the wind in a sandstorm: unpredictable and merciless.

My claws met silver, and I ignored the sting as they raked down a man's chest covered in silver chainmail.

This man was taller than the rest, and his eyes glowed faintly red. There was a stench about him that spoke of corrupted blood and dark magic. He roared and swung a stone-headed hammer toward me. I ducked. It smashed into the ground with a tremor that sent cracks racing across the cave floor. Before he could lift it again, I leapt toward him.

I hit him full-force, claws driving into his shoulder. He roared again, grabbing my arm, and trying to fling me, but I twisted so that I now stood behind him. My claws found his neck. My teeth found his jaw.

With a growl, I tore half of it away.

He dropped like a slab of meat.

I stood over his body, chest heaving, his putrid blood soaking my fur.

More of Kadin's men turned the corner but paused.

They saw what was left of the men who came before. Then their eyes went to my Lycan before going to Amara who stood proud, her sword drenched in the blood of the men she had defeated.

They saw us.

And they ran.

Rage was hot in my throat, but I knew I could not spare time to go after them. We had to get to the children.

The air here was heavier closer to the caved-in chamber. Rocks were piled high across the mouth of the passage where I knew the children had been studying.

The ceiling above creaked under its own weight, threatening to collapse with the next tremor of an explosion. We had to hurry.

"Is anybody here?!" Amara called, already climbing over the rubble.

I pressed a clawed hand to the stones. Warm. Too warm. Whatever explosion had hit this area had brought fire with it. Whimpers in reply to Amara's call told us that there was still a chance for the children caught under this.

I furtively began tearing through the stone. My paws were already raw, my claws dulled from battle, but I did not stop. Amara worked beside me.

We peeled back one layer, then another.

We could hear their small voices. The faint, muffled crying as they were thrust into a situation they did not understand.

We could not let them down.

Their innocence rested precariously on our shoulders

"Almost," Amara breathed, using her sword as a lever to move a group of rocks blocking our path to the children.

Finally, we managed to create an opening just big enough for them to get through.

Amara called to them.

"Come on, you can do it," she cajoled.

A pair of tiny, bloodied fingers reached through hesitantly. Amara grasped them gently, tugging the child toward us.

A little girl emerged—no more than eight, caked in dirt and soot, her eyes wide and unblinking. Disgust for Sorrin rolled over me in waves. He was willing to sacrifice these innocent lives yet hated me for what had happened to his daughter. What a hypocrite!

She looked up...

...and saw me.

Clawed. Blood-streaked. My teeth still bared from the fight. My Lycan's red-eyes glowing in the dim light.

A raw, piercing wail of terror split the air.

She twisted in Amara's arms, trying to scramble away, sobbing uncontrollably.

"Shh, it is all right," Amara whispered, cradling the girl close. "Shh, shh... That is Zayed. He is not here to hurt you."

The girl shook her head, tears streaking down her filthy cheeks caked in blood and dirt. She clung to Amara, staring at me with wide, trembling eyes.

Amara looked over her shoulder, calm and certain. "He is one of the good ones. He is the reason you are still breathing."

I stepped back slowly, lowering my head. I would not risk shifting back into my human form when Kadin's men could be just around the corner waiting to ambush us.

Another cry echoed from the gap. Then a boy crawled through, coughing and bleeding from a gash on his brow. Two more followed behind.

I lifted a boy into my Lycan arms carefully. He flinched at first but did not scream, just wept quietly. I set him down next to the other children and continued to help Amara.

When the last child was through, I started to move back—just as the stone above groaned.

The structure above our heads gave way with a bone-shaking crack. I threw myself toward a wooden beam and caught it with both clawed hands, my muscles screaming as I held it upright. This was the only way. I looked at Amara, sending her a message through my Lycan to GET THEM OUT. Our Lycans could not talk, but they could communicate through emotions and intentions with each other. And my Lycan could sense her reluctance to leave me here. But we had no choice if we wanted to save the children.

The full weight of the cave pressed down on me like the sky itself. The world around us shook with violence, dust enveloping us like a shroud. The cries of the children echoed in my ears, pushing me to hold on. I could not fail them—not now, not ever.

"You will be crushed—" she started.

I growled in warning. She had to get out of here. Only the goddess knew how long I could hold out.

She hesitated, eyes pleading, fists clenched at her sides. Her mouth opened, but she did not argue again.

"Stay close together!" she urged softly, a sob leaving her lips as she guided them away from the impending doom that threatened to swallow us whole.

I watched her leading the last of the children through the rubble raining down around us.

The weight pressed deeper into my bones. My muscles screamed. My legs trembled.

One heartbeat.

Two.

Then silence.

They were clear.

I let go and jumped back. But it was of no use.

The stone ceiling came down with a thunderous crash, rock and dust exploding around me. I was thrown against the wall, the impact stealing the breath from my lungs.

Darkness swam at the edges of my vision.

The world seemed to shatter around me, the ground buckling as if it were rebelling against a divine punishment. More explosions echoed through the caves. Darkness swallowed me whole, the roar of collapsing stone and dust blanketed the chaos. My last thoughts raced to Amara, to the safety of the children, and an ache blossomed deep within my chest.

When consciousness flickered back into existence, I found myself buried under rubble, suffocating in darkness. Panic surged through me as I pressed against the weight crushing my body. I could barely move; my limbs like lead weights encased in iron.

And then I heard it.

Amara's voice. "Zayed—Zayed, stay with me."

I blinked through the darkness. I heard the groaning of rocks.

I tried to moan out that she had to leave. And then I heard more voices next to her.

"Are you sure he is alive?" Ashad queried, his voice strained and followed by the movement of rocks above me. Was he helping Amara dig me out?

"He has to be!" Amara's voice was frantic. "I feel it. He is here. Keep digging!"

I struggled against the heavy stone, forcing every ounce of strength into my limbs. The Lycan within me stirred, embracing the resilience thrumming through my veins, and bucked against the worldly constraints.

With a fierce roar that shook the very fabric of my being, I moved in a blur of pain. The debris crumbled around me as I pushed upwards, shards of rock and dust spiraling with every forceful motion. And I was free.

My gaze landed on Amara. Her face was bloodied, her braid half-loose, but her eyes burned with fire and worry for me.

"Thank the goddess," she gasped, flinging herself at my bloodied Lycan form.

"We have to get out of here," Ashad hissed. "This location has been compromised, and Kadin's men are merely regrouping because they had not expected a Lycan to be here. We must move!"

"Zayed," Amara whispered, urgency lacing her voice. "We have to hurry. The others have already started the journey to the new hideout. We have to put as much distance as possible between ourselves and Kadin's men."

I grunted, refusing to change out of my Lycan form. The children might be safe. But my wife, though formidable in her own right, was still a target—and I would burn the world to ash before I let anyone touch her. I would carve their names into the sand with their own bones if they tried to rip her from me. So, despite the fact that I was severely wounded, I snarled and bared my canines, ready to battle anyone who tried to get in our way.

Chapter 12

Amara's POV

Ashad had agreed to help me. He stayed back to aid me in getting Zayed out of the caves. So while I was thankful to my friend, I was still livid at my husband. When we were finally out of the caves, I turned to my Lycan King with steely eyes.

"Never order me away from your side again," I hissed angrily, hands shaking as I clenched them at my sides. "I could have lost you!" I screamed up at the Lycan towering before me.

A rational part of me knew that we had done the right thing. Because saving the children was important. But that did not lessen the storm of anger and helplessness that engulfed me when I thought I might have to dig my dead husband out of the rocks he had been buried under.

His glowing red eyes stared down at me and I could sense his feelings radiate toward me. His Lycan was telling me through his emotions that Zayed could not have stood by while innocent children died.

"He looks angry," Ashad muttered, taking a few steps back as the Lycan before me growled low. "Watch out, Amara!" he barked out.

My Lycan King extended his clawed hands, and they closed around my waist. I was brought flush against his chest in a warm hug.

A contented purr emerged from the depths of him. "Forgive me for worrying you," he seemed to say to me.

I buried my head in his furry chest, letting my hands slide along the powerful muscles coiled with ominous lethal power. He cradled me gently in his embrace.

A sigh escaped my lips, the tension breaking between us like a fragile thread that had been stretched too thin.

"Let us focus on getting out of here," I said quietly. "Ashad knows the way to the next hideout. We must leave."

My husband released me reluctantly, and I could see the wheels turning behind those fierce red eyes. He was already making plans on what to do next. It was not until we were much further along in our journey that Zayed finally turned back into his human form.

There were few things in life less mortifying than travelling with your husband and ex-betrothed. Especially when said ex-betrothed, for reasons unknown, kept side-eyeing my husband like he knew a secret.

Zayed rode ahead on his camel, looking far too graceful atop his mount, the desert wind catching the end of the dark cotton scarf that covered his face to prevent sand abrasions. His eyes were not on Ashad, but tracking the terrain as if he expected us to be attacked at any moment.

Ashad rode beside me, his camel slightly taller, which he kept reminding me of by subtly glancing down as if I needed help staying upright.

"You remember when we used to spar on the outskirts of the city of Ilm?" Ashad asked suddenly, turning his head just enough for the sun to catch the glint of his smile. "You nearly dislocated my shoulder once." He chuckled.

I smiled, recalling our carefree youth together. Ashad was not just my ex. He was, and always would be, one of my closest friends. Ultimately, he was the one who chose to stay back and help me get Zayed out. And he did all he could to aid me. In that aspect, I knew he would always support me.

Zayed coughed discreetly from up ahead. "She nearly broke my nose once. She stopped the match, despite my protests because I sorely wanted to win. Instead, she insisted on getting me medical aid to staunch my bleeding nose."

I laughed, recalling when that had happened. Despite the spectre of Elvira and the curse looming over us, we had managed to create happy memories in the palace together.

Ashad chuckled. "What would you win? A story?"

Zayed grinned, looking back at me with warmth in his beautiful eyes. "Yes. She used to make me fight her for story rights. You and I have that in common."

Ashad leaned forward slightly, smug. Dread exploded in my belly. "See, when *I* won, I got a kiss."

My spine stiffened like a bowstring. That was not the right thing to say to my husband.

Zayed's lips briefly pressed into a thin line, but he did not reach for his sword.

There was a terse silence, and I glared at Ashad, who was smiling in triumph. Ashad looked like a vulture who had spotted easy prey—smug and slow-blinking, as self-satisfied as a dune basking in the sun, convinced it had shaped the desert itself.

Finally Zayed laughed. "So she would rather skewer you than kiss you?" He turned in his saddle, eyes gleaming. "You may have won a few kisses, Ashad, but make no mistake..." He looked dead at him, tone smooth as honey and twice as sharp. "I won her heart."

Pin drop silence. Ashad flushed red.

My camel actually stopped trotting along.

Even the desert wind seemed to pause out of respect or maybe it was shock.

Then, from somewhere just beyond the sandy dunes, a scream tore through the air.

Zayed's smile, as sharp as a knife, vanished like a mirage. He kicked his heels into his camel's sides and shouted, "Come on!"

As we drew closer, we realized the sounds of women yelling were familiar.

Zayed reached for his blade. "Trouble," he said, already urging his camel forward.

Ashad kicked his heels into his mount. "Could be bandits."

I squinted ahead, sand whipping at my face.

As we crested the dune, the scene that greeted us was...not what we expected.

Down below, we saw chaos: Katarina—*of course* Katarina—draped in pink chiffon and fury, stood atop a bejeweled golden trunk, wielding a parasol like a saber. Around her, five men, bandits, clothed in white billowing robes, were circling Katarina and her entourage of female servants. My eyes were immediately drawn to the utterly flamboyant attire Katrina wore amidst the blistering heat of the desert. Her crop top was a vivid shade of pink, intricately lined with threads of gold that glinted under the harsh sun. A gossamer veil, shimmering in delicate pink, gracefully draped over the lower part of her face, adding an air of mystique. Her loose trousers, a fluttering cascade of blended-dyed patterns in vibrant pinks and purples, danced in the desert breeze like the colors of a sunset reflected on a rippling oasis. It was not at all a practical outfit suitable for escaping an attack or even trekking to the next hideout.

Around her was a flurry of silk-clad, shrieking, and wildly fleeing female servants running in every direction. One poor girl hurled a silver tray like a discus. The bandit immediately grabbed it with unconcealed glee, happy he had been able to obtain an expensive prize.

Another servant girl held onto an armful of jeweled necklaces as if they were a tiny baby that needed protecting.

"Back, you sun-baked sand rats!" Katarina screamed, jabbing her parasol toward a man who looked moments from dismounting his camel. "I have *very* expensive face cream in my box! You cannot have it! Girls, protect the jewels with your life!"

One of the riders reached out toward a box tied to the back of Katarina's camel standing next to her, and Katarina shrieked like someone had slapped her.

"THAT IS MY ANTI-AGING SERUM!"

"Hand over your valuables and we leave in peace!"

"Never!" Katarina exclaimed vehemently.

The group of bandits circled them—clearly confused about whether this was a group of innocent females to rob or a traveling circus. The women were shrieking, fabric and bangles flying everywhere. One servant girl was haphazardly pulling out colorful bangles from an emerald encrusted golden jewelry box and throwing them at heads of the bandits, as if that could keep them away.

"Do not make me use my embroidered parasol against you!" Katarina shrieked. "I will not give you my valuables!"

"Then we will take you as well, by force!" the man who was obviously the leader of these bandits replied.

At once the rest of his followers yelled in defiance.

"We would rather leave empty-handed than take this wench anywhere with us!" his men yelled.

I could not blame them for such a sentiment.

"I think she is doing a marvelous job defending herself," I muttered, eyeing Katarina, who was poking her parasol in the air with obvious anger. It was thin and made of flimsy lace. Suitable as a shade under the unforgiving sun, but not at all suitable for battle. "But no material goods are worth her life." I eyed Zayed critically. "Surely you must have taught her some self-defense during your time together?"

Zayed coughed awkwardly into his hand. "She was not interested in self-defense."

Obviously.

Ashad had already drawn his sword. "I am not letting her fight off bandits with a parasol. Let us end this."

"Not just any parasol, it is an *embroidered parasol*," I added dryly. before drawing my own sword.

"Zayed!" Katarina shrieked, her eyes falling on her former lover. "Please save me! I-I was here...waiting for you!"

And yet she had not thought to help me save him when he was buried under a mound of rubble. She had undoubtedly been waiting here and anticipating Zayed's arrival, adorned in her finest attire and meticulously styled to catch his attention.

She had caught attention, just not Zayed's.

I did not even give myself time to roll my eyes before I was charging down the dune, sand flying behind me like a comet's tail.

"If you touch her, I will slice your hands off with my sword," I muttered to Zayed before flinging myself into the fray and straight toward Katarina.

I heard Zayed's grunt of exasperation next to me.

"If they touch you, I rip their hearts out," Zayed deftly replied. "And if you spar with Ashad again, I will rip his out, too."

The bandits noticed us and charged.

I raised my sword high above my head in a graceful arc before deflecting a strike.

"We are just friends," I replied, meeting my opponent blow for blow.

"A friend who used to be your betrothed. A friend you used to spar against and kiss," was my husband's reply, jealousy now oozing from his voice as he put one of his attackers into a headlock.

I huffed in exasperation as I parried an attack.

"Now is not the time to discuss this," I replied, letting my blade slice into the side of another opponent. The sand drank his blood like a parched man. He crumbled, holding his wound.

Honestly? Marriage could be more exhausting than battling bandits.

I lunged forward, my feet sinking into the shifting sand as the cries of panicked women mixed with the guttural shouts of the men suddenly at a disadvantage now that Ashad, Zayed, and I had arrived.

I deftly made my way closer to Katarina, cutting down one of the men who had been trying to get close enough to grab the box on her camel.

"No...no...Zayed is supposed to save me! He is supposed to be here! Not over there!" Katarina bemoaned, eyeing my husband, who was covering me from the front as I tore a path to this wretched woman.

"Sorry to disappoint," I huffed, dodging another man who lunged at me.

He turned to swipe his sword at me.

I sidestepped smoothly, pivoting to bring the edge of my sword across his pantaloons.

"But Zayed's wife will be your hero today," I ended as my attacker's pants fell to the floor under the hiss of my blade, the tip dangerously close to his manhood.

"No! You ruin everything!" Katarina hissed, tossing her head back in anger.

Well, her priorities were certainly odd. But there was no time to tell her that when the man before me was slowly reaching for his dagger.

"Take another step, make another move, and you will not be able to sire children, ever," I responded sweetly, stepping closer to where Katarina stood. "Walk away from here, you sniveling cowards," I hissed.

"Amara?" a new voice spoke. A voice tinged with disbelief.

I stilled, shocked eyes going to a man standing farther away, several lengths behind where Katarina and I stood. We had not noticed him before, for his inconspicuous attire had camouflaged him quite efficiently. His silken merchant robes and camels loaded with goods gave away exactly who he was. Even if he wore a white cloth across the lower portion of his face to protect himself from the harsh sand particles that undoubtedly flew into one's mouth on long trade expeditions in the desert.

"STOP!" He raised his voice, and his right hand.

The bandits immediately stopped fighting and retreated to gather around him. And that was when I realized that the leader of these bandits was the man who had broken my sister's heart. Because before me stood Salim, a man Asya had loved with all her heart, until he betrayed her.

Chapter 13

Amara's POV

"Salim?" I asked, my voice oozing with distaste. I kept my sword poised to attack the final marauder, letting the tip of my blade remain perilously close to his balls despite his attempt to retreat like the other bandits. My eyes narrowed on my prey in warning before I turned to look at Salim. "I knew you were a despicable man, unable to keep your word! But I did not know you and your men preyed upon travellers in the desert."

"Salim!?" Ashad exclaimed in surprise.

Zayed merely stood, watching the exchange. I could see when everything clicked into place and he realized that Salim was the man my sister had been betrothed to. The man she had loved. The reason I had volunteered in her stead to be his bride.

My eyes went to Salim's fallen face, his eyes filled with tears.

"Amara! Thank the goddess you are alive. When I got word of how you sacrificed yourself for Asya—"

"Do not speak her name, you piece of filth! You betrayed her! You left her for another woman!" I roared, so angry I nearly saw red.

Salim and Asya had been betrothed for two years, and had been in love for far longer. They first met when he was selling his wares in the market. Asya and I had gone to buy cloth so she could sew me a new outfit. It was love at first sight for both of them. Often, I had helped Asya sneak out of the house to meet Salim in secret. Asya had given him everything: her heart, her body, and her trust. And he had spat in her face!

Salim held his hands up, a bright gold opal ring glinting on his left finger. His eyes were on my sword, which was trembling against the inner thigh of his man, near his groin.

"I will explain it all, Amara. Please leave my man be."

"You mean your thief? Is this what you have come to? Stealing?" I sneered, lowering my blade.

I watched out of the corner of my eye as my prey gathered his ripped pantaloons and rushed toward Salim.

Salim cleared his throat, his eyes darting nervously between me and the trembling bandit before him. "You do not understand. I was forced into this life—"

"Forced?" I scoffed, cutting him off with a wave of my sword. "Forced to betray the one you claimed to love? Save your breath; I have heard enough."

"No, please!" Salim begged, voice rising above the chaos of my anger. "Listen, Amara! It is not what it seems! There is no other woman! There never was. I—my trading expedition did not go as planned. Why do you think I never returned?"

He looked at me pleadingly before looking to Ashad. Ashad and Salim used to have a cordial relationship, considering they had expected to become related through marriage.

"My caravan was caught in a wild desert storm! I lost all my valuables. I thought of Asya every day, I swear it!"

"Your caravan has been caught in such situations before," Ashad spoke carefully. "You have always been able to recoup any losses."

"Not this time." Salim wiped his eyes. "I was left a pauper, with only the clothes on my back. I was unable to pay my men—" he gestured to the scoundrels who had been attacking Katarina. "I...was a shadow of the man Asya knew me as. The rich merchant who would whisk her out of poverty. How could I go back to her a penniless pauper? How could I look her father in the eye and ask to plan the wedding when I could scarcely afford to feed myself?" He blew on a cotton handkerchief before turning his attention back to me. "I promised myself I would come back once I re-ammassed my wealth. I resorted to plundering passing travellers...however, I never, ever hurt any of them."

I let out a huff of anger. He never hurt them, but he did steal from them! That opal ring was most likely also a stolen trinket! My eyes went to it in distaste.

Salim kept speaking. "But as time went on I could not, and realized I might never..." he ended somberly.

"So you thought abandoning her was the answer?" I demanded, incredulously. "You broke her heart because you did not want to show your face empty-handed? That is your excuse?"

"Yes! No! I mean, it is complicated!" he sputtered, glancing nervously at Zayed, who stood next to me with crossed arms.

"Complicated?" I echoed in disbelief. "Tell that to Asya's empty, broken heart. You never knew my sister at all if you thought she would think less of you for being poor!"

His shoulders slumped as if I had struck him. Then he glanced at Ashad again.

I took a step back as if I had been visibly battered into a retreat.

"You knew," I seethed, eyes flashing angrily to Ashad and then back to Salim. "You knew Ashad was a noble. Your ego was too fragile to come back empty-handed because...you did not want my betrothed—"

"Ex-betrothed," Zayed cut in, glancing at me sharply. "You are my wife now, and he is no longer your betrothed."

He had a fair point.

"Ex-betrothed," I corrected hastily. "You did not want to be compared to him."

"My family...they always told me that wealth was my worth. That love would never feed us!" Salim argued.

"Love is not a commodity!" Ashad's voice boomed, echoing the sentiment we all felt. "And neither is it worth abandoning." Ashad shook his head in disgust.

Zayed's frown deepened over Ashad's words. He did not like the fact that Ashad's words denoted that he would not abandon his love for me. But right now I was too fixated on the man who hurt my sister.

"You shattered her heart, and left a crater in its place. Tell me why I should not gut you for what you did to my sister. Never mind the fact that you were complicit in Ashad's duplicity," I added, grip on my sword tightening as frustration boiled just beneath the surface of my skin.

His eyes shone with the brilliance of unshed tears, desperation clawing at him as he stepped forward, trying to gain sympathy.

"I did not want to live in shame! I thought she could go on without me. That Ashad would help her find a suitable noble to marry and keep her in the manner she deserved. In the manner that I had promised to keep her," Salim added in a morose whisper.

"That is not love, that is cowardice," I spat. "Love is having the courage to stand bare, with all your flaws and fears, and still choose each other. It is not about having everything; it is about weathering the storm when you have nothing. That is what makes a bond unbreakable." I glanced at Zayed and noticed the warmth in his eyes as he stared at me. My gaze shot back to Ashad then to Salim. "My husband was a king. Now he is not. And yet, I have never known him more deeply than I do now. We are learning parts of each other we never had time to see before. That is what love is! It is not built on status, but on staying when things fall apart, and choosing to rebuild *together*. That is the resilience of love. *That* is courage."

Salim stood there, his face paling as my words cut through him more effectively than any sword.

"Amara, I-I-..." he stammered, trying to form a coherent response, but the weight of my gaze pinned him in place.

"You were a fool to believe that wealth defined love," I continued relentlessly, feeling the fire of outrage shimmering in my chest. "You did not just betray Asya's trust; you strangled her spirit with your cowardice—a cowardice you chose over her."

From the corner of my eye, I could see Zayed's posture shift slightly, pride, evident in his stance, radiated toward me like a shield.

Salim took a shaky breath, his hands trembling as he lowered them in defeat. "I thought I could come back...when I had something to offer," he admitted, his voice cracking. "I was wrong. I see that now."

His gaze searched mine pleadingly before going briefly to Ashad, and then finally to Zayed.

"Do you think she would give me another chance?" he queried breathlessly. "If I could prove myself...If I could earn her trust again..." he trailed off hopefully.

I hesitated, taken aback by his words.

Zayed's nostrils flared in anger.

"She would never marry a leader of thieves," Zayed sneered. "If Asya is anything like my wife, she would marry a pauper happily, but never a man who preys upon the innocent...looting them in the middle of the desert."

Salim winced.

"I think Asya should have a chance to hear Salim out, though." Ashad's brow furrowed as he looked thoughtfully at Salim.

Salim hesitated for only a moment and then he straightened his back with new-found determination. "Please take me to her...let me prove myself."

"And why should we trust you?" Zayed growled, hard eyes on Salim.

"Because I do not want to let my love for Asya be held hostage by fear any longer."

The conviction in his voice gave me pause. Was it truly possible for him to change? The hope flickered inconveniently within me.

Was there a sliver of redemption in him? Could this be a chance for my sister to regain her happiness?

I exchanged a look with Zayed. The wariness in Zayed's eyes told me that he did not trust Salim.

"Trust cannot so easily be rebuilt," I pointed out to Salim before looking at Ashad, who winced at my double-pointed barb.

"What will you do if she rejects you?" Zayed growled out swiftly.

"Then so be it," Salim replied firmly. "I will respect her choice...even if it shatters me.

Zayed's expression rippled, conflicted between the defensiveness swirling in him and the unexpected twist of compassion sparked by Salim's confession. The growl in his throat softened slightly; perhaps even he recognized the longing in Salim's plea. There had been a time when he, too, had offered to let me go free and run away with Ashad, because he wanted my happiness.

"Well...I suppose we shall let Asya decide," I decided stiffly.

A yelp of protest from behind made me swirl to look at Katarina. I had completely forgotten about her presence.

"Are you seriously considering wasting your sister's time on this charlatan?" she exclaimed, waving her parasol in a dramatic flourish. "He is clearly a coward hiding behind his wretched bandits!"

"They did not hurt you! We were only trying to earn a living," Salim argued feebly.

My lips pressed into a thin line. Salim seemed to think there was nothing wrong in what he was doing.

Zayed was right. Asya would not want anything to do with a man who had turned to thievery.

Katarina sniffed, a haughty expression crossing her face. "I will not speak to a thief. If your band of scoundrels is to accompany us, they must make themselves useful. Rather than squabbling about love and broken hearts, help us!" She gestured wildly to her trunks of expensive belongings and then at the bandits still lurking around, bewildered by the sudden change in plans.

"Perhaps if you were not throwing your pearls around like pebbles, we would not be in this mess, would we?" Ashad said dryly, mirroring my earlier sentiments.

Katarina was a fool for travelling in this manner. Quick escapes and getaways to inconspicuous hideouts were not possible when she was like a vain peacock strutting about the dessert—colorful, dramatic, and attracting attention where silence meant survival. I had no idea why Sorrin put up with her antics.

"Let us go now," Katarina declared, ignoring Ashad and casting Zayed an innocent look. She fluttered her eyelashes at him. A low growl escaped my lips.

It was the growl of my Lycan, who had been silent as of late.

Quickly, Katarina scurried forward on her camel, putting distance between us.

I sighed wearily. I had been wrong when I thought our travelling entourage could not be any more bizarre. It was an entirely awkward ordeal to travel with my ex-betrothed and my husband. But add in the husband's ex-mistress, and awkwardness gave way to a spectacle of strained civility. Adding my sister's ex-be-trothed who was friends with my ex-betrothed turned the entire journey into a full-blown farce. The camels groaned less than we did. It was less a journey and more a battlefield in which we not only fought the heat, but the desire to throttle at least one person within arms reach.

Zayed's POV

By the time we made it to the next hideout, the chaos that awaited us was unexpected.

Another hideout location had also been compromised, which was surprising, as these caves were only for the most trusted of men. Idris informed me that Kadin's men had never infiltrated the rebellion to the extent that they were granted access to these hideouts.

In addition, most men did not have families who required residence in the caves. So such members were left to stay in camps closer to the city of Ilm.

If Kadin's royal guard had found out about the caves, it could only mean there was either a traitor among us, or the rebels were being followed.

And the rebels from our own hideout were all yelling at Sorrin.

"You nearly let the children die!"

"Hypocrite!"

"You told us all children were your children!"

"You have no right to continue being our leader!"

Sorrin stood there, the weight of accusations crashing over him like a relentless storm. His face was pale, betraying a layer of fear beneath his steely exterior.

He had become the target of their ire.

"If it were not for the king, our children would be dead!" a woman screeched as she held one of the children we saved close to her bosom.

"Enough!" Sorrin shouted, trying to assert dominance, but the rebels remained undeterred, anger fueling their shouts.

"They are innocent children!" one voice cried out, tears flooding the speaker's eyes. "How could you?"

"We trusted you! We were promised safety!" another warrior spat, fists clenched tightly by his sides.

I exchanged a glance with Amara.

"Betrayal and cowardice have no place in leadership when every choice could mean life or death!" another man shouted.

Sorrin looked around, hoping someone would take his side. No one did.

"I was afraid of losing more people," he protested feebly.

This is what happens when fear usurps loyalty. I folded my arms, watching everything unravel before me. If Sorrin did not think quickly, he would have an uprising of his own to deal with.

"So you thought to sacrifice our children?!" the same woman from before shrieked.

"Enough!" Idris shouted, intervening as the voice of reason. His eyes went to us, surprise flickering across his features as he found Salim amongst us.

I did not trust Salim. For a man who resorted to looting for his own personal gain was not an honourable man. And judging from Idris' glance-over at Salim, he, too, did not like him. Perhaps there was more to the story of Idris beseeching Asya to pick another suitor to marry. Perhaps Idris had known all along that Salim was not worth his daughter.

However, now was not the time to dwell on such things. Right now, we needed order.

"The children were saved thanks to the valour of my daughter and her husband," Idris called out to the crowd. "I believe we should retire and give thanks to the goddess that we are safe for now. Regarding the attacks now occurring in various hideouts, I believe it is best to gather more intelligence. We have sources in the palace who are to come to us with vital intel tomorrow. Now is not the time for division, but for unity."

"What should we do? Our leader was killed in the attack!" one of the men from the group of rebels who had been hiding in another cave shouted.

Idris passed a tired hand over his face before breathing in deeply.

"For now, we shall all defer to Sorrin," he murmured, gesturing to Sorrin to assign us our rooms.

"Because we do not have space to accommodate everyone–" Sorrin began, puffing his chest out like a vain peacock. "We will have to double up. Family accommodations will not be provided. And no special cases will be granted." His beady eyes went to Amara and me. "Women will share rooms with women, and men with men."

I wanted to protest. Because I was loath to let Amara out of my sight. But she placed a hand on my arm to stop me.

"He is right," she murmured into my ear. "The only way to accommodate everyone is to separate the family units."

My jaw ticked in ire. It did not escape me that Katarina was immediately granted her own room. The princess who had been enslaved by the evil king and forced to be his sex slave. And then the king fell in love with her and set her free. That was the sob story she had fed everyone. And it might have some loose ends thanks to my arrival, but Sorrin was all too willing to believe she had been forced into prostitution.

But when Sorrin announced that Amara, Asya, and four other women would be placed in a room next to a group of men who included Ashad, I snapped.

"I–will–not–be–separated–from–my wife!" I snarled out, eyes gleaming red.

Sorrin eyed me. A malicious gleam in his eye.

"Then you and your wife can take first watch outside the caves. Camp out there, too, in a tent, if you two are unable to keep from copulating like rabbits–"

He was shoved against the hard stone wall in an instant, my canines bared to him as I grasped his throat.

"Do not ever talk about her like that again!" I roared, ready to rip his throat out and damn all the consequences.

"Zayed," Amara's voice came from far away, her hand on my back. "It is alright, Zayed. Please let him go. We do not need to create this dissent. And...I would like to spend time with my sister. She needs me, due to Salim's unexpected arrival here."

Sorrin's eyes bulged, and I watched in satisfaction as his skin turned purple.

"Do it," he rasped out. "Kill me just like you killed my daughter."

I let out a roar of anguish, his eyes morphing into the eyes of my first wife. Her blood was on my hands. And if I killed her father too, then everyone would be right. Then I really was a monster. Something I had no qualms about being when it came to the safety of my wife. But I could not kill this man. Not when I saw the innocent eyes of my first wife staring back at me. The eyes of a woman who had gladly sacrificed herself if it meant her kingdom and family would be safe. So I released him, letting him crumple to the floor as his wrinkled hands clutched his throat and he gasped for air.

"Your daughter was not a miserable coward like you," I spat at him as he hunched over on the ground at my feet. "She gave her life willingly to save everyone. You, Sorrin, dishonor her with your actions."

And with those final words, I turned on my heel and left him spluttering for air.

Amara's POV

I was unable to move. Kadin towered over me, a dagger in hand. He was about to kill me. I tried to scream but to no avail.

The dagger gleamed cruelly in the light, inches from my throat, and the cold bite of fear settled in my stomach. Kadin's eyes were dark with malice, and I knew he would not hesitate to plunge that blade into me.

"You think you can escape me?" he sneered, his voice thick with contempt. "You have caused enough trouble for one life, Amara. Time to end this once and for all."

I struggled against the invisible weight pinning me in place. Panic clawed at my chest. All the training, all the battles fought—none of it prepared me for this moment. I was helpless before him. Then, a low growl reached my ears and a blur of white tackled Kadin to the floor, only to be followed by a painful yelp.

I wanted to scream but was unable to move as sorrow wracked my body. Baghel was dead!

And then Kadin was dumping his body, white fur matted with blood, on top of me.

"His blood is on your hands. If he had not been so loyal to you, he would still be alive," Kadin sneered.

All my fault. Baghel had only wanted to protect me. I tried to scream, to struggle, to fight. But to no avail. And then Kadin raised the dagger over me once more.

"I will kill you, and then your husband too...before I come for your family," he laughed mercilessly.

And then he plunged the dagger into my breast.

I shot up in bed, mouth open in a silent scream, chest heaving.

"Amara," Asya whispered, jolting upright beside me, worry flooding her gaze.

But before she could even reach out to comfort me, I was rushing out of the bed and retching into a small, empty bucket next to a bucket of fresh water situated in a corner of the sleeping room we had been assigned to. I did not care if I woke up the other two women on the bed next to us. Or the little boy who was sleeping in his mother's arms. It had been a dream, and yet...I could still smell Baghel's blood.

Still hear his surprised cry of pain. Envision how his beautiful, white, pristine fur must have become matted with blood.

I choked back a sob as I wiped my mouth with the back of my hand after emptying the contents of my stomach. Asya gently placed a hand on my back. She was trying to comfort me, but I could not help but flinch away from her touch. Why was I having this dream now? An incessant knocking made Asya get up to answer the door.

I knew who it was. My Lycan felt calm at once due to his nearness. Wordlessly I stood to go to him, grabbing a robe to throw over my flimsy cotton nightgown.

He did not even wait for me to pass the threshold before wordlessly pulling me into his arms.

"I felt it," he whispered into the crown of my head. "I felt your distress."

I burrowed my head into his shoulder. He had sensed it through our mating bond. Just like I had sensed he was still alive when the roof caved in on him. I realized that his presence next to me had been keeping the nightmares at bay. And without his comforting presence, dark dreams were wreaking havoc in my mind.

But if I told him that, it would result in another argument between him and Sorrin. So instead, I let Zayed pull me out of the cave and into the vast expanse of the desert, the stars shining like jewels overhead.

"Do you wish to talk about it?" Zayed asked silently, his arm around my shoulder as I allowed the night air to wash over me and help calm my roiling stomach.

I shook my head. I was not ready to voice the horrors of my nightmare. The guilt of Baghel's death.

"I wrote to Queen Seraphina," Zayed murmured, changing the subject to help get my mind off what was plaguing me. "I did not tell Sorrin. And she has replied. She is willing to grant asylum to the families of the rebels in Assar."

"Sorrin will cry foul," I muttered.

"Let him," Zayed responded. "These innocent children should not be living in a war zone, Amara. They are the future of my kingdom. They are our future. And they deserve to hold on to what little bits of childhood they have left in them."

I sighed, knowing that tomorrow would not be pleasant. I rested my body against Zayed's side.

"You know..." I trailed off, looking up at the stars. "Sorrin's proposition of us sleeping outside has its merits. Look!" I pointed to a shooting star going by, my finger tracing its path as it streaked across the night sky. "Is it not breathtaking?" I breathed, staring in fascination as it left behind a silver glow in its wake in the inky black sky. Like a fleeting brush of silver across the deep indigo canvas of the heavens.

"Yes...very much so." Zayed's voice held a tender note to it that was much too intimate to be praising a star. I looked to see him staring at me, transfixed.

"Who knows when you will see something so beautiful again," I admonished, gesturing for him to look up at the brilliance making a path across the dark sky. It was as though the universe had sent a sign of hope just for me. Even in the darkness, there was light.

"There is nothing more beautiful than watching you enthralled, as you gaze at something that brings you joy," he replied solemnly.

My breath caught at the love in his eyes shining back at me. How had someone I had not even known until mere months ago completely taken over my life, consuming my every thought and emotion? In such a short span of time, we forged this powerful, unbreakable bond, this connection that became etched into the fabric of my soul, into the sands of time itself. Had this been our fate this entire time? Or had it everything to do with one small decision? For if Salim had married Asya, she would never have caught the attention of the Grand Vizier. And I would have never volunteered.

"What are you thinking?" Zayed asked solemnly, staring down at me.

"I am thinking... what if I had never become your bride?" I admitted.

He grabbed both my hands, bringing them to his lips and kissing my knuckles.

"I would have been utterly lost without you. Drifting through the days, a hollow king in a golden cage, wearing a crown that felt heavier with each breath. Before you...I had already decided. I was going to let it all go. Leave the kingdom to a capable heir in the form of Seraphina's child and vanish. Disappear into the shadows."

My breath caught as I realized exactly what he had planned. He had planned to end his life. It was clear in the look in his eyes.

"I had no will to fight anymore. No reason to stay. But then you...you came into my life like the first breath after drowning. You painted color where everything had dulled to gray. You reminded me what it meant to feel alive again. To hope. To want." His forehead met mine. "When we sparred, Amara...I was not fighting. I was falling. Falling hopelessly in love with you."

And then his lips met mine in a kiss under the starlit sky as a shooting star arced over us, a sign of hope.

Amara's POV

"You do not have to decide anything right now," I murmured.

We had been back and forth on the topic of Salim. It had been an entire day and night since we had moved into the new hideout. Asya and I were patrolling the perimeter. Zayed was deep in counsel with Baba. Regarding what exactly, I knew not. But I had an inkling that Baba was in agreement with Zayed about sending the families to Queen Seraphina's kingdom. How they would convince Sorrin was a different matter entirely.

"But he wants to prove himself," Asya replied, her voice trembling with emotion. "He wants another chance. How can I? How can I trust someone who took my heart and tossed it away like it meant nothing?"

"Because you want to?" I supplied hesitantly.

The truth was, if Asya did not want him, she would not be asking me these questions.

"Love is powerful," I went on as we walked the perimeter of the caves. "It does not vanish, sister. It lingers, waiting for a chance to grow again—if you give it space."

"Does his love deserve that space?" Asya demanded, eyes narrowed on the horizon where the sun was setting.

I hesitated before answering. "It does not matter what he deserves. It matters what you want to do. If you believe he is worth giving a chance, then he is. Because your happiness can be found with him."

"Can I really forgive him? Can I put myself back together again if he walks away? What if it was Zayed who left you?"

Pain coursed through my heart at the mere thought. I listlessly withdrew my silver dagger to stare at it. I peered at it closely, able to look at it without my eyes stinging...

"We have company," Asya hissed, drawing her sword.

Immediately, I sharpened my senses, the familiar pulse of urgency flooding my veins.

And then I saw them. An entourage of travellers on their camels. My back tensed. Were they friends or foes?

The figures approached, their silhouettes framing the fading sun behind them. Sharp features and vibrant fabrics caught the last light of day, but as they drew nearer, a sense of unease settled in my stomach. The colors...were familiar.

Asya eased next to me.

"They are allies," she whispered.

I shook my head, staring at the man flanked by his lackeys. I took in his colorful clothes, his jewel encrusted gold sword...

If Zayed ran into him, it would end catastrophically.

"Zayed will not allow their leader to enter," I hissed. "It is better to turn them away."

"Why would he not allow these vital allies inside?" Asya queried, voice full of bewilderment.

I sighed, sheathing my dagger as I prepared to greet the approaching men. "He"—I pointed to the leader whose surprised eyes landed on my face, recognizing me— "assaulted me when he thought I was a lowly servant in the palace."

I met the eyes of Shain with quiet resignation. This was not going to be good.

Especially since Shain's face flushed red, and the men who flanked him did not seem at all surprised by this news. Which meant his behavior was habitual.

Zayed's POV

"Absolutely not!" I snarled out. I was sitting in the council chamber with Idris when we got word that the men we had been expecting with vital information regarding Kadin's movements had arrived. I had not expected our informant to be Shain. "That man is not allowed within an entire kingdom of you!" I boomed. "The last time I saw him, I promised him certain death if he breathed the same air as you!"

"You do not decide who gets to be here and who does not!" Sorrin blustered.

I ignored him. His opinion was going to be moot sooner rather than later.

"Zayed, listen to me," Amara urged, her voice steady amidst the tumult of my anger. "He is working as an emissary in Kadin's court. He holds information that could help us."

"Help?" I snapped, feeling the growl of my Lycan echo in my chest. "The only thing he brings is shame on men. He has no right to set foot within our walls after what he did to you!"

"Maybe so," she conceded, stepping closer with a fierce intensity that mirrored my own. "But if we turn them away now, we lose the chance to forge ties that might protect our people in the future. The rebellion cannot survive on pride alone."

"Pride?" I laughed bitterly. "This is more than just pride for me, Amara. It is about principle. You were attacked—"

"And I defended myself!" she snapped.

I rubbed my temples, frustration flooding through me like a poison as I tried to keep my temper at bay.

"Do you honestly want him residing here? Can you tell me you feel at ease knowing he is lurking within these tunnels?" I pressed.

"It does not matter what makes me feel at ease," Amara replied, sidestepping the question entirely. "What matters is how to use this opportunity while ensuring the past does not repeat itself." She held my gaze.

I exchanged a glance with Idris. Sorrin was screaming about how he was the authority.

Idris held up a hand to me, the signal for patience. I sighed wearily. As always, my old mentor was right. I had to bide my time. Now was not the time to challenge Sorrin head-on.

"If he dares lay a hand on you again," I muttered as we all moved toward the entrance where Amara paused to gather herself before addressing the incoming group of men.

Shain stepped through the cave once the signal to enter had been passed to him.

"I will rip your cock out and feed it to the camels if you touch my wife," I growled, eyes falling on Shain.

For his part, Shain took a step back and tittered nervously. Sorrin gasped in outrage.

"It is all behind us now, Lycan King. I would never ever...had I known she was your queen—"

"You would have tried to force yourself on some other unsuspecting maid?" Amara stated scathingly. "Know this, Shain. You might be Ashad's brother, but you are not my friend. And if I hear even a single female complain or feel uncomfortable due to you, I will not hesitate to skewer you through the heart with my dagger."

She brandished her dagger threateningly, making Shain gulp.

Shain's face turned a shade paler under the weight of her words, his bravado flickering slightly. "I understand," he managed, his voice shaky. From behind him, his companions shifted uncomfortably, almost as if they believed he would not behave.

"You are treading on dangerous ground," I growled, stepping closer until the air between us crackled with tension. "You have burned bridges once; you will not survive my wrath a second time."

"I am not here to forge friendships, but I bring news," Shain interjected quickly, eyes darting to Sorrin, desperate to regain his footing in this volatile conversation. "Kadin's forces are mobilizing for battle. They will come for you soon. They are slowly unearthing the locations of the hideouts. We must move quickly with our plan."

"And your intentions in revealing this are purely altruistic?" I challenged again. "You expect us to believe you come now as a harbinger of goodwill?"

"He is helping us because Kaizern wishes to align with our cause!" Sorrin stated, puffing his chest out proudly.

As if Kaizern had aligned with the rebels because of him. Delusional fool. Ashad and Shain's uncle, the king of Kaizern, only did what was in the best interest of his country. There was a chance Ashad convinced his uncle. However, aside from that, Kaizern had signed a trade treaty with me. Not with Kadin. They knew Kadin would not honor it. It was pure self-preservation masquerading as familial benevolence.

Shain squared his shoulders, determination creeping back into his expression. "I do not expect you to trust me," he admitted. "But I am supporting my brother, who wishes to help Amara." Sorrin's chest deflated slightly over Shain's words. "Kadin has eyes everywhere; he will crush any sign of dissent with merciless force." Shain's voice dropped an octave lower. "There is talk of...him using a mage with powerful, dark magic to do his dirty work."

"Elvira?" Amara queried.

I shook my head.

"Elvira is a witch. It seems Kadin has access to mages able to wield dark magic," I replied, thinking back and realizing it made sense. "A dark mage could track hideouts using spells. All he would need...would be materials to track rebels."

"All of my things must have been burned when the explosion took place in my room," Amara murmured.

"But my material possessions are intact," I clipped out. "Which means he could be using the mage to track me."

I cursed, shaking my head, then looked to Idris. What we had planned must be set in motion soon.

"We need to move the families to a more secure location—one where Kadin cannot reach them easily," I announced. "It is time to gather everyone and give them a choice," I ended, eyes on Idris.

"Choice? What choice? There is no choice!" Sorrin blustered.

But we pointedly ignored him. I looked to Asya, who was already familiar with the plan. She nodded and moved to get the word around. In two hours' time, Sorrin would finally reap the fruits of all the hate he had sown.

"I have contacts who can provide safe passage through the desert to an ally after sunset," I announced to everyone gathered outside the caves. Night had set in, and it was time to set our plan into motion. "Amara and I must move and leave for the mountains in three days' time and talk with Chieftain Lamar. Queen Seraphina will grant us her army, but we need more allies if we wish to succeed. War is near. And it is better for your families to be somewhere safe. For if we perish, our future will still be preserved.

"We will send scouts ahead to ensure the route is safe," I added, attempting to soothe some of the fears I could sense amongst the people. "But waiting for disaster to knock at our door is not an option."

"What are you talking about?!" Sorrin screamed, face red. "This...you are in no position to decide such things!"

"I am not," I agreed. Not yet. "But the people here have every right to decide what is best for their families."

"I will not allow it! As the leader in charge of everyone's well-being—"

"But you failed to take care of their well-being when you willingly sacrificed their children," Asya cut him off crisply.

She nodded toward me. I inclined my head, choosing to remain silent so the plan would work.

"I would say you were derelict on your leader duties," Asya concluded, crossing her arms.

"He is no leader!" one of the men jeered. "Not when he willingly puts us all at risk."

There were murmurs of agreement.

"We will no longer follow your orders, Sorrin!" a woman yelled out. I knew her. She shared a room with Asya and Amara.

"Agreed!"

The jeering around us increased. There was going to be a rebellion within the rebellion if things did not come under control soon.

"Zayed!" Idris yelled my name, his eyes landing on me from the throng of discontented rebels. His brow was furrowed as he looked at me across the crowd. He was feigning concern. Feigning bewilderment. "Things have unexpectedly taken a turn that could be disastrous for the workings of our rebellion. To maintain unity, we need you to take control before this spirals further."

Amara looked at her father in surprise. Then her eyes went to me. I felt her wary scrutiny of the situation, and I sent my own emotions back at her, knowing that our Lycans would communicate and she would realize exactly what was going on.

"We need someone to lead us, and I pick King Zayed!" a rebel yelled out.

"As do I!"

"AND I!"

"He has my vote!"

"What about the council's vote?"

"Silence!" Idris' voice carried above everyone's. "Until the council convenes, Zayed will lead us in Sorrin's place. The rebellion has been divided into groups for safety, and Zayed will lead everyone residing within these caves for now."

"Agreed!" came a new voice.

"LONG LIVE KING ZAYED! So mote it be!"

"SO MOTE IT BE!"

They spoke words that spoke of divine intervention. Of fate. So mote it be was the motto, the religious mantra repeated amongst us when it was clear that the goddess had willed it to be.

I was not chosen by any goddess. I was not worthy. And I would still take the position willingly. Because my wife was having nightmares, and I was not about to let her suffer in silence. If the only way to ensure I was by her side to comfort her when she awoke was to usurp Sorrin's position, then so be it.

And yet it was still humbling, because despite everything that had transpired, these people picked me as their leader. I had not expected it to be so easy.

"Zayed!" Amara's voice broke through the tumult of thoughts swirling in my mind. "You cannot hesitate now."

She was right. I could not lose myself to my thoughts.

The shouts from the crowd swirled around us—frustration, sorrow, fear—but also hope flickered in their voices.

"Zayed!" Idris' voice broke through again, drawing attention back to him as he raised a hand to quiet the crowd slightly. "You have earned their respect and trust by putting your life on the line for their children! Many of these men were unable to reach their children in time due to being assigned to defend the cave entrances. However, you stepped in to risk your life and protect their children when they could not. You did what many would not have. You deserve to lead, to spearhead a cause men would lay their lives down for because they know their children will be well looked after by you."

The crowd surged with agreement once more—shouts overlapping each other in an exhilarating blend of anticipation and urgency. Most had children. And most wanted a leader who would ensure the safety of their progeny whilst they were defending the frontlines.

"King Zayed!" they all chanted slowly.

I held up a hand to silence them.

"I am no longer your king," I called out to them gravely. "That title no longer belongs to me." I hesitated a moment, looking out at everyone.

But they kept chanting my name.

"Rebel leader Zayed!" someone called out, and the chanting changed to match those words.

And as I stood there, ready to take up the mantle of their leader, I recalled Idris' words: Trust in your people.

My eyes hardened. They deserved to know the truth. It was time to rule differently, and that began with placing my trust in them regarding the truth of the curse and the killings. I would begin this rule differently from the last.

"Zayed, the rebel leader," Amara teased as she sat on a cushion unbraiding her hair in front of a mirror in our new and very private chamber.

I grinned at her as I ran a hand through the ends of my long hair, which now fell down to my shoulders. It had been ages since I had allowed it to be trimmed. Truthfully, there was no time. Everything was moving quickly around us.

"Rebellion looks quite attractive on you, dear husband."

"And what about you? As my partner and equal, you are also their leader."

"Ahhh," Amara ran her fingers through her unbraided hair, "but it is not my name they chanted as we left to retire for the night."

She smiled at me, and it was as beautiful as the first rainbow after a long rain.

Her laughter danced around the chamber, filling the air with warmth and light. It was a sound I had grown to cherish, even in the darkest moments.

I leaned back against the wall, admiring my beautiful wife as she shook her hair out and then began to brush it.

"And what do you make of it?" I asked, my voice low. "Of these rebels rallying around me? Do you not think it hasty?"

Did she think I was wrong in planning to take Sorrin's position is what I really meant. And she knew it.

"I believe you possess all the qualities to lead, but it is your heart that makes you worthy. You have fought for their children and have stood strong against overwhelming odds. You deserve to lead. And yet, you think you are not worthy," Amara concluded, eyes on me.

"I do not know," I admitted slowly, feeling the weight of destiny settle on my shoulders once more. "As much as they see me as their leader, there is still part of me that feels lost in this tumultuous sea of responsibility."

She studied me thoughtfully, her dark eyes shimmering with understanding as she set her brush down and stood to look at me. "You are not alone in this. You have me by your side, and together we will navigate these waters. Just remember that a true leader grows through their failures, learns from them, and continues to rise. I am glad you told them the truth. They have finally heard your version of the story and will relay it to everyone else no doubt. You have revealed how truly remorseful and guilty you were over having to kill innocent women. You controlled the narrative rather than letting whispers of your evil nature keep spreading. Sorrin no doubt would never have quashed such rumours."

I inclined my head, appreciating the clarity in her voice. "But what if I lead them into disaster?"

Her expression softened, and she strode over to me. Brushing a hand against my cheek, she spoke, "Every leader faces that fear. It is part of the burden they carry—the responsibility for their people. It is why you are worthy to lead. Because you understand the responsibility."

The way she looked at me, filled with unwavering belief, stirred me. I grabbed her, holding her close to me, and allowed my lips to descend over hers. Her lips were like an elixir, a promise of calm against the chaos that surrounded us. I lost myself in the sweetness of her taste as she sighed into my mouth. I revelled in the softness of her body pressed against mine. Her intoxicating taste and scent was a unique blend that settled my raging heart. My hand went immediately to the front tie of her garment, eager to claim her as mine.

But a sudden commotion outside our chamber interrupted us. A moment later, Asya entered our chamber, giving us moments to break apart.

Her expression was stricken.

"Another hideout was attacked by Kadin's men. We have an influx of people fleeing and coming here and..." Asya paused momentarily before proceeding to speak. "There were not many survivors," she finally choked out.

At once, Amara and I were following her. Kadin was mobilizing all his resources to brutally kill everyone.

Chapter 14

Zayed's POV

I ran a tired hand over my face. I sat in the chamber designated for meetings, gearing up to put into place our next course of action. Because now, the entire rebel movement depended on me. All of the inhabited hideouts except this one had now been attacked. I was almost positive the empty hideouts had already been ransacked. It was only a matter of time before Kadin's men closed in on us here as well. We had to move, and fast.

Which is why I sat here, surrounded by anxious people worried about their families, writing a letter. Finally signing it, I passed it into the hands of Idris.

"Amara and I will leave tomorrow to meet with Chieftain Lamar. Take this letter to my uncle, my mother's brother. He will provide refuge and aid our cause." I exhaled. "These caves are no longer safe."

"But if he is tracking us through magic, we will be caught there as well."

I studied Idris guardedly.

"If Elvira truly cared for my mother as much as she stated, I am sure the witch has magical wards up in the area to block magical tracking. You will be cloaked there due to her spells placed when my mother was a child. Mother often spoke of how the home she was born in was safer than even the palace. I believe those were the words of a woman who knew that powerful magical enchantments surrounded her childhood home."

"Let me go with you and Amara," pleaded Asya.

I gave a curt nod. Amara's sister would be an asset.

"Ashad must go as well," Idris reasoned. "For as a noble from Kaizern, he can assure the Chieftain of an alliance with his kingdom as well."

I exhaled loudly again. I did not want Ashad anywhere near us.

"Ashad will not hold as much weight as Shain, a legal emissary who is the oldest son. He will inherit his father's title as prince. Remember their father is the brother of the king," Sorrin grumbled.

I narrowed my eyes at Sorrin. He was right, dammit.

Sorrin, though I did not like him, was no fool driven solely by grief. The man was forged from calculating shrewdness, honed by experience, and sharpened by loss. His daughter's death at my hands did not *make* him who he was; it merely added fuel to an already calculating mind. His choices were not only born of blind vengeance, but of strategy. He thought like a tactician, spoke like a statesman, and moved like a man who understood the weight of consequences. Yes, his hate for me had influenced his decisions. Yes, I did not trust him. I did not like him. But I respected the cold precision of his intellect. So I would continue to consult him...because power recognized power. Whether I liked him or not was beside the point.

"If he touches my wife, I kill him on the spot, no questions asked," I hissed out.

"You do, and you lose any real sway you have with Chieftain Lamar. We know he does not like you," sneered Sorrin.

My fist slammed onto the wooden table. I could feel my eyes glowing red.

"She is my crown, my oath, my fury. If he harms her, I will unmake him."

There was a tense silence as my words settled into everyone.

"Maybe we should ask Amara if she feels comfortable travelling with Shain?" Asya ventured, clearly trying to calm me down. "Where is she?"

"She is overseeing the evacuation of more families," Idris explained, eyes on me.

I was too angry to even say that Amara was doing what we should be doing rather than sitting here and discussing worthless scum like Shain.

"I do not like him either," Idris chided, eyes on me. "But Sorrin has a point."

"What if Ronan went with us?" Asya was referring to Sorrin's son.

I did not think he could be trusted, but kept quiet on the matter.

"Katarina must go too. She is the daughter of a defeated chieftain, after all," Sorrin added. "Maybe we can negotiate an alliance through marriage…"

I exhaled, eyeing Asya. I would first have to consult Amara and Asya on the plan I had formed in my head. It was no secret that Chieftain Lamar had a son. A son who refused to marry for some reason. And if there was going to be an alliance through marriage, I would prefer it to be with Asya. Only if Asya agreed, of course.

"Katarina," Asya spat venomously, "would only slow us down. Her entourage of colorful servants will get us killed before we can make it halfway across the desert."

"I have already written to Chieftain Lamar with the proposition. He will be expecting her. And as tales of her remarkable beauty are known far and wide, he will be eager to show her to his son," Sorrin stated, puffing his chest out proudly.

Of course he would have done something like this. Leave it to Sorrin to undermine me as he believed I had undermined him.

I exchanged a look with Asya. This was not going to go well at all.

I moved swiftly through the cave corridors until I reached the chamber Amara and I shared. I entered quietly, eager to see my wife, and my eyes fell on the outline of her naked form in bed. The torches had been put out, her attempt to set the mood perhaps? My frustration scattered like sand and need roared to life in my veins. With everything that had happened in the two days since we arrived at the new hideout, we had not had much time for each other. And it looked like my little tigress wanted to rectify that.

I moved, a dark chuckle rumbling low in my chest.

"What a pleasant surprise."

Amara had had an unfortunate run-in with Katarina's trunk of makeup. I had been informed she would be in the bathing rooms before coming to bed tonight.

"Did you already bathe? Or were you hoping I would help you later?" I purred, sinking into the bed and wrapping my arms around her slender frame, one hand going down to possessively grab her thigh and eagerly coax her to wrap it around my waist.

And then I stilled in shock. Too slender, too fragile...

Her thighs were not the muscular thighs of my wife. Her waist was too small....

"Zayed," she breathed, pressing her supple bare breasts against my chest as she turned into me.

Nauseatingly sweet lilac hit my nostrils, and it was like a bucket of cold water was poured on me. I had not smelled her upon entering because she had masked her scent. But at this proximity, I could smell her just fine. It was not Amara's scent in my bed.

My hardening cock went limp immediately and I moved away, snarling in anger.

"What the hell are you doing in here?"

I lit the torch on the wall and turned to look at Katarina's form spread out on my bed. The bed I shared with my wife.

Her presence defiled it.

"I just thought you might like to have some fun," she said innocently, tossing her golden hair behind her shoulder in a move that might have had me salivating after her if I was still the young boy who had fallen for her.

"Get out," I snarled. "How dare you—"

Katarina laughed.

"Look at you, trying to stay loyal to your wife. You do not have to, Zayed. All kings have...discretions. Women to please them. Your father's harem was full of—"

"I am not my father," I bit out, eyes narrowed on her. "Get out before I let my wife strangle you with her own two hands."

"Oh…" Katarina smiled like a cat who had been given ample cream. She stretched out further, showing off the glistening triangle between her legs. Her body gleamed in the torchlight. I smelled the air, and her arousal wafted toward me. The scent made me want to retch. I did not want to smell anyone's arousal except for my wife's. I did not want to look at any women naked unless she was Amara.

I turned my back to her.

"The sight of you makes me sick." I spat the words out, tone laced with revulsion.

"I did not make you sick when you were younger," Katarina argued, ire in her voice.

"I am married and in love," I replied calmly. "Stop this nonsense, Katarina, and leave."

I could not let Katarina accompany us if this was what she planned to do for the entire journey to Chieftain Lamar's.

"Maybe you do not like the fact that I am on the bed. Maybe…you want me somewhere else?" Katarina ventured.

I heard her move and then suddenly she was in front of me, bending down on all fours and turning to bare her ass to me.

"Please, Zayed…I missed you…your cock… so much," Katarina moaned, spreading her ass cheeks and offering up her pussy to me.

I blinked, wondering why she was so insistent even after being rejected multiple times.

"I need this," she moaned, moving a finger to insert it inside her pussy. "I need to come, Zayed. The drug I ingested makes me so hot."

I took another step back. Drug? Alarm shot through me as my mind quickly attempted to put the pieces of the puzzle together. No, it was no coincidence she was here right after dumping Amara with a trunk full of makeup. This was not a stupid woman trying to seduce me. This was something else entirely.

Without a second thought, I reached for her wrist attached to the hand fingering herself from behind. An attempt to give me a show that would arouse me no doubt. Fool. If it had been Amara before me, it might have worked. I wanted no one but her. So I twisted Katarina's wrist with enough force to make her stop. She cried out but I did not stop. Exerting pressure, I angled her arm so it was now pushing against her back. Her knees gave way, she fell to the floor. I pinned her there, my hand around her wrist like a vise as I made her forearm dig harshly into the small of her back.

"Oh you want to be rough now?" Katarina giggled, moving her ass in an attempt to rub against my groin. But I was careful to keep my distance, hovering above her and out of reach.

"I do not want you anywhere near me," I hissed. "Now tell me what drug? Who gave it to you?"

"Fuck me and I might tell you," Katarina replied. I could see her body beginning to bead with sweat.

She was going into some sort of state of extreme arousal due to whatever she had consumed. Her body was hot, burning up.

I wanted to slap her, but she might like it. I twisted her arm further, exerting pressure on her wrist. She cried out again.

"When I break your wrist, it is not going to feel good," I snarled. "Tell me what drug!"

"I-I do not know!" Katarina cried out, squirming under me. "Oh Zayed...please. .let me come just one time. I remember how you used to put me on my hands and knees and fuck me. Please, just one time, can we do that again? I need—I need..." she squirmed again, trying to rub her thighs together and probably relieve some of what was going on in her body.

"Tell me or I will break your skull after your wrist," I growled, my other hand going to wrest on the back of her head, pushing her face further into the stone ground below her.

She swallowed.

"It was a note! A note!" she cried out, voice muffled as she spoke into the stone floor. "A note in my room to take it and let you fuck me. You would be mine after that, because you would not want Amara after...after..." Katarina trailed off.

"AFTER WHAT?" I roared, my hand on her head tightening as I shook it so hard, I was surprised it was still attached to her shoulders. Alarm shot through me. Alarm and panic.

"After she was unfaithful to you! After another man had her body in the bathing rooms!" She shrieked in pain, angling her head to turn and look at me. Blood caked her cheek because it had grated so hard against the stone.

FUCK. Immediately, I let Katarina go and rushed to the bathing rooms.

Chapter 15

Amara's POV

I was so angry I wanted to drown Katarina in her supply of perfumes and makeup. My entire body was covered in pink and purple shades of blush and liquid lip paint. I did not believe even for a second that it had been an accident. They had purposefully upended the trunk, splattering my entire body with the vile concoctions.

Katarina had, with that fake saccharine smile of hers, offered me a drink of water as an apology before suggesting I should go clean up. She even had the gall to offer one of her blue lace outfits for me to change into. Along with a wink that Zayed loved it when a woman wore lace to bed.

I wanted to break her face. Bile had risen in my throat at her speaking about Zayed like that. It had made the water she gave me taste utterly bitter in my mouth.

So I had stalked off with the offered lace to take my bath, all the while thinking if I was willing to face the repercussions of murdering Katarina and burying her body in a deep recess of these caves. I knew I should not let her get to me. But much of it stemmed from constantly comparing myself to her.

She was the beautiful princess with her golden hair, a slim frame, and soft hands.

Meanwhile, I was the peasant with callused hands and a muscular physique, because my worth was in my ability to stay alive.

We were from two different worlds. And yet, both knew what it felt like to be loved by Zayed.

I sighed, scrubbing at a particular purple spot on my bronzed arm. It looked utterly ridiculous against my skin tone. Yet on Katarina's face, the color made her look exotically radiant.

I shook my head. Zayed loved me. Not her. I should not let my dark thoughts get the better of me. And as soon as I was done bathing, I would be back in our room. In his arms.

My body heated just thinking about it. We were fortunate that these bathing rooms had an underground spring to wash up in. I slowly moved to step out of the warm water, the coolness soaking away the heat of anger that twisted my gut. I stumbled momentarily as I attempted to make my way toward the pile of my discarded clothes that held my weapons. I braced myself and found myself on my hands and knees, unable to get my body to cooperate and move faster.

I blinked, realizing that my movements were not sluggish due to rage but something else entirely.

A slow, intoxicating heat had slowly wrapped around my limbs like the embrace of a lover.

My skin tingled and every little droplet of water cascading over my body felt like a scintillating caress, igniting every nerve ending and awakening a primal desire deep within me.

The memory of Zayed's touch and the head of his body lapped around me.

I knew something was wrong. I knew I had been drugged. But my racing heart sent arousal pulsing between my legs, and my body was not reacting the way I wanted it to. I stared at the spring as I teetered on the edge of it, trying to gain my bearings. I had to dilute the substance within me. But a heady rush overwhelmed me before I could act, making me gasp in shock. My hands bracing against the ground of the cave, but my knees gave way, and then I was lying face down on the cool ground, unable to even lift myself.

All I could think about was how alive I felt—each heartbeat pulsed with longing, my arousal making me dizzy.

Those pulses of longing began to bloom, exploding across my skin. I moaned, my hands moving to touch myself as erratic patterns of desire crashed against my senses.

I cried out in surprise when a warm body pressed itself over me, moving me slowly so that I was now on my side.

My arousal had curled across the edges of reason, whispering promises of intoxication that hung heavily in the air around me.

Images danced before my eyes of flesh and desire and Zayed's dark gaze. The thought of his body pressed against mine sent shocks of yearning skittering down my spine. I shook my head, trying to clear it.

A masculine hand trailed across my right side and came to cup my breast. A thumb flicked at my nipple. Hot lips attached to the side of my neck.

"Zayed," I gasped out, trying to turn into him. "I need you."

But he held me firm, unable to move as his erection poked into my backside. I squirmed against him, mewling in satisfaction when my backside nestled against his hard cock.

My eyes fluttered open momentarily, to look at the hand now determinedly trailing down from my breast to my abdomen and to the triangle between my legs. Something was wrong. My Lycan's senses were trying to tell me something.

It took a few moments for my brain to register that this was not the strong, callused hand I was used to. That this person was not my husband. I tried to scream in protest, but all that came out was a soft pathetic cry.

"Get...off!" I gasped out, voice hoarse as I struggled to break free.

But a wave of arousal surged through my body, locking every muscle in place.

He chuckled against my neck, his voice low and sultry, sending shivers cascading down my spine. The warmth radiating from him mingled with the heat pooling within me, but the moment sickened me. It was intoxicating yet so painfully unwanted.

His hand slid slower, fingers skimming over my thighs as I writhed against the ground in protest.

My heart thudded violently at the unwelcome sensations coursing through me. I raised a feeble hand trying to push him away. My hand uselessly fell to my side, against my pile of dirty soiled clothes.

Dirty. Soiled. My stomach churned in disgust as the man's hand came to the folds between my legs. He hissed darkly when he found me wet.

I cried out weakly as my body refused to move with enough strength to throw him off of me. Desperation creeped into my tone as my useless hand curled over the cloth of my clothes. And closed firmly around the hilt of my sheathed dagger.

I stilled, gripping the dagger tightly. The cold metal was like a lifeline amidst this chaos unfolding around me.

My reflexes were too slow. I had to wait. My heart hammered in my chest as I registered every unwanted touch, every cruel whisper that slipped from his lips.

"Whore."

His fingers played with my pussy before inserting a finger into me. He pumped it into me harshly, painfully.

"So wet for me. Queen of sluts."

He forced me onto my back. He was shrouded in darkness, the torches having been doused before he began his assault. My blurry vision, clouded by the drug, registered a glint of a long gold chain around his neck.

"He will not want you after this. I will make you my whore."

He spread my legs wide.

I closed my eyes, knowing he was wrong. Zayed loved me. But that did not give this man permission to rape me!

"So ready for me," he grunted, his voice garbled and distorted to my ears.

I had planned to wait until he was inside me. But something in me rebelled at letting the violation occur. Why did I have to wait for him to violate me to strike?

Maybe it was the right decision, because as he was preoccupied with lining himself up against my entrance, he did not notice the slow movement of my arm as my hand moved, flicking open the sheath of my dagger with my finger and slamming the naked blade into the bicep that belonged to the arm that held my hip down.

He cried out in surprise as I removed the dagger from his arm, blood falling out in rivulets. It was deep enough to have hit a major blood vessel.

His silhouette staggered back, clutching his arm as hot wet liquid poured through his fingers.

I blinked and the room spun.

"You little—" he began.

But I did not give him a chance to finish. I pushed myself slowly off the ground, feeling the cool air of the cave wrap around my naked skin.

I stumbled briefly, knowing that I was not going to be able to defend myself for much longer.

But he did not lunge at me as I expected. Instead, he swiftly backed away, running out of the bathing chambers faster than even my blurry vision could comprehend.

I breathed heavily, stumbling forward in a pathetic attempt to catch him. I barely had the strength to move. The world around me was swimming in and out of focus. I wanted to vomit.

I could hear the echo of my heart pounding in my ears, drowning out the remnants of shock that gripped me. My hands shook as I pressed my back against the cool stone wall to steady myself, panic clawing at my throat like a ravenous beast. I was spiraling. Trying to comprehend that I had been assaulted and nearly raped. Only a few seconds longer and he would have...

Zayed's face filled my thoughts—his fierce protection, his unwavering love. I could hear his voice in my mind, urging me to be strong, to fight. I needed to dilute the substance in my body, even if the urge to vomit was overpowering.

I struggled to make sense of everything. This had been premeditated. Not some desperate attempt by a random man.

Suddenly, there were hands on my body again. I lashed out, my blade cutting into skin.

"Amara, it is me!"

I thought it sounded like Zayed, but it must be another hallucination. I protested weakly, my scream coming out more like a garbled gasp of protest, limbs flailing out to protect myself.

I heard a curse as my hand hit his jaw weakly. It was not enough to keep anyone at bay. In my drug-addled state, even I knew that much. There was no strength behind my arms. They were useless. I stumbled as I tried to shrink back against the cold stone wall. I could not see, my vision distorted and blinking in and out. I could not defend myself against him.

But he...

He was still staying back.

"My love...my life...my queen..."

I heard his pleading murmurs and stilled.

"Z-Zayed?" I rasped out, finally.

I blinked, cautiously trying to concentrate on the dark form before me.

Was it really him? Or was I seeing things?

I swayed, and he cautiously wrapped his hands around my naked body, bringing me into him. I sluggishly felt his hand resting on my waist as he tried to steady me against him. I inhaled his scent but had to be sure. And when I let my fingers skim over his chest, feeling the familiar grooves of it, I sobbed in relief. It really was him. My senses might have failed me, but if the man before me felt like Zayed, sounded like Zayed, and smelled like him...then it must be my husband.

I sensed the wetness of my tears on my cheeks and let myself sink into him, giving into blissful oblivion.

Zayed's arms tightened around my trembling frame. He lifted me into his arms and I heard the gentle thudding of his heart against my ear, a steady rhythm that pulled me back from the brink of panic. My body sagged against him, and I buried my face into him, inhaling deeply.

He was here now. I could let myself lean into him, depend on him.

Zayed

I held her against me in our bedchamber, rage flooding my entire body. The scent of fear clung to her like a shadow, and there was blood on her—luckily not her own. Whoever had assaulted her masked their scent using something they had consumed. Therefore, I could not scent him out from the blood. I hoped the comfort and familiarity of our bed would help her. But she was whimpering in fear, even in her sleep. I had never seen my wife as terrified as I had seen her in the bathing chamber. I had never seen her as vulnerable as I was seeing her right now. Whoever did this to her would die a painful death.

Her body was hot, and perspiration dotted her forehead. Even in her unconscious state, her potent arousal permeated the room. My surge of anger was almost overwhelming as I pressed a wet cloth to her forehead, desperately trying to cool her feverish skin. I had done my best to administer a few sips of water to her lips as well. Nothing was working to cool her body.

My eyes strayed to the marks on her breasts—bruises already healing quickly from being touched too harshly. The stark reality of what had transpired clawed at my insides with venomous rage. Whoever had touched her, whoever had dared to lay hands on my wife—there would be a reckoning.

With every breath I took, cold fury coursed through my veins like fire.

My fingers traced the delicate contours of her face, lingering over the remnants of fear shadowing her features. I placed a kiss on her forehead, and I inhaled her scent deeply, allowing it to ground me amidst the storm brewing inside.

But as I sat there on the bed, cradling her form against me, shadows of doubt flickered at the edges of my consciousness. Had she sustained more damage than just bruises? Would she awaken bearing the weight of this violation, a burden she did not deserve to carry?

Amara moved, inching closer into me. I had no idea the extent of the violation, because I could not smell the perpetrator on her. Bastard. And even though I wanted to go and murder every man within this cave, I could not. She needed me more.

She cried out suddenly, eyes flying open to look at me disconcertingly.

"Shhh...my love...*jaan*," I whispered ardently, calling her my life, my soul. "*Jaan*, it is me. You are safe." The words, however, tasted like sawdust on my tongue. I should have kept her safe.

"Zayed," she breathed, looking at me, but not looking at me. She was not lucid. She was not fully conscious. "Zayed...I need you..."

Slowly, she slinked into my arms, like a lioness honing in on her prey. My arms went around her waist on instinct. She let out a gasp, wrapping her bare legs around my waist. Her body was burning.

"Ohhhh." She threw her head back, long dark hair flowing down her back like an inky waterfall. She was so beautiful. And then she began to grind against me. "Yesssss," she hissed, arms twining around my neck.

Her breasts were at eye-level, and though we had been in this position before, where I knew taking her nipples into my mouth would send her into ecstatic waves of pleasure, I hesitated. Because this was not her wanting to make love. This was the drug in her system.

"My *jaan*," I murmured, breathing and trying to get my hardening cock under control. Her pussy was wet, and I could feel how damp she was making the thin cotton cloth that covered my loins. She was grinding against me, panting as she undulated her hips against mine. "You need to stop. We need to diminish the effects of the drug."

"I need...I need—" Amara cried out brokenly, eyes closed as she attempted to rock against me but could not because I held her hips firm in my hands now.

I cursed, feeling my cock twitch against her warm, wet core. The Lycan in me wanted to claim her, wanted to fuck her and erase any other man's touch from her body. But I would not let her wake up to feel as if her choice had been taken from her.

"Drink," I urged, reaching for my camel skin filled with water. Slowly, I brought it to her lips.

She let out a cry of pain, moving her head away from the offered water.

"Please...it hurts!" Her eyes flew open, looking right through me. "Oh, it hurts!"

She let go of me, curling into a fetal position. Still, I offered her water, hoping it would dispel whatever the drug was doing to her. She took a few sips before passing out, her body still burning to the touch. I cursed, noting the light sheen of sweat that now covered her bare arms. I had to figure out how to bring her body temperature down. Touching my wife while she was drugged, while her mind was addled due to a concoction that forced her arousal, did not sit well with me.

There was a sudden, discreet knock at my door. Pulling the sheet over Amara's naked form, I moved to answer it, stepping out to talk to Idris and Asya, who stood with grim faces.

"Katarina has been thrown into the cells for her part in all of this, though she is completely devoid of rational thought at the moment," Asya explained worriedly. Her cheeks reddened lightly. "Whatever this drug is...it...has extreme side effects."

"News has spread through the tunnels," Idris added grimly. "The others are worried—"

"Worried?" I echoed, my voice low and dangerous. "They need to know that whoever laid a hand on her will wish they had not drawn breath. They should be terrified of my wrath."

Idris hesitated for a moment, weighing his words carefully. "We need to focus on helping Amara get better. Have you attempted to dilute the drug from her body?"

"She is unconscious!" I barked out. "I am doing my best to dispel any effects."

Asya coughed into her hand.

"The only thing that brings down the effects of the drug is to..." Asya trailed off.

"Out with it!" I barked, angry and impatient.

"She needs to find her release. It is what worked for Katarina. She finally fell into a fitful sleep after...touching herself," Asya ended, looking away.

Idris cleared his throat, wisely backing away and murmuring something about going to check on the patrols. I did not blame him. He did not want to be anywhere near this sort of conversation.

Through the haze of anger and despair, a flicker of realization ignited within me. *She needs to find her release.* The words echoed in my mind.

"She. Is. Unconscious," I grit out, narrowing my eyes at Asya. "And she was assaulted!"

"And you are her husband!" Asya snapped, eyes hard on me. "You can help her!"

The temperature spiked within the tunnel, a mix of my fury and disbelief swirling around us as I processed Asya's words.

Asya looked at me steadily.

"It is not just about release. It is about her body needing to stabilize, to reset itself. The drug complicates things further if she is left as is. We do not know what was used. We have no means of creating an antidote."

"She is unconscious," I protested, a part of me wanting to deny what she suggested, the other part raging with desperation and willing to do anything it took to help her. "How can I—"

"Wake her up then," Asya replied steadily.

I exhaled.

"I would be no better than the man who assaulted her," I murmured plaintively.

Asya inclined her head in deference and understanding. "I can assure you, you are nothing like those vile men who force themselves on women. I can also only tell you what we have been able to discover through Katarina. But...we do not know what effects this drug may have on her body if left unchecked. All we know is that Katarina's temperature normalized after she..." Asya trailed off, not wanting to complete the sentence again.

I brought a tired hand to my face.

"Have the caves been searched for men with injuries?"

"Zayed, it is not possible. Do you know how many men reside here? While we have done our best to look for any man with recent injuries or a man possessing a limp who might not have before, there is nothing. We have come up empty-handed. Stripping each and every male within the tunnels to check for fresh wounds is not only preposterous, it is not logistically possible!"

I growled. I did not care! I wanted the perpetrator to be found and then I wanted to feed his dick to my camel!

"Who could have done this? Sorrin...Ashad?" I could not help but voice my concerns, anger radiating from me. "Shain?"

I wanted to kill them all just for being suspects.

"Right now, what is important is helping Amara. We will figure the rest out once she wakes and has recovered," Asya assured me. "Hopefully, Amara can tell us more about who assaulted her. He is probably the same person who gave Katarina the note with instructions to use it on herself and to give to Amara."

Asya was right.

Swallowing hard, I bid Asya goodnight and turned back into our shared chamber where I knelt beside Amara's still form. Her breathing was shallow, her brow glistening with sweat as that insidious heat lingered beneath her skin. Every fiber of me ached seeing her suffer like this—to think of someone violating her, to imagine the terror that had accompanied that violation.

"Amara," I murmured desperately, brushing a damp strand of hair away from her face. "You need to wake up for me." I leaned closer, pressing my forehead against hers, sharing my breath with her as if my essence could reignite her spirit. "Fight this. I need you to come back to me."

Her body stirred beneath my hands, and brought a scorching against my palms as she pressed into me. A soft groan escaped her lips. I watched her eyelids flutter open briefly before closing again.

Rage bubbled under my skin. Whoever had done this had wanted her completely incapacitated like she was now. She could barely move! The only thing she wanted was to fuck, to find her release. No doubt she would not have provided much resistance. My Lycan itched to run through these tunnels and castrate every man I set my eyes on. Damn the rebellion. Damn everything. None of it was worth Amara's well-being.

Another soft groan escaped her lips, and I could see the tension in her delicate features. Was she still in pain? My heart pounded, desperate for her to return to me, to shake off the nightmare that had invaded her senses.

"Zayed..." she breathed, the softness of my name on her lips like a soothing balm. Her eyes opened, and she seemed more lucid than before.

"It is me," I confirmed, leaning closer so she could sense my presence entirely. "You are safe, *jaan*. You are home." Because her home was with me.

My heart hammered at the slight disorientation evident in her expression, but I held her gaze steady, pouring all my strength into my voice. Into her.

Those dark, soulful eyes blinked at me, filled with confusion.

"I feel... strange," she admitted, her brow furrowing as she struggled against the obvious heaviness weighing down her limbs.

She moaned again, moving into me where I sat hovering over her worriedly. I noticed the way she pressed her thighs together, the sheet falling from her form as she moved. Her body glistened with sweat, a red tint giving away how heated she truly was.

"Help..." she trailed off, closing her eyes and grimacing in pain. Her temperature was rising slowly.

"It hurts," she breathed out, desperation lacing her voice. "Please." Her hands settled onto my chest, fingers curling into my shirt like a lifeline in turbulent waters. And then she was gone, consciousness floating off, yet her body undulating against mine.

I yearned to sweep away the pain coursing through her, to banish the drug that clung to her like a shadow.

I brushed a wet cloth against her heated brow. "I will help you." Her body shuddered against mine, a wave of longing crashing over her so palpable that it sent a tremor rippling straight into my chest. I cursed, struggling for control. Her eyes fluttered open briefly again and she pulled me closer to her.

"Only you," she whispered before her head fell back onto the pillow.

She only trusted me at this moment.

Her breath came in shallow gasps, and with it, I sensed the intoxicating mixture of heat and need wrapping around her.

I reached out cautiously, brushing my fingers along the curve of her face, feeling the intense heat radiate from her skin. Even for a Lycan, this was not good. "I am right here, love," I murmured assuringly, heart pounding as I slowly began to explore the contours of her body with my hands. I was tentative yet firm, mindful of her vulnerability.

She whimpered in her sleep, a whine of need. A sound I was all-too-familiar with. I dipped lower, my lips, finding the delicate line of her collarbone, then began pressing soft kisses against her heated skin. She responded instinctively, arching toward me.

The heat rolled off her in undulating waves, pulling me deeper into the intoxicating atmosphere that enveloped us. My fingers trailed down her sides, dancing over the curves that had always captivated me.

"You are my everything," I murmured against the soft skin of her abdomen, my fingers dancing along the softness of her hips while I shifted closer to the heat pooling between her legs. "Nothing will ever take that away."

My fingers grazed lightly over the soft curls between her thighs. The warmth there beckoned me closer, a seductive promise that drew me deeper into a realm where the whispers of our hearts entwined in an unbreakable bond. Her pulse quickened beneath me, matching the rhythm of my own heart, each thump echoing through the silence like a war drum preparing for battle.

Her body responded to every brush of my lips. And I only prayed she would forgive me if this was something she did not want.

But even as I savored her softness, that familiar anger surged within me anew. Katarina's malevolent actions would not go unpunished. I gritted my teeth, forcing myself to focus on Amara and not on the fire of vengeance threatening to engulf me.

She gasped in pain under me again and I realized I had stopped to stew over my anger.

"Zayed!" she cried out in protest in her sleep.

"I am here, Amara," I said hoarsely, lips finding the folds between her legs. "Focus on me my love, my touch—" I gently pried her legs apart. "My lips—" I kissed her inner thigh. "My tongue," I plunged it between her folds, tasting her slick wetness, growling as the juices of her arousal flowed freely. She was so so wet. And I only tasted her, which meant no one had been inside of her against her will.

Her body trembled at the first contact, a gasp escaping her lips as my tongue explored the silken warmth of her core. Each flick and swirl made more arousal pool between her legs.

I lavished attention on her, noting every gasp and whine of hers that shattered the quiet of our room. I was attentive to even a singular cry or movement of protest. But she only begged for more, one hand sluggishly coming to fist the hair at the nape of my neck, moving me more firmly against her core.

I moved slowly but deliberately, teasing and coaxing her body to relax against the waves of pleasure I wove for her.

Each flick of my tongue against her sensitive flesh drew out breathy whimpers.

She bucked against me, seeking more pressure, more pleasure, and I obliged willingly, eager to guide her toward the edge of ecstasy.

"That is it," I murmured against her soft flesh, breathing warm air against her wetness. "Let go for me."

Another cry of urgency echoed in the chamber, and I could feel the tautness in her thighs as they tensed.

She whimpered, her voice a blend of desperation and longing, as though she could sense the release just beyond her grasp. Need radiated from her, intoxicatingly sweet. I was rock hard. But this was not about me. This was about helping her.

Her body began to quake beneath me, and I reveled in it. And then she cried out in sweet relief when her release finally crashed over her. But as I pulled back, ready to pull the sheet over her and keep vigil over her recovery, I heard it.

"Please," she gasped again, desperation threading between her words. "I need you inside me."

Her words were still sluggish, but my hands on her hips told me there was a difference in her body heat already. She reared up onto her elbow to stare at me between her legs. Her eyes were open and on me, though still a bit disoriented.

"I want to feel you inside me," she pleaded, breathing shallowly. "Help me forget..."

I reached for her hand buried in the hair at the nape of my neck. I brought it to my lips, placing a kiss on her knuckles before, interlacing our fingers tightly. "Focus on me," I whispered, attempting to guide her beyond the haze that dulled her senses. "We will get through this together."

I positioned myself between her thighs, feeling her heat radiate against my skin. I was acutely aware of the urgency in her gaze, the way she begged for me—body and soul. My heart thundered in my chest as I aligned myself with her entrance, pausing for a moment to meet her eyes one last time.

"Are you certain?" I asked softly, wanting to ensure she was wholly present despite the fog of the drug still clinging to her consciousness.

"Goddess yes! Please fuck me."

Her singular plea struck deep within me, igniting a fire that coursed through my veins like molten lava. Driven by desire and an instinctive need to protect what was mine, I thrust forward slowly, entering her warmth with exquisite care, savoring every inch as she enveloped me completely.

A gasp escaped her lips as I sheathed myself completely inside of her. Did it hurt her?

"Breathe," I urged softly, pleadingly.

A shadow of a smile crossed her lips faintly.

"You said that...the first time...we made love."

She said the words through her harsh pants, as if it took effort to speak.

Her body tightened around me, a warm embrace that pushed away my fears, assuring me she was still there with me.

She shifted beneath me, arching her back and urging me deeper, as if seeking to reclaim every piece of herself that I had promised to protect. That I had failed to protect.

"I could not figure out if you were commanding me or requesting me," she muttered, eyes fluttering closed as I pulled back and thrust into her again gently.

"Yes, just like that," she hissed, raising her hips to meet my thrusts.

My breath fell from my lips in ragged gasps as I attempted to hold on. But she felt divine wrapped around my dick.

Her slickness wrapped around me like some sort of intoxicating witch's spell.

Her body writhed beneath me, and I could see the remnants of the drug's influence fading under the weight of desire and connection. "You feel so good," she gasped, arching into me, urging me deeper. "I need more."

The force of our bond surged through us, heightening everything. We were husband and wife, yes, but we were also two mated Lycans. Everything was intensified between us. Her beautiful gasps of pleasure were music to my ears. And every brush of her fingers on my body sent pleasure pulsing hotly through me. I shifted my angle slightly, brushing against that spot inside her that sent her spiraling toward another wave of bliss. She cried out my name again, sweetly pleading. A begging whine. It was my favorite sound.

And then I, too, cried out as I emptied myself inside her, our bodies moving to an ancient rhythm older than time itself.

I lost myself in her, allowing myself to forget everything in that moment. Allowing both of us to transcend into a realm where nothing else existed but the two of us as we held onto each other through our shared climax.

"You are here," she breathed, voice still laced with traces of the drug's remnants but now tinted with clarity. The relief in her voice was not lost on me.

"I am here," I whispered, leaning down to capture her lips in a fervent kiss, my tongue sweeping against hers, claiming her all over again. She responded, clutching me to her before pulling away to look at me lovingly. I kissed her forehead and watched her slowly fall into a restful sleep.

Chapter 16

Amara's POV

I awoke with a pounding headache and a feeling of dread in my stomach.

Panic surged through me, and I bolted upright, scanning the room frantically.

My breathing was fast and erratic. I looked around, completely disoriented, and the world spun unsteadily. I blinked in the dim light, realizing I was in my bed chamber.

"Zayed?" I croaked out, confusion flooding my senses.

Terror clawed at me as the fragments of memory played on a loop in my head. Someone's hands on me. Someone...

"ZAYED!" I screamed, wildly searching the room, only to realize I was alone.

Tears pricked my eyes.

A memory floated into my brain.

He will not want you after this.

The words echoed in my mind, a haunting refrain that twisted my stomach into knots. I could almost feel the weight of his hands on me again, the intrusion of those rough, unforgiving fingers.

A stitch of uncertainty twinged in my chest as I swung my legs over the edge of the bed, the cool stone floor grounding me momentarily against the impending wave of panic threatening to wash over me. I blinked rapidly, realizing I was naked. My chest tightened and I willed my heart to steady itself as I frantically searched the dimly lit room that was both familiar and foreign.

"Amara!" The door swung open, and Zayed entered, disheveled but alert.

Relief flooded through me, though it was tainted by lingering dread.

He rushed to me, gathering me in his arms.

But even in his presence, the crushing weight of memories suffocated me. "What happened?" My voice trembled as I searched his eyes for answers, seeking solace in the depths of his fierce protectiveness.

He pulled back, eyes staying on my face as I stood before him.

"I—I do not remember everything," I stammered, my heart racing as fragments of the past night flickered like scattered memories before me. "There was a man...I tried to fight him off, but..."

His expression darkened, and heat radiated off him in waves. "That bastard," he growled, fingers curling into fists at his sides. "He will pay for what he did, I swear it. But tell me, my love...my *Jaan*...are you hurting? How do you feel?"

Jaan. He called me his soul. His life.

I blinked, a memory of Zayed saying this last night filled my head. I blinked in quick succession, my breathing becoming rapid again. Had it been Zayed or someone else? I could not even trust my memories or my senses anymore.

He cupped my face.

"I am here, Amara. You are no longer in the bathing area. No one can touch you."

Tears slid down my cheeks.

"I...please tell me...was it you last night? I cannot remember, Zayed!" I sobbed.

He pulled me into his chest, arms wrapping around me protectively.

"He told me you would not want me after he violated me!"

His arms stiffened around me briefly before pulling me even closer. His chin came to rest over the top of my head.

"I will always want you, Amara. Whatever he might have done would not have diminished my love for you. And I can assure you....my little tigress...I was the only man you were with last night."

He cupped my chin, tilting my head to meet his eyes.

"I tried to stop it." He searched my eyes. "But your body would not cool down until you found your release. You told me you wanted it."

Relief poured through me, and I sighed, shaking from the emotion. So it had not been a hallucination. Or another man with me in my bed. It had been Zayed.

"I was afraid it was him," I said in a small voice. "Be-because when he grabbed me in the bathing chamber...I-I thought it was you."

My voice broke, cracked. Just like my soul. I had been drugged. My senses dulled. My ability to remember was taken away from me.

More tears poured down my cheeks. I had been touched by a man I did not want touching me.

What if he tried again?

"*Jaan,* it is safe now. You are safe," he assured, placing a chaste kiss on my forehead before moving to grab me a camel skin. "Please...drink." He held it to my lips, and I allowed him to tip the camel skin up so cool water fell down my parched throat.

The cool water soothed my dry throat, but even as I drank, shadows danced behind my eyes. I could feel Zayed's gaze on me, steady and unwavering, but terror loomed in my heart.

Zayed's expression hardened, the protective fire in his eyes igniting again. "No one will touch you again."

I took a deep breath, forcing my emotions into submission. My heart was still racing from memories. But they were not memories of events. More like memories of emotions...of panic and helplessness—of being violated.

"*Jaan,* I have to ask. Do you remember his face?"

I tried to think, but all I came up with was darkness. And a skull-splitting headache.

"No," I whispered in a small voice.

I had never felt so pathetic in my entire life. Unable to recall something from the night before because someone had drugged me...

Zayed's jaw clenched tightly, a muscle ticking in his cheek. He pulled me toward the bed, setting me down there. Instinctively, I reached for the sheet to cover myself. As I wrapped it around myself, I noticed the bruises. Bruises in places I did not recall being touched. Evidence that someone had touched me against my will, because those finger imprints were not my husband's.

I choked back a sob.

"We will find him," Zayed vowed, his voice low and fierce, radiating a protective energy that enveloped me like a shield. "Can you tell me what part of him you were able to injure?"

I looked at Zayed in confusion.

"Injure? I injured him?" I queried.

All I remembered were his hateful words and then...I remember thinking Zayed was here. That... my breathing became fast again. Oh goddess. What had he done to me while I was drugged? Before Zayed found me?

"Amara."

The softness in his voice pulled me from my spiraling thoughts. Zayed crouched before me, eyes piercing but gentle, tracing the contours of my face as if trying to find the pieces of me that had been scattered. "You fought him off. You stabbed him. You fought back and defended yourself."

Horror careened through me as I recalled the intent to *let* him violate me so I could stab him.

Zayed's hands came to clutch my shoulders, grounding me.

"Trust me when I say that what you see on your body is the most he did to you. When I reached the bathing chamber, he was gone, and you held your dagger in your hand, coated with blood that did not have a scent." His nostrils flared. "He consumed something to mask his scent, else I would have been able to smell him out using my Lycan. I have questioned Katarina. Asya has tortured her to the point of breaking. But she does not know who put her up to this."

"Katarina fed me the drug," I whispered in realization. "Dumping her makeup on me was planned. Premeditated."

Zayed nodded, still kneeling before me as I sat on the bed.

"She was under the influence of whatever that man used to drug you." He spoke calmly, but I sensed the simmering anger under his calm façade.

I tried to process what he was saying. A single tear escaped, trailing down my cheek.

"I barely remember anything," I finally choked out. "I do not remember where I hurt him. I do not remember his face...all I remember is..."

"Is?" Zayed prompted, his face full of eagerness.

He thought I could give him a lead.

"Is the way I felt," I explained in resignation. Why did I feel worthless?

Zayed's expression softened as he listened, eyes glimmering with a mix of anger and sorrow. "You are brave, Amara. Braver than you know."

"I do not feel brave," I murmured. "I feel shattered." My fingers traced the bruises on my arms, each mark a reminder of the struggle.

"I remember being terrified," I confessed, my voice trembling as the memories slithered through the fog in my mind. "I remember feeling trapped...powerless."

Zayed's expression softened, his gaze intense and unwavering. "You were not powerless," he assured me, his hands clasping my own, grounding us both in this chaotic torrent of emotions.

"But I still allowed him to get so close," I whispered, shame gnawing at my heart like a ravenous beast.

His grip tightened around my hands. "What matters is you survived. You are here with me now."

He was lending me strength through the force of his presence alone. His support. He did not shame me. He did not blame me...

He...still wanted me.

I wiped my cheeks with my hands and fell into his embrace. There was so much to do. He was leading a rebellion and yet, for now, he was here with me when I needed him most.

Icy rage coursed through me as I made my way to Katarina's cell.

It was not until much later that Zayed finally told me the entire story. That Katarina had been in our bed. Trying to seduce my husband!

So when I stormed into the cell to see Asya holding Katarina's head in a bucket of cold water by gripping the back of her skull, I hissed in triumph.

Had she not cared that I would be raped?

"Amara!" At once, Asya let go of Katarina and rushed to throw her arms around me.

I could hear Katarina sputtering in the background, coughing out water.

"You vile, evil women! You think you can torture me because I have a past with Zayed? Because you want to make your sister happy?"

I paid her no need and kept hugging my sister. And once we finally broke away, we shared a smile. Asya looked at me, brimming with relief.

Her hands went to my damp hair.

"You bathed?"

I nodded. Zayed had stayed with me the entire time. I would probably not be able to bathe alone any time in the near future.

Asya and I turned our attention to Katarina, who was still sputtering in her corner of the cell, water dripping from her hair.

She was glaring at us.

"You think this is over?" she spat, still catching her breath. "You may have your precious Zayed now, but he will tire of you! I was always meant to be by his side!"

"You thought you could help someone violate me so Zayed would not want me anymore," I said calmly, staring at her with cold fury. "And all you have done is expose yourself for the coward you are. For the absolute filth you are. You. A woman. You would help a man commit such an atrocious act against another woman? You do not deserve to walk among us. You do not deserve to lead anyone. Daughter of a chieftain," I scoffed. "Hear me now, Katarina. Zayed and I are married. You cannot come between us. No matter what you do, I will always be his wife."

Katarina gave me a venomous smile.

"Marriages can be annulled," she purred.

"Bitch!" Asya hurled herself at Katarina, punching her in the jaw.

Katarina's head snapped back as she screamed in pain. Then she spat out a mouthful of blood.

"Do not waste your energy on this coward," I hissed at Asya.

"Coward?" Katarina responded in outrage and winced because it hurt her to speak now. "I had an opportunity to claim Zayed back. So I took it!

I shook my head. "You had an opportunity—a chance to grow beyond being the daughter of a defeated chieftain. You could have been the wife of a chieftain—a queen. Not Zayed's but someone else's."

That made Katarina still. Ah. Just as I had thought. She had not known about Sorrin's plan to marry her off to Chieftain Lamar's son. Zayed had filled me in on that and his alternate solution. Because if he had his way, Katarina would be beheaded at dawn.

"Chieftain Lamar's son," she murmured, a light bulb clicking on in her mind.

I nodded with a grim smile.

"Instead, you tried to shatter our bond with your petty schemes, and now you must pay the price. Know this...marriages can be annulled. But the bond between

Lycans can never be broken," I stated with finality. "And anyone who comes between two mated Lycans has signed their death warrant."

Her eyes blazed with defiance, but the tremor in her voice betrayed her. "You do not know what I am capable of, Amara. This is not over!"

I straightened, feeling a surge of empowerment. "Oh, it is very much over, Katarina. You have underestimated the strength of love—the very thing you wish to destroy."

Asya stood beside me, fists clenched at her sides. "You thought your beauty would be enough to lure Zayed back into your grasp. But he has chosen Amara—a true warrior and queen—over a hollow façade."

I turned to look behind me, beyond the cell. My eyes met Zayed's. He had purposefully been standing back while I talked to Katarina. But now he stepped forward.

"I sentence you to—"

"Imprisonment," I cut Zayed's statement off.

He had been about to sentence her to death. And Katarina knew it, judging from the horror displayed on her face.

I shot Zayed a look and then glanced at Katarina.

"You will spend the rest of your days imprisoned in this cell. No makeup, no luxuries, no beautification products. No servants." I counted them all off on my fingers idly, watching Katarina's growing horror.

She would have rather died. It was written all over her face.

"You will grow old in this cell, Katarina. And be alone, with no one to comfort you in your weakest moments. No one to keep you company when the walls start to close in on you."

My voice was firm as I delivered the final verdict.

Zayed did not interfere.

"We will find whoever your accomplice was. With or without your help. We do not make deals with women who would help lechers rape other women. You do not deserve to walk free."

Her sobs and echoes for mercy still rang in my ears hours later as we prepared to leave on our journey to Chieftain Lamar.

Chapter 17

Amara's POV

I was unable to move. I was in the bathing chamber, and someone was holding me down against my will. I tried to fight, to kick out of his hold and defend myself. But I could not move.

Suddenly, the man above me became discernible, his cruel smirk and murderous eyes gazing down at me. Kadin towered over me, a dagger in hand. He was about to violate me. I tried to scream, but to no avail.

The dagger gleamed cruelly in the light, inches from my throat, and the cold bite of fear settled in my stomach. Kadin's eyes were dark with malice, and I knew he would not hesitate to plunge that blade into me.

"Do not move or you die, stupid woman. You think you can defeat me?" he sneered, his voice thick with contempt. "You are at my mercy."

I struggled against his weight pinning me in place. Panic clawed at my chest. All the training, all the battles fought—none of it prepared me for this moment. I was helpless beneath him. Then, a low growl reached my ears. A blur of white tackled Kadin to the floor, only to be followed by a painful yelp.

"NO!" I screamed, unable to move as sorrow wracked my body. "BAGHEL!" I yelled.

And then Kadin dumped Baghel's body on top of me, his beautiful white fur matted with blood.

"His blood is on your hands. If he had not been so loyal to you, he would still be alive," Kadin sneered.

"NO!" I cried out.

"Amara!" A voice broke through the haze of despair, a familiar warmth wrapping around me like a protective cloak. The world shifted, and the suffocating weight pressing down on my chest began to relent.

"Amara!" Zayed repeated.

His voice shattered the dreamlike haze enveloping me. I shot upright in the tent we were sharing on our journey to meet Chieftain Lamar, straight into Zayed's waiting arms, heart racing. I felt as though the dagger that Kadin thrust at me pierced through my sanity. The remnants of that nightmare clung to me—Baghel's loyal form, his blood staining the ground.

And I began to sob into my husband's shoulder.

"He died protecting...me," I choked out.

My husband—strong and resolute—held me close as he let me cry.

Yet the memory of Kadin's twisted smile lingered, as potent as ever. And dancing behind it was the memory of nearly being raped.

"My love," Zayed breathed softly, leaning closer until our foreheads touched and our breaths mingled in the silence between us. "He cannot reach you here."

"But Baghel is gone," I murmured morosely.

Every day I thought of him. But in the week since everything had occurred, I had not truly embraced the grief that came with losing him. All my trauma had melded together to create one horrendous nightmare. One I feared I would never be able to escape from.

"I know," Zayed said gently, brushing a thumb across my cheek to catch a stray tear. His gaze was warm, brimming with love and unyielding strength. "But you must remember, he gave his life for the bond we share and for the hope that lives in this fight. He would want you to be strong for him, as he was strong for you."

We sat in silence for a long moment, Zayed cradling me against him, the steady beat of his heart guiding me through the storm of my emotions. Finally, he spoke again. "Baghel loved you fiercely. He would not want his memory to turn into sorrow—it should be a beacon of strength for us both. We will honor him by fighting with everything we have."

"Did he get a proper burial?" I croaked out.

Zayed sighed.

"Amara, my Lycan went feral almost immediately. I do not know. Knowing Kadin, it is doubtful." His eyes softened as he saw mine brimming with tears.

"My love. We will carry his memory with us and pay tribute to his loyalty when the time comes."

I took a shaky breath, pulling back slightly to look into his eyes.

"I do not want revenge, because that will not bring him back," I whispered, my voice trembling with emotion as I wiped my tears away. "But we need to stop Kadin before anyone else pays the same price. Before he can harm more innocent lives."

Zayed nodded solemnly, understanding my pain but offering hope at the same time. "Agreed. Because if we do not stop Kadin, Baghel's death will have been in vain."

He handed me a camel skin filled with cool water, and I drank from it.

Outside the tent, I could see dawn beginning to peek through the night. Soon, everybody would be awake. Our entourage consisted of Asya, because I trusted her the most, Salim (because he had begged to be allowed to trail after Asya), and Shain, because he was the oldest son of a prominent noble from the neighboring kingdom. Ashad had stayed back to help my father.

So here we were, travelling with two men I would rather stick my sword through and a sister who would readily help me do it.

"Why now?" I murmured. "I had not had any nightmares since you began to sleep with me." My voice was feeble as I sat the camel skin down. It was true. Zayed's presence had kept me grounded. But now even his presence was unable to keep the darkness away.

Zayed was quiet for a moment before sharing his thoughts.

"I think before, with everything going on, you were not able to process the grief, which is why the nightmares started. And now...coupled with the trauma you recently endured, your subconscious is processing everything that you have endured," he said softly, his eyes filled with empathy. "I had hoped my presence would keep the nightmares at bay, and I believe they might have for a time...but it is important to process and grieve those we have lost as well."

I looked away. His uncle had died...Baghel had died...so many other people would surely die. Was there truly no other way? Was more bloodshed inevitable?

"I am so glad we found each other again," I whispered. "When I was shifting into my Lycan...I felt so alone without you."

His hands came to cup my face, and his thumbs moved across my cheekbones in a steady caress.

"Remember, even in your darkest moments, you are never alone. We are tied together, not just by love but by every hardship we have faced and will face side by side."

I leaned into his touch, and then pulled away as we began to prepare for the remainder of the journey. Today we would reach Chieftain Lamar's lands. And I truly hoped that whatever awaited us was good news. He had seemed amenable in the letter that had reached us. But still...it was no secret Zayed and the Chieftain did not get along.

"I would like to bathe," I muttered, standing at the flap of our tent.

"Wait for me, *Jaan*," Zayed responded, eyes on the parchment in his hand. "I shall go with you."

Since he was now the rebel leader, he was constantly going over the different plans and strategies they would put into place to defeat Kadin.

"I...I think I can do this alone," I said with a confidence I did not truly feel. But I had to start bathing alone again. I could not depend on Zayed like a little child. "You need to finish your task at hand before we make the remainder of our journey."

Zayed's eyes flicked up, the warmth and determination in them unwavering. "You are my heart, Amara. No situation is inconsequential where you are concerned. Let me accompany you."

I held his gaze, feeling the pull of his steadfast love wrapped around me like a warm cocoon. Yet, within me, a small spark of independence flickered. I wanted to prove to myself that I could regain my footing. I was supposed to be a warrior. A queen. His queen.

"I appreciate your willingness to protect me, Zayed," I said softly, with an earnestness that soaked every word. "But I need to reclaim my autonomy. I can bathe alone," I assured him.

He scrutinized me for a moment, his brow furrowing as if weighing the world in his mind. "You are so strong, Amara. But strength is not just independence. It is in choosing when to lean on those who love you."

A wave of affection coursed over me, and a warmth blossomed within my chest. "You are right," I acknowledged, my voice firm. "But I would like to try."

Zayed studied me intently, the flicker of understanding behind his gaze telling me he recognized this desire for autonomy in me. "Very well," he relented, still reluctant but respecting my need to assert myself. "But I will be nearby."

I nodded before stepping out of the tent and taking in the fresh morning air. Now that we were close to Chieftain Lamar's mountains, the terrain had changed somewhat into grasslands, and there was a tiny stream we could utilize as a source of water.

Walking idly, I took in the fresh morning air. The sun was rising slowly, casting golden rays across the horizon, and for the first time in days, a glimmer of hope shifted within me.

As I made my way toward the bathing area, the rhythmic sounds of nature greeted me. The gentle rustle of sand, the distant call of a bird, and the soft whisper of the wind enveloped me like a sweet touch. I let out a sigh, absorbing the tranquility that seemed to seep into my bones, soothing the jagged edges of my frayed nerves.

The sound of bubbling water greeted me as I approached the stream. I knelt down, cupping my hands to gather the cool liquid, letting it slip through my fingers. For a brief moment, I closed my eyes, allowing the essence of the earth to ground me.

A noise from my right made me suddenly look up, and my eyes narrowed as I looked at Shain.

He stood a few paces ahead in a sleeveless thin cotton shirt, clearly just having arrived to take advantage of the stream. He inclined his head toward me.

"I did not mean to intrude," he murmured, respectfully, taking a few steps back to leave.

And as I watched him turn slowly, I froze, icy cold fear seeping into my veins. A glint of gold at his neck brought back memories from my assault in the bathing chambers. But if that had not been enough, the lone jagged scar on his upper-arm, an ugly red, brought back another memory like a nightmare. For me, it was a mark of betrayal that linked him to the man who had violated me.

Without thinking, I leapt to my feet, adrenaline surging through me. "You!" I called, my voice sharp with accusation and anger as I took a step closer, fingers curling tightly around the dagger hidden beneath the folds of my long chemise.

Shain froze, raising his hands in surrender as he turned to look at me. "I mean you no harm, Amara!" His voice was steady but strained, as if he was trying to calm a beast ready to pounce. "I truly did not intend to intrude. I am leaving—"

"Do not lie to me," I shot back, anger igniting the edges of my words. "You think you can get away with what you have done to me? You think I would not have remembered! It is you! You are the man who assaulted me in the caves! Are you the one who gave the drug to Katarina?"

I withdrew my dagger menacingly. It was Shain. He was my assaulter. And I was going to make him regret what he had done.

"I—" he stammered, glancing around as if searching for an escape. "You are mistaken! That was not me—"

"It was you!" I roared, brandishing my dagger higher, the blade glinting maliciously in the early morning light.

Shain straightened his shoulders, his fearful apologetic visage melting away. He tilted his head, a spiteful curve forming on his lips.

"And so what if it was? What can you, the daughter of a retired scribe, do to the son of a nobleman?" He sneered the words, his feeble tone evaporating and being replaced by his true self. "You think you can threaten me? You need me for the meeting with Chieftain Lamar. I am the only one who can offer him trade to my kingdom as an ambassador. What do you have to offer, Amara? You need me for your mission to be a success. For your precious husband," Shain spat the words distastefully, "to gain the support he needs to regain his crown."

He let out a cruel laugh.

I tightened my grip on the dagger, realizing he was right. "Wait until I plunge this deep into your heart, and then let us see who is laughing."

"You are a fool, Amara, if you think you can harm me and not face the repercussions. You think you matter to this world? You do not. Your precious husband knows he needs me. So do you. So for everyone's sake, you will keep quiet and pretend all is well."

I trembled, feeling a mix of helpless fury and fear. He was right.

"How many victims have you coerced in this exact manner into keeping their silence?" I hissed.

"Victim?" he scoffed as he stepped closer, a predatory gleam in his eye. "You have always been a pawn in a game far larger than you can comprehend. I am far more powerful than you."

"Powerful?" I echoed incredulously. "You think manipulating and attempting to assault women is power?"

He laughed again, a hollow, mocking sound. "It is a world of survival, Amara. If you do not adapt, you will be crushed. Look at you now, brandishing a dagger against a son of nobility. Such theatrics," he sneered. "Drop it. I will leave now, and you can continue your morning ablutions. All will be cordial between us. This will remain our secret, and tomorrow, when your husband is king, you will remember who helped you both get your crowns back."

I remained still, my dagger held tight in my hand, but I was no longer poised to strike. He was right. We did need him. But to pretend day in and day out that he had not done those horrible things to me...it would kill my soul.

A disgusted shiver rolled down my spine at the thought. But did I have a choice?

Shain smirked, realizing that his message had hit home. He then gave an exaggerated bow before turning to leave.

"Or," said a lethal voice behind me that sent prickles of fear racing up even my spine. "We kill you now, consequences be damned."

"Zayed NO!" I screamed.

But he was a blur, faster than I had ever seen him move.

Zayed closed the distance between them in an instant, his body a powerful blur of feral rage. In one swift motion, he grasped Shain by the collar, lifting him off the ground with a ferocity that made the air crackle with tension. The dagger I once brandished now felt like a forgotten relic as my husband's fury blazed before me. I had never ever seen him this angry.

He did not say a single word. Did not utter even a curse. No. He was all movement and deft vengeance. I watched as, with deadly precision, he reached between Shain's legs and gripped his manhood through the cloth of his trousers.

Shain screeched in pain when Zayed tightened his hold.

"Let him go!" I yelled. "He is right, we need him!"

My words only made Zayed angrier. I watched his eyes flash, felt his fury bubbling over in waves. And then I watched in horror as a ripping sound rent through the air and blood spurted upwards like a fountain in a grisly arc, splatting over Zayed and Shain. Shain screamed in agony. It took me one horrible moment to register that Zayed had twisted Shain's manhood clean off his body. The bloody member was now in Zayed's grip as Shain's ripped trousers revealed a bloodied stump where his cock was supposed to be.

Shain looked like he was about to pass out from the pain. Or maybe die.

Regardless, the gruesome sight of my husband holding my assaulter by the throat as he ripped his cock off would forever be seared in my mind.

"Ripping his member off is something I can agree with," Asya stated as she walked next to me. My eyes went ahead to watch Zayed leading his camel through the sand. We were not far now from our destination.

My stomach heaved at the thought of what had happened earlier today.

Zayed had abruptly disposed of Shain's body earlier this morning by burning him alive. He would not survive the blood loss caused by the dismembering of his cock. And Zayed wanted to burn him while he was still breathing, wanted Shain to feel the pain.

I shivered. Zayed's mind came up with the most gruesome punishments. In a way, Crimson King really did suit him.

"But then stuffing it into his mouth—"

"He did not merely stuff it. He made him eat it," Salim supplied, lips pale.

He was walking behind us and I heard him dry heave after speaking the words. I could not blame him. It had been a most gruesome sight to watch Zayed stuff the bleeding member into Shain's mouth.

Salim had run to the river upon hearing Shain's screams. Then he had abruptly upended the contents of his stomach at the sight that greeted him.

"I do not think Shain was lucid enough to realize he was eating his own cock," Asya pointed out primly, turning to glance at Salim.

I heard more dry heaving behind me.

"Regardless, now we have to figure out how to get Chieftain Lamar to be amenable toward us since our ambassador is dead."

I spoke the words listlessly, eyes going again to my husband's strong back as he walked ahead. Completely indifferent to what he had done earlier today.

"Killed by your husband," muttered Salim.

I stopped walking and so did Asya.

"And rightly so!" Asya yelled angrily, her death glare on her ex-betrothed as we both turned fully to look at him. "You think we should have let him live?"

"At least until he had served his purpose, yes," Salim responded in kind, crossing his arms. The leashes attached to our camels were in his hands, but the animals remained obedient and still behind him. "We could have punished him later."

"And let him assault more women?" Asya argued. She glared at Salim in disgust, "I am glad we are no longer together."

Salim paled at those words, stuttering that Shain should be punished, but that now had not been the right time.

Asya merely glared at him. I walked away, lost in thought.

It was clear Zayed, in that moment, had not cared about the repercussions. He had been overcome by anger. But now...we truly had a situation on our hands where we did not have any negotiating power to bring to the table when we met Chieftain Lamar. What were we going to do?

I caught up with Zayed, who was leading his camel.

"How long are you not going to speak to me?" I asked as I fell into stride with him.

Zayed's jaw clenched and he cast me a brief stoic glance before looking ahead.

"I know you are angry—"

"Angry? I am livid," he spat, picking up his pace to walk faster.

"It was necessary—" I began, but he stopped abruptly, turning to face me, and the fire in his eyes made me give pause.

Livid did not do justice to what my husband was feeling.

"Necessary? You truly considered his proposition to pretend he had not done anything to you. You think it was necessary to do that?" His voice was low, laced with frustration and helplessness and barely contained fury. "You would have looked at him day in and day out, at the monster who wanted to do unspeakable things to you!"

My tone was weary but resolute. "We need allies, Zayed. We could not afford to lose him. I cannot lay waste to every man who wrongs me. As satisfying as it might be, it is not practical. Not when we need everyone's cooperation."

He took a step forward, mutiny in his eyes.

"I will tell you what is not practical, Amara. It is not practical to look at a man who violated you every day. It is not practical to be expected to be civil to such filth. It is not practical to think your value is so low that his cooperation matters more than bringing you justice!"

Zayed's voice rose, all the pent-up rage and hurt spilling over in a wave that crashed against me.

"I realize your Lycan was thirsting for blood, but—"

He interrupted me again, his voice vibrating with anger.

"You think what I did, I did to appease my Lycan? No, Amara, I wanted him, and everyone else, to understand the cost of such actions—the price of underestimating someone like you! You are worth so much more to me than any crown! And the fact that you were willing to lie to me, to pretend in front of me as if Shain was not the man that harmed you has hurt my soul in ways you cannot imagine."

His fists balled tightly at his side, his body trembling with suppressed fury. "I will not allow you to think that your worth can be bartered for power. You are not a pawn, Amara. You are my queen!"

"But I am not a queen," I replied brokenly. "I am a peasant, Zayed. I was not born into nobility."

"You. are. MY. QUEEN. I care not for your parentage or what you were born into. Your worth is not defined by your lineage or titles; it is defined by the strength of your spirit, by the resilience you have shown time and again. You have fought battles others would cower from. You are my love not because of blood or birthright but because of the flame inside you. No throne makes you my queen—you were born one."

The intensity in his eyes made my heart race, almost drowning out the torment that had been swirling within me. I took a shaky breath, feeling the weight of his words squeeze against my chest like a vise.

"Zayed...I only want to protect you, to ensure we have every advantage we can get. Losing Shain, even if he is a monster, complicates things vastly."

HIs jaw clenched again.

"Is that what you are afraid of? Losing an ally over your dignity? Amara, where is the woman who punched a nobleman without a second thought? What has happened to you?"

I flinched at the reminder of who I once was. Between Kadin's betrayal, Baghel's death, and the assault, I had shattered. However, how could I tell Zayed that? The weight of his words hung in the air, pressing down on me with an intensity

I had not expected. In his fierce gaze, I saw not only his anger but also the raw vulnerability that came with love—love that demanded all of me, even when I was scared and uncertain.

"I am afraid, Zayed," I admitted, my voice barely above a whisper, the tremor in my words betraying the tempest inside me. I bent my head, looking down at the sand under our feet.

"I do not want to lose you, or anyone else I care about."

His expression softened slightly, the sharp edge of his rage blunted by my honesty. We had already lost so much.

"I carry the weight of that dread as well. However, you must understand that fighting for what is right means doing right by yourself as well." He stepped closer now, reaching to cup my chin and tilt my face up so that our gazes met. "I went through hell and back when I thought I lost you. Everything else is inconsequential to me, Amara."

"You fought to protect me, and I...I let fear cloud my judgment." I murmured the words, barely managing to hold his gaze as vulnerability engulfed me.

Zayed was right. I was no longer the woman who had resided in the castle. But I hoped through the cut of betrayal, the agony of loss, I could become something more. Someone stronger.

"I want to make the right choices for us...for our people." My hand came up to rest over his, still cupping my cheek. I leaned into his touch, closing my eyes momentarily.

Zayed's fingers traced along my jawline, his touch gentle yet igniting an electric spark of hope that surged through my veins. "The right choices do not come from fear, Amara. They come from strength and honesty. Look at what we have faced together. That power is within us. Do you not feel it? The way our Lycans are stronger? The way you can touch and look at silver without flinching in pain? Any other Lycan would find it difficult to even hold the hilt of the silver dagger. But not you. And not me either, not any longer."

My eyes flew open in shock. Zayed was right. But I had not thought much of it.

"We make each other stronger," I breathed in realization. "That is why I can still wield my dagger."

Zayed's expression softened, an undeniable warmth flooding his gaze as I spoke. "Yes," he murmured, his voice low and steady. "Together, we wield strength that transcends any single challenge. We are not defined by the battles we have lost or the scars we bear; it is how we rise from them that truly matters."

His words hung in the air like a challenge—a call to arms for my spirit. I took a deep breath. He was right. But just as I opened my mouth to say as much, an arrow flew right by us, grazing Zayed's forearm. He hissed in anger. A yell from behind us had me turning to see that the arrow had embedded itself in Salim's leg.

"Get down!" Zayed roared, pulling me to the ground. Dirt hit my face.

I hit the ground hard, the weight of Zayed's body pressing over me as he shielded me from view. The world shrank into that singular moment, adrenaline coursing through my veins as I glanced back to see Salim writhing on the ground, clutching his bleeding leg. Panic flared inside me—where was this attack coming from?

The sound of hooves pounding against the earth and angry shouts echoed around us.

More arrows rained down around us.

"Asya!" I yelled desperately.

"She is fine," Zayed whispered into my ear.

"We mean no harm!" he said, louder now. "Tell your men to stand down."

"Zayed!" Asya's sharp voice cut through the turmoil, her eyes wide with alarm as she hurried toward us, her sword drawn and ready. "What in the name of the goddess is happening?"

"Arrows came from the direction of the mountain," I managed to say, my heart racing. "Salim—"

"Salim will be alright. He has been wounded, but he is conscious," Asya reassured me, glancing at the man shifting uncomfortably on the ground. "However, we need to move now! Or else these arrows will surely meet their target soon!"

Another volley sailed through the air, and I winced as one struck inches away from us, embedding itself into the sand with a shuddering thud. Zayed cursed, grabbing Asya and pinning her down with his free arm.

Her body fell next to mine as another volley of arrows sailed over our heads. Asya's voice rose above the clamor, urgency lacing her tone. "We need to move to cover! They are trying to pin us down!"

"I cannot walk!" Salim moaned in pain.

Zayed's grip on me tightened. The message was clear. We were not risking our necks for Salim.

But in the next moment, we were surrounded.

The sound came first—a hiss of steel drawn as one, then the ring of iron settling into place. I lifted my head just enough to see the tip of a sword before my gaze. I looked around only to see swords. Dozens of them, gleaming under the unforgiving sun, their edges catching the light like shards of fire. They closed in from every direction, forming a perfect circle around us, the sharp tips angled inward exactly like the fangs of a predator poised to strike.

The world narrowed to that circle of steel as Zayed tensed over me. He cursed as one man stepped forward, his blade at a point where it hovered directly above Zayed's throat. My breath caught as I saw the steely determination in the man's eyes, so close I could see my own reflection trembling in the polished metal. He was going to kill my husband.

"NO!" I screamed, flailing under Zayed. But he was too strong, pinning me under him not in dominance but in a desperation to protect me.

Zayed moved. Slowly, deliberately, he tilted his head upward, baring his neck further to the blade before him, meeting the man's gaze without flinching. His voice was calm, unyielding, and it cut through the silence sharper than any blade.

"You know who I am. This attack was intentional. Good to know Chieftain Lamar sent his lackeys to do his dirty work."

My stomach lurched.

Chieftain Lamar's soldiers were the ones attacking us.

Chapter 18

Zayed's POV

Fury rolled over me in wave after wave, coiling in the pit of my stomach like a viper ready to strike.

"Li," I spat, my voice low and filled with disdain.

His dark eyes settled on me, flickering momentarily to Asya and then my wife. The name tasted like poison on my tongue.

"You are here to do Chieftain Lamar's dirty work?" I taunted.

He smirked, but there was a glint of uncertainty in his eyes as the circle of swords tightened around us. Li was Chieftain Lamar's commander of warriors. His formal title was Hujun (Commander).

"You were supposed to come with Ambassador Shain." Li tilted his head, silver eyebrows bunching together as he looked at us critically.

Asya let out a huff as she lay next to me on the ground. I had situated myself between both sisters, prepared to do my utmost to protect them. "Get your sword away from me," she hissed, rearing up on her elbows and staring up at a man with straight dark hair that fell below his shoulders. His blade was pointed right at Asya's throat.

"Is this the bride you brought for the crown prince?" The man who held his blade inches from Asya's jugular spoke mockingly. "I thought she was the daughter of a chieftain with hair spun from gold. This is not the woman Chieftain Lamar's son was promised."

"Ren," Li chided next to him. "Does it matter, when they will all be dead soon anyway for lying?"

Salim let out a wail behind us.

I moved swiftly, standing within the blink of an eye and pulling my wife and her sister up with me. My eyes glowed deep red in warning.

Ren's gaze danced across us, assessing, calculating. Not at all like the gaze of an obedient soldier. My eyes went to Li. Was Ren being trained to take Li's position as *Hujun* to Lamar's warriors?

Or had he been sent by the crown prince? Not much was known about Chieftain Lamar's son. He was aloof and reclusive. Often his father was at the forefront in the dealings between our two countries. Lamar's son was an enigma.

"Do you truly think this ends well for your men?" I challenged, narrowing my eyes, my voice lowering to a growl. "You intend to slaughter us when we come to you in peace? You think I will not go down without a fight?"

Li laughed—a deep, guttural sound that echoed around us. Next to him, Ren ran a hand through midnight black hair before looking from Asya to me with amusement. His eyes fell on my hand, loosely clasping Amara's. I had not even realized when I had subconsciously sought out her touch, but I had. And it did not go unnoticed by Ren.

"You were supposed to come with an ambassador. With the promise of a new trade deal and alliance for us with another kingdom. Instead, you arrive with two women and a poor merchant." Li shook his head, his short, dark brown hair falling in his eyes. His gaze went to Asya, studying her intently before looking back at me. "We had a deal. Ambassador Shain is not here..." he shrugged, his glance going again to Asya. "And neither is the princess we were promised for our prince. But I see you have brought something infinitely more interesting."

What did he mean by that?

Ren cleared his throat, eyes on Asya. "Our future Chieftain is not interested in a prospective bride, no matter how beautiful she might be. You have wasted your time, travelling all this way in hopes of becoming a future queen of our tribe."

Amara tensed next to me. I swore. She had not spoken to Asya about the proposition to marry. That much was clear.

Asya then let out a snort next to us.

"Who said I had hopes of becoming a queen? I do not need pretentious titles to compensate for my lack of courage. Unlike some people," Asya pointed out snidely, looking at Ren and then glancing at the men circling us. "It must be hard living in the shadows of greater men. For only cowards would attack an entourage that comes in peace."

An immediate hiss of anger passed through the gathered men, but Ren merely chuckled, unfazed. "And you think your biting words are enough to intimidate us? Spare me the theatrics."

I tightened my grip on Amara's hand, feeling her pulse quicken beside me. "You are making a grave mistake underestimating us," I said, my voice low and steady. "If it comes to a fight, you cannot defeat two Lycans."

Ren's smirk faltered for a heartbeat, revealing a crack in his façade.

Li took a step forward. "Perhaps we cannot, but it seems you forget that our men have no qualms in trying."

"Is this a new tactic from Chieftain Lamar?" I taunted, stepping slightly forward, ready to absorb whatever insult or attack these men had left to throw at us. "To send his pets to eliminate us? You promised us safe passage, and now you threaten our lives. How noble."

Ren's eyes darkened, rage flickering beneath his amused exterior. I cocked my head to the side. Exactly who was he? Not a warrior in training, that was evident. "You have no room to critique nobility, Zayed. You are no king; you are a mere specter of the past, reduced to a pathetic rebel hiding behind the skirts of your wife."

The implication cut deeper than I would have liked. This man thrived on provocation.

My Lycan's bloodlust rose, restless and eager, demanding to be unleashed against this cowardly group of assailants.

Ren's lip curled upwards in an amused smile.

"I heard you went feral when you thought your wife was dead. Maybe I will get to see you go feral again."

It was like a red haze slowly settled over me as I took in his spiteful words. I prepared to shift and rip this man to shreds. No one threatened Amara. However, Asya was faster, maybe because blinding rage did not cripple her in the same manner it momentarily crippled me. She knocked her bowstring, arrow ready and pointed it straight for Ren's heart.

"Try to hurt my sister and I will split you in half!" Asya's voice rang out, fierce and unwavering.

Ren paused, eyes narrowing as he measured the distance between himself and the arrow's deadly point. If she was anything like her sister, she would not miss.

A man standing next to Ren let out a dark chuckle.

"You dare point your weapon at him, at one of our strongest warriors?"

"I point my weapon at a coward!" Asya railed. "You promised us a peaceful meeting. And yet you have broken your vows!"

"That meeting was contingent on the arrival of ambassador Shain," Ren snapped. "He is clearly not here. The pact has been broken. Now lower your weapon. You think you can intimidate me with a mere bow? You must be more foolish than I imagined."

"Enough talk," I urged, my voice low and dangerous. "If you intend to kill us, then do it. But know that I will not go down without a fight."

Ren laughed, a sharp, mocking sound. "Brave words for someone whose back is against the wall."

I growled, preparing to shift. Ren snapped his fingers. From overhead, a cascade of purple-tinged darts immediately rained down upon us, a storm of sharpened steel that sliced through the air with lethal intent. My instincts kicked in, and I swung Amara behind me instinctively, feeling the urgency of the moment rush through my veins. Damn shifting and tearing out his throat. I had to protect my wife first.

Salim screamed again behind us. Asya let her arrow fly. Multiple darts embedded themselves into my skin at the same time that Asya's arrow landed squarely on the left side of Ren's chest, mere centimeters from his beating heart.

I blinked, expecting the man to crumple to the ground. Instead, he grimaced and reached a hand up, pulling the arrow out with a deep groan of pain. Blood spurted up out of his wound.

"You cannot continue to endanger yourself in this manner!" Li yelled at him as men rushed to surround Ren.

Next to me, I heard Asya fall to the ground. Amara, protected due to my body shielding hers, fell to her knees to check on her sister.

"They are doused in a sedative!" Amara screamed frantically, right as my own vision began to blank. "NO!"

I heard her scream the word as the ground rushed to meet me.

My last thought was of Asya and Amara, the weight of their lives pressing heavy against my consciousness as darkness enveloped me.

However, one last thought whispered on the edges of my mind. Ren was...not what he seemed.

Amara's POV

I was in a luxurious room, not too different from my living quarters in the palace of Elamaria. The view from the arched windows showed the rising sun. My eyes strayed to Asya, fast asleep on the canopied bed surrounded by thick velvet curtains. It was colder up here in the mountains. Much colder. I pulled my thick furskin robe tighter around my form.

Li had had us captured and dragged here. Though I had been awake, a black cloth had been tied over my eyes.

And though Ren had assured me that no harm would come to my sister or husband, or even Salim, I could not help the worry coursing through me. I had no idea where Zayed was. What if they tried to do something to him? His father had killed Chieftain Lamar's nephew.

The door opened and I instinctively pulled out my dagger, wielding it with an ease I had not felt since I had turned. Zayed was right. Somehow...I was becoming immune to the silver. Was it because our lycans were stronger together? Or something else entirely...

"I mean no harm," whispered a soft, melodic voice.

I did not blink as a petite woman with long straight black hair and midnight blue eyes walked into the room. Her form was covered by a plain brown, long, full-sleeved dress, signalling that she was one of the servants who resided in the royal fort of Chieftain Lamar. She shut the door quietly and turned to look at me warily.

"Please, I only come to help you get ready, mistress. My name is Mei, and I come with a message that Chieftain Lamar wishes for your presence in the cherry blossom garden. He would like to have morning tea with you."

"Tea at dawn?" I asked skeptically.

"Here, it is the custom to drink tea before breakfast, or rather it is served as a precursor to breakfast," Mei explained with an incline of her head. "Please, allow me to draw your bath and take out the clothes selected for you." She moved toward the wooden armoire, and I lifted my dagger higher threateningly. Mei gasped, cheeks turning bright red. "Mistress, I only mean to help you."

I narrowed my eyes at her. After Sherazi, I was wary of all maids.

"And what of my sister?" I jerked my head in the direction of Asya, fast asleep still. "And my husband?"

Mei was silent a moment before finally exhaling slowly.

"I tell you this only to assure you, mistress. Chieftain Lamar does not intend to harm your entourage. His brother, Loran, for now, merely wishes to speak with your husband once he awakes. That is all."

I raised an eyebrow.

"Mei, tell me, what does Chieftain Lamar wish to discuss with me?"

Meit coughed into her hand discreetly, cheeks burning red. "He wishes to discuss the possibility of marriage of your sister with his son. She wounded one of his best soldiers, and for some unfathomable reason, Chieftain Lamar believes..." Mei trailed off momentarily before continuing. "He believes a strong female warrior is a suitable candidate for his son. Forgive me if I am being too forward, mistress, but such a union would give you the support you require from Chieftain Lamar to take back your throne."

"My sister is not chattel to be bartered for a crown!" I exclaimed angrily. It was true. I had already told Zayed that the only way we would and could agree to a union was if the Chieftain's son and Asya were a suitable match. Otherwise, I would never agree. And I could never ask Asya to sacrifice herself.

"But I will do it nonetheless," rasped out Asya weakly.

I turned, running to her, overjoyed that she was awake.

However, in the next moment, Asya was leaning over the bed and dry heaving.

Mei rushed forward, her pale white hand disappearing into a pocket of her brown dress. When she retracted it, there was a vial filled with a pearly white concoction in her grip.

"It is a reaction to the sedative. This will help," Mei whispered, sinking onto her knees close to Asya and uncorking the vial.

Asya snarled and attempted to slap the vial out of Mei's hand.

"Get away from me!"

She lurched forward suddenly, her body convulsing as another wave of nausea gripped her. Each dry heave wracked her slender frame with violent spasms. Glistening beads of sweat pearled across her ashen forehead, catching the dim light like morning dew. I glanced at the vial in Mei's trembling hand—pearlescent liquid clung to its rim, a few precious drops splattering onto the polished wooden floor where they formed small, shimmering puddles. When I turned back to Asya, her teeth were chattering audibly, her entire body quaking as if gripped by some terrible frost despite the rivulets of sweat now streaming down her hollowed cheeks, dripping from her chin onto the silken bedsheets.

"It is rare, but sometimes the sedative makes people sick. It reacts with certain bloodlines," Mei stated quietly, her slender fingers trembling around the vial's delicate neck. Her midnight-blue eyes widened with urgency as another violent spasm seized Asya. "The medicine contains extract of mountain lotus and silver birch sap—it binds to the poison before it reaches your heart. Without it, your fever will climb until your mind fractures with hallucinations, and then—" She swallowed hard, her voice dropping to a whisper. "Please, I have seen this before. You have perhaps an hour before the damage cannot be undone."

I lunged forward, snatching the vial from Mei's trembling fingers. The glass was cool against my palm as I brought it to my lips. My lycan senses picked up on the faint scent of mountain herbs and something sweeter. Was it honey? Without hesitation, I tilted my head back and let a few drops touch my tongue, tasting bitter earth with metallic undertones.

"NO! It could be poison!" Asya croaked, her voice like sandpaper as violent tremors rippled beneath her sweat-soaked chemise.

"I am more likely than you to survive if it is," I snapped, counting heartbeats as I waited. My tongue tingled but nothing more sinister occurred. The liquid warmed my throat without burning—a harmless medication after all.

I dropped to my knees beside Asya, my knees hitting the cold wooden floor with a light thud.

"Please goddess, let this help," I whispered.

Carefully, I cradled Asya's head, her damp hair twisting around my fingers as I pressed the vial to her cracked lips. With each swallow, the violent quaking subsided—first, her fingers stilled, then her shoulders, until finally her chest rose and fell in something approaching a normal rhythm.

I let out a long, shuddering sigh of relief when Asya leaned back against the beige and gold embroidered pillows, her tense shoulders finally relaxing as she closed her eyes. The feverish flush drained from her cheeks, replaced by the tranquil pallor of exhaustion, and the furrow between her brows smoothed away like ripples settling on disturbed water. Her eyelids fluttered closed, dark lashes resting against her now-pale cheeks as her breathing steadied into the gentle rhythm of healing sleep.

"What if Zayed or Salim have the same reaction?" I asked of Mei, handing her the now-empty vial.

Mei shook her head, her expression grave. "The effects of the sedative can vary greatly from person to person, especially depending on bloodlines and consti- tution. The mountain lotus is a powerful antidote, but it can also be a toxin if not administered with care. I do not know how it will react with your husband's Lycan blood. But this reaction is not common, and we have servants standing guard with vials should the need arise to administer the medication."

"Where are they?" I demanded, my voice sharp and authoritative. "We need to find them!"

Mei bit her lip, glancing toward the closed door as if someone might burst in at any moment. She was forbidden from telling me. No matter how much she might want to.

"I swear to you, mistress, no harm shall befall your husband while he is in the sleeping quarters assigned to him."

Her words were carefully chosen, conveying perhaps more than she meant too. Or maybe she meant to tell me that for now, Zayed was safe, but she could not guarantee his safety once he stepped out of his room.

Just like she probably could not guarantee mine if I met with Chieftain Lamar in the cherry blossom garden. I glanced again toward the arched windows that gave a direct view of the courtyard where the garden was located.

There was only one person who could guarantee our safety in this gilded prison of polished wood and silk cushions. My muscles tensed as I stood with deliberate slowness, my hands brushing the fur skin wrapped around my body, my face a carefully crafted mask of composure that hid the storm beneath."Draw my bath with jasmine oil and rose water," I commanded, my voice steady despite the knot of dread coiling in my stomach. "Let us see what deal your Chieftain wishes to place before me."

Chapter 19

Amara's POV

"You must eat something," chortled Chieftain Lamar, offering me a bamboo tray filled with dim sum. I glanced at the dim sum from where I sat across from the Chieftain in a pale pink long robe with hanging long sleeves. Delicate pink petals drifted down like snow around us, masking whispered threats with beauty.

The cherry blossom garden was located in the grand courtyard, surrounded by the four watchtowers of the wooden fortress built into a side of the vast mountain. Chieftain Lamar's tribe was known as the Jade Fang Tribe.

My eyes went to the four watchtowers and then to the wooden parapets connecting them. Soldiers could be seen far above, their gazes locked outward. My eyes searched for the side of the fort where I knew Asya lay recovering. Mei had assured me she would care for Asya.

My gaze then went to the food laid before me. The translucent dumpling skins revealed hints of the savory fillings within. Some were pleated into perfect crescents, others formed into small purses with crimped edges. The aroma of ginger, scallion, and sesame oil rose from the steaming morsels, mingling with the more delicate scent of shrimp and bamboo shoots. My stomach clenched in hunger despite my resolve to refuse his hospitality. Anger rose within me as the Chieftain continued to offer me food, holding the tray before me. My husband was somewhere in this fort, and the man before me was offering me Oolong tea and dim sum to distract me.

I checked the urge to smack the tray out of his hands.

Instead, I looked away, jaw clenched in anger. A few wet tendrils of my hair, still damp from the jasmine bath, escaped from the intricate bun Mei had woven with trembling fingers.

"I admit, my men took things a tad too far. But they were worried it was all a trick."

"Your men nearly killed us," I shot back, my voice steady despite the turmoil raging within me. "You presume to treat this as a jest when we are the ones who bear the scars from your men's folly?"

Chieftain Lamar chuckled, a sound like silk sliding over steel. Indifference radiated from him as he lounged in his ornately carved chair, one bejeweled finger tracing the rim of his teacup. His golden robes, embroidered with crimson dragons whose eyes seemed to follow my every movement, glimmered under the soft amber light of the morning sun.

But they did little to conceal the arrogance that draped around him like a second skin, as palpable as the cloying scent of incense that hung in the air between us.

"My dear Amara," he drawled, his tone deceptively smooth as aged sake. "Mistakes were made, yes. Yet, you must understand that after what the previous king did...we are wary of his son."

"Zayed is not his father!" I seethed, clenching my hands until my knuckles blanched white against my olive skin. The jade bracelet Mei had placed at my wrist clinked against the lacquered table."Yes, we realize that now. Especially after you relayed to me exactly what happened with that filth Shain and why." Chieftain Lamar's voice dropped to a dangerous whisper, his weathered face hardening like clay baked in the sun.Fire ignited in Chieftain Lamar's amber eyes at the mention of Shain, a hatred so visceral it seemed to darken the cherry blossoms around us. It was the first real reaction I had seen from him during this entire meeting. "I would like to go check on my husband now," I reiterated, my words precise as cut crystal, hoping for a different response than last time.Chieftain Lamar gave me a benign smile that never reached his eyes, pushing a glass plate of glistening dragon fruit and persimmons toward me with long, bejeweled fingers."You will...soon." His voice was honey poured over stone. "Why not go get some rest? Think about my proposition for your sister to marry my son. That is the woman who injured my most talented soldier, correct? If you agree, you will have our full support. Then we may all talk. By then, I am sure Zayed and Loran will have had their discussion as well."I stood abruptly, the silk of my robe whispering against the wooden chair, my hands clenching at my sides until my nails bit crescents into my palms."You have promised me he will be safe. And yet, while giving me access to my sister, you have denied me my husband. Now you tell me that the one man who has the strongest motive for harming my husband will get to meet him alone."Chieftain Lamar merely looked at me again with that benign, patient smile of his, like a serpent watching its prey. The golden dragons on his robe seemed to writhe in the dappled sunlight."I am not your enemy, Amara," he assured me, standing to tower over me, his shadow falling across my face like a cold veil. "And Loran has no intention of killing the son of the woman he loved," the Chieftain ended coldly. "If anything, he is the reason we have still continued to provide support and open trade to King Zayed's rule. We could have joined the rebel cause at any time. But we did not."

"You did not warn us either," I replied in measured tones.

Chieftain Lamar shrugged offhandedly.

"If you are unaware of what is going on in your own kingdom, that is not my problem."

Bastard.

The air thickened with tension, the cherry blossoms swirling around us like whispers of foreboding. I held my ground, refusing to let his casual demeanor unsettle me.

"You cannot expect me to trust you so easily."

Chieftain Lamar's eyes flickered with amusement, as if he were entertained by my defiance. "And yet here we are, Amara. Your husband is but a ghost without allies. You must remember, the world of politics requires sacrifices and compromises." He leaned in closer, his tone lowering conspiratorially. "I am willing to help you reclaim your throne, but only if you play along with my game. Your sister's marriage can strengthen our combined forces, bringing you both into a position of power."

Bile rose in my throat at the thought of using Asya as a pawn. But he was right.

"My sister was in love once. And had her heart broken. I...I cannot force her into a union that is unsuitable for her."

Chieftain Lamar smiled, his long great beard flowing like cascading wisps of silver against the rugged, weathered skin of his face.

"Trust me on this one, Amara. They will be more than suitable for each other. Of that I am certain. Why else would I offer my support in exchange for this union? What else do you have to offer me at the moment?"

He had a point.

But there was something still prickling at the edges of my subconscious.

"Why Asya?" He had not even seen my sister yet. Surely it could not be because of her beauty. Not yet at least.

Chieftain Lamar looked at me, amber eyes unblinking. "Not many have ever struck Ren—he is the finest soldier I command. And yet your sister did. That is what I want for my kingdom: women with the courage to fight, to defy, to rise. For a kingdom with strong women does not falter; it endures, it thrives, and it shapes generations. A warrior queen, a fearless sister, a woman who will not bow—such strength is not only rare, it is the very spine of an unshakable empire. You both are strong women. Just like your mother, Sayla, was."

I blinked in confusion upon hearing my mother's name, feeling as if my entire world had been upended. He knew my mother?

Zayed's POV

"Are you here to kill me?" I asked, arching a brow at Loran.

He stood before me with his long hair and beard, while I sat tied to a chair. A chair made of silver in a cell of silver bars and cold wooden walls. But the metal did not burn me like it should have. There was a biting sting where my skin touched the silver chair, like the slow burn of ice against bare flesh in winter—uncomfortable enough to make my muscles tense, but not the searing agony that should have consumed a creature like me.

Loran's amber eyes narrowed, glinting like polished gold as he leaned against the intricately carved wooden wall behind him, his arms crossed over his chest. "Whether I intend to kill you or not is irrelevant to the situation at hand. For now, I have no desire to see you perish." His voice was smooth and laced with arrogance. "After all, a dead king cannot reclaim a throne."

"You wish to see me back on the throne?" I scoffed.

Loran smirked, tilting his head slightly as if observing a peculiar creature.

"Welts are not forming on your skin as of yet. Interesting."

I snarled, ignoring his comment. I would not give information away like he expected.

"What do you want?" I struggled against my binds and the rope gave away slightly. A little more and I would be free.

"To talk," Loran replied simply, unruffled by my attempts to break free. His amber eyes were fixed on me. "I am not here to harm you, son of Liliana. Not yet at least."

I stilled at his words, my blood freezing as he spoke my mother's name.

"What game are you playing?" I narrowed my eyes at him.

Suspicion and curiosity warred within me.

He leaned forward slightly, the corner of his mouth curling into a half-smile, as if he could sense the storm of thoughts brewing in my mind.

"Your mother was a strong woman," he continued, his tone shifting to one of genuine admiration, a strange contrast to the tension in the air. "She was resilient, much like the women of our tribe. She understood the value of alliances."

I shifted in my chair, the silver biting against my skin, but I refused to let the discomfort show. "And yet here you are, speaking of alliances while holding me captive."

"Life is rarely so black and white, Zayed," he replied coolly. "You of all people know better than anyone. Your mother was killed unjustly. All because...because she loved me. Was our love truly such a heinous crime?"

"You toy with the memory of my mother as if it grants you power over me? You are wrong." My voice was low, filled with fury and regret of the past. I closed my eyes briefly before opening them, unconcealed loathing in my face. "You could have protected her. Instead, you fled back to your lands and let her die!"

I exerted all my might, and the fibers of the ropes slackened, giving way success-fully. The chair toppled over, and adrenaline surged through me as I lunged for Loran. My muscles strained against the remnants of the ropes, but I was driven by a fury that eclipsed pain. I discerned the faintest shadow of regret on his face mixed with surprise at my attack.

He darted aside with surprising agility, springing off the wall to evade my grasp.

"Fool!" he hissed, eyes narrowing. "Do you think violence will help your mother's memory? You are better than this!"

His words ignited a fresh rage within me, blurring my vision momentarily. "Bet-ter?" I spat, my voice dripping with venom. "You think this is about honor? You betrayed her, left her and my brother to die while you conspired to protect your own interests!"

Never before had I spoken so freely to this man. But now, without the shackles of my crown weighing upon my brow like a band of molten gold, the words rose in my throat like a tide that had been held back for too long. The bitter truths I had swallowed down at countless council meetings, diplomatic banquets, and royal audiences now spilled forth with the force of a dam breaking. A king's face must remain a mask of marble, betraying nothing of the storm beneath, but here—stripped of title and throne—I finally tasted the sweet venom of honesty on my tongue.

I could finally voice the accusations that had festered in my heart for years, accu-sations a diplomatic king would have buried beneath layers of courtly pleasantries and political necessities.

"You left her to die!" I roared, turning on my heel to launch myself at him again. "That is not love! It is cowardice!"

Loran stood motionless this time, a statue awaiting destruction. My fist collid-ed with his jaw—bone against bone—with a sickening crack that reverberated through my knuckles. Heat surged behind my eyes as they transformed, glowing amber-yellow like molten gold. His head snapped backward, dark hair whipping across his face, a thin ribbon of crimson trailing from the corner of his mouth.

The sight only fueled my rage. I lunged forward, my weight driving him down as we crashed onto the cold wooden floor.

Dust particles danced in the air around us, disturbed by our violent descent. I straddled his chest, my knees pinning his arms, and drew back my bloodied fist for another blow.

"I begged her to run away with me," he rasped through swollen lips, his once-commanding voice now reduced to a breathless whisper that scraped against his throat. "I did not want to leave my son and the woman I loved. I did not want to leave you either, Zayed. But you were the crown prince. You could not go with us. And…" He hesitated a beat before speaking the words that damned me to my own personal hell. "And she could not leave you." His eyes, though clouded with pain, held mine with unwavering intensity, glistening with the truth.

I let out an agonized growl, my right fist coming down, knuckles hitting the hard floor right next to where his head lay. My claws were extended and missed his left ear by a hairsbreadth.

A tempest of conflicting emotions swirled within me. Loran's words hung heavy in the air, echoing the past I had long tried to forget. I let out another mournful growl and the canines of my lycan elongated across the gums of my mouth.

My emotions were heightened, I was unable to control this partial shift taking place. I lifted my fist from beside his head. Wanting to hit something, anything. To unload my emotions.

"She would have done anything to keep you safe," he continued, his voice hoarse yet fierce. "She loved you more than her own life. It was never about cowardice—it was about duty, about protecting you from the darkness that was your father's shadow. I only wish I could have protected all three of you."

I faltered, the weight of his confession momentarily freezing my rage. Duty? Love? My fists trembled above him as I fought against the memories of my mother's warmth, her laughter, her unwavering strength.

I blinked, feeling the moisture gather behind my eyes.

She had died…for me? My brother could have lived…

Loran's eyes blazed with a fire of regret I had not expected. "I was only a young lad, Zayed! I did not know—none of us did—that your father would kill the mother of his son! We thought he would never find out. And if he ever did, well…his own harem was legendary. Surely he would not be so hypocritical as to punish your mother for falling in love! He never cared for her. But we did not count on his ego filling him with hate."

"All your promises were empty words," I stated hollowly, my body going slack over his. "You told her we would be happy together one day."

Because he had. I might have been a child, but I had seen and overheard their quiet interactions. One of the last times they saw each other was in the gardens, near what was now the graveyard of my dead queens, where she handed him my little brother. Loran had promised her one day we would all be happy. Though Loran had interacted with me little when I was a child, he had always been kind. Much kinder than my own father.

"I thought I was protecting her by leaving. She was queen...what did I have to offer her as the spare, a second son? When he sent me away, he promised me everyone's safety. The safety of my lover, the safety of my son, the safety of my tribe in exchange for—"

Loran's voice broke, and tears overwhelmed him. He did not need to repeat the words of the past. I knew my father. He must have found out and threatened Loran. Told him to leave quietly, and in exchange, he would let my brother and mother live the rest of their days in peace. At that time, the kingdom was stronger than it had ever been on the heels of my grandfather's just rule. Elamaria would have obliterated Loran's tribe in a bid for revenge. Loran thought he was protecting everyone by leaving.

But then my father broke his promise. It would not be the first time he lied through his teeth.

The more I learned about the past, the happier I was that Elvira cursed him to die.

The air around us throbbed with anger and pain, and though a part of me wanted to lash out, to make him feel the agony I had borne, another part of me recognized the flicker of remorse in his gaze. This was an emotion I had seldom allowed myself to entertain—a blending of compassion and understanding toward the man who had played a significant role in my life. My mother's choices were hers and hers alone. However, if it had been Amara and me, I would never have left her. Would I? Loran was a second son, a man with no army. His lover had been the queen of a powerful king.

I looked away from his mournful gaze, realizing that his situation was far too complex for me to ever understand.

Loran used my momentary weakness to push me off him. I could not even manage to fight him. My heart was no longer in it. How could I hurt a man Mother had loved so much?

"Zayed, I refuse to let your mother's legacy die with her. She deserves to be remembered—not merely as a queen but as the compassionate, gentle woman she truly was. You carry her spirit within you. I want you to succeed, because you are her son and blood. It is why we never supported the rebellion, despite their efforts to get us to join. It is why...why I have been trying to help you."

His words struck me like a bolt of lightning.

"Help?" I snarled as I sat on the floor, the fight drained out of me as my heart ached for my mother. My brother too. I balled my hands into fists at my sides. "Your men drugged us and separated me from my wife. Is that your definition of help?"

Loran's lips parted into a sneer.

"Your rebellion is still full of Kadin's men. They are spying on you. We could not make it obvious that we wished to help. Furthermore, we had no idea who your travelling party consisted of. For one, Shain was not on your side. He was sent by Kadin. We already know, through your wife, what happened to him."

"My wife? You met her?" My head whipped up to stare at Loran. "Is she all right?"

"She has met Chieftain Lamar and she is perfectly fine. Both sisters are being shown around the fortress as we speak."

"Take me to them," I demanded, my voice steady despite the tumult raging within me. I stood swiftly, waiting for Loran to lead the way.

Loran stood across from me and regarded me with an inscrutable expression, his arms crossed tightly over his chest. "You misunderstand the situation, Zayed. You are still a prisoner here, albeit one with a bit more leeway than most." His tone was almost mocking, but the spark of concern in his eyes hinted at a deeper complexity.

"Do not test my patience, Loran," I warned, stepping closer, my fists clenched tightly. "If you truly wish to honor my mother's legacy, you will prove it by bringing me to my wife and her sister this instant."

He hesitated, then sighed, the fight visibly leaving his posture. "Very well. But you must understand, there is only so much influence I hold with my brother. He has prepared a trial for you, if you wish to get your wife back."

Amara's POV

"Mother was a spy...in Chieftain Lamar's tribe?" Asya asked me for what seemed like the hundredth time.

I nodded as we walked along the barracks, Mei leading the way. We glanced around us at the sprawling maze of weathered stone buildings with narrow windows and heavy wooden doors. They had been built on the right side of the fortress.

"The women's barracks are at the very back," Mei explained to us as she walked ahead.

"There were only a few women soldiers," I explained to my sister. "And Mother was one of them." My boots crunched under dry leaves as we walked forward, Asya by my side with her bow and arrow, the afternoon sun making me squint my eyes. "Chieftain Lamar says that Li recognized you as her daughter. You have always been the prettier sister. You look more like Mother while I look like Father. Mother's father, our grandfather, was from Chieftain Lamar's tribe. He was a well-known blacksmith. Grandmother was from Elamaria, and he moved for her."

"I do not think I am the prettier sister, Amara. For you are the one with the purest and most beautiful heart and soul."

"But you are strength personified," I replied softly, the corner of my mouth lifting into a small smile. "You have always shown courage when it mattered most."

Asya's cheeks flushed, and she brushed a loose strand of hair, it had come undone from her high ponytail, behind her ear. "I could say the same about you. We may be sisters, but we can both recognize strength in one another."

"Exactly," I responded, warmth blooming in my chest at the bond we shared, each word a thread stitching us even closer together, even in the midst of uncertainty. "That is what Mother taught us."

As we approached the entrance to the women's barracks, my heartbeat sped up. The air smelled of sweat, leather, oil, and the metallic tang of sharpened steel.

"But how did Mother end up here?" Asya queried. "She was born in Elamaria. Our grandparents lived there."

"She was a spy for the king, Zayed's grandfather, and she infiltrated Chieftain Lamar's ranks to gather intel. It is why she was given so much recognition. Her services to the crown during her days as a spy are what eventually led to Chieftain Lamar's father deferring to Zayed's grandfather." I repeated the story for my sister patiently as we closed in on the woman's barracks.

"How did she manage that?" Asya queried with a gasp of surprise.

I could not help but puff my chest out proudly as I explained everything to Asya.

"Mother enlisted here at the age of twenty with forged credentials. She posed as the orphaned daughter of a late blacksmith who had worked closely with Grandfather. People had been paid off to vouch for her. And somehow, within the span of a year, she had gained the trust of Chieftain Lamar as she rose in the ranks. Her assignment was to kill Chieftain Lamar. Instead, she became his closest friend."

I spoke animatedly, so fast I had to pause momentarily before resuming the story.

"Consequently, Mother had been a key figure in negotiating peace, trade, and protection between the mountain tribes and Elamaria. The tribes only became part of Elamaria's kingdom after Zayed's grandfather promised protection through his soldiers, should the need ever arise."

I stopped speaking, not wanting to voice that now Elamaria was on the brink of waging war against the very tribal lands they had promised to protect. We walked silently past the barracks as Asya absorbed all this information.

We were here because Chieftain Lamar had said her old possessions were still here, in an old chest that no one had been allowed to throw out. He spoke of her with affection, as if she were much more than a friend. And maybe she had been more. He had been newly appointed Chieftain at the time. Had Mother been something more to him, despite being a spy for her kingdom?

There were so many questions we still did not know the answer to when it came to our mother's past. But we could find out.

I pushed open the door to the storage rooms behind the female soldier barracks.

A musty scent greeted us as we stepped inside, mixing with the faint aroma of aged wood and dust. The room was dark, illuminated only by the narrow beams of sunlight streaming through the small, grimy windows high above.

Shadows danced across the floor as we ventured deeper into the storage room, searching for the chest I knew was here.

"Do you think we will find anything...revealing?" Asya whispered, her tone a mix of hope and apprehension. I could sense the same burning curiosity coursing through her veins, just as it was in mine.

"I hope so," I replied, glancing around at the various crates and forgotten relics hidden in the shadows. "Whatever is left behind might tell us more about who she was...and why she made the choices she did."

Her depression...her death. Something told me there was more to it than what we had been told.

We walked toward dusty crates situated next to discarded weapons and breast-plates. Asya gasped and pointed to a small wooden chest with ornate carvings placed behind a pile of old rusty armor in an obscure corner of the room. It was partially covered by a worn blanket, but from what we could see, the lid was intricately carved with an S. S for Sayla. We stared at each other briefly. Father had the same exact chest in a storage room at our home in the city of Ilm. This was Mother's, no doubt.

Chieftain Lamar had been right. Some of her belongings were still here. And he was giving it to us as a peace offering. To show he meant no ill will toward us.

The wood seemed older than the walls surrounding it, the grain smooth from countless hands touching its surface. There was something almost pulsing about it, like a reverberation of memories waiting to be unearthed.

"Help me," I urged Asya, my heart racing with anticipation as we approached the chest together. We crouched before it, exchanging glances filled with unvoiced questions. What stories lay buried within?

I grasped the edge of the blanket, lifting it gently. Dust rose up around me but I paid it no heed.

"It is locked," Asya murmured, attempting to open it. She pointed to the lock embedded into the chest.

I bit my lip, staring at the lock before reaching into the folds of my clothes and withdrawing my silver jagged dagger.

She left this here for a reason. It was waiting for someone to open it. Was it waiting for me?

No. Her time as a spy here was long before she met my father. They had fallen in love after she began working inside the palace as one of Zayed's grandfather's most trusted warriors.

With a steadying breath, I slid the jagged-edged dagger into the ancient lock's keyhole. It slipped in easily, about one fourth of the dagger becoming encased entirely inside the metal lockplate placed over the chest.

With a slow, deliberate motion, I twisted the dagger, the blade catching in the metal as I felt for the tumblers inside the lock

Asya inhaled sharply when a satisfying click resonated through the air, an echo of something long dormant finally awakening. My heart raced, anticipation thrumming in my veins like the beat of a war drum. Asya leaned closer, her breath quickening in tandem with mine.

"She placed it here for another Blade-Caller to find," Asya breathed, leaning forward eagerly to open the chest.

"It is the only plausible explanation," I said, voice trembling.

With a gentle tug, I lifted the lid of the chest. It creaked open, revealing an assortment of objects nestled within—silks, an intricately woven scarf, and several neatly folded garments, all imbued with the scent of time and memory. But what caught my eye was a small, rolled up piece of parchment with the words "The Magic Carpet" scrawled in big bold letters.

I blinked, recalling the story of Yasmin and Farid. Had Mother been inordinately fond of their story? Or was there another reason she would recount it to me frequently? I reached for the scroll as Asya began to go through our mother's material possessions. I caught her holding up an old white scarf, inhaling to try and catch remnants of our mother's scent. She sneezed instead.

"These items have been here for a long time," Asya muttered, reaching inside to delve through the pile of clothes.

A book fell out of the folds of cloth with a clunk. No. Not just any book...

"A diary. Mother never kept a diary," Asya muttered, flipping through its contents to look for anything of import.

I went back to the scroll in my hand, slowly opening it to reveal not a story but...a map.

"This is a map of the fortress," I commented, taking in the contents. "No wait..." My eyes followed a path outlined in bright crimson ink, words like "secret passage" and "behind the tapestry," clearly visible. Mother's handwriting jumped out at me. This was not a map but a clearly outlined trail to a treasure, or perhaps a test.

Above all else, a huge red X stared back at me. A red X situated underneath the fortress.

"Amara...look!" Asya shoved the pages of the diary before me.

And what I read made me realize exactly why Mother had been acknowledged not only for her bravery but for her wit. The Sword of Honor had been awarded for her services in peace, not in war. Words written in her neat and precise penmanship sprang forth, blatantly telling me a glaring truth she had been preparing me for.

There is NO weapon beneath the fortress. NO plot against our king to murder him. The accusations are LIES whispered in the ears of our monarchy. The Chieftain guards something far more dangerous. His bloodline traces directly to Yasmin and Farid, making his family the sworn guardians of the magic carpet. The carpet lies dormant, bound by Yasmin's blood oath after she wrested it from Harun's vile grasp. *LISTEN CAREFULLY: If this diary has found you, fellow Blade-Caller, our alliance has CRUMBLED. Though a formidable shifter, Chieftain Lamar is no match for a siege upon his tribe.*

Trust NO ONE from the crown! Harun's descendants have infiltrated the highest ranks of nobility—they walk our palace halls wearing human faces while concealing ancient magic. Harun's descendants infiltrated our lands with knives in their smiles. Harun's heirs walk our palace halls wearing noble faces, whispering poison in royal ears, PLOTTING marriage alliances with the crown prince that will deliver the kingdom into darkness. The crown cannot be trusted. Be wary of the man with blood-red eyes and the ruby ring. He seeks the carpet with relentless hunger. If Lamar's fortress falls, the carpet will be found, the forbidden incantation spoken, and a darkness will sweep across not only Elamaria but EVERY KINGDOM WITHIN REACH. Harun's descendants will burn everything we love to ash. For domination over all the kingdoms is possible when the carpet gives one the power to be anywhere and everywhere upon the merest whisper. The peace I sacrificed everything for rests in your hands now. They seek not just power but VENGEANCE that will drown every kingdom in flames. You MUST succeed where I failed.

As I finished reading the last line, a chilling wave of realization washed over me. It was all real. The stories she had told me...were all real. The shifters, the story of Yasmin and Farid. The magic carpet!

"This...cannot be," Asya choked out, looking at me pleadingly. "The magic carpet is but a fairytale!"

"There is always truth woven in the fabric of stories, for even the wildest fairytale springs from the heart of reality." I spoke the words Mother once said.

My mother had been a celebrated warrior, and a woman who had advocated for peace. She had not been awarded the Sword of Honor for killing countless men in battle. She had been awarded the sword for her time spent here. For her valuable service to the Crown in which she had been a key figure in the alliance between Chieftain Lamar's tribe and the Kingdom of Elamaria. Lamar had bowed to the Crown in exchange for protection and trade. And in return, she had ensured the magic carpet would remain safe, the guardians only having to worry about their job as its custodian while Elamaria protected their borders.

I exchanged a glance with Asya, the weight of our shared understanding hanging heavy in the air around us. The knowledge that our mother had once been a key player in this grand game of politics and power was staggering. What had she sacrificed for this peace? And now here we were, standing on the precipice of chaos.

Asya's brows knitted together in thought, her fingers tracing over the edge of the diary's pages that went on to explain her time here as well as her role in brokering peace.

"This is not just about Elamaria anymore, is it? There are lives at stake beyond our kingdom's."

I inclined my head in agreement, eyes going to the open map still in my lap as I sat on the old worn floor where many many years ago my mother must have sat in this exact position.

"What do we do? She specifically stated that Harun's descendants infiltrated the royal court of Elamaria. Do you think...do you think she meant Zayed's mother was from Harun's bloodline?"

My shoulders sagged as Asya voiced my own concern. It was a possibility. What if Elvira had been sent by Liliana's brother to perform the curse?

"Man with red eyes...Lycan eyes glow red," I muttered, closing my eyes.

Zayed knew nothing of this story. But what if his uncle, his mother's brother, was part of all this? What if his mother had been? Or his father? His father had not been a good king. Maybe he was the man with red eyes my mother had been warning us about. Zayed's grandfather was king when Mother worked for the crown. It was possible she suspected the crown prince, Zayed's father. But he was dead now...and he could have waged war against Chieftain Lamar at any time. Could Zayed be part of a greater plot? No. I refused to jump to conclusions. But for now, this had to remain a secret. We could not trust anyone.

"What do we do?" Asya asked.

"We find the magic carpet and hide it somewhere they will never look," I hissed through clenched teeth, slamming the diary shut with such force that dust exploded from its ancient spine. My knuckles whitened around its leather cover. "Whatever it takes."

It was then that Mei entered the storage room.

"Chieftain Lamar wishes for you to return to the cherry blossom gardens. Your husband is being brought to meet him."

I closed my eyes in remorse. Did I want to go to Zayed? Yes. But there was no time to waste. I clutched the map to my chest, closing my eyes as I made my decision.

Forgive me for what I am about to do, Zayed. For it is the right thing to do.

Chapter 20

Zayed's POV

"What is the meaning of this?" I demanded, looking around the cherry blossom garden brimming with women in veils covering the lower half of their faces. They wore gauzy two piece outfits that belly dancers from my own kingdom often wore, their laughter dancing like petals on a breeze.

I turned to glare at Lamar, displeasure evident in my stance.

Women might wear such attire in my land, but not in his. Not in the tribal mountains. Long robes that trailed behind women were the norm here.

Cascading laughter mixed with the soft rustle of blossoms above. The air was sweet with the fragrance of flowers, but my stomach churned. Where was my wife?

"We have a tradition here in our lands. When a man misplaces his wife, he must find her amongst the dancing courtesans of the harem." Lamar chortled, his silver beard glinting in the late afternoon light.

My nostrils flared.

"If he cannot find her, then he does not deserve her," Lamar ended with a taunting smile.

Bastard!

I looked back at the women gathered on one side of the garden, all talking amongst one another.

What was this man planning?

Each pair of eyes met mine and sparkled with mischievous delight, a chorus of whispers rippling through them.

"Traditions do hold weight, but this—this is a mockery!" I snarled.

Lamar's laughter echoed as he gestured toward the crowd, encouraging me to join the game. "You have but one hour to find her, dethroned king. Otherwise, welll..." He let the words hang tantalizingly in the air. A promise of consequence that sent an awareness of ominous endings.

I squinted against the afternoon sun, scanning the swirling colors and shimmering fabrics. Each face was masked, leaving only the sparkle of their eyes visible. There were too many women here. How could I possibly search for Amara? I could not even sense or smell her out here. Was it due to the sedative they had given me? Or something they had given her? I tried to inhale, but all I smelled were cherry blossoms. I cursed.

"To make it a little more...challenging, you must pick within the hour. Else you lose her...forever."

I snarled at Lamar. I was going to kill him for this!

"Your time starts...now!" Lamar announced.

With a sudden flurry, the women began to sway and twirl, their movements fluid like the petals that drifted from the branches above. My heart raced; this was no mere game. The laughter echoed, teasing and taunting, as they beckoned to me with outstretched hands.

"The king without a crown must find her," one young woman called out, her voice rich like honey. "It is not merely the prize but the journey that will test your worthiness!"

I clenched my fists, each pulse of my heart extricating frustration from my veins. This was ridiculous, a ruse to embarrass me! To see me fail, most likely! Could Amara truly be among them? My gut told me she was not here. She would have come to me on her own otherwise. But what if I was wrong?

The women undulated in divine artistry, their silk veils catching the dappled sunlight filtering through cherry blossoms overhead. Jingling gold anklets marked their movements as they blurred between reality and dream. Amidst the whirlwind of crimson, sapphire, and emerald fabrics, I forced myself to the edge of the gathering where the sweetness of blossoms hung heaviest in the air. I inhaled deeply, searching for Amara's distinctive jasmine scent, but found only the cloying perfume of flowers and incense. I looked back at Lamar's smug face before scanning the crowd for Loran's familiar silhouette. "My brother is not allowed to help you during this trial, Zayed," Lamar declared, stroking his silver-streaked beard. "This is between two rulers. Prove yourself worthy, and you shall have my support." I gritted my teeth until my jaw ached. "Finding my wife is important whether you aid me or not," I growled, ignoring the handful of women who had now formed a circle around me. They began to dance at a punishingly fast pace, their hips swaying hypnotically. Pale torsos undulated beneath sheer fabrics, tiny feet kicked up puffs of grass and colorful petals, and bangles flashed in the sunlight. My eyes flitted from woman to woman. It was impossible to discern their features...and yet, I knew with crushing certainty: None of them were Amara.

"What does picking the right woman have to do with a tribal chieftain deeming me worthy of backing in an alliance?" I called out, arms crossed and completely unaffected by the women dancing around me.

I cared not for their come hither looks. "Everything," Lamar replied, glancing at me through the dancing women around me. "A man may carry a sword, but the one who sees through tricks and guises to recognize his true wife shows the greater wisdom—for he who can walk his home in steadfast partnership is destined to guide his kingdom with unshakable strength."

"Wisdom?" I shot back, ire boiling in my chest. "You think it wise to waste time on this army of illusions when our enemies are closing in on us? You and I both know that Kadin will come for your tribe. He needs a diversion to keep the people of Elamaria preoccupied as he loots and plunders the royal coffers. The alliance would benefit you just as much as it would benefit me."

"My tribe has survived for thousands of years before we allied with Elamaria. We will continue to survive. We can wait out Kadin's rule. Can you?"

A muscle ticked in my jaw. Arrogant bastard. He did not have the men to fight off Kadin. Yet he spoke with such unwavering certainty...

Taunting laughter erupted around me, growing louder and louder as the women continued to dance. It was like a mocking symphony of giggles, swishing skirts, and bangles clanking together that echoed through the garden.

However, beneath my anger simmered a current of desperation. I had only this hour; every second ticked away like the relentless beat of a war drum, and each twirl of fabric was another moment stolen from me. I forced myself to focus, letting the chaos blur into a single thought: Amara.

She would not play along. Would she? She must be here somewhere. Perhaps farther back, behind the women dancing around me. She was merely waiting for me to find her. Knowing her, she would find it amusing to see if I found her. But not at a time like this. We did not have time for amusement right now.

My eyes narrowed, searching for something—anything—that would allow me to distinguish her presence among these vibrant shapes. Ten more women were now circling Chieftain Lamar. He paid them no heed, eyes steady on me. I inhaled deeply once more, trying to center myself amidst the overwhelming aromas. It was then I caught a fleeting hint of her scent, delicate yet distinct, layered beneath the floral sweetness.

My wife was here somewhere. I walked through the circle of women surrounding me, toward the females dancing in a line under a copse of trees. Petals fell from above, showering down on them like drops of rain. My gaze darted from woman to woman, searching for deep brown eyes that reminded me of the desert under a starry night sky. I searched for the unmistakable glimmer of warmth that could light up the darkest corners of my mind. Suddenly, a woman stepped into my path, twirling like a leaf caught in a tempest. Her midnight dark hair fell like an inky waterfall down her back. It was the same length as Amara's. Silver glinted at her hip. A silver dagger.

She moved toward me, hands pressing briefly against my chest as she circled me, her hips undulating in rhythmic movements.

I inhaled, and Amara's faint scent wafted toward me. Soft hands came around me from behind, palms pressing against my beating heart.

"Have you picked?" Chieftain Lamar's voice came as if from far away.

The woman slowly circled me again, her right palm intermittently flattening itself across parts of my chest.

"It is me, Zayed." I heard the faint whisper. Not in my ear. But in my mind. *"It is your wife."*

"I seek Amara, my wife!" I called back to him.

Silver glinted in the corner of my eye again. I sensed her moving to place her palm against me, over my heart, much in the same pattern as before. I turned swiftly to face her.

She never got the chance to touch me because I embedded the extended claws of my lycan into her abdomen. "I do not seek a fleeting shadow of her," I grit out as all the women around me stilled in horror.

The imposter also held a silver dagger in her right hand, poised to strike me.

"Your attempt was not bad, but I know how my wife rolls her hips," I hissed, eyes narrowed on the veiled woman who resembled Amara. Crimson cascaded over my extended claws embedded inside her bare torso. I twisted them viciously, revelling in the wetness that drenched my hand. The woman's flesh yielded around my talons, ripping as I twisted. More blood flowed like a river, spilling forth through the tears in her flesh.

The smooth-edged silver dagger, dropped from her raised hand with a soft thud as it hit the ground. The woman gasped. Blood spilled from her mouth, staining her pink veil.

"What is the meaning of this!" Chieftain Lamar screamed. "You have killed one of my concubines?" I turned to look at him.

"She tried to kill me first," I snarled.

"NO! My concubines are not trained to handle weapons! They are women trained in pleasure, not warfare!" Lamar yelled, eyes on the woman I had wounded. Or perhaps killed, for she would be dead soon. I pulled out my claws and allowed her to collapse to the ground.

It then struck me that if what Lamar said was true, why were these women not screaming or running in horror? Instead, they stood still...too still.

My eyes moved over the woman choking on her blood at my feet as life seeped out of her. No one was helping her...

There were no guards here to restrain me for what I had done. Lamar probably did not need guards when it was just his harem and him. Which meant...

"LOOK OUT!" I yelled to Lamar right as one of the females who had been standing in the circle around him extended a dagger to embed it into his heart. She lunged at him from his right side.

"You are not my concubines!" Lamar growled, side-stepping her in time and ripping off her veil. He reached out with his other hand, snapping her wrist in one quick motion. She opened her mouth but did not cry out in pain. Instead, she issued a direct order.

"ATTACK!"

As one, the veils were removed and weapons drawn. Weapons with jagged edged blades.

"Blade-Callers," I breathed in surprise. These women were sent by Kadin!

Lamar let out a grunt of pain, and I turned to look back at him. He might have evaded one attack, but there was now a silver blade protruding from his shoulder.

His eyes glowed dark red as he prepared to shift. "WE ARE UNDER SIEGE!" he roared.

We shifted as one.

Chapter 21

Zayed's POV

I could hear pounding against the doors as guards attempted to break them down and enter the secluded garden within the courtyard.

Some were now jumping from the windows of the fort to reach us.

Someone told Kadin we would be here. Somehow, these women had infiltrated the harem.

Where were the actual women? Where was Amara?!

More adversaries were appearing out of the shadows in the cherry blossom grove, blades glinting in the dappled sunlight as they lunged toward us with deadly intent. Male and female alike, all in servantile clothing.

My Lycan let out a howl and I ducked to avoid a slashing strike to my neck. Cool wind whooshed passed as the blade missed me by a hairsbreadth.

Lamar was beside me, his wolf sinking its fangs into my attacker, his muscles rippling beneath gleaming fur.

More growls behind me told me that Loran had arrived too. Like his brother, he could also shift. But that was not what made the fur on my body stand on end.

No. There was something else here. Something sinister and lethal that hovered just beyond my vision. I tore my gaze away from the shifting forms of enemies attacking from all sides and forced myself to focus on the task at hand. Amara. I had to find her, amidst the carnage. She was still here! As was Asya. And—

I growled in anger when my eyes landed on Salim, who materialised from the shadows with a man I recognised from the granary roof. The man who had ordered the soldiers to kill Amara.

Had Salim been captured? But he did not look as if he had been forcibly dragged here.

A sudden explosion from one of the fort lookout towers shook the ground beneath us, sending debris raining down like petals from an angry storm. The chaos erupted, familiar voices rising above the fray as shouts and snarls echoed around the garden.

Amara! Where was Amara!?

A prickly sensation travelled across my skin, and the sense of ominous death creeped up my spine. What was here that made even my Lycan wary?

And then I heard it.

Ssssssss

A sinister prolonged hiss that cut through the chaos. The sound grew louder, sending the chaos around me into a temporary stillness. The battle halted for a heartbeat, as if the entire world was waiting, holding its breath. The hiss coiled and slithered through the air, laden with malevolence.

And then it came, slithering through the shadows. Giant green scales glinted like obsidian in the light, a serpentine behemoth that looked as if it could swallow an elephant whole.

Each hiss resonated like the whisper of a death knell, foreboding and insistent. Glowing yellow eyes—sunk deep into a grotesque, elongated head—sized up the frantic figures that darted in desperation, their cries of fear echoing across the barren battlefield. Its head was as big as the entire body of the humans scattering and screaming in fear. But Lamar's men were not afraid. Rather, they looked relieved!

With a sudden, fluid motion, the giant snake lunged forward, its maw stretching impossibly wide, revealing rows of razor-sharp teeth that glistened with anticipation. The scent of terror wafted around me and seemed to be fueling its hunger as it darted out a forked tongue, tasting the air in anticipation.

Then it captured one unfortunate female Blade-Caller in its grasp, wrapping its scaled body around the unsuspecting victim. Her screams were swallowed by darkness as the beast coiled around its prey, tightening its grip until her bones cracked like brittle twigs and her screams died on the wind just like her body.

A blur of fur next to me pounced on a warrior aiming for the demon serpent.

Whatever this thing was, it was not our enemy. And it was most likely the reason Lamar was so smug about his ability to hold off Kadin's men.

And if Lamar had more beasts like this one, he might be able to.

The serpent's sinuous body moved like a shadow among the chaos, its golden eyes filled with predatory intent as it swallowed ten men in one gulp before curling its scaly body around another victim.

"The Bashe will eat you all!" one of Lamar's men cried out.

It was then that I realized, this was no mere serpent.

I heard of this creature before. But I thought it was a monster of mere legend. The Bashe was a demon serpent that brought death and destruction wherever it went. How did Lamar have access to something like this?

The Bashe unleashed its fury upon the encroaching enemies, a whirlwind of scales and sinew that churned the earth beneath its weight. The primal energy of my Lycan pulsed alongside the monstrous entity, there was a visceral connection that urged me forward. We were both demons, though of different breeds.

Screams of horror filled the air as blood painted the ground. Lamar's Bashe was obliterating the enemy. Another explosion rippled through the fort, causing me to pause momentarily. Noxious fumes of smoke reached me.

The fort had caught fire and it was spreading.

Loran's wolf form darted past the Bashe, his body a blur of flashing claws as he tore into more attackers that seemed to be endlessly materializing from the shadows beyond.

My eyes went to the side of the fort on fire. Amara was there, lost amidst the blood-soaked frenzy. I had to find her. Lamar did not need me to help him fight.

I moved forward to find my wife, only to encounter the spreading flames blocking my entry.

I growled low, ducking down and prepared to walk through the flames. I had to get to her! I would find her. My heart beat frantically as I thought of my wife, trapped inside the burning inferno. NO. I would not lose her.

Silver glinted from my right and I dodged in time as a Blade-Caller attempted to swipe at me. My claws found flesh, creating a gaping hole in her abdomen. Her blood and entrails spilled out, staining her sky blue silk dress with her intestines. She fell to the ground, gurgling up her own blood. I moved forward without a backward glance. She would meet her creator soon. Anyone who kept me from my goal would forfeit their life.

I faced the wall of fire again, steeling myself for the searing pain to come. Flesh would heal, but a life without Amara would be a wound that never would. With a deep breath, I readied myself to charge through.

Amara's POV The air grew colder the deeper we went, my torchlight shivering against walls that seemed to lean closer with every step. My boots scraped stone stairs worn by centuries of forgotten footsteps. Behind me, Asya clutched my arm, her grip tight, her breath quick in the dark.When we reached the bottom, I froze. A cavern opened before us, vast and echoing, the ceiling studded with dripping stalactites.

We were inside a tunnel. An underground cave system similar to the rebel hideouts. Moving forward in the dark, I raised my torch high, looking into the dark tunnel.

The sound of trickling water reached my ears.

"Do you hear that?" Asya croaked out from behind.

I nodded. "Is there a stream—"

But my voice was cut off as the trickling sound became a mighty whoosh of heat and fire rushed toward us, barrelling through with unprecedented speed. It did not burn the stone or moss growing in the cavern. No, its intent was to burn only us.

A searing wall of heat rushed toward us. I threw myself over Asya, trying to shield her with my body.

"Run back!" I screamed.

"No!" Asya replied, wrapping her arms around me and trying to wrestle me behind her. "No, Amara! You must go now!"

We stood there, frozen in limbo as both of us tried to protect the other. Surely we would both burn. I held my breath, shaking as we both braced ourselves for the pain of being burned alive. My eyes watered as the wall of fire neared. But instead, the fire curled around us without touching flesh. The heat surged past us, a living flame that recognized us. My Lycan power surged, heightening my senses, and merging with the fire's pulse. Magic recognized magic. And this magic was a friend, not a foe.

The flames twisted and turned as if they were alive, igniting the shadows encircling us. Instead of pain, an unexpected warmth encompassed me—a protective embrace rather than destruction. Asya's grip on my arm slackened, her eyes wide with astonishment. "What is this?" she whispered, her voice trembling. "I do not know," I managed to reply, my pulse racing as the fire danced around us before parting to reveal a path forward. It beckoned with a glow that both terrified and intrigued me. The very air shimmered; an ancient power thrummed in the depths of the cavern, wrapping around us with a force stronger than mere fire. The roaring heat intensified, pushing against my chest like an insistent tide. "We have to move!" I urged.

But we had not taken ten paces forward before a door blocked our path. Hewn from black stone, its surface was smooth and polished. The fire around us dissipated until we were suddenly encroached in darkness as I realized I had dropped my torch when the fire had come for us.

My fingers stretched toward the door's brass handle, but I jerked back with a hiss as scorching heat radiated from the metal.

"Look!" Asya gasped, pointing to the door.

Glowing script illuminated the once unblemished door surface. The words pulsed faintly, alive and waiting. I brushed my hand over them and read aloud, my voice trembling in the silence:

"I fly without wings, I move without feet, I weave through silence, yet I carry speech .What am I?"

The tunnel seemed to lean in around us, the air humming with the riddle's weight. It felt as if shadows of the flames eagerly danced on the dark stone walls, waiting to burn me.

Asya's eyes darted to mine, wide and afraid before motioning to the dark shadows curling around us. "Amara... if we answer wrong—"

"I know," I whispered. The fire had retreated for now. But it would turn on us if we failed.

My mind raced, every possible answer slipping away like water through fingers. I closed my eyes, forcing myself to listen. The silence was not empty. There was a faint shift of air, a breath brushing my cheek. I remembered whispers carried across dunes, voices borne through walls, songs drifting around me though no instrument played.

"Fly without wings..." I trailed off, muttering to myself.

"Move without feet," Asya added furtively.

The silence seemed to stretch before us as I stared at the black door with the words glowing in gold. Silence....

"This was not in Mother's stories," Asya whispered before swallowing audibly.

Whispers? Could that be the answer? But did whispers weave through silence?

I stepped forward, hands resting against the fiery door, feeling warmth pulsing through my fingertips, urging me onward. A gust of air blew through the narrow tunnel, cooling my heated body. My eyes widened.

"Wind," I declared assertively, looking up at the door as if expecting it to tell me I was right. "Wind is the answer!"

The golden script shimmered, swirling in intricate patterns before retracting. The door creaked, tremors rippling through the stone as it slowly began to shift open. Asya let out a cry of triumph, hugging me from behind.

"You did it!" Asya exclaimed.

"We did it," I corrected before stepping through the door cautiously.

Inside, the chamber was empty—no treasure, no weapon. Just stone walls of a cave and stillness that pulsed with something waiting.

And then...She appeared.

A shadow formed near the far wall. Not shapeless, but a beautiful woman with a crown on her head. Her hair flowed like ink, her robes dancing in a wind that was not there. Her face was familiar, beautiful, regal yet not fully alive.

Her eyes glowed like fallen stars, deep pools of mystery and power that pierced through the shadows. My heart quickened; she looked familiar. I knew her. But how? Visions of her face flickered in my mind, but something felt amiss. This figure was too ethereal, too distant. "Asya, stay back," I whispered, my voice barely breaking the silence that enveloped us.

"You found your way to the carpet," she said, her voice like wind against stone. "But you must understand—it is not a tool. It is a *burden*. And one not meant for all."

I started, realizing who she was.

"You...are the woman from my dream!" I sputtered, recalling the dream I had had my first night in the palace. She was the woman with silver hair and eyes that shone like the stars.

The shadowy figure tilted her head to stare at me. Then she smiled—a slow, haunting curve of her lips that sent a chill down my spine. "I am what remains of the stories woven by time. I am the guardian of the carpet." Her voice was melodic, echoing softly against the stone walls, wrapping around me like a silken thread. "I cannot travel into dreams, child, unlike my creator, in whose likeness I was molded. And if she is the one who chose to visit you in your dream, then surely you are her champion. The one chosen to wield that which no man has been allowed to wield after her."

"Who is your creator?" I asked. "Where can we find her?"

The spectral black figure shook her head.

"The one you seek no longer walks this land. She waits in a realm uncharted, where the heart's desires twist around helpless dreams. Only those who dare to embrace their demise may traverse the paths leading to her."

Asya gasped. "You mean...your creator is dead?"

A flicker of something like sorrow crossed the guardian's ethereal face. "Her name has been lost to time, buried beneath decades of treachery and longing. But many know her by the name Yasmin, told in whispers to young children as bedtime stories."

"Yasmin!" I gasped in surprise.

The spectral figure nodded before lifting a hand.

"You come for the carpet. But I can offer you your heart's desire. Turn back and do not take on the burden, for it is too much to bear."

A slow, golden warmth bloomed through the air like sunrise breaking through fog. I blinked, and the chamber around us seemed to dissolve—its stone walls replaced by something softer, dreamlike, almost sacred.

Asya gasped beside me, and I turned to find her frozen, her eyes wide and un-blinking. A small baby lay bundled up in her arms. She stood barefoot in a white, flowing dress and devoid of her black tunic, trousers, and boots.

"My-my son-" she sputtered, lips trembling as tears dropped down her eyes. "My son," she rasped, holding the newborn closer to her bosom. Her eyes met mine, and a pain like no other was reflected in them. A pain she had hidden all too well.

I blinked in confusion, unable to understand what I saw.

"I...after Salim left, I found out I was expecting our child." Tears fell down Asya's cheeks. "And-and after you were taken into the palace, I got word that Salim had pledged himself to another. I had waited for him for six months! Trying to keep our child a secret because I wanted him to know first. Maybe it was all too much stress. I miscarried." She closed her eyes in pain. "I do not know if it was fate's cruel way of telling me to forget about Salim, or punishment because I did not fight harder to stop my sister from being taken into the palace. But I wanted my son, Amara," Asya cried, nuzzling her nose into the top of the baby's head, clutching his tiny body swaddled in blankets. "And now I have him." Her voice cracked.

The visceral pain on Asya's face, the longing, the want for what could have been nearly cracked my heart in two. I had no idea this is what happened. But I could not help and think back to all the suitors she denied in Salim's absence. What must it have felt like, to try and hide this from her family? All because she believed the father deserved to know before any of us.

The air shimmered around us, bright green grass rustling beneath our feet, as if to tease us.

"Asya," I implored, stepping forward with a hand extended. She was on her knees now in the grass, holding the illusion as if only death itself could part them. "It is not real," I rasped, looking pleadingly at her.

Asya looked up at me now, ire in her eyes.

"You stand there, decked out in your queenly attire and dare to tell me what is and is not real?" She clutched the baby closer to her bosom, as if she was afraid I would hurt her child.

I looked down at myself and realized Asya was right. I was no longer in my tunic and boots, but in a long, flowing dress of sapphire silk skirts and gauzy net, adorned with golden embroidery that glimmered as I moved. I held up my hands, now adorned with henna instead of dirt. My fingers glittered with rings—emeralds, sapphires, and rubies catching the light with each trembling movement. Golden bangles clinked at my wrists as my hands shook in disbelief. The transformation felt as if I had stepped into a dream woven by the hands of fate.

The grassy glade around me melted into pillars of white marble and gold. I was standing in a throne room, wide and gleaming, sunlight fracturing through stained glass, scattering jewels of purple, red, and yellow across the marble floor.

At the end of the hall stood Zayed. Happy. Safe. Regal. His gold cloak billowed in a wind I could not feel, and his eyes—those fierce, beloved eyes the color of forest shadows—met mine with a quiet certainty.

His hand reached for me, open and waiting. Behind him stood the throne—the throne that had been taken from him, from us. The air tasted of jasmine and power. Around me, courtiers bowed. Armies waited. The crown on his head shimmered like a promise.

A small yelp from the seat of his throne drew my attention, and I nearly cried out in surprise. Baba stood to the right, Asya to the left of the throne. And there on the seat of the throne was Baghel. Alive and well. He let out another yelp, eagerly beckoning me toward him.

And for a heartbeat—just one—I wanted it all.

I wanted to take that throne, to crush every man who had betrayed us, to restore the world as it *should* have been, and to make sure all my loved ones were safe. I wanted to place Zayed where he belonged, and myself at his side.

All I had to do was say yes!

Then, Mother's voice rose like thunder breaking glass.

The peace I sacrificed everything for rests in your hands now. They seek not just power but VENGEANCE that will drown every kingdom in flames.

The illusions flickered. What had Mother sacrificed? What must I now sacrifice?

I turned my back to Zayed and looked down the hall to see Asya still on her knees in the grassy glade.

Her hand hovered inches from her son's face. Her lip quivered, tears streaming down her cheeks unchecked. She was waging a war inside herself. The ache of holding him again, and the terror of knowing he was not real. Because none of this was real. A tear slid down my cheek. I could fight and try to attain the peace I wanted. But Asya could never get her son back. I wanted to say something to her, but what?

Then, slowly, she lowered her hand. Her eyes closed, and she whispered, "I would give anything to hold him...but not like this."

The baby let out a soft coo, then vanished. Asya's scream pierced through my heart.

I looked back momentarily at Zayed and then briefly at Baghel, now standing by his side.

And then I turned away from the throne, from Zayed's open arms, from Baba's proud gaze and the prism of light. My body ached with the effort, my heart screaming in protest. But I let it all fade. I would not win our future by twisting the present. And then I ran to Asya, wailing with her head in her hands.

The vision dissolved like sand through fingers with every step I took toward her. The marble floor was stone again. The green glade filled with sunlight was gone. Only the cold of the vault remained, and Asya was no longer far away but close. I reached her within five paces and threw my arms around her, letting her cry.

Finally, when our tears were spent, Asya rose beside me, and for a moment, we could not look at each other. We had both been offered everything we had ever lost...and we both chose to walk away.

Yasmin's shadow stirred before us, appearing out of thin air, her voice no longer sharp but reverent.

"You have passed the hardest test: not of loyalty of the mind, but of the soul. May you remember this moment. For power that begins with longing often ends in ruin."

Suddenly the floor around us cracked, and the shadows rippled like the surface of a disturbed pond. The stone cavern groaned and rubble fell to the floor.

"What is this? I thought we passed!" Asya cried out, glaring at the shadow of Yasmin.

"The fort is under attack," the shadow replied calmly. "Harun's men have infiltrated and are searching for the carpet."

"We need to get the carpet and leave!" I exclaimed frantically, rushing forward, looking every which way for what we needed.

"You will not be able to escape. The walls will collapse and bury you alive. Your only hope...is the final trial. If you solve the final riddle, the carpet will bow to your will."

I gasped, turning to Yasmin's shadow.

She wanted us to activate the magic carpet?

"Where is it?" Asya asked urgently, eyes darting around to look for it.

"I do not know. You must find it," Yasmin's shadow remarked.

Her eyes—if they could be called that—seemed to shimmer with something unreadable. "Or be entombed with the others who failed."

"Why can it never be as simple as it seems?" Asya huffed, throwing her hands up in the air. "We answered your riddles, passed your trials, and yet..." She shook her head. "Imminent death still hovers over our heads."

The cavern walls trembled, dust raining down from above, mixing with the rising fear in my chest. Time was running out, and the imminent collapse of this place loomed like a black cloud ready to burst.

"Trials demand perseverance," Yasmin's shadow said, her voice echoing through the chamber like the distant whisper of a forgotten wind. "They are not merely tests of intellect but reflections of your hearts. Your desires and sacrifices have forged your strength. This final challenge will reveal how hard you are willing to fight, to bend, for what you truly seek."

Asya said something to the shadow that was rather rude and vulgar as more rubble fell from above.I dropped to my knees, palms slapping against the cracked floor.

"If politeness was part of the trials, you would have already failed," the shadow remarked dryly to Asya.

"Goddess be damned, this shadow is going to let us die here," Asya grunted, scanning the walls, tearing through bits of fallen stone.

My hands trailed over the cracks that had formed on the floor. It was then that I noticed the floor was not smooth stone.

Bend...for what you truly seek.

Beneath my fingertips, I felt faint patterns etched into stone. Not in gold, but in indigo, so dark it nearly vanished against the rock.

I traced the edge of one thin coil with my fingertips. It was like a thread woven directly into the floor."It is not hidden in the walls!" I whispered. "It is in the floor!"Asya ran and knelt beside me.

We both began tearing at the seams in the stone—loosened rock and ancient cracks. Asya found a crevice, deeper than the others, right where we had been standing previously. Her hand slipped into it and she gasped."Amara." Her voice shook. "I feel it. It is...soft."Together we pulled, and the section of floor gave way like peeling back bark from a tree. There it was.Tightly folded, dormant, a carpet of indigo and gold! Old and tattered and laying next to a...

"The Sword of Honor?" I breathed, recognizing the hilt and scabbard. Reaching for it, I unsheathed it and gasped as a scroll fell out of it. Asya bent to grab the scroll as I stared at the blade inlaid with gold engravings. Animals wrought in pure gold seemed to prowl across the steel, catching what little light remained in the chamber. Each creature—lion, falcon, serpent, deer—appeared poised to leap from the metal. The intricate goldwork danced as I tilted the sword slightly. It was then that another engraving caught my eye. The name engraved into the base. Sayla.

No. This was not just any sword.

"Mother's sword," I breathed in surprise. "We thought she had lost it on her final assignment before she had you." I turned to look at Asya, who was clutching the scroll to her chest, lips white.

"She-she came back here. It was her final act before leaving the Blade-Callers," Asya explained. Her lips trembled as she spoke. Something in that scroll had left her reeling.

The sound of the explosion echoed ominously through the cavern, rattling the stones overhead and sending more debris crashing down around us. My heart raced as I gripped the hilt of the sword, recognizing its weight both as a weapon and as a symbol of my mother's legacy.

There was no time to read the scroll. We had to get out.

But as we tried to navigate through the cavern falling in on itself, rubble barring our path from all around us, one thing became startlingly clear.

"We cannot escape!" Asya exclaimed, clutching the scroll in one hand whilst cradling the rolled up carpet in the other.

I reached for the carpet, laying it flat out on the floor. Ancient and weathered, its once-vibrant indigo had darkened to midnight, its golden threads dulled by centuries. Frayed edges whispered of forgotten journeys, torn patches revealing it had barely survived the test of time.

"I do not think this...is in any position to carry us," Asya finally stated, eyeing the carpet critically.

I had to agree. But if there was anything this journey had taught me, it was to never give up.

I touched it and a rush of power flooded my fingertips.

The gold threads began to pulse faintly like veins. As if...the carpet were alive.

And then they began to move, forming words in the center of the carpet. *I am worn not on the head, but in the soul.I leave no jewels, but I shape the course of kings.I am not given—I am chosen, again and again.Teachers, healers, warriors, parents, and prophets have carried me not for glory, but for the future they may never witness.You must possess it to wield me—yet once you do, you may never set me down.*

What am I?

The carpet shuddered. It was breathing.And it was watching. No. It was *listeni ng.*My mouth went dry. I knew the answer, but it was not something you could fake.Asya looked at me, her eyes wide as rubble rained down around us.

"We are going to die under a mountain because we did not read more poetry growing up."I looked away, focusing on the carpet.

"Duty," I said with absolute finality, the word hanging in the air between us as thunder cracked through the cavern and an avalanche of stone crashed down mere feet away.

A shimmer pulsed from its center, like sunlight rippling over water. Threads began to twitch, pulling taut. The fabric stiffened, colors deepening like ink dropped into clear water.Dull midnight indigo lightened to royal purple, gold brightened into firelit brilliance. Dust fled from it in all directions. The worn patterns unraveled and rewove themselves into symbols of suns, rivers, wings, and eyes, blooming across its surface like memory returning to flesh. My eyes widened as I realized, this was the carpet Yasmin had woven with such diligence.What had once looked ancient and broken now gleamed as if freshly woven by unseen hands. The edges curled upward gently, fluttering with their own will.Then it rose from the floor, hovering, ageless. Awake. Yasmin's voice returned, soft as silk."M any have craved thrones. Few have embraced duty.You have done both—and that is why the carpet listens.

The carpet obeys only the pure of heart.You are daughters of Sayla...and your hearts are truly pure."

More stones rained down around us, coming down hard and fast.

"It is caving in!" Asya yelled, throwing an arm around my shoulders as she jumped onto the carpet and pulled me along.

We braced ourselves, half expecting it to fall to the ground with a thump under our weight but instead...instead, it lifted us upward. The air around us shimmered and crackled as if we were being transported through the threads of time itself.It surged beneath us—not like riding a horse or a ship, but like being caught in a tide that knew exactly where to go. Threads beneath our legs hummed with life.We soared upward.The ceiling gave way as we flew through it in one great burst of speed so fast that even to my Lycan eyes it was a blur. The world burst open above us, a rush of cold air slamming into my chest. My stomach plummeted as we rose ever higher. Smoke spiraled around me as we left the collapsing part of the fort behind us. We did not fall. We flew.I could feel the carpet beneath me, reading our fear, our need, our purpose.

*I had to get to Zayed.*The fortress fell away below us, the entire right half collapsing slowly like a dying beast.But we? We rose.

Chapter 22

Zayed's POV

"Zayed!"

I heard her voice right as I began to move to walk through the fire.

My Lycan turned in surprise, and for the briefest moment, I thought it was a mirage before me.

Amara rushed toward me from the sky overhead, with Asya behind her. The Sword of Honor flashed gold in Amara's grip as she descended into the chaos atop the carpet. With one fluid motion, she cleaved through an attacker, then circled her weapon overhead, blade whirling to meet the men converging behind her. Beside her, Asya nocked and loosed arrows in rapid succession, each finding its mark among the enemy ranks.

"Sayla sent help even from the grave. They have come to help us!" cried out an elderly soldier, grunting as he speared through one of Kadin's men.

My eyebrows knitted together, recognizing the name instantly. What did Amara's mother have to do with any of this?

Right as I moved to go toward my love, who was weaving through our enemies and cutting them down with efficient speed, white-hot agony ripped through my back and burst through my chest like molten metal poured into my veins. I looked down in disbelief to see a silver blade jutting from between my ribs, its polished surface now slick with crimson. The metal gleamed obscenely in the sunlight, my own heartbeat sending fresh pulses of blood to coat the intricate engravings along its edge.

I turned to throw off my attacker who had stabbed me in the back, the blade missing my heart by what seemed to be a hairsbreadth, only to still in shock when my eyes fell on—

"SALIM!" Asya yelled in anger, jumping off the carpet and tackling him in anger right as he prepared to strike me with a second blade in his left hand.

She landed atop him with a hard thud.

"You betrayed us!" she screamed, a blade held to his neck.

"I had to! I was promised riches beyond my wildest imaginings by King Kadin!" He rasped out the words as Asya held her blade dangerously close to his neck.

I fell forward onto the magic carpet as Amara's hands pushed down on my wound in an attempt to staunch the blood flowing out of me in rivulets.

"No, no, no," Amara muttered, shaking her head. "Zayed...it is merely silver. You have to heal! Remember, our Lycans are...together now. Silver does not hurt ...Zayed...Zayed!" Her voice was garbled, and I could not understand what she was saying.

I turned to look at Asya, still on top of Salim, her face contorted in fury. He must have gotten word to Kadin's men somehow that we were here. But how did they infiltrate Lamar's palace so easily? There must be spies within as well.

"The dagger is dipped in poison. He will die soon! And I will be rich!" Salim cackled insanely.

Asya reared back and punched him, making his head snap to the side violently.

I tried to scream for Asya to leave. For the man with one eye, Darrius, was nearing her from the side. She was too engrossed in threatening to kill her ex. However, more blood spilled forth from my mouth, blocking my words so that only a feeble gurgling sound escaped. Luckily, the Bashe arrived with a hiss that echoed through the chaos around us. Its green scales glinted menacingly against the fire's light as it surged toward Darrius, who was aiming his blade at Asya. The Bashe's maw opened to eat him and snapped over air. I blinked, wondering if the blood loss made me hallucinate. Just like that, Darrius had disappeared as if he had been nothing but a spectral figure. The Bashe's fangs closed over air a second time, snapping together in frustration. Even the Bashe was confused.

Another explosion ripped through the flaming wall I had been ready to walk into to find Amara, sending molten debris arcing through the smoke-choked air. A wave of blistering heat washed over us as fire roared toward our position, a hungry orange-gold beast with writhing tendrils that reached for our flesh. Asya was in its direct path.

"Sister!" Amara cried out.

But the Bashe laid its form around her right as its tail coiled itself around mine and Amara's form. The demon serpent took the brunt of the blazing onslaught. There was ringing in my ears as my vision dimmed momentarily.

"Focus, Zayed. Use our bond to heal yourself!" Amara's voice seemed to come from far away, distant yet unmistakable as it reached me in the depths of my fading consciousness.

I felt it, felt our bond, felt her Lycan calling to mine. Helping to heal me.

My eyes snapped open to see Amara, furtive eyes on me.

"Ren!" Asya gasped.

We both looked as one to find Salim had vanished. So had the demon serpent. In his place, Asya cradled Ren, the same soldier whose flesh had met her arrow during our capture.

"It was Ren!" Her arms wrapped around his torso as she tried to drag him away from the battle. "The serpent was Ren!" she gasped out in disbelief, trying to pull him along. That was why Lamar valued Ren. He was a shifter! Wolf shifters I was familiar with. But this was the first I had heard of men being able to shift into demon serpents.

Fire erupted around us, and now part of the tribal warriors were attempting to douse the flames. Kadin's men were still fighting, still trying to win, though their numbers had dwindled.

Asya looked up at Amara and me, eyes firm.

"Amara, leave. Take Zayed and do what must be done." She turned then, notching her bow and arrow. "I will stay here to help Chieftain Lamar."

"But—"

"Go, Amara! Stop Kadin! We both know he will send an army sooner rather than later to this fortress. Mother had two daughters. You go help our kingdom while I help the tribe of her friend. Obviously, both were dear to her. We both have our own part to play."

I knew Amara did not want to leave Asya. But her sister was right.

I leaned over the carpet, coughing up blood before looking at my wife. Tears shimmered in her eyes as she exchanged one last glance with her sister. Sometimes I was envious of that bond between siblings, something I had never experienced. The bond the two had was so deeply rooted that even silence between them held meaning. They did not need to explain their pain, their loyalty, or their love—it was written in years of shared memories, whispered arguments, inside jokes, and griefs no one else would ever fully understand.

And watching it, I could not help but feel like a stranger to something I had never been given but somehow still mourned.

"Go!" Asya urged again, her voice steady but laced with an urgency that pierced through the tumult. Loran arrived, still in wolf form, crouching protectively over Ren and Asya. "I will catch up later. I promise, sister!"

Finally, Amara nodded, and we were suddenly soaring up into the sky, away from the fire and smoke and chaos. The scent of ash and burning wood trailed behind. My heart pounded in sync with the carpet's rhythmic movements. The threads beneath me pulsed like a heartbeat, alive with ancient magic. We were not riding it. No, it was carrying us, guiding us through the sky like a current knows how to cradle a leaf. The wind kissed my face, cool and sharp, yet pain throbbed inside my chest as more blood spilled from my body.

"Your bleeding has slowed somewhat," Amara whispered, clasping my hand in hers firmly. She pressed her cool lips to my forehead as she cradled my head in her lap. "Stay with me, my love."

I brought my left hand to her cheek, "I am here," I murmured, my voice barely audible above the rush of wind.

I closed my eyes, allowing her presence to envelop me. Our hearts had intertwined in ways I could have never comprehended; we were two threads woven into a single tapestry.

"Feel our bond, let it heal you," Amara whispered.

Her presence was a beacon, drawing me back from the brink of darkness threatening to swallow me whole. With every heartbeat, I felt our connection. I focused on that bond, feeling it ripple through us, merging our strengths, our lycan energies intertwining, fueling the healing process. The pain from the hot metal of the blade began to recede.

The pulsing of the carpet beneath us matched the rhythm of my heart, as if it too recognized the power of our union and sought to aid us.

"I love you more than all the grains of sand in the vast desert of Elamaria. We are going to win this. We are going to take down Kadin, and...Zayed, do you hear me?!" she screamed.

The icy grip of pain was receding, but in its place, a healing sleep was taking over.

Her arms wrapped frantically around me, and I sent her reassurance through our bond. I would be fine. But my Lycan demanded sleep to recuperate from the severe injury. A stab through the chest was not something that could heal within minutes. Then there was the matter of my body fighting off whatever poison Salim had laced his dagger with.

"Sleep, my love," Amara whispered, realizing my body would heal. She gently combed her fingers through my hair. "Sleep and when you awaken, we will reclaim what is rightfully ours. We will fulfill our duty to our people and give them a safe home once again."

Amara's POV

Getting word to my father was harder than I had expected. While the carpet took us wherever I wanted, it did not guarantee stealth. And in the kingdom of Elamaria, Zayed and I were wanted rebel leaders. However, somehow, I managed.

As Zayed lay in a tent on the outskirts of the city of Ilm, his body wrought with fever, I managed to get word to the right people. Queen Seraphina, my father, Ashad, and even Chieftain Lamar.

They all would hopefully be ready to deploy troops. I wondered if any other nobles were still on Zayed's side, if they would also rally behind us. That task was left to my father and Ashad. For now, I had to make sure my next move worked meticulously.

Hopefully, the plan I was formulating in my mind would buy enough time for our allies to surround the palace. I did not want to lay siege to my home, but if it had to be done to take down Kadin, so be it. It was now more than clear that Harun's descendants were working through Kadin. A noble perhaps? Who was Darrius? How had he managed to disappear when Ren, in his serpent form, tried to eat him? He knew magic, of course. But was he the man with red eyes we had been warned of?

Or was it Zayed's uncle, his mother's brother, we had to be wary of? There were so many questions, and I felt as if I were lost at sea. My eyes strayed to the partially open tent flap to peer into the night. The sky seemed to mock me as the stars twinkled down on us. I could almost feel the weight of every star, each one perhaps a wish unfulfilled.

My mind strayed to Asya, and worry for her gnawed at my insides. How was my sister doing? Part of me wanted to take the magic carpet and go back to her. But I had to trust that she could hold her own.

Sighing, I glanced again at Zayed. His breathing had evened out. I had done my best to administer antidotes for various poisons, but my access to supplies was limited to what I had stockpiled before we began our journey to Chieftain Lamar's fortress.

"Come back to me, my love," I murmured, reaching out a hand to comb it through his hair. "I would trade every star in the sky to see you awake again."

His body lay still, yet I felt a pulse of energy surge between us. It vibrated with an intensity that thrummed through my fingertips as I stroked his hair. I squeezed his hand, feeling the warmth of our bond wrap around me like a cloak.

"I will fight for you, Zayed," I promised softly, letting the tears I had been holding back flow freely. "I will fight for us."

I could feel my husband's consciousness flickering between realms. As I gazed down at his pale form, I could not shake the feeling that my mere presence was a lighthouse in the storm for him, guiding him back to me.

A soft rustle caught my attention, drawing my gaze from Zayed's peaceful face. My heart quickened, and I instinctively reached for the hilt of the sword resting beside me. Slowly, I crept outside, careful to remain low and concealed in the shadows of the night.

Someone—or something—was here. Slowly, I moved farther away from the tent in hopes that whatever was here would follow me rather than aim for my injured husband inside.

I kept my eyes honed in on the direction I believed to have heard movement. Finally, a figure emerged from the deepening shadows—a cloaked silhouette, the folds of black fabric swirling like smoke around them.

The figure stepped closer, the air turning so cold that I could see my own breath. It was as if I were back in the mountains. My breath caught as I realized that whatever stood before me was not entirely human.

A bony hand, with fingertips as dark as night, pushed back the dark hood slightly to reveal a face as ancient as the desert itself. Skin like parchment, eyes clouded white yet knowing, and black hair streaked with gray peeked out from beneath the hood. All was eerily still around me, and I realized that her presence made even the night hold its breath.

Her head snapped toward me with unnatural precision, milky eyes fixing on mine despite their blindness. Lips peeled back from bare gums in what could only be described as a predator's smile.

She stepped closer, and I could smell the forest on her. Moss, smoke, and something old, something that hummed with forgotten magic.

I knew her. Even before she spoke, *I knew.* I stood from my crouching position, refusing to bow, and held my golden blade steady.

"You are the old crone of the forest," I breathed, puffs of visible air emitting from my lips as I spoke. I recalled Elvira's story. "The one who taught Elvira magic."

The crone's laugh was dry and papery, like wind through dead reeds.

"Clever queen, but your husband is cursed. I come to tell you to prepare for the worst."

Her words slithered into the air like venomous serpents, each syllable dripping with ancient, malevolent magic. It poured out of her and toward me like noxious fumes. The suffocating darkness clawed at my skin, invading my lungs with each desperate breath, threatening to drown me in its putrid, unholy essence.

"Speak plainly. Why have you come?" I asked, though the answer already trembled at the edge of my mind.

Her grin widened, became more macabre. *"What will you rule, when you win the war? Your king is cursed, your lands decay, The kingdom you love will fade away."*

I tightened my hand around the hilt of my blade. It was exactly as I thought. "What do you want in exchange for breaking the curse?"

I swallowed audibly. She was not here to help.

Her voice lilted like a song—half prophecy, half warning.

"Learn the dark to set things right. I can help you win the fight."

"You want to teach me magic, so that I may break the curse," I deduced. My eyes hardened, I lifted my sword higher. "But at what price?"

She laughed—a brittle sound that sent shivers crawling up my spine. Every word she spoke settled in the air between us before grating against my skin. The sensation was like venomous spiders crawling over every inch of my body. *"You wish to mend what fate has spun, But every gift demands what is won. My gift must be repaid, Amara."*

She pointed a black-tipped finger at me. It was then that I noticed that around her wrist hung charms of bone, feathers, and teeth that whispered against one another.

"Break his curse, and the land shall bloom, The rivers will flow, dispelling gloom. But every light must cast a shade— A price in pain must still be paid."

"What is the price?" I demanded, not able to keep up with her riddles. "Speak plainly!" I exclaimed.

The old crone tilted her head, her milky eyes glittering with cruel amusement. *"For life to heal, something must die. The kingdom you seek to free from blight— Will burn what is dearest in the night."*

I recalled Elvira's story. She had lost her baby, the one thing that had been dearest to her.

"I cannot sacrifice the life of a loved one," I finally stated.

There had to be another way! The right way!

She cackled, the sound so macabre it was like rattling teeth inside a skull. I grit my own teeth against the sound, against the suffocating darkness clawing at my skin, invading my lungs with each desperate breath, threatening to drown me in its putrid, unholy essence.

"Learn the dark to set things right. For who would wear a crown so fine, When all that is left is dust and twine?"

She took a step back, her cloak billowing in a nonexistent breeze as shadows began to spiral around her.

Then, with a whisper, like smoke fleeing the flame, she was gone.

Only her words lingered, curling through the night like an incantation:

"Save your king or save your soul, The path you choose will take its toll."

Chapter 23

Zayed's POV Warm hands gently cupped my cheek before cradling my head. I tried to open my eyes, but it was as if they were sealed with honey, and my limbs might as well have been carved from stone.

"Drink," her soft voice beseeched me, floating through the haze in my mind, and I obeyed without question. As the cool liquid slid down my parched throat, a sharp citrus tang lingered on my tongue, which denoted this was some healing concoction, not simple water.

"The healing herbs should help quell the fever," Amara murmured, hands now trailing down to my chest where a bandage covered my wound.I sucked in a sharp breath when she splayed her hand, palm down, against my abdomen."The wound has healed," Amara muttered, relief evident in her voice.I finally managed to peel open my eyes to find her hovering over me, exhaustion etched into the lines of her face. She must have tended to my wounds without rest and kept vigil over me for only the goddess knew how long.My beautiful, perfect wife. Even now, in her disheveled and worried state, she was the most beautiful vision to wake up to. She was my radiant, strong queen.

"Do not overexert yourself," Amara warned cautiously, her anxious eyes meeting mine. "Does this hurt?" she asked, moving her hands over my bare abdomen, feeling my muscles tense beneath her touch .

"No, *jaan*, it does not," I rasped out, reaching out to bring her to me in a hug.

"Then why do you tense up in such a way when I touch you?" Amara queried, her voice tight with worry. Nevertheless, she returned my hug, melting against me as if this was where she belonged. Her body draped over mine as she rested her head on my chest. She released a sigh that seemed to release days of fear, her palms pressed flat against the bedding on either side of me, careful to hover rather than press her weight onto my healing body.

I looked down at my wife with a heavy lidded gaze and feline smile."I do not tense up due to pain," I clarified, moving in one swift motion so that she was now pinned under me.Amara let out a surprised gasp when she sensed my hardening member against her thigh.I allowed my nose to nuzzle against her neck briefly, breathing her in and enjoying this moment. Because I knew this would be the last time I held her like this for awhile.

"I was so worried." She sighed, arms going around me. "Hold me, Zayed. Hold me as if everything is going to be alright."

I gently tilted her chin, compelling her gaze to meet mine,"It will be," I vowed, before placing a kiss on her soft, wonderful lips.

A rustling outside the tent sent ice through my veins. My body, forgetting its weakness, moved on instinct, shielding Amara behind me as my muscles coiled tight, ready to spring despite my wounds.

"Wait," Amara whispered, her fingers circling my wrist from behind with surprising strength. "Your body needs rest. The fever only broke a few hours ago."

The fabric of our tent whispered again with movement from outside. I allowed my eyes to glow red. If needed, I would shift into my Lycan. I did not attempt to stop an instinctive growl from emitting through my lips. It was a warning to any approaching enemy. Who was here with us in this vast desert?

"Zayed, do not attack," Amara warned from behind me, a hand going over my arm as if to restrain me. "You have been in and out of consciousness for three days."

I stilled in absolute shock. Three days? What might have happened in that time?"Baba arrived earlier today with Queen Serafina's troops. Asya is on her way. We have a plan, but..." Amara trailed off hesitantly right as Idris entered the tent

.

"You are awake," Idris commented, his face pale and haggard.His eyes went to Amara, who I still shielded with my body.

"That is good. We can put the plan in motion now." Idris' posture relaxed.

"What plan?" I asked.

Idris looked at Amara before looking at me.

"The one where you challenge Kadin to a battle to the death to take back your crown."

I cocked my head to the side. That was easier said than done.

"And how do you propose I get into the castle to do this? Kadin will not let us anywhere near him for an opportunity to do that."

"You will have to sneak in, Zayed. Amara has a plan."

I glanced at Amara and then at Idris.

"And how does my wife plan to get me inside the palace?

"You are not going into the castle alone," Amara spoke up, moving forward to stand beside me and smile at her father. "We go in as traders, selling goods."

I scoffed, eyes on Amara.

"And what goods are we selling? Weapons? Jewels? Silks? None of those things will appeal to Kadin." My eyes went to her sword, the Sword of Honor, laying on the ground in our tent. It was sheathed now, but it was a magnificent weapon. There was a story there I had to ask Amara about. But right now, this plan she had formulated was more important to discuss.

Because there was no possible, viable plan in existence that could enable us to parade as traders and sneak into the palace.

Amara smiled, her white teeth glinting in the fading evening sun that peeked through the flap in the tent. For a minute, her fatigue seemed to vanish.

Her voice oozed pride when she spoke her next words. Words that made my lycan go insane.

"You will be posing as a trader and selling me, in disguise, as a concubine to Kadin."

Amara's POV

I finished sharing the entirety of my plan with Zayed as we sat, crosslegged, across from each other on the floor of the tent. Asya was on her way with two other women. We would all go into the palace with Zayed, who would pose as a trader looking to sell us off. It was the only way to get into the palace. If the rumours were anything to go by, Kadin loved amassing concubines for his harem.

Baba had made a quick exit as soon as Zayed's thunderous refusal echoed off the tent walls, leaving me alone to face the storm of his anger.

"You stay here. I will go with Asya and the other two women she brings with her," Zayed gritted out.

I shook my head, hands on my hips.

"Zayed, we are a team. And I am your queen. I either ride into battle with you, by your side, or we do not go at all."

He looked away, his hand flexing over the hilt of my mother's sword. Zayed's jaw was tight, anger radiating off him like heat from a furnace.

At some point, whilst explaining my plan, I had also managed to convey to him everything regarding the magic carpet and my mother.

He had to understand. I was part of this whether he wanted me to be or not. This was my mother's legacy. Zayed also assured me that his uncle from his mother's side did not have red eyes or a ruby ring. He explained his father had many prospective wedding proposals from many nobles. But eventually, Zayed's mother had been decided on. Perhaps the man with red eyes and ruby ring was a noble in our court. We had yet to ferret him out as Harun's descendant.

Regardless, right now I had to convince Zayed to follow through with my plan. For one, he was certain that Kadin would recognize me. But my face would be covered. Also, he would not even be involved in the purchasing of the concubines.

From what we knew, he had deployed others on his behalf to deal with the harem and his concubines. We simply needed a way in, and this was a way into the palace. After that, Zayed would challenge Kadin. Besides, there were women prettier than me who would grab Kadin's attention. I was not there to be a distraction. That would be the job of one of the women Asya was bringing with her.

"I understand that this is important to you. Your mother was a spy for my grandfather," Zayed stated. "But do you honestly think I would let you go to Kadin? To that monster's clutches?" he growled, his voice deep and resonant. "Amara, he will see through this charade! He will not hesitate to take what he wants. He will hurt you!"

"I know the risks," I countered, my resolve hardening even further. "But you must realize, this is our only chance to turn the winds in our favor. Kadin has an army, and while we gather our forces, he will remain untouchable, holed up in the palace." I gestured to the heavy canvas of the tent, our illusions surrounding us, trapping us in this bubble of fake peace and tranquility. "Zayed, the world outside us is suffering. And it will take time for all the troops to gather and formulate a plan of attack. Time we do not have. Even now, Kadin plans to storm Chieftain Lamar's fort. And though the carpet is safe with me, we cannot let them be lambs for slaughter. Besides, the kingdom is suffering greatly under Kadin's reign."

I shuddered, recalling what Baba told me. People were starving. And Kadin was hoarding all the food for himself. Famine and drought ravaged the kingdom of Elamaria. The curse strangled our people like a serpent, crushing the life from our kingdom while Kadin watched them writhe and gasp their final breaths. He was indifferent to their plight.

"I know you are upset I did not come for you in the cherry blossom garden when I was told to, but—"

"You think that is why I am angry?" Zayed asked in disbelief. He shook his head. "Amara, I understand that you chose to go find the carpet. It was the right thing to do. Lamar might have thought you were there among his women, but I understand why you were not. You did what had to be done." He passed a hand over his face and took a great big exhale before handing the Sword of Honor back to me.

"It still feels unbelievable that the story of Yasmin and Farid is rooted in truth, not merely a children's fairytale." He shook his head before meeting my gaze.

"She was preparing you," he stated with finality. "Your mother was preparing you, should the need arise."

"Do you think she knew...that this would happen?" I queried, my voice barely above a whisper as the glow of the full moon seeped through the open flap of our tent and reflected off Zayed's warm brown skin. "Maybe," he mused.

I gripped my mother's sword tighter in my hand, feeling its history whispering into the depths of my soul.

"Your mother was a harbinger of peace. A boon to our kingdom. And it is no wonder that such a remarkable woman bore two such extraordinary daughters," Zayed said with a small smile. Pride, fierce and profound, was laced in every word. "Maybe she did not expect her daughter to be the Blade-Caller who found the magic carpet, but she had a contingency plan in place to protect everyone," he added. "We have the carpet and the blade. They are gifts that carry the potential to shift the fate of this war in our favor. But I do not want you putting yourself at risk, Amara. We will win."

I gazed at Zayed in concern. We would win, but the curse loomed over us like a harbinger of death. The grim reaper, willing to destroy everything we had fought for. Winning would not get rid of the famine or drought.

"What is it, *jaan*?" he queried.

I was silent for a moment, but right as I opened my mouth to speak my concerns, the tent flaps drew both our attention. A shadow fell across the entrance. I turned to look at the new intruder.

"Ashad!" I explained to Zayed, moving to stand and rush to him.

But Zayed placed an arm out to stop me. His eyes glowed red and my stomach plummeted.

"I do not trust him," he grunted, eyes on Ashad, who stood at the entrance to our tent. "I murdered his brother."

And then Zayed let out a low growl of warning, a warning for Ashad to run.

Chapter 24

Zayed's POV

I was going to kill this man and feast on his entrails, but Amara was pleading with me not to harm him.

"We have already discussed his brother while you were recuperating from your wound!" Amara huffed, trying to move past me. "He arrived with Baba and the other rebels that follow you."

That did not assuage my distrust of him. I would not budge and continued to block her way. I was not letting my wife near this man.

"I am sorry for what Shain did," Ashad said mournfully, eyes on his best friend before switching to gaze at me. "I have apologized to Amara many times already for his part in all of this." Still I was wary. We had been betrayed too many times.

Ashad merely stood where he was and spoke solemnly to us.

"I have been in touch with our informant from inside the palace. She will meet you tomorrow morning on the outskirts of the palace, where she will guide you," Ashad explained. "I wish I could offer troops from my own kingdom, Amara, but my brother's death has complicated things. Father will not talk to my uncle to support Zayed. Salim got word to Kadin's people that Zayed murdered my brother. Of course, Kadin immediately sent word to my father and offered an alliance with him. I—" Ashad hung his head. "There were rumours about my brother. But I always thought they were simply rumours. I should not have turned a blind eye to the accusations."

He sounded broken. And guilty. He should be. If he had taken the accusations more seriously, he could have stopped his brother from hurting countless women.

"How can we be sure you are trustworthy?" I challenged, eyes on Ashad. "I killed your brother. You might be seeking revenge."

Ashad looked at me, aghast.

"He assaulted my best friend and most likely countless other women. I do not fault you for what you did."

"Still," I insisted, crossing my arms and looking at Ashad with a hard glance. "I do not want you inside the palace with us. Only Amara and I will go inside, along with a few females. Asya will go with us as well." She was the only other person I could trust implicitly.

"Asya cannot go," Ashad said quickly, too quickly.

I narrowed my eyes at him. Why was Asya unable to go with us?

"For that matter, how can we know our informant from inside the palace is trustworthy?" Amara asked challengingly.

Ashad met my eyes as he answered Amara's question. "When you see her, you will know why she is the most trustworthy."

When we saw her? Who was she?

"What is taking Asya so long to arrive?" Amara queried. "I sent the magic carpet to get her."

I noticed the way Ashad shifted uncomfortably, as if he were hiding something. My eyes remained on him, scrutinizing his movements. What was he hiding?

"Asya had some injuries during the fight. She needed time to recuperate as well. They were able to overpower Kadin's fighters after you left, but—" Ashad stopped short, swallowing hard.

"But what?" Amara pressed.

"You will know when you see your sister. She will explain it all. For now, we must move forward with the plan."

I heaved a sigh of consternation. I did not like Amara's plan.

Not many men would be keen to pose as a mere tradesman, looking to sell his wife and a few other females into Kadin's harem.

Once night fell, and when they least expected it, I would shun my disguise and challenge Kadin to the death. Challenge him for the crown. Amara would open the gates from the inside to let troops sent by Serafina and Chieftain Lamar into the palace. We would surround Kadin and his fighters from all sides in hopes that he would either surrender or take my challenge. For refusing my challenge in front of so many witnesses would deem him unworthy. However, if he did refuse the challenge, we would have troops as a backup plan to help us fight him and his men.

I would, of course, defeat and kill Kadin.

It was actually a very good plan. But I did not want Amara inside the palace. I did not want her posing as a concubine for Kadin either.

My blood boiled at the mere thought. But my eyes went to Amara, whose stance permeated determination. And I relented.

Because she was never meant to be hidden. She was born to stand beside me, not behind.

Marriage, or any relationship, is not about shielding the one you love. It is about standing equal, even when every instinct in your body screams to keep them safe.

My queen would not wait in silence while her king rode into battle. Amara was the woman who would ride with me with her blade drawn, eyes steady, and heart unflinching.

And though every part of me ached to protect her, I knew this was what respect truly meant. To let her fight. To trust her strength as I trust my own.

If she was to face the storm, then I would face it with her not as her savior, but as her equal.

Amara's POV

It was dawn when we made our way to the outskirts of Ilm with Baba, dressed as peddlers. I wore a dark brown flowing dress with a plain hood to cover my features. Zayed was in a similar garb, carrying a bag of trinkets on his back. Baba tugged along an ancient camel whose eyes had long since dulled with the weight of too many desert journeys. On the camel's back was a tattered bag of fake jewels. We stood, waiting a good distance from the entrance of the city, hiding behind a vast dune.

"Asya is supposed to meet us here with the two women she picked for the mission," I huffed, looking every which way. My eyes fell on tents and encampments in the distance, littered sparsely across the perimeter of my beloved city.

"What..." I trailed off in surprise.

"Due to the famine overtaking Elamaria, Kadin has forbidden anyone who is not born a citizen of Ilm from entering the city. They must go back to the tribes they were born in. But most do not have the funds or the energy to manage the journey," Asya spoke up from our left.

So relieved was I that she was before me in one piece that I did not even get a good look at her until I pulled back from our hug. Her dark hood fell back against her shoulders, revealing her face, and I gasped.

Angry red burns twisted across the left side of her face, forming a jagged scar that began at the corner of her eye, carved down her cheek in a sharp V-shape, and disappeared beneath the collar of her garment, where it continued along her jaw and neck.

"What happened?" I breathed, raising a hand to her face and stopping a hairsbreadth from the ugly red welts and boils.

Asya shrugged, trying to make it seem as if she did not care. But I knew my sister. Her beauty was known far and wide in our city. I looked at her with tears in my eyes.

Asya's eyes flared with defiance, yet the pain in them betrayed her bravado. "It is nothing. There was one final explosion, and I was too close. But I survived, did I not?" Her voice trembled, a mixture of pride and sorrow threading through her words. I could tell she was struggling to mask the pain that surfaced whenever she spoke of her experience.

My heart ached for her. "You are still beautiful, sister. Scars are just marks of strength," I whispered, taking her hand in mine.

Asya nodded, though it was not the confident nod I was used to. "Now you know why I cannot go inside with you as a concubine for sale. For no one wants a scarred woman." She spoke hollowly, as if she spoke in more than one context.

"That is not true," I grit out, gripping her hand tightly in mine. "Any man would be lucky to have you!"

Asya gave me a trembling smile.

"I suppose that is why Chieftain Lamar only promised his troops if I agreed to wed his son."

I gasped, realizing exactly why she had been able to secure his troops.

"No, sister! You sacrificed yourself?"

Asya shook her head. "I did not sacrifice myself, Amara. I tried marrying for love one time. Where did it get me?" She motioned to Zayed, clearly reminding me what Salim had done to him. "Maybe...I am not meant to find love? This is for the best. We now have Chieftain Lamar's troops and his backing. And once you have the throne, it will cement an alliance with the wardens of the carpet. He wants it back, by the way. Chieftain Lamar has made it clear that though you are the one who activated it, it rightfully belongs to his family." Asya sniffed. "He has agreed to give it to me as a wedding gift to reach a compromise."

"So he has given himself a gift. Because giving it to his daughter-in-law means keeping it in his home," Zayed deduced, crossing his arms.

"What need do you have of it once the war is won?" Asya challenged with a raised left brow. It was then that I noticed the tip of her eyebrow had also been singed off. She winced, the pain from the burns causing her expression to fall.

"He does not want us to become too powerful," Zayed deduced, rubbing his chin. Finally, he gave a nod. "Let us get through defeating Kadin first. Once he is defeated, we have no need for unchecked power. Peace is what we aim for. Not war. And if the carpet in my hands makes Lamar uneasy, we shall give it to Asya, who will be the future queen of his tribe and the custodian of the carpet."

I opened my mouth to agree, but a shrill cry from my right made me look beyond the sand dunes we stood behind.

A few feet away, a woman was walking with a toddler and babe wrapped in deep blue blankets clutched to her chest. Her baby was sucking his hand and letting out intermittent wails.

She came forward, spotting us behind the dunes.

"Please," she begged, dropping to her knees as the sun rose high over our heads. Her gaunt face looked up at us beseechingly as her tattered dark clothes rustled against the sand. "I beg you," she whispered, her voice barely audible above her baby's cries. "My name is Verona. I used to live in Ilm. We have gone three days without food. King Kadin banished me for not city-born, but my little ones..." She clutched the wailing infant tighter to her chest while the toddler clung to her skirts. "They were born in Ilm, yet they starve in exile with me. There was no one to care for them." Her cracked lips trembled as she gestured weakly toward the endless dunes beyond. "We have wandered the sands aimlessly, searching for anything to eat."

"Behold, Kadin's rule," Asya stated in disgust. "Starving the citizens of Elamaria."

Asya and I both reached for our skins of water, handing them to the toddler and woman.

The wails of the infant continued as the two drank.

Zayed reached into his bag, pulling out dried meat.

"Here." He handed over the tiny pouch to the starving woman. "Take it."

"Goddess bless you all," Verona sobbed, quickly scarfing down what little food we had given her. She handed a few pieces of meat to her toddler, who began to chew ravenously. It broke my heart to see their emaciated faces and hollowed eyes.

Without hesitation, once she had eaten, the poor woman lifted up her tattered long shirt to nurse her baby, who began to suckle greedily at her breast. "I have not had any milk since yesterday to feed my child. Goddess bless you and shower you with all the world's riches."

"Where is the father of your children?" I asked hesitantly, wondering if he was starving somewhere.

Verona, sitting on the ground cross-legged before me as she fed her baby and took sips of water, looked up at me. Her face was crumpled into a visage of utter despair.

"My husband is dead. He was sent on a mission as part of Kadin's army to hunt down and destroy the rebels. He died at the hands of the rebel leader Zayed. Without our house under the name of a born resident of Ilm, we were evicted."

Behind her, Zayed took a step back, utter shock on his face. I set my lips into a grim line. That was the fact of war. You think you have killed an enemy, but you have taken what someone loved most: a father's hands that built, a husband's arms that held, a son's laughter that filled a home.

"In war, you are not killing enemies. You kill the love that someone was living for," Baba said, standing next to Zayed, weary resignation on his face.

I let my shoulders drop forward before stepping away from the woman. What would she say if she knew we were her husband's killers?

"We must move," Asya urged. "We have an important meeting within the hour."

My last glance back at the poor widow was of her feeding her toddler son strips of meat given by the man who had killed their whole world.

We made it through the gates of Ilm rather quickly, the soldiers giving us a once-over and glancing at our forged papers that Ashad had handed over before bidding us goodbye early this morning.

Asya had brought two females with her, both actual concubines from Lamar's harem.

"He confided to me that he bought them for his son. But the tribal prince had no interest in them," Asya informed me as we walked through the streets of Ilm.

Streets I could hardly recognize. There were no joyful faces shopping casually in the markets. No produce being sold or even silk traders lounging in the bazaars.

It was almost like an eerily deserted ghost town.

"That is why the soldiers said we would not find any business within the city," I breathed.

The few people who I did see on the streets had gaunt, drawn out faces and bags under their eyes. Were these the same colorful streets I had walked down where street performers breathed fire and merchants traded goods? It did not seem like it.

"This is not good," I breathed.

"It is the curse," Zayed added grimly. "It is my fault."

"Your fault?" I exclaimed, incredulous. "You did not conjure Kadin's madness! You had a contingency plan set in place to reserve water and grain! A plan Kadin did not execute due to his thirst for power!"

Zayed's gaze was distant, shadows dancing across his features as he clenched his hands into fists. I could see the weight of responsibility pressing down on him, like an anchor threatening to pull him into the depths of despair. He would not listen to a word I said.

"Do not lose hope, my love," I urged, taking in the dark thoughts in his mind. My Lycan could sense them.

I gripped the hilt of my sword, hidden under the folds of my clothes. "We will fight for them. For every child, every widow. We will bring Kadin down."

Zayed did not reply. We traversed deeper into the heart of Ilm, closer to the palace.

"Ashad said we were to meet her here," I murmured, stepping into an alley not far from the palace. My heart twanged as I recalled that this was the same alleyway where the doctor resided who had treated Baghel.

"You are late," stated a disapproving voice.

I stiffened, looking into the alleyway to my left and seeing a figure stealthily step out of the shadows. She wore a cape of fine beige silk, and jewelled rings glittered over the fingers that gripped the edges of her hood placed over her head. The shadows concealed her features, but I did not need to see her face to know who she was.

And yet, she still drew back her hood to reveal the elaborate pearl necklace adorning her neck, strands going down from her breastbone to her waist.

"Dornia," I hissed, pulling out my dagger on instinct and pointing it at her.

Chapter 25

Amara's POV

Her gaze did not waver, though pain flickered there. "Put that down, child," she murmured. "If I wished to betray you, you would already be in Kadin's dungeons."

Zayed moved first. "Amara," he said softly, laying his hand over mine, gently lowering the blade. "She is not our enemy."

"Not our enemy?" My voice cracked, disbelief and fury lacing the edges.

"You are the one Ashad said was trustworthy," Zayed stated, eyes on Dornia.

Eyes full of...affection? He moved forward, embracing her in a hug.

I watched helplessly, dagger hanging limply in my grasp as Dornia stiffened for a moment, then broke, her body shaking as she clutched him like a mother clutching a lost child returned from the dead.

"My boy," she whispered into his shoulder. "You are safe. You are alive!"

My mouth fell open in shock. This woman...she was the one who had accused me of cheating on Zayed!

"You were the one who wanted me dead!" I whispered fiercely, angry that Zayed was so quick to embrace MY enemy.

Dornia flinched in Zayed's embrace as if I had struck her. Her painted lips trembled, but she slowly extricated herself from Zayed to look me directly in the eye. She stood tall, shoulders squared beneath her silks.

Her voice dropped to a whisper, yet each word struck like a hammer against steel. Purposeful and direct. "Everything I did—every choice—was to protect the only son I have left in this world." Her eyes went to Zayed. "For him, I would move mountains...even if it meant moving the wrong ones."

One jewelled hand came out to rest against his cheek.

"I am sorry, Zayed. I only thought I was helping you to maintain your rule. My biggest fear was seeing the crown fall from your hands."

Zayed gently covered the motherly hand on his face with his own.

A storm of emotion crossed his features—grief and gratitude.

Finally, she lowered her hand, eyes gleaming wet in the dim lighting filtering into the alleyway we were hidden in.

"I am the informant," she stated, looking in my direction. "The one who has been sending word to the rebels. Every message, every warning has come through me. However, I am not privy to everything Kadin plans. I am simply in charge of his harem." Dornia shuddered. "I choose and manage the women. I try to hide as many as I can, so I can protect them from him."

Her hands trembled as she spoke, and she clutched them together in an attempt to still their shaking. Her eyes took on a haunted, far-off look as she continued to speak, rings clicking together. "He has sent Blade-Callers who refused to comply with his orders to be part of his harem, punishing them in the worst way. And any harem girl who refuses Kadin's...demands, he makes examples of them."

Her voice trembled as well now as she spoke of the horrors of King Kadin. "He forces them to dance before his court barefoot, on marble floors dusted with salt until their feet split open and stain the white marble red. And when they slip over their own blood, he laughs. Says the desert has no mercy for prideful women." Bile rose in my throat.

Dornia continued, tears streaking the kohl beneath her eyes. "Some he keeps locked away for days without food or water. Others he parades through the halls with their faces veiled, so no one sees the bruises on their faces. Rather they see only their bodies, bared for his men." Her bottom lip shook. "It is cruel. It is inhumane."Zayed clenched his fists. "And you have stayed through all this?"

"He trusted me due to my friendship with his father. So I took advantage of it to watch. To save what and who I could. To help you return." She reached into her cloak and withdrew a small bundle of linen masks, stitched with intricate gold thread work. They were beautiful and delicate, covering the eye portion but leaving the nose and lower face bare."Disguises. For the women posing as harem girls. Veils will hide the lower portion of your face, Amara, but do not underestimate Kadin. Conceal as much of yourself as you can." Dornia's eyes went to Zayed. "You look different enough, with the long hair and untrimmed beard. But you should wear one too."

Dornia held out a black mask that extended down to cover his nose as well. His untrimmed facial hair would do the rest.

I took the masks from Dornia, ready to don them with the rest of my disguise.

However, I could not help but think...how had Dornia managed to pretend to be complicit to Kadin's cruelties? I surely would have skewered him by now.

Dornia spoke to me then, pulling me back from my thoughts. "You think me a monster," she said quietly. "But tell me, Amara, what would you do if the only way to protect a few was to damn yourself before the many?"

Her question hung heavy in the air like a blade of truth swiping quick and true between us.

Zayed reached out again, resting a hand on her shoulder. "You did what you had to," he murmured. "You always have."

And now I realized that while Dornia might be posing as the perfumed keeper of Kadin's pleasure halls, she was actually a woman fighting a losing war in silence—her battlefield lined with mirrors, concubines, music, and bleeding feet.

"Here are the papers I managed to smuggle from a group of traders who passed by earlier this week. You will pose as traders from the Isle of Varethra."

I started a little at the name. The Isle of Varethra was shrouded in secrecy. The inhabitants were said to worship a goddess of rebirth. In a time when gods walked the earth, the goddess of rebirth was the one who cared for the dying sun each night and lifted it again at dawn. When the gods fell silent and retreated to their heavenly abodes, her isle sank beneath the fog, guarding the last flicker of her divinity. Not many ever reached the isle. And those that did rarely returned home, choosing to reside there for their remaining days.

"How did you manage to get these?" I asked sharply. For such papers would not have been given up by such reclusive traders so easily.

Dornia looked away swiftly.

"We were expecting your arrival. You have allies amongst the soldiers as well. We did what had to be done. It was our only chance to manage a disguise and believable backstory for you."

The pit of my stomach dropped. Were those traders still alive?

But before I could ask, Dornia was quickly handing over a satchel that had been resting at her feet previously. It was brimming with colorful silks.

"Clothes from the Isle of Varethra. Kadin is not a fool. You must dress as if you are from there as well. Zayed, you were taught the customs. I am sure you can teach them." Dornia nodded her head toward us, still standing a few feet behind Zayed.

"I can also aid them in regards to the customs of Varethra," Baba spoke up finally, his voice strong and unwavering. "I know the customs and nuances they observe. We will meet you at the palace in a few hours time as true Varethrans."

"Baba," I gasped, turning to glare at him where he stood, farther off behind the rest of us and in the shadows. "You are too old to go into the palace—"

"If my daughter is rushing head first into danger, I will follow her," he retorted sharply. "I let you go alone into the palace one time, Amara. Never again. We go in together, or we do not go in at all."

"I am perfectly fine with Amara staying back with you," Zayed said gently. "But you need to realize she will not sit idly by in this fight."

Baba's chest puffed out proudly as he stepped into the light.

"And neither will I. I will enter as your assistant, Zayed, and we will free everyone from Kadin's clutches together."

I opened my mouth to argue, the words dying on my lips as I realized the fire in his eyes matched my own determination. Baba was right; he would not stand idly by while his daughter faced potential peril. That was not the man he was. I knew because it was not the type of woman he had raised me to be.

I glanced at Zayed, and he sent me a feeling of reassurance through our bond. He would protect Baba. Besides, the plan did not involve Baba fighting. It was Zayed who would challenge Kadin.

Dornia wordlessly held out a second mask, exactly like Zayed's. I reached out, taking it from her to hand off to Baba.

I closed my eyes, resigning myself to the fact that Baba would go with us.

"Go now, before we are seen here," Dornia hissed. "I will see you before dusk at the palace. You must arrive in the next few hours if you wish the guards to allow you in for an audience with me. They will purposefully make you wait. Be patient, and do not give yourself away."

With those final words, she was gone, like a whisper on the wind.

Zayed's POV

I touched the black mask tied to my face as I looked in the dusty mirror. Dornia was right. It was efficient in hiding my identity. In my dark green shirt and dark brown pants, both articles of clothing clearly smudged with dirt from days of travel, I was already unrecognizable, but this mask, which covered the upper portion of my face, made it nearly impossible to discern my features. I made sure to hide the evil eye necklace under my clothes. It was a talisman I always wore in some shape or form, and I knew it would alert Kadin if he saw it. The evil eye symbol kept Elvira's magic from harming me. Something told me I would need this protection now more than ever.

"Remember, the people of Varethra value artistry above all. You must showcase your love for intricate details, the textures, the colors, the architecture around you." Idris spoke up from behind me. He wore matching drab dark brown attire.

I listened only with one ear as he spoke, my attention drawn to our surroundings as I looked around. We were inside a mud hut with cracks spiderwebbing across the walls like ancient veins. The thatched roof sagged in one corner, yellowed stalks poking through in places. The sitting room barely fit the three of us, its packed dirt floor worn smooth by countless footsteps. A tiny iron stove squatted in the corner, its surface flecked with rust, the scent of old ashes still lingering. The wooden shutter over the window hung brokenly from a single rusted hinge, allowing dusty shafts of golden afternoon light to filter through, illuminating dancing motes in the stale air.

This was the home Amara had grown up in. My wife's childhood home. Nostalgia tugged at the corners of my heart. It was as if I could hear her laughter echoing in the sunlit beams. A rocking chair on one side close to the stove drew my attention. Is that where she would sit as her mother braided her hair and told her stories?

"We would sit on the floor here to eat," Idris spoke up, making me realize he had stopped talking about Varethran culture. He pointed to a small rug on one side of the room. "When their mother became too unwell to move about the house, I set up a tiny bed for her here." Idris pointed to where we stood. "The mirror was here as well so she could easily brush her hair instead of going into the girls' room. I--" Idris hesitated before speaking. "I had hoped the presence of a mirror would spur her to see what her condition was doing to her. She had given into such dark thoughts closer to the end. And no matter what I did..." Idris shuddered, eyes haunted by the past. "I could not bring her back from it." He hung his head.

I placed a hand on Idris' shoulder.

"It is not your fault."

A lump formed in my throat. Amara's mother had been a formidable woman. Her bravery and selflessness lingered in the air around us like the sweet scent of blooming jasmine. I still felt the weight of that legacy; it was woven into the very fabric of who Amara was.

"We are ready," came the sweet voice of my wife.

I turned to look at her, dressed in billowing, dark blue gossamer silk. Layers of midnight-blue tapa cloth wrapped around her like rolling tides. The material was hand-beaten from the inner bark of mulberry trees, as was custom on the Isle of Varethra, then softened and painted in shifting hues of ocean blue and moonlit silver. In the dim light, the faint brushstrokes of waves, stars, and crescents seemed to ripple across it as she moved.

Her top was a long strip of silk and tapa intertwined, crossed over her chest and tied behind her back, leaving her bronze shoulders bare and gleaming. The fabric hugged her breasts and torso like a second skin. An intricately woven sash of pandanus fiber cinched the clothes at her waist before it flared out below in dark blue silk. Deep indigo threads glimmered over the sash with silver embroidery that traced constellations once used by island navigators to find their way home.

The sash's long ends brushed against her thighs, decorated with tiny shells and bits of polished coral that clicked together like soft chimes when she moved. The skirt beneath was layered—thin panels of gossamer silk and tapa cut unevenly so each piece lifted and fell like the surf curling upon the sand.

Her dark hair was gathered loosely to one side in a braid threaded with white hibiscus blossoms, and across the crown of her head was a single line of mother-of-pearl beads that gleamed when she turned. She looked as if she had risen from the sea itself. She was not a child of the sand here, but a daughter of the ocean...a daughter of storms and coral, clothed in the language of waves.

She smiled sweetly at me, holding up her white mask threaded with gold filigree.

"Goddess of the moon, grant me the strength to not claw the eyes out of any men who look at my wife tonight," I said, saying the prayer out loud and watching Amara smile at me as I took the mask from her hands.

She turned her back to me so I could tie the mask. I resisted the urge to kiss across the expanse of her sun-kissed shoulder-blades glowing in the light filtering through the window. I wanted to press my lips against the smoothness of her skin, to sink my teeth into the curve of her neck as I had done countless times before. Her body glowed like polished amber, and It took a great amount of concentrated effort to tie the white silk ribbons behind her head, securing her mask in place.

I knotted the ribbons with deliberate slowness, resisting the urge to press my lips to her spine, to taste the sweetness of her skin where it disappeared beneath the midnight-blue tapa.

"I am not the distraction. You forget we have much prettier women, dressed more elaborately than I, for Kadin's men to look at," Amara muttered, turning now to face me with her mask in place.

She gestured to the two women standing behind her next to Asya.

I had not even noticed them.

The one who was supposed to sing for Kadin, Anya, stood before us, her pale white, creamy skin displayed in dark pink see-through silk. A crown of diamonds and rubies rested on her intricately braided head. The other woman, Sanya, was dressed in dark green. She would be the musician. She could play the Dizi, which was a transverse bamboo flute, held sideways and blown across a hole. We would have both of them showcasing their skills and honoring Varethra.

Amara could not sing, play a musical instrument, dance, or paint. And I found I had never been more thankful than I was at this moment. She did not have any such skill we could use to distract Kadin. I would not need to parade her in front of that vile man. She was mine. All mine.

And though both of the other women did look like visions in their own right, for me, there was no brighter star in the midnight sky than my wife.

"We should go," I said, forcing myself to focus. I met Asya's eyes. "Wait for Amara's signal, and then lead the soldiers into the open gates of the palace."

Asya gave a nod, swallowing audibly. I could tell something was bothering her. But there was no time to ask her what.

"Take these bottles so Kadin does not recognize your scent," Asya said, handing over two indigo vials. "I was able to get the scent-masking bottles from Katarina. She is still held prisoner at your uncle's home. This concoction holds a new scent, as well as what Katarina used. The contents of the vial will mask your current scent and replace it with a new one to fool Kadin and any other shifter enemies within the palace."

Amara slipped her hand into mine and smiled at her sister.

"Thank you, Asya. For everything you have done. And please, dear sister, remember what we talked about on our way to find the carpet. You will always be beautiful."

Asya looked away, her jaw clenching.

I watched Idris go to her. He took Asya's hand between both of his, his voice dropping to a gentle murmur that somehow carried more weight than a shout. "These scars," he said, lightly tracing a fingertip along the ridged flesh at her cheek, "they're a map of your courage, not your shame. The most beautiful gardens grow in soil that has known lightning strikes and forest fires."

His eyes held hers, unflinching. The eyes of a father willing his daughter to understand how special she truly was. "Your heart beats with a warrior's rhythm, Asya. That is what I see when I look at you. Not damaged skin, but a courageous spirit that refused to let others get hurt. And there is no greater beauty in this world than the selflessness you showed at the battle in the mountains."

Asya was still coming to terms with her wounds. It would take time, but we, as her family, would be there to help in any way we could.

Her gaze softened, and for the first time since we encountered her after her injuries, I saw her smile genuinely.

"See you soon, Baba," she whispered, moving to place a kiss on his cheek. Then she turned to face me and Amara. She raised a hand to her brow in salute. Then a hand went to the arrows at her back before faltering and moving to the sword at her hip. It was then that I realized she did not have her bow with her. Had she lost it?

"I will be waiting, Amara. Take back the crown and bring back peace to our kingdom."

With a final look exchanged, we bid our goodbyes and stepped out into the bright sunlight once more. It was time to take back our city and our kingdom.

Amara's POV

People lingered in doorways of the mud houses as we passed. They stared at us with eyes hollowed by hunger and fear.

"Stay close," Zayed whispered, his grip tightening around my hand. I nodded, my heart racing as we navigated through the narrow alleyways, a maze of uncertainty where danger could lurk around any corner. With every step, I recalled Dornia's warnings about Kadin's cruelty, her tales of women silenced beneath the weight of tyranny. The memory of the widow and her children flickered through my mind, urging me onward.

My heart raced as I approached the palace, its towering walls looming overhead like a predator waiting to ensnare its prey. This was my home. And yet, fear wrapped around my heart like a vise, squeezing the breath from my lungs. My eyes scanned the expanse of the castle, eyes resting in the direction of my room. I could not see whatever remained of it, as it was situated at the back of the palace, but still, my eyes seemed to search out the location from where I stood.

"You are the merchants who come with women?" a soldier inquired in a bored voice as we approached the front gates.

"Yes," Zayed replied smoothly, his voice steady as he stepped forward in his black mask, positioning himself between us and the towering gates. "From the Isle of Varethra, we have heard of your king's proclivity for the finer things. We bring gifts of beauty." Zayed moved, gesturing toward us. "Women who can sing like canary-winged parakeets and play musical instruments more soothing than the rhythmic lullaby of the ocean waves. These women are entertainers to keep your king's court intrigued."

The guard squinted at us, his brow furrowing. "You have trade documents?" His voice was low and rough like gravel.

Zayed produced the papers Dornia had given us with practiced ease, presenting them with an air of confidence that I desperately hoped would be enough to convince the guard of our authenticity. The soldier took the documents and examined them closely, his eyes narrowing as he read over the details with a meticulousness that made my heart race.

"Hmm," he muttered, his face unreadable. "And how do I know you will not run off with my king's money, handing off women with no real unique skills?" The guard then leered at us. "Perhaps you should allow me to test one out?" Hungry eyes rested on Anya's ample bosom displayed in her frothy pink dress.

Zayed's jaw tightened, but he remained composed. "We would not dare insult the king by allowing wares meant for him to be used by another. These women are treasures beyond measure," he said smoothly, a confident smile tugging at his lips. His poetic sentences were strung together purposefully, depicting the Varethrans' love of poems and rhymes. "Trained in song and skilled in the musical arts of our people, they will ensure your king's court is never dull. Is that not what a king desires? The attention and admiration of his subjects, as opposed to their ire? And do you not want to be applauded as the harbinger of such unique jewels added to the king's harem? "

The guard's skepticism remained, but deep in his eyes, I saw an ember of interest.

With a flick of his wrist, the guard motioned for us to move forward. "Let them through!" he called to the ones behind him. "If King Kadin does not want them, know that I would gladly buy one from you."

The eagerness in his voice made disgust swirl through my veins. Zayed moved smoothly past the guards, his posture regal despite the peasant garb, and I focused on keeping pace behind him, my stomach tightening with each step. We had made it through the gates and into the courtyard, the same courtyard where I was picked by his uncle to be his bride.

And here I was again, hoping to be picked as a concubine.

The air on the palace grounds was vastly different from the last time I had stepped in here as a mere peasant. Even from the last time I walked these halls as queen. Back then there had been an ominous aura. But now there were vibrations of cruelty. There was a tangible weight of hate pressing down on my chest, heavy with the scent of the burnt incense of fear. The walls around us loomed like silent witnesses to atrocities unseen. Yet, through the haze of dread lacing my mind, I spotted the intricate tapestries placed across the palace's expanse. The colors that once sang with stories were now muted by neglect and cruelty, frayed threads and dust coating the beautiful artwork that had once been in pristine condition.

"Now we wait for an audience with the woman in charge?" Baba asked, clearly referring to Dornia.

The doors to the once opulent courtyard flew open. The same doors I had been led through when chosen by the Grand Vizier.

"No, now you show me what you have brought me and I decide whether I send you back to your wretched isle or hang up your beheaded bodies for the kingdom to see what happens when someone displeases the king," said Kadin as he walked confidently through the doors with his soldiers by his side. My blood froze and breath caught at the sight of him. Last time I saw him, he tried to kill me.

But I stood my ground, banishing the horrid thoughts. Now was not the time to let fear choke me.

He strode through the doors and into the courtyard, with rosy cheeks and a healthy pallor lacking in every single one of his subjects. It was evident that only one person in the kingdom was being well fed.

"What do you think, uncle?"

His eyes slid to a man next to him, dressed as finely as he was. A man with light brown eyes and an iris tinged with blood-red. A ruby ring glinted on his left finger.

"I think if there are any women of worth here, you should gift one to your uncle," the man chortled, red eyes gleaming maliciously as his eyes went to rest on us. "As your only surviving maternal relative, I deserve one."

Chapter 26

Amara's POVI inhaled sharply, realizing with acute clarity what this meant. Kadin's mother was one of the evil mage Harun's descendants. The man with the ruby ring and red eyes was Kadin's uncle! It was completely within the realm of possibility that he had tried to marry his sister off to Zayed's father. And when that had not worked, she had ended up betrothed to Zayed's uncle.

Which meant...

I took a step back involuntarily. Baba's hand came over mine, gripping it reassuringly. I glanced at him. He kept looking ahead, eyes on Kadin. But his grip tightened over my hand, anchoring me.

I had to stay put together. I could not falter. However, it was more than evident that everything Kadin's mother had done had been with the specific aim to invade Lamar's lands and obtain the magic carpet.

The air around me was heavy with unspoken truths, and it was as if a lump of lead had been dropped into my stomach. My mind swirled with the implications. Kadin's mother had woven a web of deceit that ensnared not just her family, but nations as well. It was clear now: Kadin was not merely a tyrant drunk on power; he was a pawn in a far more sinister game, played by those who had planned and plotted for centuries!

But I had to remain calm, even as soldiers fanned out around the courtyard and Kadin smirked at Zayed. His form was cloaked in silk that shimmered under the midday sun.

Kadin's voice broke through the tense silence like steel scraping against stone. "Traders bearing gifts," he taunted, his gaze sweeping over us with an unsettling cruel twist of his lips. His eyes glinted, sharper than the cut of a dagger. "I see you bring fresh offerings for my court. But I shall not pay you until I see the skills possessed by your women. Uncle Jevan, we cannot buy them until we are sure of their worth."

My eyes shifted to Zayed, who had purposefully positioned himself between the two concubines meant to distract Kadin. How could Zayed bear this? His knuckles whitened as he clenched his fists at his sides, jaw muscles twitching beneath his skin. The crown that should have rested on his head now adorned the brow of a usurper, while he—the rightful king—stood before his own throne like a common merchant begging for scraps. Every fiber of his being screamed through our bond for justice, for vengeance, for blood.

Dread twisted inside me, a cold knot in my stomach, as Kadin leaned against a white pillar, crossing his arms nonchalantly.

"As the representatives of the Isle of Varethra, we offer talents befitting the highest courts, mighty King Kadin," my husband stated, voice steady, unwavering. He maintained the slightly lilted accent which was possessed by the Varethrans to mask his true voice which Kadin would have recognized. Pride blossomed in my chest. And anger. It was not fair that Zayed had to pretend to bow and scrape before this man. "Allow them to showcase their skills, and you shall be rewarded with treasures to fill your harem."

"Let us see if these women are worthy of my attention, shall we?" Kadin's eyes darkened, his gaze flitting over the concubines like a hawk looking for wounded prey. "Sing, entertain...prove that you are not another set of ample breasts and empty minds."

I focused on the two women in front of me, feeling the tremor of uncertainty bouncing between us.

But to their credit, both performed, taking turns to showcase their talents. Their performance was astounding. By the time both had finished their performances, the sun had travelled across the sky and dusk was upon us. Kadin now lounged on a throne-like chair which had been brought in by two emaciated servants. Their bones jutted out of their skin grotesquely as they performed Kadin's bidding. It was disgusting. He sat there in good health while his people starved! His loathsome uncle sat next to him on a smaller version of the chair Kadin sat on.

Both men studied the concubines eagerly. Both would have to be fools not to buy women with such talent. But then what about me?

"Is the third one merely for show? Or does she have any artistic talents as well?" Kadin queried from his makeshift throne, eyes going to me where I still stood next to my father.

"She is training, my King," Baba spoke up gruffly. "But should you buy the two, you would have obtained the third. We have no need of her and would willingly throw her in for free."

Kadin threw his head back and laughed.

"So you have a talentless, good-for-nothing woman amongst you that you are looking to get rid of." He shook his head. "She would just be an extra mouth to feed. If she does not possess any talent, she may leave and crawl back to whatever gutter spawned you all. The singer and musician I will buy gladly. But this worthless, empty-eyed parasite can leave with you on the morrow."

Kadin stood briskly. "We have arranged lodging for you as a thank you for bringing such unique treasures to add to my harem. Tomorrow morning, you must leave. Food is scarce in these parts. We cannot feed you for more than a night."

I could not help but smile, glad the veil covered the smirk.

One night was all we needed. We had our way into the palace. It did not matter if he would not buy me.

Vast sums of gold exchanged hands, and Zayed played the part of a greedy merchant quite well. He eagerly took the money, eyes glinting in relief. I knew the real reason. He was relieved I had not caught Kadin's eye.

"Your generosity is noted, my King," Baba replied eagerly, ensuring his voice carried the sweetness of honey.

I forced my expression to remain passive, masking the thrill coursing through my veins. Soon, we would be led inside the palace and our plan could be put into motion.

Female servants, scantily clad so that their protruding ribs were prominent, arrived directing the two concubines to follow them.

The doors had been thrown wide open to the inner sanctum of the palace, the same doors I was led through many months ago as the chosen queen. The two concubines disappeared ahead of us.

But right as Baba, Zayed, and I moved to follow, guards stopped our descent.

"You three are not allowed inside of my palace. Your lodging has been arranged in a nearby inn," Kadin said off-handedly as he turned his back to us.

My stomach plummeted. No. We had to be inside to open the gates. I was the only one who knew this palace well enough to do it. I had to get inside.

"Thank you, my King," Baba replied respectfully. "But we also carry fine silks and trinkets we wish to trade or possibly sell to the nobles in your court."

He was trying to find a way into the palace.

"The nobles in my court have no interest in your baubles unless they can provide an unlimited supply of grain. When famine is wreaking havoc in the kingdom, jewels hold no value to them."

I exchanged a glance with Zayed. The plan would not work unless we were allowed inside the palace. And if these two would not be allowed, I had to get in somehow. The other two women did not know this palace like I did. And once inside, I could manage to get Zayed inside as well.

"Wait, nephew. Why would they bring the third one if she was of no value?" his uncle asked in a raspy voice. He was still sitting in his chair, peering at me.

Kadin paused at the threshold of the open doors, his gaze on the women being led away. He turned to frown at his uncle, annoyed. Obviously Kadin cared more about his new purchases than me.

Panic fluttered in the pit of my stomach, but I quickly quelled it. Jevan had a point. I was a liability they were travelling with if I was of no value.

With a slow, calculated breath, I stepped forward, drawing the attention of both men. "Perhaps I can offer a demonstration," I suggested, keeping my voice steady even as my heart raced. I purposefully altered the pitch of it, so Kadin would not recognize me. The words floated into the air, light but purposeful, like the silk of my costume swirling around me as I moved. "My masters do not think my skill holds value. But maybe, two men of your calibre will think otherwise?" I suggested smoothly.

Kadin turned to look at me now, a flicker of interest sparking in his eyes. "Oh? And what sort of trick do you possess, little one?" He chuckled, amusement lacing his voice. "Can you dance?"

I shook my head.

"Something far more captivating," I replied, my tone confident as I gestured toward the open courtyard. "A show of power, if you will allow it." My heart thudded against my ribcage.

I stepped forward, feeling the weight of their scrutiny but pushing through the wall of apprehension. This was my moment to seize control—to not only prove my worth but to ensure our plan remained intact.

Kadin raised an eyebrow, curiosity piquing beneath his haughty facade. "You, a woman, possess power? Let us see this power," he scoffed, but I detected the slightest tremor in his voice, a flicker of interest.

Even if he expected me to fail, he would enjoy watching me prove him right.

I stood in the courtyard as the sun dipped toward the horizon, staining the sky in molten orange. Servants now moved quietly around us, touching flame to torch after torch until the courtyard flickered with dancing light. Shadows lengthened, stretching like dark fingers across the white marble beneath us.

Kadin now waited near the edge of the fountain, arms crossed, lounging again in his chair, watching me through lashes lowered in that half-amused, half-ominous way. Like a predator waiting to pounce on his prey.

I shot a brief warning glance in Zayed's direction before taking a step forward in his direction.

"Are you done stalling?" Kadin taunted.

I drew a slow breath that filled my lungs to burning and twirled in place, feeling the weight of my body shift as the elaborate blue silk of my skirts caught the evening air. They billowed outward in rippling layers, spilling like a breaking wave across the sun-warmed marble. The movement echoed what I imagined to be the rhythm of the ocean—relentless, hypnotic, and the ancient pulse of something that had existed long before either of us drew breath. I had never seen those vast waters myself, only heard travelers speak of endless blue horizons, but I was certain Kadin had witnessed their power. My fingers trembled slightly at my sides. I only had one chance to get this right.

"No," I said softly, completing my elaborate twirls and finally facing Kadin, silk settling around me like rippling water. "I am preparing."

"For what?"

"To tell you a story about power. And how too much power can be one's downfall."

His brow creased. "Then tell it."

Now he sounded impatient. As if he could not wait to get this over with. I cleared my throat and then I began.

"When I was a child, my grandmother told me a story from the old islands. Long before kingdoms were created, before the first canoe sliced through the sea, there was a girl named Hina'ele. She was born in the season when storms chased each other across the horizon and when the ocean was said to dream."

A cool evening breeze shifted past us as I spoke, lifting the silks of my clothes. Torchlight reflected the edges of my attire as if the fire itself was listening attentively to my story. Kadin leaned forward, intrigued.

"Hina'ele had a gift," I continued. "She could hear the ocean speak. Not in words but in rhythm. In the push and pull of the tide." I moved my arms from side to side, allowing the sway of my skirt to mimic the ocean waves. "In the heartbeat of waves crashing on volcanic stone."

Kadin's expression softened, curiosity pushing aside all skepticism. For that was the power of a good storyteller...the ability to captivate their audience.

"But there was a darkness," I said solemnly. "A spirit that lived deep beneath the reefs. Te Manawa-kai, the Devouring Heart. It fed on fear, on the fear that grew in silence when storms swallowed the sky."

The final torch flared to life behind me, casting the courtyard in warm gold.

"One year, when the storms grew too strong, and Te Manawa-kai had devoured countless islanders who had ventured too far during the storms, the islanders lost hope and cried out for a saviour. That was when the ocean spoke to Hina'ele. It revealed to her the truth of the Devouring Heart. The spirit thrived on despair, and with each life it consumed, it grew stronger, feeding on the darkness that suffocated the islands. Hina'ele understood then: if she faced it with fear, she would be devoured; but if she embraced the power of light, she could defeat Te

Manawa-kai. Hina'ele dove into the depths to confront the creature. She carried nothing—no spear, no shield, nothing to fight with—only the blessing of the fire goddess whom she had prayed to for strength."

Kadin shifted in his seat. "Fire goddess?"

Even his uncle was now leaning forward in his much smaller ornately carved golden chair. I had them where I wanted them. Entranced by my storytelling.

I paused, feigning a slight cough. A servant was quick to hand me a drink. I turned away from my audience, lifting my veil to take a sip, letting the wine soothe my nerves.

"Yes," I said, the cup of wine held tightly in my hand. "For only fire can make the ocean listen."

As I spoke, I stepped toward the nearest torch. Its flame bent toward me, drawn by some unseen breath.

"Hina'ele found Te Manawa-kai in the darkest trench. The spirit roared, sending currents swirling, but she answered with the fire given to her. Fire she carried inside her lungs."

My fingers closed around the wooden shaft of the torch. Heat curled up my wrist.

"And when the spirit lunged," I said softly, "Hina'ele exhaled."

I lifted the torch.

Kadin's eyes widened.

I inhaled deeply, so deep that I barrelled past all my fear, all my doubt. I beckoned one of the concubines over to help me. Handing her the torch, I positioned her so that she stood before me, obscuring my face from Kadin's view.

"And the ocean," I whispered slowly, trying not to waste precious breath, "bowed."

Then I moved my veil aside to take a final sip of wine. I handed the cup of wine to the girl with a smile and took the torch back from her, motioning her to move aside once I was sure the fire and torch would obscure my face from Kadin's view.

Then I blew.

A torrent of flame erupted from my lips, blooming outward like a dragon made of sunlight. The fire curled and roared, illuminating the courtyard and Kadin's stunned expression. The silk of my outfit swirled like living ocean foam around me as I twirled in place. The veil fell back over my face with no one the wiser of my features as they were all still looking at the fiery spectacle lighting up our surroundings.

The blaze finally faded into embers floating on the wind as I completed my twirl and faced them.

"And that, your highness, is how a hero rises to defeat the darkness," I concluded, the last flickers of flame dancing in the air, illuminating me where I stood.

Kadin's astonished expression remained transfixed as he processed what just transpired.

I held my breath, knowing that the fate of our plans hinged on this moment.

The silence was punctured by clapping. His uncle was clapping.

"Bravo! Bravo! Much more intriguing than any song or dance! This one! I want this one!" his uncle crowed delightedly.

"No, Uncle," Kadin stood, peering down at me with an odd expression. "She will belong to my harem."

His eyes went to scrutinize Zayed, then Baba. For a moment, I thought he had caught us in the act. And then his next words sealed my fate.

"You said she was free with the other two. I take you up on your offer."

And then he turned to leave.

I exhaled. It worked. I would be allowed to reside in his harem tonight.

The servant girls moved to guide me inside once Kadin and his uncle were gone.

Zayed's hand clapped over my wrist like a vise.

"Be careful," he hissed.

I did my best to keep my expression neutral, that of a slave taking orders from her master to behave.

"I will get you inside later tonight," I whispered back.

My eyes went to Baba. I wanted to go hug him. Instead, I gave him a reassuring smile. Realizing he would not be able to see my smile, I simply placed a hand over my heart and looked at him with nothing but love in my eyes. He lifted a hand to his brow, as if saluting a soldier going off to war.

The doors shut behind me with a resounding click, Zayed's angry face and Baba's confident smile seared into my mind's eye.

I followed the servant who led me through winding hallways I had to pretend were foreign to me, my mind a whirlwind of thoughts and plans. This was not just a game of survival; it was a quest for liberation, not only for myself but for the countless others trapped within this gilded cage.

They led me past a hallway where my old room had been in and toward a corridor leading into the old harem. It was a wing of the palace I had not visited as queen. My eyes went out to the gardens, clearly visible from the windows, the garden where Zayed and I had kissed under the moonlight when I refused to leave with Ashad.

My heart twanged at the memory.

Mutely, I strode forward, my mind whirring with possibilities of what could go wrong.

Hopefully nothing. Once I was settled into the chambers within the harem, I would wait for nightfall, and then we would strike.

My pulse quickened as we approached the end of the corridor and took a right rather than the left that would lead us closer to the harem. I blinked twice. This was not...my blood chilled as I realized exactly where we were going.

I recognized the heavy wooden door at the end of this hallway, flanked by two guards standing as still as statues. An ominous dread settled over me, weighing down my limbs. "Where are you taking me?" I asked, my voice steady despite the rising panic in my chest.

I knew where. But I had to pretend I did not know.

The servant girl did not reply, keeping her head down.

Right as we reached the door, it was thrown wide open before anyone could even knock.

Kadin lunged forward, his fingers digging into my shoulder with such force I nearly cried out. "My most exquisite prize!" he crowed, his breath hot against my face as he yanked me inside. His eyes gleamed with a predatory hunger that made my skin crawl. "Those fools practically threw you at me," he hissed through a smile that never reached his eyes. "A diamond cast before swine. But I—" His grip tightened until I thought my collarbone might snap. "I recognize exactly what you are worth, my little fire-breather."

My stomach turned to lead as the doors were shut behind me and I was suddenly trapped inside Zayed's room. No, this was not Zayed's room for now. It was the room of King Kadin.

Chapter 27

Amara's POV

Kadin's grip on my shoulder was unyielding, his fingers digging in like a vise as he propelled me further into the room. His laughter echoed off the marble walls, a grotesque symphony that mocked my existence. I forced myself to stand tall, to hide my anger. I squared my shoulders against the invasive heat radiating from his body. The room was opulent, draped in silks that shimmered like deceitful stars under the dim torchlight. My heart raced, not with fear, but with a defiance that surged like fire in my veins.

I wanted to get rid of him. Could I do it? I could try, but the guards standing outside his room would be in here within the blink of an eye.

I had to time it just right. The pit of my stomach dropped at the mere thought of potentially letting him violate me so I could strangle him in his sleep. That was not something I wanted to do.

"It has been so long since I have had a woman with..." His hand trailed down my shoulder to rest on the swell of my hip.

His eyes roved over me like a hungry lion. "Your body is delectable," he murmured, fingers pressing into the softness at my waist, his thumb making small, circular motions that left trails of revulsion across my skin. "No sharp angles, no bones—all woman. You are soft where a woman should be soft, curved where a woman should curve. You are meant to be savored slowly, like the finest honeyed wine." His eyes were now trained on the swell of my breasts.

His voice, thick with desire, made me want to retch. He starved his harem women and dared say that to me?

Woodenly, I allowed him to lead me onto the cushions placed before a low-lying table where food was waiting. So much food. It spilled over in sweet pastries, wine, honeyed snacks and platters of meat.

"Eat, for the king's room is the only place where food is abundantly served still." He laughed, as if this was something to be proud of. He towered over me with a benevolent smile on his face.

"As long as you are the king's favorite, you will not go hungry, fire-breather."

I reached for a salted almond in a golden bowl before me.

I had to fight back the urge to vomit, and yet, I carefully slipped it under my veil and chewed on the dry fruit as if I was starving. My mind raced with possibilities. How was I going to get Zayed inside if I was here with Kadin?

"You like to tell stories," he murmured, dipping to speak into my ear from behind. His hot breath wafted over my ear and neck as he spoke. I blinked as images of being assaulted in the bathing room invaded my senses. I breathed deeply, attempting to remain calm. "Let me tell you one. One that I find you will rather enjoy.

"There was a man, a mage, who possessed the greatest carpet on earth," he began excitedly, standing tall and slowly making his way around the table I sat at. "His name was Harun. But an evil king and queen believed the carpet to be theirs. It was not. It rightfully belonged to Harun. He might have taken it from the queen when she was still a maiden. But it was his right, as he had helped her escape a tyrant who had been after her for the magic carpet." Kadin completed one round and came to a stop to stand behind me again.

"See, this magic carpet possessed great powers. Powers that could be harnessed by the mage Harun. Unfortunately, the queen and king wanted to keep all the magic for themselves. The king was jealous because his wife had loved Harun. He wanted to punish Harun and become more powerful. So he attacked Harun's lair, killed him, and seized the magic carpet. But Harun—" Kadin threw his head back and laughed before continuing, "—Harun was not a fool. He made a ring in which all his power manifested. It also held a piece of his soul, so any of his descendants, and he had many due to his love for women, could use his power to continue his work to retrieve the carpet and take back what was rightfully his.

And now…we can not only take the carpet, we can also use its magic to rule the world."

Kadin laughed some more and began to walk around the table again. "So you see, fire-breather, unchecked power is not a downfall—it is a tool. A weapon. And with it, I will ensure that no one ever rises against me again." His voice was a low, menacing hum that slithered through the air, wrapping around me like a serpent poised to strike.

I forced myself to remain calm, my fingers tightening around the stem of the wine glass I held. The room felt smaller now, oppressive, the weight of Kadin's ambition pressing down on me like a tombstone. I needed to think quickly, to find a way out of this before his darker impulses overtook him.

"You speak of power," I said slowly, my voice steady despite the storm raging inside me. "But true power is not about domination. It is about understanding, about knowing when to wield it and when to let it rest."

Kadin paused, his eyes narrowing as he studied me. "And what would you know of power?" he sneered, pulling me up from the cushions I rested on and turning me in his arms. His eyes glittered with venomous madness. "With the carpet, I will be unstoppable. Uncle Jevan has the power of Harun through the ring. A ring which has helped us perform magic. You will watch us overtake the world and weave fantastical stories of our victories."

I forced myself to remain calm, my mind racing. Kadin's delusions were dangerous, but they revealed something crucial: he believed the carpet was his by birthright. He did not just want power…he felt entitled to it.

Kadin leaned closer, his breath hot against my ear. "You see, my little fire-breather, you have stumbled into a game far greater than you realize. But do not worry," he whispered, his tone deceptively gentle. "You will play your part beautifully."

My stomach churned, but I forced myself to remain calm and not push him away. His nose went to nuzzle at a spot under my ear. He inhaled deeply.

"You smell of sea salt and ocean breeze," he murmured, lips cold against the pulse of my neck.

I wanted to push him away.

His arms wrapped around my waist tightly.

"Come, show me what women do to stay the king's favorite." He chuckled expectantly.

I froze, eyes going to the doors of the far balcony. The crescent moon hung high in the sky. By now, I was supposed to have opened the door for soldiers to enter. Instead, I was here. And I refused to give in. To use my body in a manner I was not ready to.

There was a knock on the doors and Kadin swore, pulling away from me abruptly.

"What have I told you about interrupting me when I am entertaining myself with my concubines!" he roared, turning to watch soldiers enter. No, not mere soldiers.

Blade-Callers. My breath caught in my throat.

"As captain of my Blade-Callers, I would expect more common sense from the likes of you," he sneered.

My gaze fell upon Nora. Despite her crisp white Blade-Caller uniform and the gold headcovering marking her as captain, I could see that no amount of fine titles could hide the weight she had lost in a span of a few months. Her cheekbones stood out like knives beneath her skin, and dark shadows hung beneath her once-vibrant eyes.

She approached Kadin with a bow, her voice steady. "My king, we have urgent news from the northern border. Our scouts report movement, suspected rebels gathering on the outskirts. I believe immediate action is required. Your men await your orders."

Kadin's face twisted with irritation, but beneath it, there was a flicker of concern. He glanced at me, his grip tightening on my arm as if reluctant to let me go. "This better be worth my time," he growled, releasing me abruptly. "Stay here," he ordered, his eyes locking onto mine with a warning. "Do not move. You—" he pointed to Nora "—keep an eye on her while I go consult with my war advisors. Women, always creating a fuss for nothing."

His movements were sharp with frustration. The two Blade-Callers who had been flanking Nora followed him out of the room, leaving the door slightly ajar. My heart raced as I realized this was my chance. I glanced at Nora. I could take her out, though she had once been my dear friend, I would have to. I knew I was stronger than her. But before I could act, she moved with purpose toward me.

"What is your plan, Amara? We need to move quickly."

I blinked, disconcerted, and took a step back. Was this a trick?

"I-I do not know what you speak of," I replied, instilling my voice with as much bewilderment as I could.

"Who do you think managed to get Dornia the papers of traders from Varethra?" Nora asked in frustration. "It was me. Who do you think has been getting word of Kadin's movements through Dornia? Her knowledge is limited since she is only in charge of the harem. And who do you think created this distraction to get Kadin out of here? There are rebels gathering on the northern perimeter. There are also armies on their way, spotted on the southern pass. We have not informed Kadin of that, however. But we need to move quickly. Let us go."

She grabbed my hand. I moved away from her, shaking my head.

"You are the captain of his guard," I accused.

"Because if I am not, there are many women who would gladly trample on the rights of other women to get ahead. Half of our women are already in the dungeons for insubordination, being raped by the guards regularly down there. Some have been sent to his harem. The rest of us have to fall in line or meet the same fate. It is why so many volunteered to go to Chieftain Lamar's fort and attack. It was a last-minute attack, because Salim got word to Kadin using an enchanted ring. I could not warn anyone in time. However, as captain, I can help you in any little way possible. Be it helping get information to your rebel faction or to help you with your plan. "

"Get Zayed into the castle," I whispered. "I will stay here. We cannot sound the alarm yet. He needs to be here. He should be waiting in the back servants' entrance behind the harem."

Nora began moving away from me. Then she paused hesitantly, gaze going to me in concern.

"What if he hurts you?"

"I can save myself," I replied tilting my chin up, hand reflexively going to the dagger concealed in my skirts.

"My Blade-Callers are ready to fight Kadin's men on my command," Nora added. "Give the word, Amara, and we fight. Any who might have resisted have already died in the battle at Chieftain Lamar's fort."

I gave a shake of my head.

"We want the least amount of deaths possible. Zayed will lead the charge, and once Kadin is surrounded by the armies, he will have to surrender and take Zayed's challenge. That is the plan. If there is no other option left but to fight, only then should they raise their swords."

Nora gave a nod and raised her good arm in salute. It was right as she lowered her hand that Kadin re-entered, agitated and upset.

"They think they can come seize my crown." Kadin laughed. "But I have something they do not."

His gaze held a gleam of triumph in his eyes.

"Uncle has made sure the demon witch knows it is time to attack. She will get her pound of flesh. Zayed is close, I can feel it. "

He was speaking to Nora and probably did not know I understood exactly what he meant. My mouth fell open in shock. Kadin was right. He had magic. We did not. The old crones promise of magic teased at the edges of my consciousness. But at what price...

"Send your worthless Blade-Callers to man the perimeter. They can be used as fodder to wear down the armies coming for us. Women who are warriors are of no use anyway. Once they are dead and have exhausted the enemy, the men will come in and finish them."

Anger rose inside of me. Kadin was despicable. He held no respect for women, even though he had been born from one.

My eyes went to Nora, who bowed low in front of Kadin before walking away.

As the doors shut behind her, I noticed more guards than usual gathered outside Kadin's room. He had increased security for himself.

"Useless woman with only one good arm. Only thing she is good for is taking orders," Kadin muttered, shaking his head as the doors closed behind Nora.

Kadin's eyes then went to me. I still stood close to the balcony, teetering on the threshold. It would take a simple swipe in his direction to end this all. A shift into my Lycan would take him by surprise. But what if I could not defeat him? He had been born one, I had been made one by Zayed. Kadin was stronger than me. But could the element of surprise be enough to overpower him?

In the moments it took me to ponder, and to hesitate, he was by my side. His arms went around me and he hauled me against him, against the proof of his want for me. I winced, feeling it become more prominent against my thigh.

"Nothing like a quick fuck before going to kill the scum who dare threatened me." His hands reached for the ties of my skirt to undo them.

I twisted in his grasp on instinct, my hand unconsciously reaching for the hilt of the dagger hidden beneath my skirts. But before I could act, Kadin's grip tightened, his fingers biting into the bare flesh of my waist like steel. He chuckled darkly, his breath hot against my neck.

"Ah, the fire-breather thinks she can resist," he murmured, his voice dripping with malice. He leaned closer, his lips brushing against my ear now. "But you see, my dear, you are not in control here. I am."

My heart raced as I struggled to maintain my composure. The dagger was within reach, a shift would take seconds, but the guards outside the door were just moments away. And I had to wait for Nora to open the gates!

Kadin laughed again, his hands going to squeeze the swell of my rear-end. I gasped in revulsion, pushing him away in disgust and escaping his grasp. I could not do this. The mere thought of letting him grope me or use my body made me want to retch.

"Do not come near me," I hissed, anger flaring in my eyes as I took up a protective stance. I could still fight off his sexual advances and pose as a woman sold to him.

I only needed enough time for Nora to get Zayed inside.

"I had my doubts. But now I know. You think you can fool me, Amara?" he sneered. Shock paralyzed me at his revelation. "I must admit, I expected you to whore yourself out before revealing yourself. Pity. I would have enjoyed that traitorous pussy of yours while you believed you were fooling me."

He laughed darkly as I grappled with the implications of his words. He knew who I was? How? The veil...I reached for it, it was still over my face. So was the mask. How?

"I will give you one last chance. You can surrender. Join me. I will keep you here, as the king's favorite whore. You can suck my cock every night while your husband is trapped in the dungeons below us." Kadin tilted his head toward the door that led to the silver-lined room Zayed had used for his lycan. "Or maybe we can keep him there, close enough to listen. Maybe even watch as his wife whores herself out to me, for power." He leered at me.

"Go to hell!" I hissed, reaching and withdrawing my dagger. I would kill this man.

"I believe someone has to go before me," Kadin said with ominous amusement.

The doors opened to reveal...

"Baba?" I gasped, watching as he was hauled inside flanked by two guards.

This was why there were so many guards outside his room. They had been waiting outside with Baba!

"Where is Zayed?" Kadin barked out, evidently surprised to only see one person.

"He was not in the inn when we arrived there," explained a guard holding onto Baba.

"Where is he?" Kadin turned to me, livid.

I raised my dagger higher in defiance. I truly did not know. But even if I did, I would never tell Kadin.

My heart thudded painfully against my ribcage. Why was Baba here? He was not supposed to be here!

I had to get Baba away from Kadin. From this place.

"Put that silver dagger away. You, a mere human, cannot over power me," Kadin sneered, his eyes glowing red menacingly.

I bit my lip. Of course! Kadin did not know I could shift. Back then, he had thought I was sick with fever. Word had not reached his ears, which meant we still had a way to overpower him.

I reached out a hand to Baba. The guards jerked him back roughly. Pain flitted across Baba's face, but he did not cry out.

"This old man is your father, huh?" Kadin said off-handedly, coming to stand between myself and my father, a barrier to the man who had made me what I was today. And he was in danger!

I took a step forward.

"Let him go!"

Kadin sneered, his eyes glinting with a malevolent light. "Oh, I think not. You see, Amara, your father is quite useful to me. He is the perfect pawn to ensure your cooperation." His gaze flicked to Baba, who stood tall despite the guards holding him roughly by the shoulders. "Tell me, old man, where is your son-in-law? Where is the traitor-turned-rebel leader?" Kadin angled his body toward my father.

I took the opportunity to move closer.

If I could move fast enough, I could grab Baba. I could shift and fight them off. I could give Baba enough time to escape. But he would never escape uninjured in the scuffle. I bit my bottom lip. Why was it that every time I faced Kadin, I felt utterly powerless?

Baba's eyes met mine over Kadin's shoulder, and I saw the resolve in them, the same strength that had carried him through countless trials. The same strength he always infused in me. "I do not know," Baba said firmly, his voice steady despite the danger. "And even if I did, I would never tell you."

Kadin's laughter echoed through the room, cold and devoid of any warmth.

"You think your silence will protect him?" Kadin sneered, his voice dripping with venom. He leaned in closer toward my father and spoke in a mock whisper. "Your daughter will watch you suffer. That is the price of defiance."

I lunged forward, dagger in hand, but the guards moved swiftly, drawing their swords, sharp and gleaming under the torchlight.

"Halt," one of them growled, his voice low and warning as the blade hovered precariously close to Baba's neck. I froze. They would kill him.

Kadin chuckled. He had not moved a muscle. He did not need to. These men would do the dirty work for him. His laugh was a dark, twisted sound that sent shivers down my spine.

"Such fire, Amara." Kadin crossed his arms and stared at me. I now stood mere inches from my father, with Kadin still positioned between us. And yet, I could not save him. For if I moved to take Kadin down first to get to Baba, the guards would not hesitate in harming him.

"I knew it was you from the moment you breathed fire. For you are the only one who flares like the desert sun—scorching, untamed, and forever doomed to set." He threw his head back mockingly. "Amara, even fire can be snuffed out. You are outmatched. You always were. Weak woman that you are."

I whimpered, watching the blade tilt slightly to dig into the side of Baba's neck. No, no, no. I had to save him!

"Stay strong, Amara," Baba called out, his voice steady despite the circumstances. "Remember who you are."

The old crone's words came back to me. If I had magic, I would be powerful enough to defeat Kadin. But at what cost? Was that really who I was?

My eyes met Baba's, and it was as if he could see into my very soul. He gave a firm shake of his head as if warning me to not fall into the lure of darkness.

Then Baba straightened his spine despite the guards holding him.

"I have lived long enough to see true kings," Baba said, allowing the blade to dig deeper into his neck.

I gasped. What was he doing?

"You stand there, pretending to be the terror of the desert," Baba said, voice steady, "but you are merely a frightened child wearing a stolen crown."

Kadin's nostrils flared in rage.

"Watch your words, old man! You speak that way to the one who holds your life in his hands? One word from me and your head will roll."

Baba narrowed his eyes, tilting his chin up defiantly. He was shorter than Kadin, yet at this moment, he seemed taller. More noble.

"You cling so tightly to fear, because without it, you are nothing. And deep down, you know it. You know you could never match the men who came before you. So go on, *boy*," Baba spat the words out viciously. "Prove me right. You only feel powerful when someone else bleeds for you. Your father would weep if he saw what you have become. Your mother was always a venomous bitch, plotting and—"

"NOT A WORD AGAINST MY MOTHER!" Kadin roared. Now he was screaming in Baba's face, his face inches away from my father's. Kadin's back was to me now, but I could see that even his ears had turned red from anger. His entire body shook with rage. "SHE DID IT ALL FOR ME! FOR ME! SO I COULD BE KING. SO I COULD OWN THE MAGIC CARPET."

"Your uncle will kill you before giving you the magic. You think he will help you become powerful when he could have all the power for himself?" Baba challenged, laughing in his face. The lines in Baba's face hardened and his tone became stern. "Your mother deserved to die after everything she did. It is poetic justice that she passed away due to a plague that happened because of the curse she was the cause of. And you will die in the same way, Kadin. Your uncle is using you. You are a pawn to him. Give up the crown. Return it to its rightful ruler. For even the desert wind whispers what you cannot face—you are unworthy of the crown you wear."

Kadin's expressions twisted, rage sharpening every line of his face as he screamed in anger.

"I dare you to say it again," Kadin hissed, hands balled at his sides.

Baba did not flinch. "You wear a stolen crown," he repeated, voice steady. "You are a false king."

Kadin lunged.

In a single furious motion, so fast only my Lycan senses registered it, Kadin grabbed the hilt of the blade being held at Baba's throat.

The guard stumbled back, startled, but Kadin was moving forward with a predator's speed.

Steel flashed—one violent, merciless arc—and the sound that followed was sickening: the heavy thud of impact, the scrape of metal through resistance, the sharp gasp that rippled through the room as the bodies of the two guards flanking Baba recoiled.

Baba's head snapped back, his knees buckling as the sword tore him away from life in one brutal strike. His head fell to the floor before his body collapsed, limbs folding under him in a heap at Kadin's feet.

I did not scream. I could not. Because I could not comprehend what I was seeing.

Kadin stood over Baba's body, chest heaving, the sword dripping with the weight of what he had done. The guards stared in stunned silence, as if even they had not expected him to go that far. A thin, terrible smile curved his lips.

He said something, but I could not hear his words. Lightning struck as if from far away, illuminating the twisted grin on Kadin's face.

All I heard was the ringing in my ears. It was shrill, and endless. All I felt was the sensation of my lungs collapsing. No. My mind refused to accept what my eyes saw. Baba's head lay on the stone floor, the stump on his shoulders spilling waves of crimson on the polished floor. This was wrong. It was impossible. My knees hit the floor. My breath fractured in my chest. I could not stand. I could not breathe. There was nothing except a terrible ache in my chest. My world tilted.

"No..." The word scraped out of me, thin and useless. "No, no—Baba—get up!" I yelled, wet tears blurring my vision.

But he did not move.

A crack split down the center of my world. Down the center of my very being.

"BABA!" I screamed, hands held out helplessly toward his body.

This could not be. He would smile at me any minute. It was a trick. A magic trick! He was supposed to stand by me as I ruled as queen. He was supposed to be our advisor!

The man who carried me on his shoulders...the man who was supposed to be able to live his final days in peace with his daughter as queen...

I was breaking. My soul was breaking. Shattering. I lost my mother early. But Baba...he promised to *stay*. He still had many years with us.

"Baba," I croaked out brokenly, one hand extended out to his mangled body, the other toward his severed head.

Superimposed over the bloodied, severed head and his lifeless body was the image of his smiling face. His silver eyebrows were raised in amusement as he smiled at me when we reunited in the caves.

Then I will stand by you.

I might be a frail old man, but I will fight for you with all I have, my dear daughter.

"You said you would stand by me!" I screamed as I fractured into a million pieces.

And still, he would not get up. This was no mirage. This was the ugly truth. He was gone. No.

And then something in me snapped. Like a dam breaking, my disbelief gave way to a new emotion.

Rage—pure, ancient, feral—surged up so fast I tasted blood on my tongue. Or maybe I was just thirsting for it. My hands shook, not with fear anymore, but with the kind of fury that could burn the desert to ash. My vision blurred, then sharpened. Everything inside me screamed.

Kadin turned toward me, wiping the blade as if Baba's life were dust he could brush away.

I lunged.

"You coward!" I roared, the words ripping from my throat. "I should have torn you apart the moment you touched me!"

I cursed myself for freezing, for standing rooted to the floor while Baba died. Guilt sliced through me, but I did not let it stop me. I let it *feed* me.

Heat pulsed under my skin. My bones trembled, reshaping. The world narrowed to instinct, to the thundering of my pulse, to the way the air tasted like iron and vengeance. My nails lengthened, scraping against stone and as I ran to him on all fours more animal than woman. My teeth ached, they sharpened, my muscles coiled tighter and tighter until they were ready to snap.

A low and feral growl tore out of me, vibrating in my chest. My vision tunneled red.

I did not think. I did not care.

I let the Lycan take me.

My body twisted, expanded—fur bursting through skin, limbs stretching, spine arching. Power flooded me so violently it stole my breath, and for one perfect, brutal moment, I felt unstoppable.

Kadin stumbled backward toward the exit, eyes wide. "You—" His voice cracked. "You can shift?"

Only partially shifted, I hit the ground on two feet and two hands, claws screeching against the stone as I launched myself at him with a snarl that rattled the windows and doors.

He wanted power?

He was about to learn what real power looked like.

Remember who you are.

"I challenge you for the crown in a battle to the death!" I growled out right before my snout elongated and lips disappeared. My words ended in a triumphant howl as I pounced on him.

Chapter 28

Zayed's POV

I crouched low against the rough stone wall of the palace, the shadows clinging to me like a second skin. The night air was thick with the scent of impending danger, the distant clamor of guards' boots on stone echoing through the silence. My heart pounded in my chest, not with fear, but with a furious determination that burned through my veins like wildfire. Amara was inside, and Kadin was a viper coiled around her, ready to strike.

I had left Idris at the inn, unwilling to risk her father's safety further. The man was brave, but this was my fight. My responsibility. And now, with Amara trapped inside the palace, I could not afford to wait. The plan had unraveled the moment Kadin refused to let us inside earlier today. Now, I had to improvise.

The low hum of voices reached my ears, and I pressed myself tighter against the wall, my Lycan senses sharpening as I focused. Two guards patrolled the perimeter, their conversation drifting toward me like whispers on the wind.

"The king's got a new toy," one of them laughed, his voice dripping with malice. "Some fire-breathing concubine. He is holed up with her tonight. No one is allowed near his chambers."

My claws dug into the stone at my sides, the thought of Kadin's hands on Amara igniting a rage so fierce it threatened to consume me. She could fend for herself, but the thought of Kadin's hands on her, his breath on her skin, made my blood boil. I clenched my fists, forcing myself to focus. Panic would not help her. I needed a plan. I forced myself to breathe, to think. I could not afford to lose control now. Not when she needed me here.

The guards moved on, their laughter fading into the darkness. I waited, counting the seconds until their footsteps disappeared entirely. Then, I moved.

This was my home. My palace. I had grown up here, and I knew every hidden corner that could conceal me as I skirted the castle walls looking for a way in.

It was clear now that Kadin had pretended to not be interested in Amara to avoid paying for her. And now that he had her, what would he do? He was capable of anything. I had to get to my wife!

I crept along the wall, my senses heightened, every sound amplified. The faint scent of incense wafted from an open window above, and I paused, tilting my head to listen. Soft murmurs drifted down, too faint to make out words. I was close to the harem. But how was I supposed to get in? These walls had been constructed as such to be unscalable even by shifters. There was a back door that Amara had promised to let me through, but now that she was with Kadin, it would be impossible.The sound of footsteps echoed closer now, heavy boots settling into the dirt. I pressed myself deeper into the shadows, my lycan senses honing in on the guards patrolling the perimeter. My muscles coiled and ready to spring.

Their voices carried faintly.

"Do you think she will fight him?" one chuckled.

"It would be an interesting story to hear from the men guarding the king's bedroom tonight. He loves it when they fight." The reply grated against my frayed nerves.

I forced myself to not react and to wait for the perfect moment to strike.

One guard paused a few feet from my hiding spot, his hand resting on the hilt of his sword. His companion continued walking ahead.

I waited, my breath shallow, until the second guard was out of earshot.

Then I moved.

In one fluid motion, I lunged from the shadows, my claws extended. The guard did not even have time to scream. My hand clamped over his mouth as I drove my other hand into his chest, piercing through armor and flesh with ease. His body went limp in my grasp, and I lowered him to the ground silently, my heart pounding in my ears.

The second guard I did not even give enough time to turn his head before I was on him. My hand clamped over his mouth, muffling his startled cry as I dragged him into the darkness provided by the walls of the palace. A quick, efficient twist of his neck, and he slumped to the ground, lifeless.

Neither guilt nor hesitation slowed me down. They were obstacles, nothing more. My purpose was singular—get to Amara. Quickly, I donned his uniform, making sure to hide my evil eye talisman under my clothes after securing it around my neck. After Amara's run-in with Elvira in the desert, we were careful to keep the talismans on us at all times. And here, in this palace, I had a feeling she was close.

After hiding both bodies so that it would take a considerable amount of time to find them, I moved forward with purpose. The path to Kadin was clear now.

The palace was a labyrinth, but I knew its secrets. I knew the procedure for guards required to be relieved of their duty.

Resolutely, I turned toward the barracks, knowing that if I were to get anywhere, it would have to be through there. But if the guards on duty did not recognize me when I asked to be let inside, it might cause problems.

No matter, I would have to kill them as well. More blood on my hands meant nothing now. Anyone who stood between Amara and me would meet the same fate as those guards. I stalked toward the barracks, my jaw clenched with grim resolve, when a metallic scraping sound froze me mid-step. The stone door leading from the servants' quarters— adjacent to the harem wing—was being unbolted from within.

The door creaked open, and I tensed, ready to pounce. But instead of a guard or servant, a familiar figure slipped through the gap, her movements swift and deliberate. My eyes went to her disfigured arm, strapped in a sling at her side because it was of no use in battle. She was the woman Amara had become friends with during her training. But my jaw hardened in recognition of her attire. She was captain of Kadin's Blade-Callers? Which meant she sent the women to attack us at Lamar's fortress!

Her eyes widened when she saw me.

"Are you not supposed to be patrolling the perimeter clockwise?" she queried, turning her head to look for my missing companion most likely.

I paused in hesitation. What was I to do? Kill her too?

"I received orders to report to the barracks for a change of duty," I replied gruffly.

Her head whipped toward me, eyes narrowing as they studied my face.

"You are not one of the royal guards." She took a step closer, her hand hovering near the hilt of her blade.

I hesitated, weighing my options. Was she innocent or part of Kadin's supporters?

She drew her sword. I tensed.

"There is no time to waste, Your Highness. Amara sent me to get you inside. Someone has to give the signal and open the front doors for the allies to surround the castle. We must move fast. They have her father."

I exhaled. She could be trusted, for she would not have come here if Amara had not sent her. There was no time to waste on entertaining doubts.

"Where are they holding Idris?" I asked quickly.

"I saw him being hauled toward Kadin's rooms, which means the man has been caught and is being brought to Kadin. I do not know if it is because he suspects that he has Amara in disguise, or if it is because they caught Idris and have been ordered to present him in front of Kadin. But we have to move fast. Amara wanted us to stick to the plan. You must go challenge Kadin now. Tell me what to do. Not all Blade-Callers are under Kadin's command. Most will follow me. We can give off the signal for your allies."

I nodded, my mind racing. We did not have time for hesitation. "Do as Amara planned. Signal the allies and open the gates. We need to surround Kadin before he realizes what is happening. And Nora—" I paused, my voice lowering to a growl. "If any of your Blade-Callers stand against us, they will meet the same fate as Kadin's guards."

Her expression hardened, and she gave a curt nod. "Understood."

I moved swiftly to free my wife from Kadin's clutches.

"Be warned, Your Highness," she cautioned as I moved stealthily down the corridor of the servants' wing. "Kadin is not alone. His men are stationed everywhere. He is expecting an attack."

"Then we better not keep him waiting," I growled, my lycan instincts surging to the surface. The beast within me snarled, eager to tear Kadin apart limb by limb. But I forced myself to stay focused. Amara was in danger, and Idris' life hung in the balance. This was no time for recklessness.

The shortest way in was to step out of the servant quarters and cut across the gardens in front of the harem, where Kadin was with Amara. I quickened my steps, boots hitting the grass.

I glanced up at the night sky, where the crescent moon hung high overhead. The hour was late—midnight approached, and the gardens stood eerily silent, not even a whisper of wind disturbing the leaves. Time was slipping away from us.

I could not stop an anxious gnawing in the back of my mind. Something was wrong. The hairs on the back of my neck shot up as a cold, electric awareness slithered down my spine. Eyes—predatory, calculating—were boring into me from somewhere in the darkness, tracking my every movement with lethal intent.

I turned to look behind me. There was no one.

I froze, my lycan senses honing in on the source of the threat. The shadows around me shifted, and I shot my gaze to the sky, where the clouds took the shape of a circular face with angry eyes staring down at me. The air was charged with a malevolent energy that prickled my skin. The clouds twisted and coiled, forming into grotesque shapes of a sinister smile and narrowed eyes. Lightning struck overhead, illuminating the garden for a brief moment, and the clouds dispersed.

A figure moved toward me from the depths of the garden. Elvira emerged from the shadows, her skin a patchwork of decay—gray flesh peeling away in strips to reveal blackened sinew beneath. One eye socket was hollow with a jagged scar running across it. Her remaining eye gleamed red ominously.

"Let us end this, you vile scum!" she cackled, her voice like broken glass scraping against stone. Yellow ichor oozed from cracks in her cheeks as her lips pulled back in a gruesome smile, revealing teeth filed to jagged points.

Her hands were raised, fingers curled like claws. The stench of death and decay wafted from her, choking the air around us. The sheer magnitude of the dark magic she commanded—the kind that twisted reality, defied nature, and corrupted souls—pressed down on me. It was magic she had learned from the old crone, but amplified into something monstrous.

I could not afford to falter now. She lunged, her movements unnaturally fast, her claws slashing through the air toward my throat. I dodged, allowing the instinctive reflexes of my lycan to take hold of me. But I did not shift.

No. I wanted to kill her in my human form. She was the cause of all this. And due to the curse, she had some sort of sway over my Lycan form.

Elvira laughed, the sound echoing eerily through the garden. She raised her hands, and the ground beneath me began to tremble. Vines burst from the earth, writhing like serpents as they coiled around my legs, anchoring me in place. I snarled, thrashing against their hold, but they only tightened, thorns digging into my flesh.

"Is this all your lycan strength amounts to?" she mocked, stepping closer, her decaying features twisted into a macabre grin. "I will enjoy tearing you apart piece by piece."

I roared, summoning every ounce of power I had. With a violent jerk, I ripped the vines apart, their tendrils snapping like dried twigs. Elvira's grin faltered for a moment, but she quickly recovered, her hands weaving intricate patterns in the air. Shadows coalesced around her, forming into ghastly shapes—creatures of nightmare that lunged at me with gaping maws and razor-sharp claws. It was as if she had unleashed the gates of hell itself for demons to crawl out of and feast upon me. I met them head-on, my claws slicing through the shadowy forms with brutal efficiency. They disintegrated into wisps of darkness, but more took their place, an endless tide of malice. I could not keep this up forever. I needed to get to Elvira.

With a burst of speed, I darted past the shadow creatures, closing the distance between us in the blink of an eye. Elvira stumbled back, but not fast enough. My claws raked across her torso, tearing through rotting flesh and releasing a foul stench that made my stomach churn. Green puss oozed from the wounds I inflicted on her.

"You betrayed my mother by targeting her son," I growled out angrily. "She would abhor you if she were alive today."

Her laughter was a hoarse, guttural sound as she staggered back, clutching her bleeding side. The ichor oozed between her fingers, but her grin remained, cruel and unyielding. "Your mother was my world, and your father ended her," she spat, her voice dripping with venom. "I want my revenge! Die!"

I lunged at her again, but she raised a hand, and the air crackled with dark energy. A wave of forceful malevolent energy slammed into me, throwing me backward into the stone statue of myself within the garden. Somehow, during the fight, we had ended up here, in the deep recesses of the garden. Pain exploded through my body, but I forced myself to my feet, my lycan strength pushing through the agony.

"You think you can defeat me?" Elvira hissed, her voice a cacophony of madness and hatred. "I am the embodiment of death itself! You need magic as powerful as mine to defeat me. Your wife was given a chance to learn when you lay recovering from your wounds, but she refused the old crone. Pity. If she had accepted, *you* would already be dead!"

Startled at this revelation, I paused to absorb this piece of news.

And Elvira used my surprise to pounce. The air exploded from my lungs in a rush as if my chest had been crushed in an iron embrace, my air violently ripped away as Elvira's dark shadows slammed into my chest with the force of a battering ram, hurling me backward into the night. White hot pain lanced through my ribs as I fell back. The unmistakable crack of my rib bone sent dizzying pain shooting through me. I fought the urge to retch.

In what seemed like seconds, she was on top of me, her red eye gleaming in the night as she stared down at me triumphantly.

Her rotting fingers closed around the evil eye talisman at my throat, ripping it away with such force that the chain sliced into my flesh before snapping. The silver disk arced through the darkness, disappearing with a distant clink. Instantly, ice flooded my veins—my muscles seized, locked rigid as stone. I could not even scream as her magic invaded me like thousands of burrowing insects beneath my skin, paralyzing everything but my consciousness. Her face lowered to mine, putrid breath washing over me as her lips peeled back in a victorious snarl.

"Time for dinner. I wonder what a Lycan will taste like!"

And then she opened her mouth wider than should have been possible, revealing rows of jagged teeth dripping with thick, black saliva. Her breath reeked of decay, and her one good eye glowed with a malevolent light as she leaned closer. I tried to fight her. Tried to move. But my body remained immobile, trapped by her dark magic. I could do nothing but watch as she descended toward me, her teeth poised to sink into my flesh.

And then, she stilled. Her mouth, stretched wide with jagged teeth glistening, froze inches from my throat as she remained bent over me, staring at me. Elvira's body violently snapped backward, spine arching at an impossible angle as though yanked by demonic chains. Her eye bulged from its socket, bloodshot and wild with a primal terror that contorted her face. A strangled sound—half-scream, half-gurgle—caught in her throat as her rotting jaw clamped shut with such force that blackened teeth shattered in her mouth, fragments spilling from between her lips like putrid grains of sand.

Her despair slammed into me with her agonizing wail, a raw force that hollowed my chest and settled in my bones. The sound echoed through the garden, a sound so full of anguish it made the very air tremble. Elvira's body convulsed, her limbs twisting unnaturally as her body writhed in what seemed to be pain. Her magic loosened its hold on me and I stood, poised to defend myself.

But there was no need, because she did not attack. Her body contorted as if wrung by invisible hands, then began to disintegrate from the feet upwards. She collapsed to the ground, her form blackening like ancient parchment caught in flame, crumbling inward from the edges. When her trembling lips parted, the voice that emerged was no longer the witch's cackle, but something fragile and fractured. Something heartbroken.

"Those eyes," she whispered. "They are hers. My flower's eyes. I cannot... *I cannot take them from this world again.*"

"Lift the curse before you disappear to hell!" I growled, realizing what was happening.

She was a demon who had been created as part of the curse. If she was dying, did it mean the curse was lifted?

She gazed at me now, not as a demon witch but as a helpless woman, red-eye no longer malicious but helpless. "I gave my life to fulfill the curse and make it unbreakable. But by giving my demonic life now, I can alter it. The curse cannot be broken unless paid for in blood. If your bride cannot survive one thousand and one nights, the rightful king must kill one final bride before the curse is lifted for good. You must kill your current bride."

"NO!" I screamed, reaching out my hand. "Let the curse kill me instead! Will it break upon my death?"

Her head only remained now as the blackness spread over her neck and chin. She gave a sad smile.

"Your death can never break the curse, but it will cement it forever if the curse is not broken. The curse would continue to plague the land. My flower's eyes will not leave this world until the goddess has deemed it your time." And then the burning black hand of death extended over her lips and nose, quickly followed by her head crumbling into black ash. She was gone.

"NO!" I screamed. "NO NO NO!"

This could not be! My people would suffer for another two years under famine and plague if Amara had to survive one thousand one nights. All was lost. My heart was cleaving in upon itself in the face of the decision to let countless innocents suffer. But if that was what it took to keep Amara by my side, could I do it? I would have to be the monster. Have to be the one thing I had tried not to become. I would have to let children, babies, mothers, wives, husbands, and fathers all suffer until the curse was broken.

A familiar roar reverberated through the grounds as I stood there, helpless and in anguish.

Amara's roar.

My heart thundered. Whatever it took, we would survive those nights together. Right now, I had to get to Amara.

As I ran through the gardens, the turrets around the castle lit up in fire. The Blade-Callers had given the signal. Our allies were closing in sooner rather than later.

And when I reached the clearing that led to the gardens outside the King's wing of the palace, there was my wife in her Lycan form, teeth bared as she fought Kadin's Lycan.

I recognized it for what it was. It was a challenge to the death for his crown.

"He killed her father," Dornia said from my right. I turned to look at her and did a double take. She was no longer dressed in finery but in the soft, plain cotton warrior outfit of a Blade-Caller. An ornate jewel-encrusted blade gleamed in her hand. She smiled.

"You think I would not take up arms to help you fight? An old woman I may be, Zayed, but I will fight to the death to put you back on the throne."

A fierce howl rent the night, and I jerked to see that Amara had been injured. I moved to intercede but stopped when I met her eyes as her clawed hands came up to wipe her bloodied snout.

The pain of a thousand years was reflected in them. That was when I realized that the anguish engulfing me was not only my own but my wife's, and the look in her eyes, as well as the feeling through our bond, warned me to *stay back*.

"This is her fight," I whispered in realization. "Her revenge."

Chapter 29

Amara's POV

The scent of blood filled the air, mingling with the copper tang of my own wounds. My fur bristled, my muscles coiled tight, every fiber of my being was screaming for vengeance. Kadin's lycan form towered before me, his massive frame silhouetted against the moonlight. His lycan's red eyes gleamed with malice, his lips pulled back in a snarl.

We had ended up out here in the gardens. Or rather, I had pounced on him, and as we swiped and clawed at each other, I had maneuvered him out into the open, where everyone could witness his demise. Because I was going to smash his skull into the ground. A man like him did not deserve to live.

Kadin lunged, his claws slashing through the air with brutal precision. I ducked, barely avoiding the strike, and countered with a swipe of my own. My claws grazed his flank, drawing blood, but he barely flinched. He was stronger, faster, and more experienced in his Lycan form than I was. But I had something he did not—rage. Pure, unrelenting rage, fueled by the image of Baba's head being severed from his body by Kadin's hand. Rage for Baghel's death, rage for everything Kadin had done to Zayed. Rage for everything he had done to our people, our kingdom.

I charged, my growl tearing through the night as I tackled him to the ground. We rolled, dirt and blood spraying between us. His claws raked across my snout, and my howl of pain rent the air. Retreating momentarily, I used my clawed hands to wipe the blood away. It was then that my gaze landed on Zayed, moving to interfere. My heart jumped in relief. Zayed was here. But I did not want him to intercede, so I sent him a warning with my eyes and through our bond.

Claws suddenly raked down my left shoulder, and I bit back the howl of pain threatening to spill over. I moved swiftly, ducking and retaliating with a vicious bite to his foreleg. He roared, thrashing as he fell to the ground, but I held on, my jaws clamped tight.

He twisted, throwing me off with a brutal kick. I skidded across the dirt, breath knocked out of me from the jarring impact. But I scrambled to my feet right as he lunged again. This time, I was ready. I sidestepped, his claws missing me by inches, and lashed out with a powerful swipe to his ribs.

He staggered but did not fall.

The sound of distant shouts and clashing weapons reached my ears—our allies must have breached the palace. But I could not focus on that now. My entire world was focused on Kadin and the fight for vengeance.

He circled me, his movements predatory...calculated.

I surged forward, my claws extended, aiming for his throat. He parried, our claws clashing with a metallic screech, sparks flying between us. He shoved me back, but I did not relent. I pressed the attack, my strikes relentless, fueled by the memory of Baba's smile, his laughter, his unwavering love.

Kadin faltered, a flicker of uncertainty in his eyes. I snarled triumphantly. I, a "mere woman," had him worried for his safety. I was pushing him back, each strike of my claws sending him stumbling a few steps back.

Shock was etched across his face. He had never expected me to fight like this, to *be* this. Kadin might be a Lycan, but he was no Lycan King. I had practiced fighting Zayed's Lycan, and his skills far outmatched this pathetic man.Finally, finding an opening, my claws sank into his side, ripping through fur and flesh alike. I felt the resistance give way, felt muscle tear beneath my grip. Felt my claws rend flesh from bone. Blood sprayed hot and thick in a crimson arc.

Kadin staggered, slipping in the slick dirt beneath us—dirt now soaked black with blood. His blood streamed freely from the gash I had opened. He snapped at me wildly, desperation creeping into his movements, but I slammed my shoulder into his chest and sent him crashing into the stone edge of the fountain behind him with a crack.

Stone shattered. His spine struck hard, and I heard it—the wet, sickening crunch of something breaking. He screamed in rage.

I was on him instantly.

My claws raked down his chest, splitting skin open in four brutal lines. Flesh peeled back. Blood poured like a waterfall now, soaking into my fur, matting it down, dripping from my elbows as I struck again and again. I tore into him with my teeth, sinking them into his shoulder and wrenching hard. Copper and iron flooded my mouth as he howled in pain. I did not recoil. I leaned into it, carving my rage into his body as I bit into his shoulder again.

Something gave way with a sharp snap, and his roar turned into a choking, broken sound.

He tried to claw at my eyes. I reared back and caught his wrist between my canines. Then crushed it.

Bones snapped under the force of my bite.

He howled, the sound raw and ragged, as his clawed hand bent in a way it was never meant to. I shook my head violently, tearing my mouth free, and spat blood and fragments of his flesh onto the ground. His clawed hand now hung drunkenly, held onto his wrist by a mere sliver of skin.

I bared my fangs bloodied from my assault. He let out a pained angry roar. But he did not admit defeat. Kadin was a snake. And snakes survived by striking when one least expected it. Kadin's Lycan retreated from my advances, and a sudden whistle cut through the air.

Before I could turn, something slammed into my shoulder and pain erupted, hot and burning. I grunted, reaching to pull at an arrow, silver-tipped. It was fired from the balconies above. The force of the pain spun me sideways, breaking my momentum. Gasps rippled through the clearing; they thought it would fell me instantly.

I met Zayed's eyes as I feigned a stagger whilst holding the arrow in my hand.

He was smiling. Because he knew what they did not.Silver could burn me.But it could not end me.

However it hurt like the fire of a thousand suns searing into my flesh.

As I stared at my husband, his words from one of our spar sessions resounded in my mind: *"A true warrior does not stop when wounded. Justice is worth the last breath."*

This was no longer just vengeance for Baba. This was justice for every life Kadin had crushed under his stolen crown.

Heat rippled through my limbs. My vision sharpened once more, and I swiftly lunged, arrow in hand.

I feinted left, then darted right, catching him off guard. And then I tackled him to the ground. In one deft move, I closed my canines over his partially severed clawed hand and ripped it clean off his wrist, leaving nothing but a blood stump. Even if he shifted back into his human form, he would not have a hand. Kadin roared in pain, thrashing wildly to dislodge me. But I held on, my grip unyielding. With a snarl, I used my other hand to plunge the silver arrow, still in my grip, into his left side. His roar turned into a pitiful howl as I twisted the arrow and tore through muscle and sinew. Blood poured from all his wounds, soaking his fur and pooling on the ground beneath us.

Twisting, his body began to turn back into his human form. I pulled back from him, knowing the battle and the war had been won.

"U-uncle!" Kadin screamed like a little girl as he searched wildly for the man who was supposed to protect him with his magic. "H-help!" His hand went to the arrow that remained embedded in him. But I knew it was hopeless to try and fix it. The silver would poison him. And kill him. His wounds would not heal with silver in his body.

I grimaced from the pain in my shoulder as I stood and shifted back to my human form. Scraps of blue still hung off my frame, the rest of my fine silk having been destroyed due to my sudden shift.

"What is wrong, Kadin?" I taunted, towering over him as blood spilled from the wounds on his body. "Could you not defeat a weak woman?"

Kadin's breath came in ragged gasps, his eyes wide with a mix of fear and fury. Blood seeped from the stump in his hand, staining the ground beneath him. His remaining hand trembled as he tried to push himself up, but the strength was draining from him fast. The silver arrow had done its work; his body was failing him.

I crouched down, resting my elbows on my knees as I leaned forward, my face inches from his. "You thought you could take everything from me," I whispered, my voice low and dangerous. "My father, my kingdom, my dignity, my loyal companion Baghel, my husband. But you underestimated me, Kadin. You underestimated *us*."

My eyes found Zayed across the blood-soaked clearing. His face was stone, jaw set with the certainty of executioners. A single nod from him sent one of the Blade-Callers rushing toward me, her ceremonial silver dagger catching the moonlight as she approached. It might not be mine, but it would finish the job.

Before me, Kadin's lips curled into a snarl, but there was no power behind it now. "You...you think this is over?" he rasped, blood bubbling at the corners of his mouth. "My uncle...he will destroy you. He will destroy everything you love to get the carpet."

I smiled, a cold, predatory thing. "Your uncle is next. And when we are done with him, there will be no one left to carry on your legacy of cruelty."

The Blade-Caller reached me, and I held out my hand. She placed her dagger with its naked, jagged blade in my palm. I closed my fingers over the blade with purpose. Kadin gasped when he realized it did not hurt me to touch it.

"How is this...possible?" he gasped, panic creeping into his gaze.

Casually I tossed the blade into my other hand before tossing it into the air and catching it again by the hilt. There was a reason Zayed's grandfather made sure the blade was silver. It was the final answer to tyrants who thought themselves immune. And how fitting that it was in the hands of his elite female warriors.

Kadin scrambled back haphazardly, sliding on the grass, his blood soaking the ground beneath him. "You...you do not understand. The curse...it is not broken! You think killing me will save your kingdom? You are a fool! The curse requires you to die so the famine can end!"

I leaned closer, my breath hot against his face. "The curse will be broken. And if my death is the price I pay, then so be it. But tonight, Kadin, you pay for what you have done."

I moved the blade in a slow graceful arc before stabbing him in the stomach.

"For Baba," I hissed as he cried out in pain when the silver burned through him. Coupled with the arrow in his side, it would only speed up his death. But I did not want to speed it up. I wanted it to be as agonizing as possible for him. I pulled the dagger out and went in for another hit, this time embedding it deep into his ribs. "For Queen Lillanna," I gasped, tears now pouring down my eyes. I missed my father. I wanted to carve out his eyes and cut off his ears. Prolong his pain for decades. Just as I would have to live with the pain of my father's death.

Remember who you are.

"And this—" I pulled the dagger back, flipping it in the air and catching the hilt swiftly.

Kadin's mouth was open, a gurgled gasp of pain escaping his lips as blood poured forth. I had punctured a lung. He was suffocating in his own blood. If I did nothing, he would die on his own eventually. But that was not who I was. I would give him what he had never thought to give anyone. A merciful death.

"This is for Baghel." I plunged the blade deep into his chest and twisted it for good measure to make sure that beating, black heart of his would never beat again.

He did not cry out. Did not flinch. No. He froze, then took one final, gasping breath before his body went limp, his lifeless eyes staring up at me.

Chapter 30

Zayed's POV

Kadin was dead. And so was Idris. The silence that followed was heavy, the weight of victory mingling with the grief that clung to the air like smoke. I moved toward Amara, my heart aching at the sight of her trembling in the aftermath of her grief. Justice may have been served, but that would never bring her father back. She stood over Kadin's lifeless body, her chest heaving, the silver dagger still clutched in her hand. My own eyes burned with unshed emotion. I could feel how shattered she was through our bond. She lost her father. And though he was not my father, Idris was someone I, too, had cared for deeply.

But I was only halfway to her, slowly closing the distance when she tilted the tip of the dagger up and toward her own chest. I froze.

Behind me, I heard Asya's sharp gasp of "No". She had been an onlooker as well since the Blade-Callers had opened the gates to allow them in.

"Amara," I began, my tone rife with warning. "It is over. We have won."

She looked at me and shook her head, tears streaming down her face, mingling with the blood there.

"Do you not see, it is not over. WE have not won." Amara's voice trembled. "The curse is unbroken. And we cannot doom everyone to starve. Do you not see, Zayed...this is the only way." Amara pleaded with me to understand.

"And you would do what then, allow him to wed another, who he will kill? WE cannot continue this cycle, Amara! It must end!" Asya's frantic pleading voice reached Amara. But I knew it fell on deaf ears.

Amara's eyes locked with mine, her voice breaking as she clutched the dagger. "I love you, Zayed. Beyond death, beyond time," she whispered. "But you must swear to me you will step away from the shadows. Tell our people the truth of what you are, of the curse, and let them choose to follow you. Let the daughters of our kingdom choose their fate." A tear fell from her eye. "They will not disappoint you. For they are the daughters of the desert, just like me. We are forged in heat, tempered by storm, and heirs to a legacy of unshakable will. Trust them to do the right thing. Give me your word."

But how could I promise her that? And how could I tell her that Elvira had altered the curse with her insufferable life so that Amara's death would end the curse? How could I tell my wife this, knowing it would only cement her decision to sacrifice herself? I swallowed and looked away briefly.

"You...there is something you are not telling me." Amara's piercing gaze seemed to look into my very soul. "Something you do not wish for me to know."

The dagger in her hand trembled.

I looked to Asya, who was stealthily walking closer to Amara.

I hesitated, the weight of Elvira's revelation pressing down on me like a stone. Before I could speak, Nora's voice cut through the clearing, sharp and frantic.

"Your Highness!" she called urgently, rushing toward us, her face pale with fear. "Jevan—Kadin's uncle—he is gone. He has vanished into the night. We tried to apprehend him..."

It took me a moment to comprehend that she was not speaking to me, but to Amara.

Amara and I gasped simultaneously as a splitting pain erupted in my chest.

At first, I thought an arrow had lodged itself in my heart as a sharp jolt shot through my body and stole the air from my lungs. But no...this was different. This was deeper. A pressure I had not felt in years, one I almost did not recognize.

Then the pain hit.

Not the dull, choking agony of the curse I had grown accustomed to... No, this was a rising, tearing burn, as if my very bones were cracking open from the inside. I staggered, fighting to stay upright, but the force of it nearly drove me to my knees.

"Not now," I hissed under my breath, though I had no control. The pain surged again, sharper and brighter. The curse was forcing me to shift into my Lycan. I was going to lose control and kill Amara. This was the blinding agony and rage that overtook my Lycan. It had remained at bay for so long because Amara's Lycan had been able to help control it. Why was I about to lose control now?

Another wave of pain crashed through me. I dropped to one knee, gritting my teeth hard enough to crack them. My hands trembled as pure power, raw and primal, stirred beneath my skin. This was not the muted echo I had lived with, but the full force of what I was. The full power of my Lycan.

Lightning crashed above me, streaking the sky purple. Amara gasped. She was shifting back into her Lycan as well. I drew a shuddering breath and realized that there was nothing but a pitiful nudge of bloodlust in her direction from the curse. Like a flickering flame thrashing to stay alive.

The curse was breaking. I closed my eyes, embracing the feel of the curse cracking inside my very soul.

Light, actual bright, white light, flashed behind my eyes. My blood was too hot for my veins, pulsing like wildfire through every inch of me. I doubled over, gripping my chest as the curse thrashed, fighting to survive.

But I could feel it slipping. Splintering. Cracking like old stone finally crumbling.

Hope—terrifying, impossible hope—clawed its way up my throat. It had been so long since I felt this much hope. I had forgotten its taste.

Amara's shifted Lycan howled into the night. And all around me, people knelt down before her.

And my Lycan did not want to kill her. My Lycan was filled with pride. Pride in his mate. If I had not already been on my knees from the pain of the curse fighting to keep going, I would have knelt, too.

"Amara..." Her name tore from me in a hoarse whisper.

She was the key. She was the storm tearing the curse from my soul.

Something inside me snapped. It was loud as thunder, as bright as fire and the force of it punched the breath from my chest. I gasped, head thrown back as a lightning bolt of strength rushed through me so violently, it felt like I was drowning and breathing at the same time.

I screamed.

Not from fear. Not from weakness. But from release.

I could feel myself expanding, rising, every inch of me flooding with the true power of my Lycan that had been stolen when the curse was placed on me. The weight that had anchored me for years lifted in a single, breathtaking instant like a boulder lifted from my soul.

I took a shaking breath. And for the first time in so long, I could breathe freely, without the weight of the curse in me.

I lifted my head. My vision pulsed with light. My heart roared like a drum of war.

The curse was gone. Shattered. Broken.

Because I was no longer king. Amara was. She had defeated Kadin in a battle for the crown. He might have been a fake king, but defeating the usurper gave her the right to claim the crown for herself, and there was no one more worthy than her.

And her willingness to sacrifice herself for the good of the people made her the rightful claimant to the throne. The land had claimed her as its true ruler.

A self-deprecating smile tugged the corner of my lips as I recalled my words from long ago.

Love and sacrifice to break the curse. As if such things ever existed.

They did. In her.

"Long live Queen Amara!" Nora yelled out.

All around us, rose the chants, building to a crescendo as her Lycan howled up at the moon.

The moonlight bathed the garden in a silvery glow as Amara's Lycan form stood tall, her fur glistening with the remnants of the battle. The air was thick with the scent of victory and grief, the weight of her father's death still pressing heavily on her heart. But amidst the sorrow, there was a newfound strength, a resolve that burned brighter than ever.

"Long live the Lycan Queen," I called out, rising to my feet and walking toward the woman who had become my reason for breathing.

She was the reason I lived, the reason I fought, the reason I would burn the world if she but asked.

"Long live Amara, the Lycan Queen!"

The chants repeated and rose around us, filling the air with a fervor that could not be ignored.

Her Lycan form was magnificent, yes, but it was the woman beneath the fur, the woman I loved more than life itself, who held my heart irrevocably.

She shifted back into her human form, her transformation seamless, her body glowing with the residual energy of her Lycan strength. The crowd fell silent, their awe palpable as they watched their queen stand tall, her naked body draped in scraps of her torn gown, her hair cascading down her back in wild waves. She was a vision of power and grace, her bronze skin glistening with sweat and blood, those beautiful dark brown eyes blazing with the fire of a thousand suns.

She stepped forward, her bare feet pressing into earth, her gaze never leaving mine.

"Zayed," she whispered, her voice hoarse but steady, her eyes searching mine for something—understanding, reassurance, love.

"Amara," I replied, my voice trembling with emotion. I reached out, my fingers brushing against her cheek, wiping away the smear of blood that marred her beautiful face. "You did it. You broke the curse."

Her eyes filled with tears, but she blinked them away, her resolve unwavering. "We did it," she corrected, her voice firm. Then she raised her voice, addressing the people who stood around us. "This victory belongs to us both. To our people."

Amara's voice rang out clear and strong. "Tonight, we have reclaimed our kingdom. Tonight, we have taken back what was stolen from us. But this is only the beginning. We have suffered greatly. We will rebuild. We will rise stronger than ever before. Together."

The crowd cheered. My wife closed her eyes momentarily before opening them to look up at me.

"This is it. We won. It is the end."

I grinned down at her, bringing her into my embrace, allowing her to lean on me.

"This is only the beginning, Amara. This is the rise of the Lycan Queen."

Chapter 31

Zayed's POV

The grand hall of the palace was bathed in the golden light of midday; the high-arched windows casting dappled sunlight across the polished marble floor. The air was thick with the scent of incense and the murmur of voices, a sea of nobles and dignitaries gathered to witness the coronation of their new queen.

I stood at the foot of the dais, my heart pounding in my chest as I waited for her. The crown rested on a velvet cushion beside me; its intricate design catching the light, glinting with the promise of power and responsibility. My eyes scanned the crowd, taking in the faces of those who had fought alongside us, those who had endured Kadin's tyranny, and those who had come to pledge their loyalty to the new queen. Ashad stood by, a smile on his face. Asya stood next to him, the scarred part of her face obscured by the colorful scarf draped over head and veil that purposefully covered the lowered part of her cheek which was also scarred from the fire. I did not like that she hid her scars. She should show her battle wounds proudly, but it would take her time to become comfortable.

I caught the eye of Loran standing in the front row. Chieftain Lamar had been gravely injured in battle. He could no longer travel, having lost the ability to walk in the explosion. Loran was here in his brother's place to pledge fealty to Amara. And then he would whisk Asya away to meet her new betrothed. Lamar's son had asked for one month to get to know his new bride before we would be invited to attend their wedding. I sincerely hoped this new chapter in Asya's life would pave the way for happiness for her. She had endured enough heartache. My eyes briefly flicked to Ren, who stood in the back with soldiers who had accompanied the nobles and emirs for today's coronation. Ren would be in charge of Asya's security detail as she travelled on horseback to the mountains. Though she had the magic carpet, she said there was a reason it had been hidden away. And with Jevan still on the loose, it was best not to use it or let anyone know who was in possession of it and where it was.

The doors opened. A hush fell over the room as Amara stepped into the grand hall, her presence commanding the attention of every soul present. She did not wear fine silk or gold trinkets on her person. She came forward in her simple, white Blade-Caller attire. And behind her trailed people from the city of Ilm. Amara had personally picked one representative from each neighborhood within the city to attend her coronation. But that was not what surprised me. What surprised me was that she had picked representatives of varying ages. Old women, young men, teenagers from both sexes, and even a few women who were clearly new mothers cradling their infants against their bosoms.

I smiled. This was Amara.

She moved forward with a grace that belied the weight of the crown she was about to wear. Her Blade-Caller attire, pristine and white, contrasted starkly with the opulence of the grand hall, a testament to her humility and connection to her people. Her dark hair was swept back into an intricate braid, adorned with queen of the night flowers and simple gold pins that caught the light with every step she took. Her face was serene, but her eyes burned with determination, the fire of a leader who had fought and bled for her kingdom.

As she approached the dais, the crowd began to whisper, clearly taken aback by the entourage of common folk trailing behind her. Their whispers of disbelief followed her like a wave. She simply held her head higher and only stopped when she reached the steps leading up to the dais where our thrones were.

She looked back at the peasants behind her and gestured for the nobles standing up front to take a step back.

They did so, unable to deny their queen. Though moving aside to make way for the commoners was a bitter pill to swallow for most.

Satisfied, Amara turned to me, her gaze meeting mine, and for a moment, the world seemed to fall away. There was no grand hall, no crowd, no crown—just the two of us, and the unspoken promise we had made to each other.

I reached for the gold crown, lifting it with both hands, its weight a reminder of the burden she was about to shoulder. "Amara," I began, my voice steady despite the emotions churning within me, "today, you become queen, and I, your king regent." My voice shook with the weight of all we had survived. "But you are more than a ruler—you are the beating heart of this kingdom, the flame that will scorch away the shadows."

I drew a ragged breath, my eyes never leaving hers. "The last time you walked toward me, you were a sacrifice—a bride with death in her eyes, convinced my hands would deliver your execution. I never imagined I would instead fall to my knees before your strength. It was your defiance that first burned me, your courage that turned me to ash, and your heart—by the goddess, your heart—that resurrected me from nothing. I love you with everything I am and all that I will ever be."

Amara looked up at me, tears in her eyes, and then she climbed the steps toward me. She knelt before me, her head bowed, her hands resting on her thighs. The importance of the moment pressed down on us both. I could see the strength in her posture, the unyielding determination that had carried her through the darkest of nights. The crowd watched in rapt silence as I raised the crown high, its golden glow catching the light and casting a halo of radiance around her.

"By the will of the land and the grace of the goddess," I declared, my voice resonating through the throne room, "I crown you, Amara, the Lycan Queen of Elamaria. May your reign be just, your heart steadfast, and your kingdom prosperous. So mote it be, under the watchful gaze of the divine goddess, may our allegiance be steadfast and true; now and forevermore."

The words I said were repeated by the gathered crowd in hushed, reverent tones. I lowered the crown onto her head, the gold gleaming against her dark hair. The moment it settled, a roar of applause erupted from the crowd, the sound echoing off the walls and ceilings of the grand hall. The commoners behind her cheered louder than anyone, their voices filled with hope and gratitude.

Amara rose to her feet, turning to face her people. The crown rested perfectly on her brow, a symbol of her strength and resilience. Her eyes swept over the crowd, and she raised her hand, silencing the cheers with a single, graceful gesture.

"My people," she began, her voice steady and commanding, "today marks the dawn of a new era. An era built on the foundation of unity, justice, and hope. We have endured great suffering, but we have also proven our strength. Together, we will rebuild our kingdom, not as it was, but as it should be—a land where every voice is heard, every life valued, and every dream nurtured."

The crowd erupted into cheers once more, their voices unified in their support for their queen. Amara stood tall, her Blade-Caller uniform a symbol of her commitment to protect and serve, her crown a testament to her rightful place as their leader.

As the cheers subsided, she descended the dais, walking among her people. She paused to speak with the commoners she had brought with her, her gestures warm and her words kind. The nobles watched in awe as their queen, dressed not in finery but in the garb of a warrior, connected with those who had suffered the most under Kadin's rule.

I followed her, my heart swelling with pride. This was Amara—the woman who had fought for her kingdom, who had sacrificed everything for her people. She was not just a queen; she was a beacon of hope, a leader who would guide Elamaria into a brighter future.

As she reached the end of the hall, she turned to me, her eyes soft with gratitude. "Thank you, Zayed," she whispered, her voice barely audible over the din of the crowd.

"For what?" I asked, my voice equally soft.

"For believing in me when I no longer did and the world wanted me silenced," she said, her voice raw with emotion. "For standing beside me in the darkness when even I could not see my own worth. For being not only my king, but the man who would rather burn his crown to ash than see me diminished. For being a husband willing to lift me higher rather than dim me."

I squeezed her hand, my heart full. She had come into my life like a blazing star, and today she stood before me, shining brighter than the sun. "Always, *jaan*. Always."

"Do you remember when you asked me to fight you?" Amara asked as we linked our arms together and prepared to walk down the hall.

Behind us, Ashad made the announcement for tonight's feast in honor of Amara. I distinctly heard invitations being handed out to the commoners as well. I smiled. This was Amara's way to rule. And I would support her.

"You mean when we had to fool the nobles into thinking we had consummated the marriage?" I replied, recalling the utter revulsion I had felt over having to scare my wife into thinking I would rape her.

She nodded, head resting against my arm as we walked down the hall toward our room, where we would change for the feast.

"I think that was when I realized...you would never let my light die out. You wanted me dangerous—even to you—rather than me be safe for you and unable to defend myself. That—" Her voice broke, and she swallowed hard, the sound cutting through the air between us. "That was when I think I fell in love with you. That was when I realized I wanted to stay with you. Forever."

We paused outside our room and she lifted herself up onto her toes to kiss me on the lips. Her lips were soft, warm, and achingly familiar, yet the kiss felt different this time. It was not the fiery urgency of passion or the desperate cling of fear. It was steady, grounding, a promise etched into the quiet space between us. It was the promise of forever.

"Forever," I echoed her word, my voice rough with emotion. I cupped her face in my hands, my thumbs brushing away the tears that threatened to spill from her lashes. "You are not just my queen, Amara. You are my heart. My light. And I will spend every breath of my life making sure you never doubt it."

She smiled then, a small, private smile that was just for me. It was the kind of smile that made the world fall away, leaving only her and me and the unspoken vow of unconditional love between us. Her fingers curled into the fabric of my robes, grounding me as if she feared I might vanish if she let go.

"You have already done that," she whispered, her voice steady despite the tears shimmering in her eyes. "You have given me everything I never thought I could have. A loving husband. A chance to change the lives of my people. Your love." Her gaze softened, her fingers tracing the line of my jaw. "And now, you have given me a kingdom."

"I gave you nothing. You earned it," I replied solemnly.

"Only because you empowered me to. In a time when women are nothing...you did not use your power to keep me down but to lift me up," Amara reminded me gently.

The sound of soft footsteps belonging to someone walking down the hallway made us both look up. Amara smiled.

Katarina, with her sour face, moved about, holding a mop and bucket of water.

After we had won, the question of what to do with our prisoners had come up. And for Katarina, Amara had decided she would be a paid servant within the castle walls. It was a way to keep an eye on her as well as put her to some type of work rather than sitting in the dungeons.

"I did not mean to disturb you, Your Highness," Katarina responded primly, bowing low. The look on her face made it seem as if she was violently ill.

"You are not disturbing me and my husband," Amara drawled, fitting herself against my side and placing a possessive hand on my chest. "I hope you have finished cleaning the hall for the feast, which is to occur for my coronation party?"

Katarina nodded stiffly, leaning forward to pick up the wooden bucket full of brown water.

"I have done it. But I have never in my life had to clean," Katarina mumbled in disgust with a shake of her head. "It is beneath me."

"First time for everything," Amara chirped with a smile. "Nothing should be beneath you, Katarina. Earning an honest living is something you should be proud of."

Katarina's eyes narrowed on Amara. She looked like she wanted to say something but was holding herself back.

"Yes, Your Highness," she replied through gritted teeth, though her tone dripped with barely-concealed disdain. "I know since you grew up a peasant that cleaning is not a hard task, but for me it is rather difficult."

My nostrils flared.

"You dare insult the queen?" I asked calmly, wondering what was the best method to rip her tongue out.

"I do not think it is an insult. I did grow up a peasant. I should not be ashamed of it. I should be proud of how far I have come. For if I can become queen, so can anyone else," Amara responded evenly, her hand still resting against my chest, though now she did it to hold me back from throttling Katarina.

A yelp of excitement, followed by the sound of pawing against a wooden door distracted us.

"Noor must want to be let out," Amara murmured, moving to open the door to her room. "He was napping when I left for the coronation."

Though the castle was safe, Noor was still a puppy, and Amara preferred to keep her watchful eye on him.

Once the door opened, Noor zipped out of it, a blur of white fur. But instead of taking a turn to go down the corridor, which led to a door into the back gardens where he could relieve himself, as we were teaching him to do, he stopped in front of Katarina, lifted his left leg, and promptly peed on her before the woman could even realize what was happening.

Amara covered her face with her hand. I did not hold back in letting out an uproarious laugh as Katarina screamed in disgust.

"He is just a puppy, still needs to be trained," Amara explained to Katarina, who was wailing because now, she had dog pee on her.

Something told me Noor knew exactly what he was doing.

Amara's POV

The feast had been perfect. Commoners and nobles had mingled together. I spent a wonderful evening with my sister and we spent our last few hours together reminiscing about Baba. And now I stood bidding Asya goodbye as she prepared for her departure in her room.

"Why are you dressed in men's clothes?" I asked, tilting my head to the side curiously.

Asya looked me dead in the eye.

"Amara, we both know I am scarred and not the attractive, beautiful woman a prince would want to marry. If he rejects me upon seeing my face, we could potentially lose the alliance."

I blinked wondering where my sister was going with this. She gathered up her long,midnight black hair and tied it atop her head in a bun.

"Did you know that when I was recovering from my burns, I found a distant cousin of ours working to help wounded soldiers in Chieftain Lamar's fortress? She bears an uncanny resemblance to me. It is how we recognized each other as relatives. And when I came here, she accompanied me."

Asya now moved to pull on her black boots.

"No, Asya. You are going to ask her to pose as you while you pose as...a soldier?" I asked blankly. Asya nodded, fixing a cap over her head for good measure.

"Nobody knows the extent of my burns. I wore a scarf that obscured my face today during your coronation, so even Loran and Ren do not know. I will go posing as a soldier sent for Asya's protection. Furthermore," Asya said, her face suddenly somber, "we do not know who the spies are inside Chieftain Lamar's court. As an obscure soldier, I will be able to pick up more information from the shadows." Asya smiled at me. "Just like what I was able to do when jailed in this palace not as your sister but as a rebel."

I let out a choked sound of disbelief.

"You cannot be serious...what will you do...marry your doppelganger off to Chieftain Lamar's son when the time comes?"

Asya looked at me seriously.

"Sister, if he is a good man, you will come to our wedding. And if he is not worth being partnered with, I will respectfully ask you to stand with me when I refuse him after the month is up. While my copy masquerades as me, I will assess for myself and send word to you on how I wish to proceed. It will give you time to strategize on negotiating a new alliance, depending on which way the wind blows. I made a mistake with Salim. I do not want to make the same mistake again. I know it is foolish and wishful thinking, but I want what you have with Zayed. And if I cannot have that, then I am better off alone."

"Oh Asya, it is not foolish thinking." I moved to hug her, and when we embraced, the gold embellishments on my pink shirt snagged against the black cotton shirt she wore. "Sorry. I decided to dress up for the feast," I explained, quickly freeing the gold beads from the black threads they had snagged against. "Where is your lookalike?" I queried, wanting to meet this distant cousin.

Asya smiled and held up a finger.

"Rowena," she called out.

The adjoining door to her bathroom opened, and out walked a woman dressed in gold silk and pale blue net. I blinked in surprise. She looked nearly identical to Asya. Rowena smiled at me. If I had not grown up with Asya...I would have been fooled.

Asya smiled at me in triumph when she realized what I was thinking.

"I still have my reservations about you posing as a male soldier," I began cautiously.

"Trust me, sister, this is the perfect plan. What could go wrong?"

I shook my head. Quite a bit could, but I wisely held my tongue and moved to greet this new relative of ours.

It was past midnight. Asya was gone, and I now stood alone in the throne room, eyes on the two thrones where, starting tomorrow, Zayed and I would hold court. Butterflies erupted in my stomach at the mere thought. Sitting there in a position of command in front of people who probably thought the same as Katarina—that I was nothing but a mere peasant—had me extremely nervous.

Not to mention I was still a little worried for Asya. I tried to tell myself that Asya would be fine. She would have a grand time pulling one over on Lamar's men and, worst case scenario, she would come up with grand stories to tell. Which was not the worst scenario. Best case scenario would be that she would fall in love with someone, be it the prince or someone else, and decide to stay.

She had the magic carpet. She could escape if need be, though she told me she would not use it unless absolutely necessary.

"What are you thinking?" asked Zayed.

I turned to look at him and smiled. He must have come in here after sensing my trepidation through the bond. For the coronation feast, he had donned a light pink outer robe which was embellished in gold with the same beadwork as my *lehenga* and *choli*. The robe was open to reveal a light beige silk shirt and trousers underneath. The silk caught the torch light as he moved, flowing like liquid gold around his broad shoulders. His dark eyes sparkled like a midnight forest, and the pendant with the evil eye at his throat gleamed against his bronze skin. He looked handsome.

"I was thinking about Asya," I admitted the half-truth, my voice soft as I turned to face him fully. "She has always been so strong, so resilient. This plan of hers...it is bold."

Zayed smiled and stepped closer. And I knew from the way he looked at me that he could tell Asya was not the only thing I was worried about. His eyes flicked to the thrones before going back to me.

"Asya knows what she is doing," he reassured me, his voice low and soothing. "She has survived worse. Dressing up as a man is nothing compared to what else she has gone through. And we have sent some of our best soldiers to help keep her safe. She also has the carpet."

"I want her to find happiness, Zayed. Not just live for duty or sacrifice but to experience a life of real happiness."

Zayed raised a brow and crossed his arms. "And what if that happiness is with the prince?"

"We do not even know him!" I replied vehemently. "How can you be so sure"?"

Zayed clicked his tongue and moved forward.

"I have done some research of my own. The prince is a recluse. And what I discovered was something very interesting. Did you ever wonder where Chieftain Lamar's wife was the entire time we were at the fort?"

I shrugged my shoulders helplessly. "I had assumed she was no longer alive. Or maybe purposefully kept somewhere else for her safety."

Zayed grinned, grabbing my hand and pulling me up the stairs to the dais. He sat down on the throne before pulling me into his lap.

"Ah, so many times I wanted to hold you like this when we held court before the nobles during my reign," he grinned, arms wrapping around my waist. His hands skimmed the sliver of skin exposed from my *choli* riding up.

"Zayed!" I reprimanded him, astonished, and slapped his hands away. "Tell me what you know of Chieftain Lamar's wife! It must be important, and it has to do with the prince!"

Zayed chuckled, lips moving to skim the column of my neck. My breath hitched. But I would not give in until he told me what he knew.

"Chieftain Lamar's wife does not live with him. Actually, they separated, and she left to go back to her people. Theirs was not a love match but a union he made out of necessity with a small tribe that lives at the foot of the mountains on the opposite side bordering the eastern region. That tribe is about one day's journey from where Lamar's is located on the side of the mountain bordering Elamaria. You need to know this since you are queen now."

He gently pushed down the sleeve of my dress and bared my shoulder, placing a kiss there. "That tribe is also very reclusive, and with good reason." I shivered when his tongue swirled around the skin of my shoulder before he bit down lightly there. The hand that had been pushing my sleeve down now reached for the neckline of my *choli*.

"What does this have to do with Chieftain Lamar's son?" I queried, arching into Zayed's hand as he pushed down the neckline of my shirt so that my breast sprang free.

He palmed my breast.

"Everything," Zayed whispered, placing another kiss on my neck. "His ex-wife left when Lamar's son was old enough. The prince would sometimes visit his mother but mostly stayed with his father, since he is the heir to his father's position. I found out something quite interesting about the tribe known as the She Zhu Tribe. She Zhu, in their language, means serpent ruler. They have the ability to shift into a specific animal."

I stilled, my breath catching as I realized exactly what Zayed was saying.

"So Lamar's son can shift...into a snake...because he inherited it from his mother's tribe?" I queried, jerking back and turning my head to look at my husband.

Zayed nodded, his other hand suddenly reaching to hike up my *choli* and bare my pussy to his view. "I think the reason Lamar's son is a recluse is because the young prince has been posing as a soldier. A soldier who can shift into a beast of a serpent. And they want to keep it a secret from the outside world."

"Ren," I breathed in realization. "Ren is Asya's betrothed." And then I broke into a peal of laughter at the realization that Asya would be under his command since she was posing as a soldier and Ren was leading the security for Asya's entourage back to the mountains.

"Let us wait and see how their story unfolds. It is going to be an interesting adventure for Asya." Zayed grinned at me. "And I do think she is in good hands, else I would have stopped her from going after finding out the truth."

I nodded, leaning into his touch and adjusting myself so that I was now sitting in a way that all he had to do was free his erection from his trousers and enter me from behind as I sat on top of him. My husband chuckled into my ear.

I felt him divest himself of his pink robe, and then one hand returned to my breast while the other began to finger my wet pussy.

I gasped, arching into his touch as his fingers teased and stroked, igniting a fire that burned deep within me. Zayed's breath was hot against my ear, his lips tracing a path down my neck, leaving a trail of goosebumps in their wake. His chest pressed against my back, the heat of his body seeping through the thin fabric of my *choli*. The hard length of him pressed against me, demanding attention. "Zayed," I whispered, my voice trembling with need. "Please..."

He chuckled darkly, his fingers continuing their torment as he whispered against my skin, "Patience, *jaan*. I want to savor every moment of this. Do not worry, I will fuck you on this throne in due time. For now, I want to see you writhe against my hand and beg."

My breath caught as his words made me hotter. He pinched my nipple and laughed behind me, his hot breath wafting over the back of my neck. Then he spread his legs slightly, using them to spread mine wide open and give better access to his hand.

"Look *jaan*. Look out into this throne room where all our subjects will bow to you. You are their queen, their ruler," he murmured, his thumb rubbing my clit. "But when we are alone, you are at my mercy. You are my queen, my wife, mine."

I turned my head to meet his gaze, my breath catching at the intensity in his eyes. There was so much love there, so much possessive devotion, that it stole the breath from my lungs. "Yours," I whispered back, my voice trembling with emotion. "Always yours. Now fuck me on this throne, Zayed, please."

I gasped as he slipped one finger inside me, curling it just right to send waves of pleasure crashing through me. "Zayed," I moaned, my hands gripping the armrests of the throne as I arched into his touch.

"Let go, *jaan*," he coaxed, his voice a seductive whisper in my ear. "Let me take you to the edge and watch you fall."

I surrendered to him completely, letting the sensations wash over me as he brought me closer and closer to the brink. My legs were spread wide as his thumb circled my clit, applying just the right amount of pressure. The tension in my body coiled tighter and tighter.

I gasped, my eyes fluttering closed as Zayed's fingers worked their magic, teasing and stroking me to the brink of ecstasy. His touch was deliberate, calculated, and achingly familiar, yet it felt new every time. The throne room, usually a place of power and authority, was now an intimate, private haven where only the two of us existed.

"Look at them," Zayed urged again, his voice low and commanding. "Imagine them all kneeling before their queen, their heads bowed in respect. And here you are, sitting on your throne, my fingers buried deep inside you." A moan escaped my lips as I obeyed, my gaze drifting to the grand hall before us.

The moonlight slashed through the high-arched windows, colliding with torchlight to create an ethereal glow in the throne room. The marble floor gleamed like ice beneath us, cold and unforgiving—this sacred chamber where kings had plotted wars and signed death warrants now witnessed a different kind of conquest. The massive stone pillars that held up generations of royal legacy trembled with each gasp that escaped my lips, as if the very foundations of our kingdom quaked beneath the force of the passion between us. For there was nothing more beautiful, nothing stronger than the love this man had for me and I for him.

Zayed's fingers curled inside me, finding that sensitive spot that made me gasp and arch against him. His other hand teased my nipple, pinching and rolling it between his fingers, sending jolts of pleasure through my body. I writhed in his lap, my breath coming in short, ragged gasps as he pushed me closer and closer to the edge.

"Zayed," I whispered, my voice trembling with need. "I need you..."

He chuckled darkly, his lips brushing against my ear. "Patience, *jaan*. I want to see you come undone first. I want to feel you tremble in my arms before I take you."

His words sent a shiver down my spine, and I bit my lip to stifle a moan. His fingers continued their relentless assault, driving me closer to the brink with each stroke. My hips moved of their own accord, grinding against his hand as I chased the pleasure that was just out of reach.

"Please," I begged, my voice barely above a whisper.

Zayed's breath hitched, and I could feel his restraint slipping. His fingers stilled inside me, and he leaned forward, his lips brushing against my ear. "Tell me what you want, Amara."

"I want you," I confessed, my voice trembling with desire. "I want you to make me yours, here and now."

Zayed's lips curved into a wicked smile.

"And when you sit here tomorrow, in my lap as you hold court, I want you to know this is what I am thinking about. About fucking you here, on this throne, about making you come all over my hand as you cry out my name and beg for more."

I snapped.

I screamed his name, my body shuddering against the force of my release. Zayed held me through it, his arms wrapping around me from behind as I rode the waves of ecstasy. When the tremors subsided, I slumped back against him, my breathing ragged, my heart pounding.

"You still have not fucked me," I finally said breathlessly as I lay back against him, my back pressing into his chest with my legs still splayed wide open and breast hanging out in the cool night air.

He kissed my temple.

"My *jaan*. I will soon. I want to savor the feeling of you letting go after so long."

He was right. We had not done anything since the first night back inside the palace. We had been so busy.And after getting one taste of him tonight after so long, I wanted more. I wanted it all. I was beyond impatient for his cock to sheathe itself inside of me. And though I had just found my release, my body hummed with desire, every nerve ending alight with anticipation of feeling him inside of me. I shifted in his lap, grinding against him, seeking the friction I so desperately needed. Zayed groaned, his erection pressing insistently against the curve of my backside.

"You are playing with fire, Amara," he warned, his voice rough with restraint.

"Then burn me," I challenged, turning my head to capture his lips in a kiss.

I moaned into his mouth, my hands tangling in his hair as I deepened the kiss, pouring all of my pent-up desire into it.Zayed adjusted himself, freeing his erection from the confines of his trousers. His eyes never left mine, the intensity in his gaze setting my skin alight. He reached for my hips, gently guiding me to stand on trembling legs before standing himself. Then he positioned himself behind me, bending me over so that I faced the throne, my back to the hall. My breath caught as he guided my hands to grip the armrests, then his hands slid down my sides to grip my hips.

"Hold on," he murmured, his voice rough with desire.

I gripped the edges of the arm rest, my heart pounding as he lined himself up behind me. The anticipation was almost too much to bear, my body aching for him. And then he was there, pressing into me with slow, deliberate thrusts that made me cry out. The sensation was overwhelming, a mix of pleasure and relief that left me gasping for air. Zayed's hands tightened on my hips, holding me steady as he began to move, his pace steady and unrelenting.

The throne room echoed with the sound of our breathing, the rhythm of our bodies coming together in a symphony of passion. Zayed's lips found the nape of my neck, his teeth grazing my skin in a way that sent shivers down my spine. Each thrust was a reminder of the connection we shared, the love that bound us together. The tension built inside me, coiling tighter and tighter until I thought I might burst.

"Zayed," I moaned, my voice trembling with need. "Do not stop..."

He growled in response, his pace quickening as he drove us both closer to the edge. The throne beneath us creaked with the force of his thrusts, but neither of us cared.

A wave of pleasure threatened to drown me. He reached over and began to thumb my clit so that stars danced before my eyes.

He gave me a sharp slap from behind and I cried out in pleasure.

"I have their queen bent over her throne, taking my cock inside her cunt," he panted. "Do you like it, Amara? Do you like the way I claim you?"

"I like the way you fuck me," I replied, my fingers digging into the throne's armrests.

He gave me another slap from behind, hiking my *lehenga* up higher.

"When you sit here tomorrow, remember I had you bent over it the night before," he grunted with a particularly harsh jerk of his hips that sent me soaring.

My body began tightening around him as the first waves of ecstasy crashed over me, Zayed's thrusts becoming more erratic as he followed me over the edge.

In that moment, as our bodies joined in rapture on the ancient throne, I sensed a power greater than any royal decree. I felt the sacred, unbreakable bond between a man and a woman. I had always been told the acts of the marital bed were dirty and unseemly. But there was nothing more divine in my opinion than allowing oneself to let go in this way. To have someone to be vulnerable with in the way I was vulnerable with Zayed.

My husband's groan echoed through the throne room, a sound of pure satisfaction that sent a final shiver through my body.

We stayed like that for a moment, our breathing ragged as we came down from our high. Zayed's hands moved to my waist, gently guiding me to turn and face him. His eyes were dark with desire, but there was a softness there that made my heart ache.

"You are everything to me, Amara," he whispered, his voice rough with emotion. "Everything."

I reached up to cup his face, my thumb brushing against his cheek. "And you are my everything."

He leaned in, capturing my lips in a tender kiss that spoke of the love and devotion we shared.

As we pulled apart, Zayed's hands lingered on my waist, his gaze searching mine. "Ready to face the kingdom, my queen?"

I smiled, realizing any nervousness I had had about holding court tomorrow here had all but disappeared. This place was no longer daunting.

"Let us get some rest," Zayed suggested, squeezing my hand. He moved to right my *lehenga* and pulled the neckline of my *choli* up to cover my breast. Then he began to right his own clothes. "Tomorrow is a new day, and we will need all our strength to face it."

"Will you come to bed with me?" I asked. Oftentimes he had stayed up late, making arrangements for the coronation and for Asya.

He placed a gentle kiss on my forehead.

"*Jaan*, I will be right beside you."

I smiled, letting his warmth settle into my bones. And as we walked toward our chamber, hand in hand, the quiet truth settled over us like starlight:

Our story would not fade at dawn. Not in a hundred nights. Not in one thousand and one nights. For I was his, and he was mine— The Lycan King and Queen, bound for all the nights yet to come.

Epilogue

Six months later...

Amara's POV

The throne room was alive with the hum of voices, the air thick with the scent of incense and the faint rustle of silk robes. The grand hall, once a place of fear and oppression, now buzzed with the energy of a kingdom rebuilding itself. Sunlight streamed through the high-arched windows, casting a golden glow over the polished marble floors and the intricate tapestries that adorned the walls. My throne was solid beneath me—a symbol of the strength we had fought to reclaim.

Zayed sat next to me on the bigger throne, which was better suited to his stature. He sat tall and regal, his presence commanding yet grounding. His hand rested lightly on the arm of his throne, his fingers brushing against mine occasionally, a silent reminder of the bond we shared. His dark eyes scanned the room, ever vigilant, ever protective. The gold crown upon his brow gleamed in the sunlight, his sharp gaze softening whenever it lingered on me.

Today, the throne room was packed with nobles, merchants, and commoners alike, each seeking an audience with their queen and king regent. The petitions had been varied—requests for aid, disputes over land, grievances against corrupt officials—and we had listened carefully, weighing each case with the fairness and compassion that had become the cornerstone of my reign. But now, the room fell silent as a nobleman stepped forward, his posture stiff with entitlement, his eyes narrowed with disdain.

"Your Majesty," he began, his voice dripping with a confidence that bordered on arrogance. "I come before you to seek justice. My wife—" he gestured dismissively toward a woman standing silently behind him, her eyes downcast, her hands clasped tightly in front of her, "—has failed in her most sacred duty. She cannot bear me an heir. I demand an annulment."

My jaw clenched, but I kept my expression neutral, my fingers tightening imperceptibly on the armrests of my throne. Out of the corner of my eye, I saw Zayed shift slightly, his body tensing with barely restrained anger. The nobleman's words hung in the air, heavy with implications, and I could feel the weight of every gaze in the room fixed on me.

"And what does your wife say to this?" I asked calmly, my voice steady despite the storm raging inside me.

The nobleman scoffed, waving a hand as if her opinion were irrelevant. "What can she say? She is barren. A wife who cannot bear children is no wife at all."

I took a deep breath to calm myself, air filling my lungs as I fought to keep my composure. The woman, her face pale and drawn, took a hesitant step forward, her voice trembling as she spoke. "Your Majesty, I...I have tried everything. Physicians, potions, prayers..." Her voice broke, and she swallowed hard, her hands clutching at her skirts. "But I cannot give him what he desires. I...I understand if he wishes to dissolve our marriage."

Her words, spoken with such resignation, sent a pang of sorrow through me. I could see the exhaustion in her eyes, the weight of her failure pressing down on her shoulders. I turned to the nobleman, my gaze sharp and unyielding. The delicate crown on my own head had never felt heavier. What good was I when I could not protect innocent women from vile men like him?

"And how do you know she is the one who is barren?" I queried, standing from my throne. "Do you have any children born out of wedlock that prove you are not the one who is barren?"

The nobleman's face turned tomato red over the mere mention of him being unable to sire children.

His jaw tightened, face flushing a deep crimson. "Your Majesty," he said through gritted teeth, "I assure you, there is no need for such baseless accusations. I may not have sired children out of wedlock, but that is because I have always been careful. My mistresses all take a contraceptive."

My eyes flashed, he spoke in present tense. Which meant he slept with women despite having a wife.

The odious man was babbling, not realizing how angry he was making me with his words. "My lineage is pure, my bloodline strong. The fault lies solely with her. She is worthless to me as she is."

My expression hardened. "You…" I said, my voice carrying the weight of my authority, "do you truly believe a woman's worth is measured solely by her ability to bear children?"

He shifted uncomfortably, his bravado faltering under my scrutiny. "Your Majesty, it is the way of our people. A wife who cannot bear heirs is useless to a nobleman."

"Then the way of our people must change," I interrupted sharply, my tone cutting through his words like a blade. "A woman's worth is not defined by her womb, nor is she a vessel for your ambitions. She is a woman deserving of respect, dignity, and love. If you cannot see her value beyond her ability to bear children, then you are the one who fails as a husband." I moved purposefully, unsheathing my mother's gold sword which had been resting against the side of the throne.

"I propose we cut off your head and allow your wife to marry someone else to see if what you say is true. If she is barren, she will not conceive and you are correct, and if she conceives, then it was you who was barren."

"We cannot kill someone for wanting an annulment," Zayed said in a bored voice from behind me. I could tell he was enjoying himself immensely. "The blood will stain the newly polished floors."

"You have a point," I conceded and grinned down at the nobleman. "How about I allow an annulment and marry this woman off to another noble? Then we will see who is truly barren. Or—" I smiled, showing my straight white teeth. "You can always stay married to her. She may sleep with someone else to see if she conceives or not. If she does, then that child could be your heir, since you are sterile."

"I cannot allow my wife to sleep with other men!" he exclaimed, aghast and horrified.

"But you can sleep with other women?" I retorted, raising the blade and pointing the tip at him.

The nobleman's face turned pale, his bravado crumbling as he stumbled back a step. The weight of the blade in my hand seemed to magnify the silence that had fallen over the throne room. Every eye was fixed on me.

"Y-your Majesty," he stammered, his voice trembling. "Surely you cannot be serious—"

"I am entirely serious," I interrupted, my voice cold and unwavering. "You come before me with arrogance, demanding justice for a perceived failure that may well be your own. You speak of lineage and worth as though your wife is nothing more than a tool for your legacy. But let me remind you, sir, that a queen sits before you—a queen who has fought for her kingdom, who has bled for her people, and who has proven her worth far beyond the confines of her womb."

The nobleman's gaze flicked to Zayed, as if seeking support, but my husband's expression was stone, his eyes hard and unyielding. He gave no quarter, no reprieve. The nobleman swallowed hard, his throat bobbing as he struggled to find words.

"Your Majesty," he began again, his voice softer now, laced with desperation. "I meant no disrespect—"

"Disrespect?" I cut him off once more, my tone sharp as the blade I held. "What you have shown is not merely disrespect. It is cruelty. It is a failure to see the humanity in the woman you vowed to cherish. You reduce her to a single purpose, discarding her when she does not meet your expectations. That is not the way of our people—not anymore."

I stepped down from the dais, the sword still gripped firmly in my hand. I stopped before him, my gaze piercing through his façade of entitlement.

"Your wife," I said, my voice softer now but no less commanding, "has stood by you despite your failures. She has endured your neglect, your disdain, and your cruelty. And yet, you dare to stand here and demand justice? You, who has failed her in every way that matters?"

The nobleman's mouth opened and closed, but no words came out. He looked like a fish gasping for air, his arrogance replaced by sheer terror. I turned to his wife, extending a hand to her. She hesitated, her eyes darting between me and her husband.

"Come forward," I urged gently. "Speak your truth. No harm will come to you, the crown will ensure it. Do you wish to remain bound to this man, or do you seek freedom from a marriage that has brought you nothing but pain?"

The woman trembled, her hands clutching at her skirts as she stepped forward. Her gaze flicked to her husband, then to me, and finally to the crowd that watched with bated breath.

"Your Majesty," she whispered, her voice trembling but resolute, "I...I do wish for freedom. I have given everything I have, but it is never enough. However, I have no choice but to remain with him. My family will not care for me, and I have no means to earn a living for myself. But I also cannot bear this burden any longer. Every moment with him is torture."

I nodded, my heart aching for her but also swelling with pride. I had given this woman courage to speak, and she spoke her truth.

The nobleman's face drained of color, his arrogance replaced now by embarrassment. In front of all his peers, this woman announced she wanted to leave him. And yet he had not cared about her pride when he embarrassed her by claiming she was unfit to be his wife.

The silence in the throne room was deafening, every eye fixed on the scene unfolding before them.

"Very well," I said, my voice steady and clear. "By the power vested in me as queen, I grant your request for an annulment. You are free from this union and no longer bound by the chains of a marriage that has brought you nothing but suffering. We shall help you by giving you coin until you are able to find a means of earning for yourself. What is your name? And what are your hobbies? Is there anything in particular you enjoy?"

She gazed at me with a relieved smile. "Zarina, your Highness. And...I have always wanted to paint. I dream of creating pieces so inspiring that one day I will see my paintings hung up in the castle walls."

Her stupid ex-husband laughed snidely behind her, and Zarina hung her head in embarrassment.

"I know it is too fanciful a dream," she mumbled.

It seemed her ex-husband had belittled her in the past for wanting to paint.

"I see," I said, nodding thoughtfully. "Zarina, art has the power to move hearts, to inspire change. If painting is your passion, then you shall have the opportunity to pursue it. The crown will provide you with the materials and space needed to pursue your passion. Verona is head of the aid committee, which helps women become financially independent." I paused and smiled briefly as I recalled how later we had found Verona, along with every other Ilm resident that had been exiled during Kadin's rule. We had then helped them settle into a new and better life within Ilm. Verona was now head of helping the women who wished to seek financial independence. I cleared my throat and continued. "She will guide you and, in time, you will find yourself able to support yourself and perhaps even inspire others to follow their dreams. I hope to see your works on these very walls one day soon."

Zarina's eyes filled with tears, her hands trembling as she clasped them together. "Thank you, Your Majesty," she whispered, her voice thick with gratitude. "You have given me more than freedom—you have given me hope."

I turned back to the nobleman, who stood frozen, his face a mask of humiliation and disbelief. "As for you," I said, my tone sharp, "you will return to your estate and reflect on how you treated your first wife. Maybe you will do better with the next woman, if you remarry." I arched a brow and gave him a stern glare. "However, should I hear of any mistreatment of other women under your care, you will answer directly to me. Do you understand?"

He nodded hurriedly, his arrogance thoroughly deflated. He had lost his wife and dignity all in one day. "Yes, Your Majesty," he muttered, his gaze fixed on the ground.

"Then you are dismissed," I said, waving a hand. The nobleman bowed shallowly and retreated, his shoulders hunched as he slunk out of the throne room. The crowd watched him go, murmurs rippling through the hall as people whispered their thoughts on my judgment. Some agreed, others (mostly men) did not.

Zarina was led away by Dornia, who cast me an approving glance. I did not care what people thought. But the fact that Dornia now respected me and was one of my staunchest supporters meant a great deal. As I turned to make my way back to my throne, I thought I saw him, his hands folded before him as he stood to the left of my throne. He looked down at me with a smiling face and approving eyes. But I blinked and he was gone. A gust of wind blew in from the windows, and for a moment, I thought I heard his voice.

"Well done, Amara."

Baba's voice was like a balm to my soul. I would make him proud.

I purposefully walked up to the throne and sat down on Zayed's knee, holding my sword by the hilt and letting the tip of it rest menacingly against the floor.

From the base of the throne, between my skirts, a small yelp of excitement came. I looked down to see Noor nestled between the space of Zayed's ankles, the pink chiffon of my skirts brushing against his ears.

Zayed smiled, taking a sip of his wine while his other arm wrapped around my waist protectively.

"Well, Noor seems to be the most vocal about agreeing with your decision."

I exchanged an intimate smile with my husband before turning to the crowd before me.

"Now," I said, narrowing my eyes, daring them to challenge my decisions. "Who is next?"

Afterword

This book was difficult to write and meet deadlines for. It was initially meant to be published in the fall. And then my father was diagnosed with Acute Myeloid Leukemia and passed away a week later. It was exceptionally hard to write the death of Baba which I planned since chapter one of book one.

I hope I did justice to the father and daughter relationship within the story. I hope I did justice to the message I wanted every women to read. We are all fierce warriors and goddesses. But sometimes, the patriarchy of this world and entitled men bring us down. However, with the right people by our side, we can learn to rise above it. And with the wrong person, we end up a shadow of our true selves.

Never let your light die out.

About the author

Ruby K. is married and a mother of school-age children. When she isn't writing, she can be found hiking, swimming, and daydreaming. A country girl at heart, she's grown up in a small town but has travelled extensively as an advocate for social change. An environmentalist by profession, Ruby loves to also write (under a different penname) about topics such as saving the amazon rainforest, conserving indigenous cultures, and issues pertaining to endangered species.

Ruby K. loves writing about stories of true love triumphing over evil. You can keep up to date on her latest writing projects through her social media listed below.

1. Rubyk12author (IG)

2. Ruby's Reading Room (Facebook Group)

3. Whispers from Ruby's Reader Room (Quarterly Newsletter)

Join the facebook group, join the spirals, and look at all the character art for our favorite couples!

Also by...

RUBY K

I also have a contemporary shifter PNR series called the Bloodfire Phoenix Series

1. His Fated Luna (on KU)

2. His Warrior Mate (release date TBA)